I0526327

DESPERATE VOYAGE

Paul J. Stam

To
All those that go down to the sea in ships,
That do business in deep waters.

CHAPTER ONE

TUESDAY – 13 January 1942

In the oven like heat of his quarters, Captain Jeffrey Chipman sat at a gray, steel desk. He was a large man. He had always been a large man, but now at the age of fifty-five he had added two pounds of weight for every one of his thirty years at sea. His light blond hair was beginning to turn gray but was not noticeable because he kept it cut short and the gray was not much lighter than his natural hair. In school he was called "Sandy" because of the color of his hair. No one called him Sandy, or Jeff, or Jeffrey, any more. Officers of equal, or higher rank, called him Chip. Everyone else, including his wife, called him Captain.

He sat at his desk wearing only his undershorts and one towel around his neck and another underneath him to absorb the sweat that ran down his body. Two fans attached to opposite bulkheads swung back and forth moving the air around much like two spoons in a bowl of hot soup might do. He wiped his face with the towel around his neck and then stood, pulling the towel off and then wiping the rest of his head. He threw the towel over the edge of the hamper and grabbed a fresh towel. He stood looking out the porthole as he wiped his shoulders.

Above the harbor the midday, summer sun seemed to be trying to suck the life out of everything it touched. The water in the harbor was as still and smooth as butter. Wakes that were created by the occasional small boat that ventured across the harbor settled back into the smoothness almost as soon as they were created. The ships, shimmering in the heat, appeared more like paintings than the tons of iron, weapons, arms, and fuel that they were.

Beyond the buoys marking the submarine net at the entrance to the harbor, there was some action, some motion, and a movement rising up and undulating in defiance of the oppressive blanket of the sun. From inside the harbor it was only a hope that there would be at least a little breeze determined enough to inch forward against the tyranny of the heat.

The steward stopped just outside the doorway and reached in to knock on the open door.

"Come in," the captain grunted heading back to his desk. "Bloody hot in here."

"Yes, sir. The passenger list, Captain," the steward said holding out a white envelope.

The captain grunted an acknowledgment while reaching for it and sitting down. The steward left and he dropped the envelope on the desk, took the end of the towel that was around his neck, and again wiped the sweat from his face and hands. When he took the paper from the envelope, he held it by the edges with two fingers so as not to get it damp. It was the standard shipping agents' form giving the name, occupation, citizenship and cabin assignment for each of the passengers.

Duer,
    Mr. Rudolph L. (Teacher)   United States – Cabin (C)
    Mrs. Rose G. (Wife)   "   "   "
    Master Robert B. (Son-7)   "   "   "
Harwell,
    Lady Marisha B.   British – Cabin (B)
    Master Nicholas B. (Son-4) "   "
Jenkins,
    Miss Margaret (Harwell maid) "   "

At the side of the form was a hand written note from the agent as though some explanation was needed, but the explanation didn't explain anything. His note said, "Lady Marisha is wife to Colonel Ransom A. Harwell, Earl of Chatham."

The captain frowned a little wondering why a British officer was sending his family, along with the maid, to Argentina. No matter how well intentioned the colonel might be, the captain thought it less than honorable to be sending his wife and child to the safety of a neutral country known to be pro-German.

Stanley,
    Miss Helen L. (Nurse) United States – Cabin (B)
VanderMeer,
    Rev. Harold G. (Missionary) United States – Cabin (A)
    Mrs. Mable M. (Wife)   "   "   "
    Miss Mary R. (Daughter-18) "   "   " (B)
    Master Matthew P. (Son-16) "   "   " (A)
    Master Mark T. (Son-13)   "   "   "
    Master Luke J. (Son-11)   "   "   "

He wondered what Reverend VanderMeer's denomination was. He wasn't comfortable with clerics that were not Church of England. Because all the children were named after saints, he feared they would be straight-laced and strict. He hoped VanderMeer wouldn't ask permission to conduct services.

He read over the list a second time. Except for the Harwell party, he had a shipload of Americans. It was not that he disliked Americans; it was just from what he knew of them they had no sense of propriety. On the other hand, if there were ever any need for one, it would be good to have a nurse aboard even if she was American. The rest of the passengers, including Lady Marisha, were each just one more thing for him to worry about. He would have preferred not to have any passengers. Passengers were a liability.

There was a time when he had looked forward to meeting the guests who would be sailing with him. In those days, each passage was an opportunity to make new friends. But that was before the war, before he'd had a ship blown out from under him. He was certain the only reason a U-boat had spotted them on that dark, winter night was because some passenger had lit a cigarette on deck. He wondered a little if the war was getting to him, if he was beginning to think every new face who came aboard his ship was a saboteur, or spy. He wiped his hands on the towel hanging around his neck, put a piece of paper on top of the list to protect it, and then picking up his pen he scrawled along the edge, "Passengers are to be aboard no later than noon tomorrow, Wednesday, 14/1/42."

***

Although the sun was almost set, the heat of the day was confined and motionless in the small, one room flat. Just three hours before, the landlady had called Rudy to the phone and the agent from Cooks had informed them they were confirmed for passage on a ship that would be leaving for Buenos Aires. They would have to stop by Cooks first thing in the morning to get the final details and be prepared to board before noon the same day. If they were not at Cooks by 8:00 a.m., the booking would be given to someone on the waiting list.

Having prepared dinner and washed the dishes, Rose Duer had three suitcases opened on the bed. Two large trunks were closed and sitting in the corner by the door. For more than three months one of those trunks had served as a table in the tiny flat in which the three of them were living while waiting for passage. The agent said the cabin to which they were assigned was small, but at least they'd be on their way.

For Rose, the shipboard accommodations couldn't be any worse than this one room with its tiny bathroom and hot plate. For more than three months she'd cooked all their meals on the hot plate and washed the dishes in the bathroom basin. During that time, they hadn't eaten at a restaurant once because Rudy said it was too expensive. It was wartime. Everything was expensive. Even this horrid little flat was outrageously expensive for what they got. Rudy said they couldn't afford a better place to live, but he always had enough to go down to the pub for a couple of beers in the evening. She hated the flat and she couldn't hide her excitement at the prospect of leaving. She had read in a recent magazine that living was cheap in Argentina. It said you could get a complete steak dinner in a restaurant for a peso, the equivalent of twenty-five cents American. Waiting for passage to the United States in Argentina couldn't be any worse than waiting for it here.

In a way, this flat was representative of her married life. Her life, and the apartment, was confining, oppressive, poor and shabby. Tomorrow, if Rudy didn't ruin it somehow, she'd be free of this hot, smelly, depressing place. When they were aboard the ship, she wouldn't have to cook a single meal.

"Rose," she looked over at her husband who sat next to the window in the only comfortable chair in the room. He was a handsome man with wavy, light-brown hair, narrow face and a pencil line mustache. He put down the magazine he was looking at and said, "Go down and get me a paper."

"I'm trying to do the packing. You're not doing anything. Why don't you go get it yourself?"

"Damn you, Rose, go get me a paper," he said reaching into his pocket and counting out the exact number of large copper pennies.

"I'll go if you want me to," Robbie said standing up, looking fearful from where he was pushing his car around the patterns in the rug on the floor.

"No. Your mother will go. You can go with her if you want," he said. Throwing the coins onto the bed, he leaned back in his chair and picked up the magazine.

Rose dropped the piece of clothing she was folding on the bed. "Come on, Robbie," she said while picking up the coins. She was not angry. She'd been ordered around so long she was beyond getting angry. What she wished was that he was dead. It was a passion that had been with her for years now. There was nothing she wanted more than to be rid of him. She didn't care how it happened, just so it happened. She was beyond the point of hating him; she loathed him. She often thought of killing him. She had heard people could die of lead poisoning and for a while she put lead pellets in his orange juice and any other acidic food that would absorb the lead, but it hadn't worked. She read medical articles hoping to find some way she could cause him to have a heart attack. His death had to look natural or she'd be taken away from Robbie and she couldn't stand the thought of never seeing her son again. She walked to get the paper thinking maybe aboard ship she would have the chance to push him overboard. But even as she began to be excited at the thought of being free of him, she knew she wouldn't do it. She was too weak. She'd never do anything to him. She didn't even feel like a real person anymore. He had made her into a nothing. She knew she had to do something to protect Robbie, but didn't know what she could do. She was even afraid to try and get a divorce because they might give Robbie to him. No one ever listened to her.

***

Marisha Harwell pushed the tab on the phonograph, watched the record drop, and then turned and walked across the room. The music was a classical arrangement of Russian folk tunes. It was music she had grown up with, music that soothed her, music she had danced to at her wedding. She sat down on the couch, the yellow-gold brocade of the upholstery and the elaborately carved legs and carved arch over the back of the couch contrasting elegantly with her simple, black, linen dress. Around her neck she wore a double strand of perfectly matched pearls that were in the Harwell family for more than two hundred years. They were a wedding gift from the first Earl of Chatham to his bride and were handed down to each succeeding Harwell bride. Ransom had given them to her on their wedding day and when Nicky marries, he would give them to his bride.

She hoped she was as attractive and lovely as she wanted to be. She sat in the corner of the couch waiting for him to come down, her ankles crossed, knees together, hands folded in her lap. She sat poised and straight without any sense of stiffness. It seemed the most natural way to sit, as though there were no other way. Her luxuriant, shoulder-length raven hair fell in soft waves around her face. From the folds of her hair and clothes came the scent of his favorite perfume. She sat staring straight ahead listening to the music, remembering. Tears started to form and she closed her eyes to control them.

She heard his footsteps before he entered the room and she looked that direction, the moisture of her eyes adding a sparkle in the evening light. He entered and she smiled at him, a smile that was both hopeful and resigned. He had that freshly bathed and shaved glow about him and the scent of cologne. He was a tall, slim man with angular features. He had a mustache and his properly brushed, brown hair was just beginning to show touches of gray. He was dressed for dinner with black tie and dinner jacket.

He went over to the sideboard and poured the drinks, gin and orange for her and a scotch neat for himself. He sat down next to her, handed her the glass and then raised his and said, "To us."

"To us," she answered and was thankful for the swallow of the drink that helped push back the lump in her throat.

He set his glass down, stood and held out his hand. She set her glass down and taking his hand, stood also. She fitted herself against him as he put his arm around her and they started dancing. She held on tightly, following him around the room, the two of them only stopping when they had to wait for another record to drop and letting go of each other only when he had to go to start the stack of records over again.

A houseboy came to the door and said, "Dinnah is served, Sah."

The colonel nodded and they continued dancing until the record came to an end. They separated when the music stopped and he put out his arm and walked her to the dining room. He pulled out the chair and held it for her as she sat. The light from the four candles in silver candlesticks arranged in a square in the middle of the table reflected off the silverware and sparkled through the carved goblets. He went and sat at his place across the small table from her. The houseboys entered with the plates of food and stood silently as Marisha and the colonel each served themselves from the dishes held for them. The last houseboy in line poured them each a small glass of wine and then the houseboys all filed out on silent, bare feet. Ransom started to cut his meat and said, "Rumors are the Yanks are going to double the amount of desert equipment they have been sending us and ship it right here to Cape Town."

"That should make Monty happy."

They sat not talking for a few moments, neither of them knowing just what to say, both of them toying with their food rather than eating it. It was their last night together and neither of them had any appetite. "I found out the name of the ship," he said finally: Port Jefferson. It's one of ours. I managed to find out where she was berthed and went by to have a look at her. Decent looking enough. Very good, actually. Couldn't board, but I know you'll be safe aboard her."

Everything he had said was true, but he wished it could have been a better ship. It was a freighter and she would be thrown in with all kinds of people. But proper travel accommodations were just impossible to find. His greatest consolation was that it was a British ship and its cargo was vital to the war effort so it had probably been well maintained.

"Thank you, dear," she said, knowing he had gone by the ship out of concern for her and Nicky, but she didn't want to know the name of the ship that was going to separate them. They left the table before the dessert was served; neither of them interested in food so they went back into the parlor. He put the records on the phonograph again and then went and sat next to her, putting his arm around her. She leaned against him, her head resting on his shoulder. They sat, not talking, letting the music soothe their fears, living in the present and the closeness of each other.

Margaret appeared at the door with Nicky in his pajamas. They separated a little as Nicky ran across the room and climbed into his father's lap. "Well, son, scrubbed and combed and ready for bed are you?"

"Yes, Sir," he said snuggling against his father who pulled him closer. "Mummy and I go on the big boat tomorrow, don't we?"

"That's right."

"And you're going to meet us later," he said looking up at his father.

His father nodded, reassuring him and Nicky in a singsong voice and quoted the rhyme his father had taught him long ago.

"The captain told the colonel,
The colonel the brigadier,
The brigadier told the general
That the weather would be clear."

At his son's words, Ransom experienced a strange apprehension, a fear. They had always used the rhyme with reference to Margaret taking Nicky to the park the next day, or for a pony ride, or some other thing Nicky was looking forward to. He had never taught his son the second half of the rhyme, even his wife didn't know it, but the words forced their way into his mind.

The captain told the sergeant,
The sergeant the grenadier
Tomorrow we go to battle
Because the weather will be clear.

"The weather will be perfect for going on a boat tomorrow," he said. "Now kiss Mummy goodnight and then run along to bed."

The houseboys had cleared the table, finished in the kitchen, turned the bed down in the master bedroom, checked the front door was locked, said good-night and left through the servants' back door and still they sat there. The phonograph turned itself off and Ransom got up to turn down some of the lights. They sat in the dimness, their last night together, savoring these moments of each other's closeness which was the only thing important to them. She cried silently once and he gently stroked her hair, kissing the top of her head as he held her a little more closely to him. Margaret passed by the door on her way to the kitchen to get Nicky a drink of water. When she returned they got up from the couch, Ransom turning off the lights as they walked arm in arm to the bedroom.

***

Helen Stanley sat in one of the four wicker chairs arranged around the white wicker table at one corner of the verandah of the Victoria Arms Hotel. She had chosen the Victoria because her agent at Cooks had assured her it was not downtown. The hotel was high ceilinged and sprawling, with large verandahs and wide lawns. It was one of the oldest and best-known hotels in Durban, dating back to early colonial times. Before the war, it had begun to decline, but Cecil Rhodes and other luminaries had stayed there and so there were always those who had to visit the Victoria for a drink or dinner. Now with the war and the shortage of hotel rooms, the Victoria was again operating at near capacity.

She sat with her back to the square, corner pillar where she could look along the front, or the side verandah, with equal ease. Except for a couple of wicker couches against the wall, the side verandah was empty. The front verandah was filled with neatly arranged groupings of four wicker chairs around a matching table. In the center of the building was a wide set of double doors over which was an elaborately carved coat of arms painted in red, black and gold. The area between the door and the steps that led down to the front lawn was void of tables and chairs, leaving a highway for those coming and going. Along the edge of that highway, several army officers had disrupted the evenness of the porch arrangement by pulling two tables together. They all sat on the backside of the table so they could watch anyone entering or leaving the hotel. From where she sat behind them she could hear them talking and laughing without being able to make out what they were saying except for an occasional word. She wished they were not quite so noisy. She did not resent their laughter, nor did she want to join them. She was not at all lonely; she was not a woman given to feeling lonely. It was just that sometimes their laughter drowned out the sounds she was listening for.

She heard the twitting of the small birds in the thick foliage of the bougainvillea growing along the pillar behind her. It was a familiar sound, exactly like a bird back home … home … Angola. Now so far away on the other side of the continent. Somehow, the call of the bird made her feel more homesick than anything that had yet happened and she hadn't even left Africa.

From the road in front of the hotel came the voices of the blacks walking to their homes in this cooling time of the early evening. The native language was not the one, which she spoke fluently and was accustomed to hearing, but the lilt and the inflections were familiar. She listened now with a sort of reverence. She was not inclined to sentimentality, but she might never again in her life hear these evening sounds. They were sounds familiar to her for most of her adult life and because they were familiar, she didn't want to take them for granted. She was on her way to the States now. Just half an hour ago a native messenger from Cooks had brought her the slip of paper saying she was to board a ship the next day. She didn't even know the name of the ship. No one ever mentioned the names of ships, or when they were sailing in these times, but some unnamed ship was taking her away from the Africa she loved. She didn't want to go, but she had made her decision and having made it, she was resigned to it.

***

The slow rhythmic click-clack, click-clack of the wheels only accented the slowness of the train's ascent as though each click-clack was the last heart beat of some great, tired, primordial creature of wood, metal and steam that had risen out of the salt marshes of the coastland of Cape Town and was making one final attempt to ascend to heights where it had no place to be. At dusk another engine was added to the end of the train, one pulling and one pushing, for the steep ascent over the mountains. It was not a long train, only five cars, but in places the grade was so steep it took two engines to move those five cars.

In compartment D of the middle car, Mable VanderMeer lay on her left side in the bottom bunk, staring in the darkness at the emptiness of the bunk across from her. It was a second-class car with six bunks in each compartment. In the upper four bunks, her children were all asleep. The bunk across from her, where her husband should have been, was empty. She had the overwhelming urge to go looking for him, but she controlled the urge, forcing herself to stay in her bunk and wait patiently for his return. She knew he wasn't in the lounge car. He still avoided crowds of strangers, but he was getting better. He was much better than he had been, but crowds still upset him.

She wanted to go look for him, but was afraid it would only add to his feelings of being hounded. Yet, how could she know? Maybe her being there might give him the sense of being wanted, be just the companionship he needed, but there was no way to know. There were times in the past when she was sure he was capable of committing suicide. He had never said anything to indicate he would do it. He never would say anything. Still, there were times when he had become so despondent, so depressed, she was afraid he might do it. That was two years ago, but she was still cautious not to do anything that might trigger one of his depressions.

It had been a day that would have tested the patience of a person in the best of health and with the steadiest of nerves. At eight in the morning there was a call from Cook's telling them there was passage available for the whole family on a ship out of Durban. If they wanted it they should get to the agency right away. Breakfast was just being served at the *Andrew Murray Rest Home* when they got the call, but she and Harold left without breakfast in order to be at Cook's as soon as they opened.

They were kept waiting for almost an hour while the agent kept making phone calls. From time to time, he would look at them and nod to reassure them he was working on getting them passage. In the past, there had been room for three of them, or two of them, but Harold had always insisted the family not be separated. When the agent finally did call them to the counter, he acted as though they were imposing on him and said, "Well, we have finally gotten you passage, Reverend VanderMeer. You're booked on a ship sailing from Durban to Buenos Aires. There's room for the whole family. You have to board her tomorrow, which means you'll have to catch this afternoon's train to Durban. Here are your train tickets. A Cook's agent will meet you when the train arrives and tell you how to get to the ship. All of you will be in one compartment on the train. Just what you wanted, Aye? Please sign here."

***

Harold VanderMeer stood with his elbows resting on the wood-capped boarding gate of the open platform at the end of the car. Behind him, the wall of the carved out mountain rose straight up. If he had been on the other side, he could at times have reached out and touched the wall of rock that was the mountain. On his side of the train, the sheer mountainside fell away from the roadbed into fathomless darkness.

His thin hands clasped tightly together as he looked down at the passing roadbed below him. From time to time, a breeze passing up the side of the mountain would add to the combined coolness of late night and mountain height, sending a chill through his tall, thin body. Occasionally, something would catch his attention and he would look one direction or the other. To the right he could see the forward engine and two cars. On a tight curve, he could even see into the cab of the engine, the red glow from the firebox brightly illuminating the glistening, black body of the stoker swinging back and forth, throwing shovel-full after shovel-full of black coal into the flaming cavern. In the other direction there were three cars with the headlight of the second engine shining over their roofs. At times, the beam of light would glare harshly against the side of the mountain against raw exposed stone, or shine on grass and shrubs. The train would follow the twist of the track and the beam of light would swing over the tops of the cars, sending its powerful ray searchingly into the darkness.

In either direction the cars were identical with the windows of the back half of the car brightly lighted where the corridor had crossed over from one side of the car to the other. The windows to the compartments were dark while the light from the corridor shown down illuminating the roadbed below. A couple of times a light went on for a little while in one of the compartments. Occasionally a shadow would move along the windows of the corridor as the conductor walked the length of the train.

He knew where the window to his compartment was. If a light had flickered on for just a moment in that window he would have gone back and asked Mable if she wanted to join him. He would so have liked to have her close to him. But he couldn't wake her up to ask her to come to the platform with him. She deserved her rest. From the moment they had left Cook's she had taken charge, making the decisions, protecting him and all the time making it appear to the children and to others he was capable. He was still a burden to her. He tended to get flustered when faced with responsibilities that should have been his. He was not as great a burden as he had been, but he knew it was Mable who had nursed him back to at least not feeling like a total failure.

He remembered when he had felt he was of no use to her, of no use to anyone, not even to God. In the hour of the Church's greatest crisis, he had broken down. He had failed. He had become afraid. He remembered those terrible days when he was afraid of everything, of standing in front of a congregation, afraid to talk to strangers, to meet new people, afraid he would not have enough money, afraid someone would give him the wrong change, even afraid, and he knew no reason for it, of his own children. But slowly he had come out of those fears. During the past year, from the times when he was his weakest until now when he was so much improved, it was Mable who was the one who brought him to where he was.

The solid sound of the slow click-clack changed to the open metallic sound of a trestle as the train passed over one of the many gorge-spanning bridges. Directly below he could see the ties and the darkness of the seemingly bottomless gorge. He shook his head when he remembered how just a few months ago he thought it would be so easy, so trouble free, just to step off into one of those gorges. Just open the gate of the platform and step off the train was all he'd have had to do. But now he had no desire to open the gate and step off. There were still times when he was frightened and unsure, but it felt good to realize he was no longer afraid of the responsibilities of living. He was back to where he could handle his own life and he wondered if he would ever again be able to help others handle their lives.

CHAPTER TWO

WEDNESDAY – 14 January 1942

It was just a little after ten in the morning when the captain looked out of a porthole and saw them walking along the dock toward his ship. All of them were loaded down with two pieces of luggage. He knew it was the VanderMeer family the moment he saw them. Reverend VanderMeer, a tall, gaunt man, was dressed in a khaki bush jacket and shorts, Wolsey helmet and knee-length stockings. He looked like someone who had just come out of the veldt.

The three boys were dressed exactly the same way except each of them had wide-brimmed felt hats instead of helmets. The left stocking of the youngest boy had slipped down and was a wad of material around his ankle. Mrs. VanderMeer, as plump as her husband was thin, wore a blue dress and white cork helmet. There was no way he could see the girl's face, but he guessed she would be plain looking with no make-up and mousy hair.

They all set their luggage down for a moment and stood looking up at his ship while Reverend VanderMeer talked to the sentry at the bottom of the gangplank. Their luggage was scarred and worn with labels and stickers from previous journeys and almost every piece had at least one leather strap around it to keep it from popping open unexpectedly. The only new piece was a wicker suitcase carried by the youngest boy. The captain wondered how long they had been traveling, living out of those suitcases, and if their luggage would last 'til they got to wherever it was they were going.

Reverend VanderMeer turned back to his family and they all picked up the pieces they had set down and walked up the gangplank, Reverend VanderMeer in front, his wife right behind him and the children following according to age. They all had a little trouble climbing the narrow gangplank with their luggage bumping the railing on either side. He saw Travers trying to tell them just to leave the luggage on the dock, but they were concentrating so hard on handling it themselves they didn't understand him. The captain knew that same procession had been seen walking through railway stations and in and out of hotels. He turned from the porthole and started getting dressed. He could never tell when one of the young ones might pop into the passageway outside his quarters despite the sign at the bottom of the stairway that said **CREW ONLY**. It wouldn't do for them to see him in his underwear.

***

Carrying her two suitcases, one held in front of her and one behind, Mary VanderMeer walked up the steep gangplank behind her mother and looked up at the ship. In the pit of her stomach she had the feeling that was a combination of excitement, fear and anticipation. It was a feeling there was something missing in her, but she could never identify what it was she needed. The whole trip had been interesting, even exciting some times, but never satisfying. She looked at the ship, not knowing she was hoping that emptiness she felt would go away.

Climbing the gangplank, she leaned to one side a little to see around her mother and *he* seemed suddenly to materialize at the top of the gangplank. She had not seen him when she was looking at the ship from the dock and she felt unexplainably strange inside. He was dressed all in white. His cap was white except for the black peak and gold band. He wore a white, short-sleeved shirt, open at the neck with black shoulder boards with one gold stripe and circle. His white shorts were sharply creased. His white, knee-high socks did not look as white as everything else because the thinness of the material permitted the flesh tones of his tanned legs to show through. She stared at him and the yearning that always seemed to be there rose up inside her, concentrating itself painfully in her chest.

He turned his head a little to look at her and smiled. She was suddenly embarrassed he had caught her staring at him. The tightness in her chest seemed to dissolve and flood to her neck and face. She knew she was blushing terribly, obviously, and that added to her embarrassment. She looked quickly down, hiding her face behind the wide brim of the helmet, looking intently at her feet and thinking how ugly her shoes were.

Ahead of her, she saw her father step off the gangway to the deck and then the officer reached out to take the suitcases from her mother. "Oh, Thank you, young man," her mother said. He set the suitcase down quickly and then his hands were reaching out to take her suitcases. She handed them to him without looking at him and stepped down to the deck.

He set her suitcases next to the other ones. He did not offer to take the cases from her brothers as they stepped off the gangplank behind her. The officer took the papers her father handed him, opened them and said, "Good morning, Reverend VanderMeer ... Mrs. VanderMeer. I'm Third Mate Travers. Welcome aboard the Port Jefferson."

"Well, thank you, Mr. Travers. We're glad to be here."

"Did I hear you speaking Afrikaans to the sentry down there?" Travers asked.

"Well, I was trying to. I grew up speaking German and Flemish, so Afrikaans should have come easily, but I still don't have it down yet. Just trying to get in one last practice session. You don't speak Afrikaans, do you?" he asked hopefully.

"No. I'm afraid the only thing spoken on this ship is English," he said tipping his head a little. Looking at the papers he added, "All of you except Miss VanderMeer will be together in cabin A." He put the papers on a clipboard on the little stand just to one side of the gangway. "John, here, will show you to your cabin. The captain will be meeting with all the passengers sometime this afternoon. Until then, we ask that you restrict yourself to this deck. If there is anything you need, or if you have any questions, please don't hesitate to ask."

The steward, dressed in long white trousers and a long-sleeved, mandarin-collared white jacket, stepped forward and picking up her mother's two suitcases, started to lead the way forward. Mary picked up her two suitcases. "You may leave your bags here if you wish, Miss VanderMeer. The steward will be back in just a moment to show you to your cabin," he said.

"Oh," she said setting her luggage down and watching her family move away from her. She was being left alone with him and she both wanted to leave and to stay. She glanced over at him. He was writing something in a book on the little stand. She looked past him to the dock along which they had just walked. She felt another trickle of perspiration run down the back of her neck and she knew her hair was soaking wet underneath the helmet. It was a long hot walk under the blazing sun from the gate to the ship and she was afraid that any minute the perspiration would be seeping through the layers of clothing. He stood there so neat and crisp without the slightest appearance of being warm. *How dowdy we all must appear to him.*

He closed the book and looked up at her just as another drop of sweat started to run down the side of her face. "It is frightfully hot, isn't it?" he said.

"Yes."

"Oh, please forgive me. I didn't mean for you to stand here in the hot sun. Let's get into the shade," he said, leading the way forward along the deck to the shade of the bridge wing. It was cooler out of the sun. He reached into his back pocket and took out a neatly folded, white handkerchief, took off his cap with one hand and with the other he carefully daubed his brow. He put his cap back on, made sure the handkerchief was correctly folded before he put it back in his pocket and said, "I understand you are missionaries. Where was your father stationed, Miss VanderMeer?"

She reached two fingers into the puff of her sleeve for a handkerchief she knew was already wet and wadded. She shook it out a little and under the brim of the helmet wiped her brow, her cheeks and neck and then stuffed it back in her sleeve. "We were in the Belgian Congo."

"I don't know much about the Congo. Does it have a coast, or is it a totally interior country?"

"It has a small coast line at the mouth of the Congo River."

"Ah, yes, now I remember. Were you along the coast, or in the interior?"

"Not far from the Uganda boarder."

"Ah. Well now, that's way inland, isn't it? Way back in the bush, so to speak."

"Yes," she said and thought he probably considered them very provincial. She wanted to take her helmet off, but didn't dare because she knew her hair was a mess underneath it.

"I should like to go to the interior sometime," he said. "All I've seen of Africa is Cape Town and Durban and they are not the real Africa. It must have been exciting, even frightening, living where you did."

"I guess," she said.

"Was it very primitive and wild where you were?" he asked.

The steward came out and picked up the luggage she had left by the gangway. "Oh, yes," she said and turned to follow the steward.

"You must tell me about it sometime," he called after her as she stepped over the high lip of the hatch frame. She followed the steward a short distance along the passageway and turned left into the cabin. He set the suitcases down to one side and she stood in the middle of the cabin. She only vaguely heard what he was saying about the other passengers that would be with her, or about the bathroom, or the dresser and extra towels. The steward was polite and trying to be helpful, but she didn't hear him. She didn't notice when he left, but continued to stand in a daze. Through the side porthole she could see the back of Mr. Travers' cap, his neck and shoulders. He had said, "You must tell me about it sometime." In her mind she could hear the sound of his voice and his words. Inside her, the yearning was more intense than it had ever been before, but there was an excitement, a hope and an expectation.

***

Marisha Harwell sat at a small table playing solitaire. In the adjoining room she could hear Margaret playing with Nicholas. He was laughing, the high, animated laugh that was more from an excitement of things he didn't understand than from the game he was playing. She turned over the last card in the deck and again looked at her watch. She had been looking at her watch at the end of every hand for more than an hour. Fifteen past ten. He had promised he would be back by ten. She had the sudden excited thought that if he didn't get back she wouldn't be able to leave. But she knew it would never happen, he wouldn't let it happen. He was determined she and Nicholas go some place "where it's safe" and nothing she could say had changed his mind.

He was not convinced, as Churchill kept saying that, "the darkest hours were past." If the bombing of England had subsided somewhat, it was only because Germany was temporarily concentrating on the Russian front. Leningrad and Sevastapol were still under siege. It did not seem likely the Russians would very soon break the German hold. Nor was he optimistic the entry of the United States into the war would be of any immediate help in Europe. In the five weeks since the attack on Pearl Harbor, the Japanese had taken Luzon, Guam, Wake, Hong Kong and Manila. General MacArthur and the United States forces had retreated from Manila to Bataan. It was Ransom's opinion that initially the United States was going to be much too busy in the Pacific to lend much aid in Europe. The air raid sirens might not be blowing as insistently in England right now as they had in the past, but they would sound again and he was convinced those wailing sirens would herald the worst bombings the little British Islands had ever seen.

She knew, though he never said it, that he did not expect to return from North Africa. His death somewhere in the desert to the north was not something he dreaded, or feared, but something he accepted stoically, as one of the little things the fates had ordained must happen before the Allies were victorious. She also knew his concept of a safe place for her was not just physical safety, but comfort. Not just comfortable surroundings, though he certainly wanted that for her, but the emotional comfort she would need when she learned of his death. His parents had never totally approved of his marriage. By any standard, it was a good match in every way except she was Russian. Because he did not trust his family's prejudice to permit them to treat her with the kindness and sympathy, he felt she deserved to be close to her cousin Andrei in the United States. She knew his thinking, but there was no way she could dissuade him from the idea of sending her and Nicky away. He was sending them away because he was convinced he was going to be killed. She could not confront him and say she knew he was wrong, that he was not going to be killed and consequently there was no reason for their leaving. He was so sure he was right he refused to discuss the matter.

She started laying out the next hand when she heard him open the front door. She swooped up the cards and dropped them in the wastebasket as he came through the door. From where she sat she saw him standing with his cap in his hand as the houseboys carried out the waiting luggage and then he came into her room. "All ready?" he asked.

"Almost. Give me a moment will you?" she said and went into the bathroom. She dabbed at the perspiration around her neck and the beads of perspiration along her hairline. She wanted to look as lovely as she could these last few minutes in this house, but it was impossible to remain fresh in this heat. Just sitting still one perspired. She wondered how long it would be before they were together again in their own house. His stupid fear was sending them half a world away. If she had stayed here, or returned to England, they could, at least, have been together whenever he got furlough. This way she would not see him until it was all over. She didn't want to think of that. It seemed too far away. She would just get depressed if she started thinking about the long separation. The arguments and the pleadings were all over with. Now was the time to be as pleasant as possible. She checked her lipstick, put the last-minute items in her case, snapped it shut and carried it into the living room.

She stood for a moment looking at the furnishings in the house in which they had lived for the past six months. It was amazing how intimately familiar things that did not belong to you could become in that amount of time. Ransom's cap and swagger stick were on the foyer table. They were always there when he was home. He had placed them there the first time they had walked into the house to look at it. She wondered if she dared ask him for the stick. No, she couldn't do that. His father had carried it at Saint-Lo in the previous war.

She heard Ransom talking to Nicholas in the other room and went in there. He was standing next to the window holding Nicky while the maid put the few remaining toys into a bag. She went over to them and took one of Nicky's hands. "He's beautiful, isn't he?" she said.

"Yes he is."

"Remember how wrong you and the doctors were about my having him? You are just as wrong about this."

"Then we shall have a great deal to be thankful for, shan't we?"

She smiled a little and looked over her shoulder. "Are you ready, Margaret?"

"Yes, m'lady. Have everything," she said and left the room taking the bag with her.

They stood looking out the window for a moment, not saying anything, each with an arm around the other. Even Nicholas was quiet with one arm around his father's neck and the other hand resting on his father's chest. From the other room they heard Margaret giving the houseboys their final instructions and the farewell envelopes with money. They turned away from the window and walked out of the house.

***

The driver jumped out and opened the door for them when they got to the ship and the sentry came to attention. He saluted as the colonel approached. Ransom touched the beak of his cap with his swagger stick and handed the sentry his papers while the driver started unloading the car. The sentry looked over the papers, handed them back, saluted again, and Ransom picked up Nicholas and followed Margaret and Lady Marisha aboard. Travers met them at the top of the gangway, holding out his hand to help the women step down to the deck. "There will be a lorry here shortly with the baggage," the colonel said. "Is there someone who could help with the bigger things? The trunks are rather large for even two chaps to handle."

"Certainly, Sir. We'll get some of the crew to help with them."

"The big trunks may be put in the baggage compartment straight away. Lady Marisha won't need them during the voyage."

"Yes, Sir," Third Mate Travers said bowing a little as he took the papers from the colonel. "Lady Marisha is in cabin B, Sir. The steward will take you there now if you like," and the steward started along the deck ahead of them.

Colonel and Lady Marisha came out and sat in deck chairs in the shade of the bridge after they had seen the cabin. They sat quietly, hardly speaking. Occasionally the colonel would reach over, take his wife's hand, and squeeze it gently. Margaret joined them when the unpacking was finished. She sat apart from them playing with Nicholas and going after him whenever he wandered too far away. The steward came up to them after a while and said, "Begging your pardon, sir, but will you be staying for lunch?"

"Why, ah, that would be very nice. Thank you. Can some arrangement be made for my driver to eat, too?"

"I think so, sir."

"Thank you, my good man."

***

Helen Stanley stepped out of the cab and stood looking up at the ship while the driver got the luggage and set it at the foot of the gangway.

"What do I owe you?" she asked.

"Eight and ten, ma'am."

"What did you do, jump the meter ahead when I wasn't looking?" she said jokingly and handed him a ten shilling note, waving off the change which he tried to return to her. She walked over to the sentry, showed him her boarding papers and said, "What are you supposed to be doing, keeping somebody from stealing this thing?"

"Something like that, ma'am," he said smiling. She took her papers back and picked up her suitcases. "Why don't you leave them here, ma'am. Someone'll take them aboard for you."

"Oh, I can manage," she said starting up the gangway. The steward took her bags as soon as she got to the deck. Travers greeted her as she handed him her papers and she said, "Do you really think this ship will get us there, matey?"

Third Mate Travers looked up at her wondering if she was genuinely concerned. She was a big woman, not fat, but big-boned and almost six feet tall. "Oh, yes, Miss Stanley," he said frowning, "It's a very good ship."

"Oh, I'm not worried about the ship," she said. "It's the crew. The captain's probably a drunkard and if the ship were to sink, how would a skinny guy like you save me?"

He smiled then and said, "Oh, I'd do my best, ma'am, I'd do my best."

"Huh," she grunted jerking her head back a little and smiling. She followed the steward, nodding at the Harwells as she went by. Nicky stared up at her curiously and she smiled at him, but refrained from touching the top of his head.

Inside the cabin, the steward set her suitcases down at the foot of the inside bunks and said, "The lower bunk here is yours. Miss VanderMeer has the bunk above you. She's a very nice young lady and I'm sure she would be willing to change with you if you wanted the upper bunk, but I think you'll find the lower more comfortable."

"Who else is in here beside Miss VanderMeer?"

"The Harwells. You saw them on deck. There is Lady Marisha with her son, and the maid, Miss Jenkins. The colonel will not be accompanying them. They are over here in these two outboard bunks and the child will be there," he said pointing to the short bunk along the forward bulkhead. It had originally been intended as a settee, but was made into a bunk when the two upper bunks were added after the war started.

"Will there be anything else, ma'am?"

"No. Not just now. Thank you."

The steward left and she stood for a moment looking out through the forward porthole, across the well-deck, and beyond the bow to the stern of the ship. She was going home. No, she was leaving home. For the past twenty years home had been two suitcases thrown into the back of a truck, or a land rover, headed for some village with an epidemic of some kind, or another. She loved Angola and the people. She knew she was loved, respected, needed, and she also liked not having to compete with beautiful, sophisticated women. Every two or three years she would take her accumulated vacation time and go home to visit her parents. Those trips were made out of a sense of duty, rather than because she wanted to go. She was going now out of that same sense of duty. Her mother had died and her father was sick. She was leaving the Africa she loved to take care of her sick, widowed father for whom she had no real affection. She was honest enough with herself to know she was hiding in Africa, but knowing it didn't make it any easier to leave. She lifted the first suitcase to the top of the dresser and started putting her things in the two drawers the steward had said she could use.

***

It was just before twelve when the Duer's taxi pulled up. He was wearing a crisp, white shirt and white trousers that he had somehow managed to keep wrinkle free despite the taxi ride. He looked like he had just stepped off the verandah at an afternoon garden party. His wife did not look as wrinkle free. She was wearing a light green dress and a wide-brimmed straw hat with a black ribbon. Seven-year-old Robert climbed out of the taxi and started for the ship and then thought better of it and stood next to his mother. She reached down and took her son's hand while they waited for the luggage to be unloaded. The driver was having trouble lifting the two trunks down from the rack in back and Duer stood there saying, "Careful now, don't drop it."

Duer came over to the sentry as the cab drove away and smiled. "Good morning, Corporal. I'm Doctor Rudolph Duer. We have passage on this ship."

"May I see your boarding papers, sir?"

"Certainly," he said holding a hand out toward Rose who reached into her purse for a brown envelope, which she handed to her husband. He opened it, took out the papers and handed them to the sentry. "I imagine these are what you want," he said pleasantly. "Are we the first to arrive?"

"No, sir," he said taking the papers. "Others are here." He looked from the papers to each of them and said, "Thank you, sir," and handed the papers back.

"You may go aboard now, Robbie," Duer said smiling.

Robbie walked up the gangplank, turning from time to time to make sure his mother was behind him. At the top he stood quietly to one side looking, apprehensively at his father. Travers held out his hand to help Rose step down and then Duer held out his hand, shaking hands with the third mate as he stepped off. "Good morning," he said jovially. "I'm Doctor Rudolph Duer and this is my wife Rose and our son Robert. Robbie for short. And you're?"

"Travers, sir. Third mate Travers."

"We'll need to have someone bring our luggage aboard," he said looking toward the dock.

"We'll attend to it, sir. May I have your papers please?"

"Oh, certainly, certainly," Duer said handing him the papers.

Travers took the papers and said, "Doctor? You said you were a doctor, are you a physician, sir?"

"No, no. Nothing that important, I'm afraid. Just a physicist. I've been lecturing at the University of South Africa in Cape Town for the past year." He spoke just loud enough for everyone on deck to hear him.

"Will you want things out of those trunks, or can they go directly to the baggage compartment?"

"They can go right to the baggage compartment, can't they, Rose?"
She nodded.

"I'm afraid your cabin is rather small, so after you've taken things out of the suitcases you may want to store the suitcases in the baggage compartment as well."

"Oh, I'm sure we'll manage just fine," Duer said cheerfully.

The steward arrived and the three of them followed him to their cabin. The Duer's cabin had originally been intended as an easy-access baggage compartment where the passengers could put their steamer trunks during the trip. It had been transformed into a small cabin with an upper and lower bunk when the extra bunks had been added in the other cabins. The other compartments had at least been intended as cabins, but everything about the Duer's cabin had a make shift look to it. The bathroom was so small you could hardly turn around in it. All you could see through the porthole was the gray steel of a bridge support and the smallness of the cabin was emphasized by the fact that the child's bunk was on the top of the dresser. Rudolph Duer took one look around the cabin and as soon as the steward left said angrily, "This is terrible. Do they really expect us to live in a place like this?"

"This isn't bad. It's not as though we have to be in here all the time. All we do is sleep in here."

"God, you're dumb, Rose. Of course all we have to do is sleep in here, and shower in here, and get dressed in here. It's bad enough having to sleep in the same room with you, not to mention I'll be bumping into you every time I turn around. For the amount they're charging us, they could at least have given us a decent cabin. I'll bet that hoity-toity Colonel out there isn't stuck in a cabin like this. Get the suitcases unpacked. I'm going on deck."

The room steward appeared at the opposite end of the lounge and Duer headed for him. "Where is the bar, My Good Man?"

"We don't have a bar, sir, however, I can have the dining steward bring you something if you like."

"Thank you. I'd like a gin and tonic. I'll be out on deck."

He waited until the steward was gone, then stuck his head back into their cabin. "Robbie, you stay here with your mother," he said and left.

All of the deck chairs were in use on the dockside of the ship and Duer stood in the shade of the bridge leaning back against the rail. From the corner of his eye he could see the Harwells to his left and from time to time he glanced that direction. He had greeted them when he came back on deck and the colonel had nodded a little in acknowledgment while Mrs. Harwell had looked straight ahead, completely ignoring him. He was not used to that. He was a strikingly handsome man; the kind women could not avoid looking at. He was occasionally stopped and asked if he was an actor. He was used to being looked at and admired by women and it annoyed him Mrs. Harwell did not look at him. She was the kind of woman he liked admiring him. She had the look he equated with absolute Grecian beauty and her disinterest irritated him.

Margaret started to get up to go after Nicholas and he watched out of the corner of his eye when her legs spread a little as she swung them from the chair to the deck. He watched her as she walked by him. On the way back, holding onto Nicky's hand, she glanced at him. He smiled at her and she looked at him for an instant, smiling a little and then quickly looked down at Nicky.

The turning of a page of the book she was reading attracted his attention to Helen Stanley. She sat with her head bent forward, her straight brown hair pulled back into a bun on the nape of her neck. She wore rimless glasses and reminded him of his sixth grade teacher. He had always been afraid of that teacher and so immediately disliked Miss Stanley. He walked over to her and said, "Excuse me."

She looked up.

"My name is Dr. Rudolph Duer. Since we will be sailing together, I thought we might as well start introducing ourselves to each other."

She stared up at him for a moment. "I'm Miss Stanley. Now if you'll excuse me," she said turning back to her book. Just then the steward came through the hatch sounding the lunch chimes.

The salon was crowded. The ship was designed with two cabins that comfortably accommodated two people each. The salon similarly was equipped with one table that could easily accommodate the four passengers and the officers. But with the addition of extra bunks plus the

Duer's cabin, the accommodations for passengers had more than tripled. Consequently, another table had to be fitted into the salon.

There was some confusion because although the colonel was invited to lunch, there was no place set for him. The steward had shown the VanderMeer family to their table and then realized there were too many people for the other table. The steward got flustered. It was Duer who settled things by announcing Robbie and he would eat sitting on the settee.

"Oh, no. I can't let you do that," the colonel said. "I'm not even a passenger. I can't put you out of place."

"Oh, come on, Colonel. Sit down next to your wife. Your not being a passenger is even more reason why you should have lunch with your family. It will be like a picnic for us here won't it, Robbie?"

"Thank you, Dr. Duer," Lady Marisha said looking directly at him for the first time.

"My pleasure, Ma'am."

***

An hour after lunch was over a steward came up to where the Harwells were sitting and said, "Begging your pardon, Colonel, but the captain requests you join him on the bridge for a moment."

"Thank you," the colonel said getting up.

"This way, sir," the steward said leading the way inside and up the stairway to the bridge level. "Colonel Harwell, Captain" he announced and left.

The captain turned away from the chartable "I regret, Colonel, that the time has come for us to take in the gangway," he said.

It was a gesture of courtesy on the part of the captain to tell Ransom himself rather than sending one of the stewards, or a junior officer, to tell him and Ransom appreciated that. "I understand, Captain."

"May I ask where you are posted, Colonel?"

He hesitated for a moment and then said, "My regiment has been ordered north."

They looked into each other's eyes both knowing all the implications of being ordered north. "Success, Colonel," the captain said.

"May I ask when you will be sailing?"

"I don't know for certain, but within twenty-four hours."

"How does it look?"

The captain shrugged his shoulders. "In these times, Colonel?" he said and wondered if the colonel knew the latest intelligence information was there were still three U-boats waiting outside the harbor. "Things can change from one day to the next."

"Yes. Of course," the colonel answered, paused for a moment and then added, "Watch out for them, will you?"

The captain nodded. He knew the last was something spoken on impulse, a breach of decorum, something the colonel would not ordinarily have said to a stranger. It was a plea that was the sharing of a confidence that deserved a shared confidence in return. "I lost my only son over the Channel three months ago," the captain said. "Shot down coming back from a raid. You may rest assured, Colonel, I will do everything in my power to deliver your wife and son safely to Buenos Aires."

"Thank you, Captain," he said reaching out to shake hands and then turned and left.

The captain went over and stood looking out of the wheelhouse porthole. The colonel would go now and say good-bye to his wife and son and he knew the parting would be passionless and emotionless. It would be much the same as his parting when he was about to start on a voyage. His wife would just pat him on the cheek as though he were only going down to the corner to post a letter and would be back in a few minutes. He stood there until he saw the colonel walk down the gangplank and get into his car without even turning to look back at the ship. The car drove away and the captain turned back to the chart table. "Take in the gangway, Mr. Renshaw. Single up all lines."

***

Captain Chipman walked out of his cabin and went down the inside stairway leading from the bridge level to the ship's lounge. He crossed the lounge and went into the dining room where the passengers were waiting for him. They sat in crowded clusters around the tables while the officers stood in front of the sideboards on either side of the large double doors. The captain squeezed his way through the salon and what little talking there was stopped as he passed. He stood with his back to the central porthole hoping to get any little breeze that might find its way through it.

"Good afternoon, Ladies and Gentlemen," he said and paused to look around the room. In that instant he knew who each person was without having been introduced to them and he formed opinions of them. He had seen the VanderMeer family when they arrived, but this was the first time he was seeing the rest of the passengers. There was no mistaking Lady Marisha. She sat with the poise and serenity that only came with good breeding. She was one of those women who for the first thirty-five years of their life become increasingly more beautiful. He was certain she had never been more beautiful than she was right then. He wondered when the colonel would see her again and if she would still be as perfect as she was at this moment. The maid sat next to her holding the colonel's son on her lap.

"I want to welcome you all aboard and I thought it would be good before we get under way to introduce you to the officers and tell you a little about the ship." Helen Stanley had put down her book when he started to speak and he thought she was the no-nonsense kind who didn't approve of wasting time.

"From left to right, my left to right," the captain said pointing and the passengers looked where he pointed, "is First Mate Renshaw and Second Mate Parkington. Third Mate Travers is on the bridge at the moment, but you all met him when you came on board. Over here," he waved his hand to the other side of the double doors and said, "is Mr. Martin, our radio operator. He's the one who will keep us informed as to what's going on in the rest of the world. Next to him is Dr. Bowman, the ship's medical officer." the captain wished Bones had worn whites instead of wrinkled khakis. "Mr. Harvey is our chief engineer and you will meet him later. He is the one who keeps this ship moving and … I'm Captain Chipman."

He noted the VanderMeer family had all changed into fresh clothes and looked considerably more presentable than when he had first seen them walking toward the ship. He thought that with a little good advice the VanderMeer girl could be very attractive. She had a pleasant face with lovely, large eyes. With the helmet gone, he could see the heavy, brown hair pulled over one shoulder that reached almost down to her waist.

The captain noticed Dr. Duer sat in such a way that he could, without being noticed, look the direction of Lady Marisha and her maid. Mrs. Duer sat next to him, looking down at her hands folded in her lap. She was not unattractive as much as uninteresting. Her hair was not disheveled, just not well kept. He couldn't say she was a plain woman and yet, at the same time, he wondered how the two of them had gotten married. He wondered if she just seemed less attractive because her husband was so handsome.

"The Port Jefferson is a twin-screw, motor vessel. For some of you who might not understand what that is, I'll try to explain. Twin-screw means we have two propellers. Motor vessel means we are powered by internal combustion engines, such as autos have, rather than steam, so you see we are not a steam ship. She is a refrigerator ship designed to carry food. She's a fairly new ship, launched in May of 1938 to be exact and has a cruising speed of around twenty knots. For a ship that is very fast. It means we are too fast to travel in convoys because a convoy can only travel at the top speed of the slowest ship. It also means it is almost impossible for a submarine to hit us with a torpedo, especially if we are sailing a zigzag pattern.

"The passage from here to Buenos Aires will take twelve to fourteen days and may, at times, be a little rough due to the fact that we have no cargo which is the way it usually is between here and Argentina. The ship's complete voyage is from England to South Africa with munitions. Then we scoot across to Buenos Aires where we pick up meat to take back to England to feed the troops. So, you can see we are vital to the war effort going both directions.

"Naturally, a ship with such a vital cargo would be a prime target for enemy submarines. Our latest information is there are three German U-boats operating between here and the Cape. There may be more." The captain paused to look around the room. "Once we head across the Atlantic there is not known to be any enemy shipping or U-boats. Nevertheless, we can never be sure. There is always the possibility of being spotted by the enemy. These conditions put some restrictions on you as passengers.

"First, there is to be no light of any kind; no torches carried on deck, no smoking on deck after sundown. I cannot emphasize that enough. The flare of a match, or the glow of a cigarette can be seen as far as three miles on a dark night. Secondly, once we are at sea, the room steward will go around every evening closing all the porthole covers. These are not to be opened. They will be opened again after sunrise. It is too easy for someone to get up in the night and inadvertently turn on a light not knowing someone else has opened a porthole. There will be other inconveniences. During gunnery practice, do not expect any service from the stewards. They will be aft passing ammunition. Incidentally, we only have two stewards so there are times during meals and in your cabins when you are just going to have to fend for yourselves. It would be most appreciated, for example, if you could see to making your own beds.

"Now about lifeboat drills. The first one will be at three this afternoon. This is to make sure everyone knows where their lifeboat station is and to issue you your life jackets. You will each get two. One is to be kept at the foot of your bunk so you can grab it quickly in the dark and the other will be left at the boxes by the lifeboats. If an emergency should arise when you are not in your cabin, do not go to your cabin for your life jacket, or anything else. Go directly to your boat. You will have a spare jacket there. After today, lifeboat drills will be held frequently, and without notice day, or night.

"While we are in port, we ask you confine yourselves to this main deck. After we are underway and have cleared the harbor, you may go on any of the decks except the bridge and the gun deck in the stern.

Conditions permitting, you may, a few at a time, be invited to tour the bridge and the engine room. Are there any questions?"

"Can you tell us how soon we will be sailing?" Duer asked.

"You're Mr. Duer, is that correct?"

"Doctor Duer."

"Certainly. Probably within forty-eight hours, Dr. Duer. Any other questions?" He paused for a moment, looking around the room and said, "Again, welcome aboard and if there is anything we can do to make your time with us more pleasant, please don't hesitate to ask one of the stewards. We'll do what we can. If we can't do it, we will tell you so, but we will say it with a smile."

***

The jangling of the bell was startling even though they were warned there would be a lifeboat drill. They had all located their lifeboats when they were dismissed from the meeting and then, almost immediately, forgot about the drill. With the persistent jangling most of the passengers hurried to their boats, arriving before the crew did. The VanderMeer family was divided. Harold, Mary and Luke were in boat number one and Mable, Matthew and Mark in boat number three directly behind it. They stood in the small space between the two boats, indicating which boats they were in, but still a family. Luke stared at each of the crew as they arrived. "Aye, what yeh gawkin' at, laddie," a stocky, gray-bearded man asked smiling.

"Are you really a sailor?"

"Aye, that I am. Ship's bosun's what I am. Been sailin' all me life."

"How come you're not wearing a sailor suit?"

"Keepin' it clean and tidy, laddie."

"Like for Sunday?"

"Aye, that be it. Savin' it for Sundays. Which boat yeh in, Laddie?" Luke pointed.

"Ah, then 'tis shipmates we are. Think yeh kin help me sail it?"

"I don't know," Luke said shrugging his shoulders.

"I'll teach yeh all yeh'll be needin' to know."

"Then will I be a sailor, too?"

"Well now, laddie, there's a heap of knowin' to bein' a sailor. The first thing is knowin' how to greet the Cap'n. Next time yeh see him yeh say, 'Good mornin' to yeh, Cap'n. 'Tis full of fishcakes yeh are, Cap'n.'"

"It's full of fish cakes you are, Captain," Luke repeated looking puzzled.

"Aye. That be it, laddie. That be the proper way of greetin' the captain."

"Hawkins," Parkington called coming up behind them.

"Aye, Sir," the Boatswain said turning and touching his hand to his forehead.

"Belay it."

"Aye, Sir."

From the boxes behind the smokestack the stewards started breaking out the life jackets and handing them to the passengers. They showed them how to tie and adjust them. They found two to fit everybody except Nicholas. Even the smallest one hung around his knees. He stood for a moment enveloped in the bulky orange life jacket and then, grinning slyly, put his hands out to his sides and skipped around in a circle, his black, wavy, page-boy hair bouncing with every step until Margaret was able to catch him.

"That'll never do," Renshaw said and turning his head shouted over his shoulder, "Bosun."

"Aye, Sir," Hawkins shouted back cutting diagonally across the cargo hatch toward boat number four. "Aye, Sir," he said again stepping off the hatch and raising his closed fist to his forehead.

"Hawkins here can sew anything," Renshaw explained to Lady Marisha and then pointed to Nicholas and said, "Can you make a proper fit of that jacket, Boats?"

"Aye, Sir, that I ken," he said sitting down on the hatch cover and motioning Nicholas over. He took a stub of a pencil out of his pocket and made a mark waist high on both sides of the jacket and some marks on the shoulders and front. Nicholas reached out and touched the gray beard and Hawkins winked at him and turned him around to make some more marks on the back. He turned Nicholas around again and undid the ties slipping the jacket off. "Ave it back to yeh in an hour, Mum," he said standing up and touching his hand to his forehead.

"Thank you, Mr. Hawkins," she said and he turned and dug through the bin until he found another small jacket and walked back across the hatch with two small life jackets under his arm.

CHAPTER THREE

Thursday – 15 January 1942

The subconscious awareness that something was supposed to happen aboard his ship woke the captain. He opened one eye to look at the bulkhead clock and when he saw it was four remembered he had left orders engines were to be started at 0400 hours. He swung his legs over the side, put on a robe and went down the stairs to the galley to get a cup of tea. He noticed as he passed there was a line of light along the crack at the bottom of the door of the VanderMeer's cabin. His first reaction was they had fallen asleep with a light on and then he reconsidered thinking they were not the kind to waste anything, not even light.

It was hotter in the galley. The residual heat from cooking during the day was still evident between the steam urns and the long, eight-burner stove. He drew a mug of tea, added milk and sugar, and then as he turned to leave he saw the doctor slumped in a chair in the corner sound asleep. An open bottle of gin was on the floor next to him and a finger was hooked in the handle of a half full mug of tea that rested on the chopping block. He thought of waking the doctor and sending him to his cabin, but knew the first thing the doctor would do when he woke up was reach for the bottle of gin. At least when he was asleep he wasn't drinking

He went back to his cabin, taking sips from the mug of tea as he bathed, shaved, and got dressed. He crossed the passageway and stepped into the pilothouse. "Good morning, Captain," Travers said as he entered. "Engine room just reported engines are started and warming, Captain."

"Very well," he said and walked out to the starboard wing. It was pleasant out there with the coolness of night and a slight offshore breeze. The sky was absolutely clear. To the west, a sliver of a moon was just setting. He wondered if this was the kind of sky his son was looking at the last time he came back over the coast of France. *Had it been clear that night? Did the sky look different from the cockpit of a bomber than from the bridge of a ship? What was the boy thinking when the shells from the German fighter cut through his plane?* The report said they had taken some flak and were heading home in a crippled plane. They had tried to make it home, but had only gotten as far as the Channel. It didn't do to think of those things too much and he forced himself to think of Elizabeth. If he were home, she would be sneaking out from under the covers to light the fire so the room would be warm when he got up. It was winter up there and he wondered if they'd had any snow during the night. When she crawled back into bed, he would pat her plump shoulder to let her know she had not been able to do it without his being aware of it. But sometimes he would refrain from reaching out his hand so she could have her little victory at breakfast. "I managed to light the fire this morning without you knowing it, didn't I, Captain?" He would nod and smile a little knowing there are times when little victories are more important than an affectionate pat of gratitude. *Ah, sweet Elizabeth, I'll be home in time for your birthday, Love.*

***

In cabin A, Harold VanderMeer slowly closed the book he had been reading since waking up at two in the morning. It had not been a frightening waking, just the discomfort of a hot night. He had gone out on deck for a little while and then returned to read. His eyes were tired and he felt he would be able to fall asleep. He had an hour and a half or more before the others would be stirring. He put the book in the rack at the head of his bunk and turned off his reading light.

***

On the other side of the cabin, Mable VanderMeer felt relieved when her husband turned off his light. She had awakened the moment he turned it on, but she had remained quiet, pretending to be asleep. She remembered when he used to be doubtless and decisive. She couldn't say exactly when he had started to change. They had been in the field ten years this time without a furlough and four years ago he had started to have little doubts. The doubts started small with questions as to whether or not he had made the right decision about something. Little fears about things that had never bothered him became more frequent and then became large fears until there was the greatest fear of all: that God had rejected him and he was damned.

At the time, she had not known how to deal with his doubts and fears except to try and comfort and console him. Then one Sunday two and a half years ago, he had fallen completely apart. A "complete nervous breakdown" is what the Doctor Haslett had called it. She could not understand the explanation he tried to give her for it. All she knew was Harold had changed completely. For seemingly no reason at all, he would break down and sob uncontrollably. Everything he had once liked and enjoyed, he suddenly disliked, or feared. For the first few months he had sat up all night with a kerosene lamp burning in his room, staring at the walls and fearful of going to bed. Then during the day he would hide in the bedroom all day, fearful of meeting someone. Before his illness, he used to spend at least one hour a day playing the piano, but he hadn't touched a piano since that Sunday. He used to love to play with the children after work and read to them every evening before they went to bed, but for a long time he had even been frightened of his own children.

His hair was turning gray and he was an old man at forty-two. Although they had said the best thing for him was to get home, it was two years before the mission doctor said he was well enough to travel. She'd had her doubts when they had started out, but Harold had done remarkably well. Now she was overwhelmingly relieved that after the six months of waiting around Cape Town, they had finally been able to book passage. It wasn't directly home, but at least it was in the right direction.

**

In Cabin B, Marisha Harwell woke up out of a lonely sleep. *Ransom, Ransom, where are you? Why are you there and I here?* She got up and walked over to look at her sleeping son. She reached out her hand and gently straightened the bangs along his forehead. She rested the back of her fingers on his damp warm cheek. *Fever? No, just perspiration from sleeping under the covers.* She turned the covers back and gently lifted him from his settee bunk. He stirred a little without waking, put an arm around her neck, and lay his head on her shoulder. She bent over to gently lay him in her bunk and then crawled in beside him.

**

On the opposite side of the cabin, Helen Stanley saw Lady Marisha get up and move Nicholas to her bunk and she felt an envious resentment. Her resentment was not against Lady Marisha personally, but against the injustice of life. From what little she knew of Lady Marisha, she liked her, but she was jealous that another woman could have position and money and beauty and a husband and a child. Most of all, she was jealous of having the child.

**

At six-thirty, John Archer swung back the blackout panels located at each end of the passageway. They were painted black and when in position, reduced the six-foot width of the passageway to just a little less than three feet. The first panel extended aft, the second forward and the third, like the first one, extended aft with their edges overlapping so a ray of light from inside could not reach the door leading to the deck. Anyone headed out to the deck at night had to turn abruptly right, then left, then right again before reaching the door. They were set up at sunset the night before, but a light was left on between each panel so the passengers could get used to walking through the maze before the ship got underway.

An hour and a half after the panels were out of the way, a steward went through the passageway and around the main deck striking a tune on the hand-carried chime announcing breakfast was served.

By ten o'clock the steel decks of the Port Jefferson shimmered under the glare of the hot sun and the humidity lay over everything like a heavy blanket. There was no escaping it. The passengers tried to find shady places on deck moving from one place to another hoping the new place would be cooler than the last only to get up after a while and go look somewhere else.

Only Nicholas did not seem to notice the heat. He got up from where he was quietly playing between his mother and Margaret and went over to Helen Stanley. "I know how to read," he said.

"You do?" she said looking up from her book.

He nodded his head solemnly and Margaret said, "Don't bother Miss Stanley, Nicky."

"Oh, he's no bother. How old are you, Nicky?"

"Four, almost five," he said holding up a hand with the fingers spread.

"And you can read already?"

"Ah-huh."

"Well, that's marvelous. What do you like to read?"

He pursed his lips thinking seriously and said, "Winnie the Pooh, I think."

"Oh, yes, that's a good one. That's one of my favorites, too. Maybe you'll read to me sometime."

"I can say some of it. You want to hear me?" he asked cocking his head to one side, his dark pageboy hair falling away from his face.

"Why, yes. I'd like that very much."

"Half way down the stair is where I sit." He walked over to the cargo hatch and sat on the edge of it.

"There isn't any other stair quite like it, I'm not at the bottom," he paused pointing to the deck," and I'm not at the top," His other hand pointed up behind him. "So this is the stair where I always stop." He pulled back his outstretched hands and shaking his head he pointed to the deck and said, "This isn't a real stair, you know, you have to pretend like it is."

Helen Stanley nodded. "Oh, yes. I know. I know."

With his hands again pointing directions, he started the second verse.

"Halfway up the stair isn't up, it isn't down,

It isn't in the nursery, it isn't in the town."

He sat with arms extended as a perplexed frown came to his face. "Don't help me," he said, "I know it. I know it." He turned his head to one side, pursed his lips and started over.

"Halfway up the stair isn't up, it isn't down.
It isn't in the nursery, it isn't in the town
And all sorts of funny thoughts,
Run round and round my head.
It isn't really anywhere, it's somewhere else instead."

"That's very good. Do you know any more?"

"Some. A little bit. But not as good as I know that one." He said getting up from where he was sitting. He brushed off the seat of his pants and said, "I have to go now. Maybe we can talk some other time."

"All right. I would like that."

He went back to playing with his toys again and Lady Marisha said, "If he ever becomes a bother, please don't hesitate to call Margaret. I'm afraid I tend to spoil him."

"Oh, he's no bother," she said raising a hand to tuck a loose strand of hair into the bun at her neck. "He's very mature for his age, isn't he?"

"Everyone tells us that. I imagine it's because we have been on the move ever since he was two. He has never really had any other children his own age to play with."

Nicky started to climb into Margaret's lap and she said, "Oh, Nicky, it's too hot."

He crossed the few feet over to his mother and said, "Is it too hot for you, Mummy?"

"Of course not," she said helping him up.

He sat for a moment twisting the pearls on the string around her neck. "Mummy, where's Daddy?"

"Why, in town, I imagine."

"Why isn't he coming with us?"

"We've been over that, Darling, he can't come this trip."

"But he's going to come later."

"Oh, yes."

"Soon?"

"It will be quite a little while, I think."

"Why can't he come now?"

"We told you, Darling. General Montgomery needs him here."

"Up in the desert?"

"Yes, Darling."

"Why does he have to go to that silly old desert anyway?"

"I don't know, Darling. I really don't know."

***

At precisely 2:30 the captain, dressed in uncomfortably stiff, starched, whites, crossed the passageway from his cabin to the pilothouse. Second Mate Parkington was just hanging a pair of binoculars around his neck as the captain entered. "The sea detail has just been posted, Captain, and the engine room reports all engines are on line and standing by."

"Very well," he said taking his binoculars out of the rack and going out to the starboard wing. He stood with his legs apart, the binoculars to his eyes, scanning every ship, trying to determine which ships would be leaving. He knew there would be ships going out because none of the harbor pilots were available. Afternoons and early evenings were the preferred time to leave because it put the sun in the eye of the periscopes. He turned to the sailor wearing earphones and a sound powered mike and said, "Take in lines two, three, four and five."

The sailor repeated the order and a short time later said, "All spring lines are in, Captain."

On the deck below, Luke VanderMeer ran through the passageway exclaiming, "We're leaving. We're leaving. I saw them pulling in the ropes. We're leaving."

The passengers got up from where they were and went to stand by the rail, but after a few minutes in the sun they turned back to where they had been before.

It was half an hour from the time the spring lines were taken in that the captain saw what he was looking for. Across the harbor a large Dutchman with the tug still alongside came out from between two piers. The tug separated itself from the ship as soon as they were clear of the piers. "Take in number six line," the captain said and the talker repeated his order and then almost immediately said, "Stern line is in, Captain."

"Very well," the captain said and stepped into the pilothouse with the talker following right behind him. "Starboard ahead slow, port back slow," he said as he passed through the pilothouse.

The helmsman acknowledged the command, swinging the handles on the telegraph to the engine room and then said, "Starboard engine ahead slow, port engine back slow, has been rung up and answered for, Sir," and even as he said it, there was a shuddering throughout the ship as one propeller pushed while the other pulled. The captain stepped out on the opposite side of the pilothouse and hung over the wing watching the stern of his ship foot by foot ease away from the dock. His head kept turning back and forth looking at the stern and then at the bow where the bowline was stretched to its absolute limit. All the time he cautiously eased his ship away from the concrete and wood of the dock there was the urgency to hurry as the Dutchman was making its way toward the entrance and he had to catch up with her. It would do no good to follow him at a distance. He had to be in the slick of the Dutchman's wake to know he was in the channel through the minefield.

He saw the stern finally clear the bow of the one tied up behind him. "All stop," he said when the stern was clear. The shuddering stopped and he waited until the bowline was no longer taught. "Take in the bow line," he said and almost as soon as he said it, he saw it drop into the water. "All engines back one third," he said and the ship eased diagonally away from the dock. He wanted to run to the other side to see how far ahead of him the Dutchman was, but he stayed on the port side watching the dock slipping away from him until it was far enough away for the ship to make her turn. "All engines stop," he said and waited just long enough to hear the bells respond, not waiting for the talker to inform him his orders had been carried out. "All engines ahead one third, right full rudder."

The ship made its turn and he saw the Dutchman almost at the net and gave the command to increase the speed to fifteen knots. He saw Renshaw' look of disapproval, but he ignored it. Renshaw was a by-the-book man. He knew Renshaw did not approve of his leaving without a pilot. Not only because it was dangerous, but also because the rules stated you had to have a pilot. The rules also prohibited doing more than five knots in the harbor.

When he saw the Dutchman dead in the water by the entrance he was relieved. It would give him that many more seconds to catch up with her. The Dutchman was waiting for them to open the sub net. He looked around the harbor, but didn't see anything else headed for the entrance. He slowed as the distance between him and the other ship decreased. The Dutchman started up again and he closed until he was within a ship's length of her and slowed to three knots to maintain the distance. He mentally noted when they passed through the net, which meant they were in the minefield outside the harbor. He wondered if the passengers crowding the forward rails of the main deck also knew they were in the minefield, or were they just caught up in finally being underway.

The ship moved forward making turns that seemed to send them back the way they had come, always staying in the slick from the wake of the ship in front of them. He thought once that if they were not in the channel, at least the ship in front of them would hit the first mine. He was immediately angry with himself for the thought.

It took them almost an hour to get through the minefield and he had a great sense of relief when he finally saw the Dutchman come to a stop and the small pilot boat come along side to take the pilot off. He looked back and saw three other ships making their way through the minefield. Ahead of them in the open waters, two destroyers were sailing back and forth in front of the harbor searching for U-boats. Behind him he heard Parkington saying, "We have cleared, Captain. Ship's heading now due east. Speed three knots."

"Very well, Mr. Parkington. All engines ahead full; show turns for eighteen knots. Come to base course one-eight-five, zigzag pattern George. Secure the sea detail, set the regular steaming watch."

"Yes, Sir," Parkington said and went back into the wheelhouse and the captain could hear him giving the orders. He felt his ship turning under him as it picked up speed and felt the pressure of the cool ocean wind against his body. It was good to be back in the open again and by tomorrow evening they would be far enough South that they could start wearing their blues instead of the hot weather whites.

***

The sea, unmindful of hopes, or fears, unaware of wars, or rumors of wars, careless of what passed over it, or through it, rose and fell in a slow and easy rhythm as nightfall settled slowly upon it. Harold VanderMeer stood looking down as the bow of the Port Jefferson rose and fell like a great cleaver folding back layer after layer as it cut through the flesh of the ocean. Pearls of spraying phosphorescence splashed outwardly with every hack of the cleaver. He was not aware of anything except the physical: the sea-salt underneath his hand on the rail, the wind against the bare flesh of his arms and neck, tears provoked by the constant wind, the movement of his hair on his head, his weight increasing and decreasing as the deck pushed up against the soles of his feet and then fell away again giving him an instant feeling of being suspended until it rose again to lift him up. Under the hypnotic spell of the steady rising and falling and the constant sight of the water being curled back, he was devoid of all thoughts, as in a sleep, but without troubling dreams. Yet, without actually thinking of it, he was acutely aware of his existence and there was some significance to it. He did not know what that significance was, nor did he want to know. He felt free and alive and though he knew rationally it was impossible, he wished he could stay at the bow for the rest of his life. He felt alone and in tune with the universe with no one else around to make demands on him, or to whom he had to be attentive.

***

On the bridge, First Mate Renshaw lowered the sextant from his eyes and was at ease with the fixed absolutes of the sightings of the first stars of the evening. They were sure and unwavering and he felt comfortable in the knowledge of their dependability. He opened the door to the pilothouse just a crack to make sure the automatic switch, which turned off the lights when the door was opened, did indeed do what it was supposed to do. Automatic switches were not dependable. Inside at the chart table he computed their position and on a chart of that coastal area of the Indian Ocean placed a small X. Next to it in precise printing he wrote, "Star fix. (1800) 15 Jan. 1942." To the west of him on the starboard beam there was a land mass that was still barely visible, but land could shift and change and was undependable whereas the little X on the chart had been established by the stars.

***

Alone in cabin B Lady Marisha did not feel any relief, or excitement, only emptiness and a dread. Up until now, she had known this moment would come, but emotionally had not accepted it. She had hoped something would happen, Ransom's orders might be changed, or he might change his mind. They might find something wrong with the ship and they would all have to go ashore again. Now all the futile hopes were gone. She stood looking at the circle of the porthole that just a little while ago the steward had closed. She didn't see anything, or feel anything except the emptiness inside her.

***

At the starboard rail of the main deck, Mary VanderMeer stood leaning against the forward davit of lifeboat number 3. She was almost completely hidden from anyone else who might be on deck. She wanted to be hidden, though she didn't know what she was hiding from. She felt somehow flung free like the sea around her, the sky above her. She felt scattered like the stars that were beginning to invade the sky, little unconnected spots in the endlessness. She felt empty and that she was waiting, but she didn't know what she was waiting for; perhaps something to end, or maybe to begin. The feeling was not unpleasant, but lacking and lusterless. She wanted something to happen, but all that was happening was the wind pressing against her and whipping her long loose hair. She knew it was getting mussed and would have snarls in it, but she didn't care. She enjoyed the wind playing with her hair.

From the other side of the ship, she heard the soft tones of the dinner chime as the steward made his way around the deck. The notes became louder as he crossed over between the smokestack and the cabin-structure and she pushed back against the lifeboat just a little more as he passed. She waited for a moment after the notes ended and she heard the metal door slam behind him as he entered the passageway. She stepped out from behind the lifeboats and stopped suddenly, startled by the sight of Third Mate Travers coming up the well-deck ladder. He seemed to glow in the darkness: long-sleeved white tunic with stiff, upright collar, long white trousers, white shoes. He took three quick steps from the top of the ladder and slowed as his right hand went to touch the beak of his cap. "Ah, good evening, Miss VanderMeer."

Her breath caught for a moment. She stood almost paralyzed, anticipating and wondering. *Oh, no! Did he think I was waiting for him?* She finally managed to respond, "Good evening."

"In to dinner?" he asked.

"Yes," she said feeling awkward and tongue-tied and wishing she could think of something else to say.

"Lovely evening, isn't it?"

"Yes."

He didn't say anything more as they walked the short distance to the hatch. She wished she could think of something to say. She thought she could say something about it being much cooler now that they were out of the harbor, but it was too late for that. She should have said that when he mentioned the evening. "I wonder what we're having for dinner." *Oh, no. How boorish. Why can't I think of anything to say?*

"I don't know," he said opening and holding the hatch for her as she passed through. He followed her and the hatch clanged loudly as it slammed shut behind them. "Frightfully dark in here," he said and his voice filled the absolute darkness completely surrounding her. She felt pleasantly vulnerable as though he was on all sides of her in that small, totally-dark, six by six-foot area between the hatch and the first blackout panel. "I always have to put my hand out in front of me to keep from bashing into the partition," the voice surrounding her said.

"Me, too," she said and then felt his hand on her waist. *Was it accidental? Did his hand just accidentally land there while reaching out to feel for the panel? Then why doesn't he remove it?* She was certain she had felt a slight pressure from his hand as though trying to guide her. It had to have been intentional and her heart started beating even faster than it had been before. She started feeling weak, then her outstretched hand felt the panel in front of her and she felt both relieved and disappointed. She moved to the right, felt its edge and then was around it and could see the gray area to the side of the next panel. They emerged into the brightly-lit passageway and he was right alongside her. They came opposite her cabin door and she turned toward it and then thought she should make some explanation for leaving him so abruptly. "Have to brush my hair. The wind made a mess of it," she said.

"See you at dinner then," he said and walked on. She watched him walk away, his cap tucked under his left arm, his tailored tunic narrowing from the shoulders to the waist and flaring out over the hips. He set his cap on the armchair next to the salon door and entered the salon. She hoped he had not seen her looking after him.

She stood in front of the mirror brushing her hair, aware once again how dull her clothes were. She had picked out her prettiest dress before going on deck, but it didn't compare to any of Miss Jenkin's dresses. "Practical," or "wears well" were the terms her mother had used the two times they had gone shopping for clothes. She wished she had one really pretty dress that wasn't practical.

She was determined she would not look at him when she entered. She stepped into the salon ready to go to her place at the table with the rest of her family and suddenly stopped. First Mate Renshaw and Mr. Martin were at her table. The officers had never been at meals before this. The only other place was at the other table and he was at that table. He stood up and said, "I think the only place left is over here with us, Miss VanderMeer."

His standing drew attention to her arriving late, but it was still nice. Her mother was always reminding her brothers to stand when a lady entered the room. No one had ever stood when she entered a room before and it made her feel rather special. "Sorry I'm late," she said quietly.

"Oh, you're not at all late, Miss VanderMeer," he said sitting down and picking up his napkin, but she knew she was late because her father's prayer had been said and the food was beginning to be served.

The two tables were crowded so close together it was almost impossible not to overhear the conversation at the other table. Her father continued after she was seated and everyone was listening to him. "You were saying, Mr. Renshaw?"

"Oh, yes. We will follow the coast down to the thirty-fifth parallel and then straight across. We should be off the Cape in two days, or so."

"How come the table's wet?" Luke asked reaching toward the center of the table to see if it was also damp there.

"The tablecloths are dampened to keep the dishes from sliding when the ship rolls. You wouldn't want to have a plate full of fish slide into your lap would you?"

"Oh," he said trying to comprehend the logic of damp table clothes. "Do you like being a sailor?" he asked leaning his head to one side and looking at Renshaw intently.

"Why, yes, I suppose so. If I didn't I'd probably be doing something else."

"Did you always want to be a sailor?"

"Really, Luke, you mustn't bother Mr. Renshaw with so many questions," his mother said.

"Oh, it's quite all right, Mrs. VanderMeer. Yes, I think so. My father was in the Royal Navy so I guess I just sort of followed in his footsteps, though I must say he was quite disappointed I didn't go into the Navy, too. My mother didn't want me to be a sailor, though."

"What did she want you to be?"

"Well, now, I really don't know. Do you know what your mother wants you to be?"

"Oh, yes! She wants me to be a girl," he said and looked around surprised when everyone burst out laughing.

"Oh, Lukie, what makes you say that?"

"You always say that. Every time I spill something, or break something, you say. 'Oh, why couldn't you have been a girl? You do say that, Mommy. You do.'"

"It's only an expression, dear. I'll try never to say it again. I love you just the way you are."

"Then is it all right if I be a sailor?"

"Well, I think you should find out a little more about it before you decide definitely."

"Oh, I will. I will. I'll find out all about it on this trip."

CHAPTER FOUR

Friday – 16 January 1942

Just before six in the morning John Martin stepped out of the radio room with a handful of the ship's newssheets: two stapled mimeographed pages containing the essentials of the news broadcasts of the night. He slipped one under each of Renshaw's and Parkington's doors and then knocked on the captain's door knowing he would be awake. He went in when the captain answered and said, "Good morning, Captain," and handed him a set of the papers.

"Good morning, Sparks. Anything unusual in the news today?"

"Not really, sir," he said and left. He went down the stairs to the passenger lounge and put half a dozen copies on the table just outside the door to the dining room before taking the rest of them to the crew's quarters back aft.

The captain turned to the second page. He was familiar with Spark's format. The news he was interested in was always toward the end, just before the American Communiqués.

LONDON - 15 January 1942
Home Security Ministry Communiqué
There was a little enemy air activity in some coastal areas of England in the early part of last night. Slight damage was caused in the Southwest. No casualties have been reported from this area. One enemy aircraft was destroyed.

Southwest. Probably the Plymouth area. Well that's far enough away Elizabeth should be all right, besides, no casualties have been reported.

Shortly before dusk this evening enemy aircraft dropped bombs at points on the Northwest of England. Some damage and casualties have been reported.

He looked up the page and read the section directly above.

Air Ministry Communiqué
Aircraft of the Bomber Command were over Northeast Germany in force last night. Hamburg, Emden and other German ports were bombed. At Hamburg, which was the main objective, very large fires

were left burning in docks and shipyards. Attacks were also made on docks at Rotterdam and on enemy airdromes in Holland.

Five of our aircraft are missing from these operations.

Five aircraft missing. How glibly they print those words. They're always at the end of a report; always a separate one or two line paragraph as though it is just something mentioned in passing. Five aircraft. Lockheeds probably. Bombers with ten men each. Fifty men gone.

For a long time he read that one line paragraph with a certain feeling of dread, a fear he always tried to tell himself was unwarranted. He tried to tell himself if he didn't fear it, didn't dread it, it would never happen. But it did happened, an official notice that one of nine bombers that had been mentioned so casually the day before had been Ronald's. Those one-line paragraphs no longer evoked fear, but an ache.

He set the paper aside. He didn't want to read any more just now. No matter how glowing the first few paragraphs reported the successes to be, the last paragraph always managed somehow to refute the good reports.

***

Harold VanderMeer came out of his cabin just a few minutes after Martin had delivered the newssheet. He bent over the table without immediately picking up one of the papers. He noted the line's letterhead, the same logo that was on all the china, which showed a flag flying from a ship's staff. The flag had a blue P in the center of a white diamond on a red field. Right under the flag was the date, Friday, 16 January 1942. He decided it was something he was allowed to have and was just picking one up when he saw Miss Stanley come out of her cabin. "Oh, good morning, Miss Stanley." He picked up another set of the papers. "Seems to be some kind of ship's news flyer here," he said holding the papers out to her. "Would you like one?"

"Thank you," she said looking down at the paper. "You're up early."

"I'm an early riser. I like to have a little time to myself before the day starts," he said turning toward the starboard blackout panels and hoping she would take the hint he wanted to be alone.

"I know what you mean," she said heading the opposite direction. She wove her way through the blackout panels and stepped out into the coolness of the early morning and wind. She pulled her shawl more tightly around her. The sun was just coming up and she pulled one of the deck chairs over to where it would be in the warming rays of the just breaking sun. She sat and started reading the paper.

CAIRO - 15 January 1942
British Middle East Headquarters Communiqué

Although the advances of our columns in the coastal sector about Gaar El-Brega was delayed by the difficult country and strong resistance from defended localities, further South progress was made. As on the previous day, the enemy air activity against our columns was on a considerable scale. Throughout the day our Air Force carried out protective steps over the area of operations together with successful attacks on enemy concentrations of mechanical transport in the rear.

In the Halfaya area, in cooperation with our Air Force, British, South African and Polish artillery continued their bombardment of the enemy defenses as a result of which an important enemy ammunition dump was destroyed and a number of direct hits were registered on a gun emplacement. Under cover of this bombardment, our infantry moved forward to new positions that are now being consolidated in the face of enemy patrols and artillery activity.

She lowered the paper to her lap wondering why she had started reading it. There were so many other pleasant things with which she could have started her day.

With the ship headed in this southwesterly direction along the coast, the rising sun was off the port quarter. Seated where she was, the sun now radiated its full warmth. All around her was the brilliant blue of the deep ocean. At home, she was almost always up before dawn just to watch the sun rise and here she had also let the war force itself in upon her. As a rule, she tried to ignore the war. If it ever came to her, she would handle it just as she handled any catastrophe, emergency, or epidemic. She seldom listened to news reports, or read a paper, yet this first morning when it would seem the most natural to enjoy the tranquility of the early morning and the restful sea, she had let news of terror, horror and stupidity, all of which war was, be first in her thoughts. Now that she had started, she felt for some reason she should read more.

Royal Air Force Communiqué

Bomber aircraft of the Free French Air Force and Royal Air Force fighters continued their attacks on objectives at Halfaya during yesterday. The bombers scored direct hits on gun emplacements and an ammunition dump while the fighters effectively machine gunned enemy motor transport vehicles. In the El Agheila area fighter aircraft of the Royal Air Force and Royal Australian Air Force were active in combats that developed. One FE-109F and an Italian fighter were destroyed. Other enemy fighters were damaged.

During the night of January 13-14, our bombers attacked a column of enemy motor transports West of El Agheila causing fires and explosions. Other bombers raided objectives at Tripoli where fires were seen to breakout in the harbor area and at the railroad station. In the Central Mediterranean yesterday bomber aircraft attacked an   enemy merchant ship that was escorted by destroyers. Clouds of smoke were seen coming from the merchantman after the attack was pressed home from a low level.

Enemy aircraft raided Malta during the night of January 13-14 and again yesterday causing some damage to civilian property. In daylight raids, our fighters intercepted enemy formations and damaged a JU-88 that, however, escaped into the clouds. From these   and other operations, nine of our aircraft are missing, but four pilots are believed to be safe.

She checked back over the material she had just read. *One FE-109 fighter and one Italian fighter. That's a total of three if I count the Junker 88 bomber that escaped into the clouds. Three for the Allies and nine for the enemy. It's not a very good score.*

She read the Air Ministry Communiqué. *Five more planes missing. Five more points for the enemy.* The Home Security Communiqué reported there had been some damage and casualties and one enemy plane destroyed. *How many casualties? Probably bad enough they didn't want to say.* No matter how she read it, it didn't look good. The final score was fourteen for the enemy, four for the Allies.

WASHINGTON D.C. - 15 January 1942
War Department Communiqué - Philippine Theater
Nine heavy Japanese bombers attacked the fortification on Corregidor Island and Manila Bay today. Two of the enemy bombers were shot down by our antiaircraft artillery and others were hit. Damage to fortification and casualties among our troops was slight.

Aggressive enemy ground activities continues with attempts at general infiltration all along the line. Although greatly outnumbered, American and Philippine troops are holding well prepared positions with courage and determination.

Atlantic Theater
The menace of enemy submarines off the East coast of the United States remains substantial.

She folded the paper and sat on it so it wouldn't blow away and wondered what they meant by "substantial." Behind her, she heard the blackout panels being turned back and she knew she had wasted her quiet time of the day reading the paper.

***

On the way into breakfast, Lady Marisha picked up one of the papers, saw what it was and immediately put it down. She did not want to be reminded about the war, most particularly not about North Africa. Ransom had never been enthusiastic about the second drive into Libya that had opened early in December. Other officers had been elated when the offensive had reached Benghazi by Christmas, but not Ransom. He felt their celebration was premature and the Imperial forces were successful only because Rommel's reserves had been depleted due to the German drive into Russia. When the Russian campaign settled down, Rommel would be reinforced and Imperial forces would be driven back because they did not have the strength to hold what they had taken. Ransom would be there when Rommel opened his counter-offensive.

***

At ten in the morning, almost all of the passengers had moved the deck chairs to sunny areas. They had finally been able to take off the sweaters that had been necessary earlier. The swells were still long and easy as they had been all through the night, giving a gentle rocking motion to the ship, but now those waves were capped with white, foamy coronets caused by the strong breeze out of the southwest.

Luke VanderMeer, with nothing to do and no one to do it with, walked to the edge of the forward well-deck and saw Ship's Bosun Hawkins sitting on the hatch sewing on the edge of a large piece of canvas. Luke ran down the ladder and Hawkins looked up. "Mornin', Laddie."

"Whatcha, doing, Mr. Hawkins?"

"Mr. Hawkins is it now? Shipmates don't call each other 'Mister'. Jack's what me shipmates be calling me. Jack, or Boats."

"Whatcha making?"

"Mendin' a kite, laddie."

"A kite?"

"Aye, laddie, a kite."

"Like the kind you fly?"

"Aye. The very same."

"How come you're making it out of canvas? Will it fly?"

"Aye. It'll fly, laddie. Powerful big it is. More than two fathoms long it is."

"What's a fathom?"

The Bosun jabbed the needle into the canvas and stretched his arms out to the side. "Fingertip to fingertip, that be the measure of a fathom."

Luke turned his head to one side looking puzzled for a moment. "That can't be, or else a short man's fathom would be less than a tall man's."

"Aye, right yeh are, laddie. Now-a-day 'tis six feet make a fathom, but in my time fingertip to fingertip was the measure of it, and a man kin drown as quickly in a short fathom as in a long."

"Are you going to fly the kite when you get it mended?"

"Not today, laddie, but the cap'n'll be wantin' to fly the kites."

"The captain likes to fly kites?"

Hawkins smiled a little. "Aye, laddie. Boat drill and kite flyin', them's his favorite pastime yeh might say."

"You're kidding me."

"Is that so now? Is it lyin' yeh think Ah am?" he said winking broadly so for a moment his arched, bushy eyebrow was a straight line before it assumed its normal curve.

"What's it really for?"

"Ah tell yeh true lad. 'Tis a kite to keep the aeroplanes from bombing the ship."

"Oh, it is not."

"Nay, 'tis God's truth. Sent aloft till only a speck in the sky they are, held to the ship with only this wee wire," he said holding up the end of a spool of piano wire. "One kite from the bow, two here," he said waving and hand back and forth to indicated the sides of the ship, "two amidships and two aft we fly 'em. 'Tis said twill cut the wings off the plane that hits the wires. 'Tis also said they twist in the propeller blades and stop the engine."

"Really?"

"Aye. 'Tis so Ah'm told."

"Can't the planes fly over the kites?"

"Aye, but 'tis said they no kin hit the ship from so high up. And if low in they come they hit the wires."

Luke sat there, his elbows on his knees, his chin in his hand trying to visualize a plane hitting the wire. He'd only seen three airplanes in his whole life and they had been so far away they were just specks in the sky. From the pictures he's seen it was hard to understand how a thin wire could do damage to a large plane.

"Does every sailor have to know how to sew?" he asked.

"No more, laddie. Ah'll be wagerin' there ain't anothah tar aboard kin stitch his name to his seabag with neat and steady hand. But in me day, sewin' was the sailor's way. Four on and four off it was with no end oh sail that be needin' mendin' when yeh was off."

"On sailboats?"

"Ships, laddie, ships! Great sailin' ships. Ah've shipped aboard some of the biggest and some of the fastest. Ah shipped aboard the Falls of Clyde to India and 'twas aboard the Pride of Belfast through the Strait of Magellan. Sails was the way of it, laddie. Sails." He pulled a knife from his belt and cut the twine, took the sewing palm off his hand and handed it to Luke. "Hold these for me, laddie," he said standing up. He spread the piece of canvas on the hatch, laid the bamboo poles inside attaching the wire to one of the poles. He folded the canvas over the poles and then rolled the canvas around the poles. "Aye, laddie, 'tis a far come down from mendin' sail to mendin' kites."

"What are you going to do now?" Luke asked when Jack had lashed the kite in its storage place along the rail.

"'Tis the rope locker for me, laddie."

"Can I come with you?"

"Yeh best be checkin' with yehr muthah, laddie."

"I'll go ask her," he said running across the deck and up the ladder to the main deck. "Mother! Mother, can I go to the rope locker with Jack?" he asked panting excitedly.

"Don't interrupt, dear," she said putting a hand on his arm. He waited impatiently, shifting his weight from one foot to the other until Miss Stanley finished what she was saying. "Now, what is it you wanted?" his mother finally asked.

"Can I go to the rope locker with Jack?"

"May I go to the rope locker with Jack," she said correcting him.

"Yes. May I? Huh, may I?"

"Who's Jack?"

"Beggin' yehr pardon, mum," he said arriving at the top of the ladder and touching his hand to his forehead. "That be me, mum. Ah'll be seein' to it that he nay hear any profanities, or the likes of that, mum."

"He won't be in your way?"

"Nay, mum. Not ah-tall. Not ah-tall. 'Twould pleasure me to have his company."

"All right, Luke. Now you do exactly as Mr. Hawkins says and don't get in his way. If he gives you any trouble, Mr. Hawkins, Just send him on his way."

"Ah, he'll be no trouble, mum. Come along with yeh, laddie."

They crossed the forward well-deck and stopped in front of a steel, water-tight door next to the ladder leading to the foredeck. The door squeaked as it swung open. "In yeh go, laddie." They stepped over the high lip and the door clanged shut behind them cutting off the outside brightness. Inside there were lights in glass covers along the ceiling. Everything: top, sides and floor were painted white. The only sounds were the creaking of the ship and slapping of the waves hitting against the hull and the scraping of the dogs being pulled down tight on the door. "Would yeh be likin' to go below and see the chain locker, laddie?"

"Sure," he said his eyes wide with wonder.

"This way, laddie," Jack said and walked forward almost to the end of the passage. He opened another steal hatch in the deck and disappeared through the hole as he started down the ladder. "Come along."

At the bottom of the ladder they were in an area that was bigger than the salon and Luke was suddenly aware of the sides of the ship and the bow sloping up and away from him. The sounds were much louder. The slapping sound of the waves was almost a pounding with the constant sound of water flowing by the hull. "Are we under water?" he asked unbelievingly.

"That we are. Bout there be the waterline," he said pointing half way up the hull.

"Wow!"

"Aye, laddie. So wee little hull holding back so great much ocean. Ah no ken understand it, but it be so."

Luke looked away from the hull to the chain that was hanging down from above him. It fell into a pile that spread out underneath the steel grate on which they were standing. The links were a foot long and the chain swung back and forth a little with the rolling of the ship. One link at the top of the pile clinked every time it was pulled back and forth by the swinging of the chain.

"Seen enough, laddie?"

Luke nodded.

"Up yeh go then," Jack said and they climbed back up the ladder. Jack closed the hatch behind them and then led the way back to a hatch halfway along the passageway. When Jack opened the steel door there was a stinging smell that caused a little burning feeling in the back of Luke's nose, but was not unpleasant. Inside, the smell was stronger. "Is that the rope that smells like that?" Luke asked.

"Aye. Pitch it is. Put in the hemp to keep it from rottin'."

The room was filled with ropes. There was a large table in the center of the room with coils of rope underneath it. Other coils were stacked on the deck around it and smaller ropes hung from spools on the bulkheads. On one of the bulkheads there were four large rolls of canvas, but everywhere else was ropes. There was everything from spools of thread to lines as big around as Jack's arm.

"What are we going to do?"

"Makin' up some moorin' hawsers is what Ah'm about, laddie," he said pulling an end out of a coil of one of the largest ropes and dropping it on the table. "Sit over here and how to make an eye splice Ah'll be showin' yeh." He unwound the three strands that made up the rope and then whipped the end of each with some twine. Then he started weaving the strand back into the rope forming a large loop. Luke sat with his elbows on the table, his chin in his hand, watching as Jack wove the rope back in on itself. He tucked each strand three times so that part of the rope was twice as big as any of the rest of it. "There 'tis. Taint nevah goin' ah pull out, nor break. Not there it 'taint. Reach me the knife out of the drawer by yeh there, laddie."

Luke looked around and found the drawer under the edge of the table and pulled it out. "Neath the canvas there. Careful now. Sharp as a north wind the edge be."

Luke lifted up the folds of light canvas, found the knife and handed it to Jack who cut off the ends of the strands. He coiled the line back up with the loop sticking out of the center of it and laid out another line to be spliced. "What yeh gawkin' at, laddie? Is it a spider in my beard Ah have?"

"What's that thing around your neck?"

'This?" Jack said sticking a thumb under the braided lanyard than hung in a loop around his neck and disappeared into one of his shirt pockets. "'Tis for me bosun's pipe," he said pulling the end of it out of his pocket. A long, curved, silver tube with a ball at the end was attached to the lanyard. He held the tube in his closed fist, raised it to his mouth and blew into the pipe causing different tones by raising and lowering his finger over the ball. He lowered the pipe saying, "Nay much use fer it now-a-day, laddie, what with 'lectric talking boxes and all, but in me day twas the pipe here be tellin' the crew what to do." He lifted the lanyard off over his head and handed it to Luke. "Fer every job there be a different call. To the fore skysail, no matter how the wind be whistlin' and screamin', a man could hear the bosun's pipe."

Luke examined the pipe and the lanyard. He wanted a lanyard, a real bosun's pipe lanyard, but he didn't dare ask for it. "Where do you get these?" he asked holding up the lanyard.

"Aye, yeh make em, laddie."

"I wish I knew how to make one."

"Aye, anyone ken make it if they've a mind to. 'Tis a simple nine strand plat. Diamond knots these are and a Turks head that."

"Will you show me how?"

Jack looked up, smiled a little and winked. "Aye. That Ah will, Laddie. That Ah will." He stepped over several coils of rope to get to the seine twine and cut off nine six foot lengths. He tied them together at one end and hung them from a hook. "Now see the way of it, laddie," he said separating the strands. "Five in the left hand there be, four in the right. Keep em flat and take the top left and weave it through, under two, over two. Now 'tis five in the right hand yeh have. 'Tis the same, take the right top and weave it, under two, over two. Back and forth like that, laddie. Back and forth." He worked quickly so the braid seemed to grow out of his fingers until he had more than an inch done. "There yeh be, Laddie," he said handing the braid over to Luke. "Keep them pulled tight and flat and 'tis a fine lookin' sinnet yeh'll be having when 'tis done."

Luke kept working on it, his fingers getting tired. He made a couple of mistakes and had to pull it out and start over, but little by little he saw it grow. "Aye, 'tis fine work yeh're doin' laddie. Neat and tidy keep it with no mistakes till as long as yeh're arm it be and then 'tis anothah plat Ah'll be showin' yeh. And when 'tis all done right and proper 'tis a bosun's pipe Ah'll be puttin' on the end of it for yeh."

"You will?"

"Aye, laddie, that Ah will."

Half an hour later it was lunchtime and he had only done six inches on his lanyard. It would take him a long time to make it as long as Jack said it should be.

"What are we doing after lunch?" Luke asked.

"Ah, on watch it be for me, laddie."

"Can I take this with me?"

"Aye. That yeh ken. An' when yeh've nothin' else to do yeh kin be workin' on it. An when yeh put it away, tie it off like so," he said tying the two bunches of cords together so they would not come undone, or tangled. "Put the knife and canvas back in the drawer for me will yeh, laddie?"

"Sure," he said. He had to lift a piece of canvas out of the way to put the knife in the bottom of the drawer. Lifting it out the piece of canvas slipped out of his hand, unrolling as it fell. The canvas was a foot wide and four feet long. On one half of it were the light pencil marks of the sketch of an eagle with wings outstretch, head turned to one side. The body and one wing had been stitched in black and white thread; the stitches so close together Luke reached down to feel it, certain it would have the softness of feathers. He picked up the canvas and put it on the table not knowing if he should roll it up to put it away. He looked at Jack not knowing what to say, wanting to express how special he thought it was and also apologize for having dropped it. "I wish I knew how to do something like that," he said. "Can you teach me to do that, too?"

"Ah, laddie, a locker-full oh time be needed to learn to sew like that. But Ah kin teach yeh a stitch, or two if yeh be wantin' it," Jack said folding the canvas up again and putting it away.

"Oh, yes, I do. I have to learn all this stuff."

"Well, come along now, laddie, or 'tis no lunch yeh'll be gettin'," he said swinging open the steel door and stepping out into the passageway.

***

Matthew VanderMeer sat by himself on the port side of the main deck. It was after lunch and almost everyone was taking a nap. The ship rocked easily back and forth with the passing swells. He wasn't thinking of anything in particular, but wondering what there was to do. He was just going to get up and go to see if he could find someone to play shuffleboard with him when Margaret Jenkins stepped out of the hatch. She smiled as she approached, pointed to the chair next to him and said, "May I sit here, Master VanderMeer?"

"Ah ... yes ... sure," he said. Both embarrassed and excited and then when she was seated asked, "How come you always call my brothers and me master?"

"It wouldn't do for a maid like me to call the likes of you by your Christian name," she paused for just an instant and smiled coyly, "unless you asked me to. Then I could do it."

"I don't like being called Master VanderMeer. I want you to call me Matthew."

"As you wish, Matthew." she paused for a moment and then said, "It looks like everybody but you and me is taking a nap. M'Lady and Miss Stanley fell asleep right after lunch. Took the little one a while, but now he's asleep, too."

They sat silently, Matthew feeling awkward, wanting to say something but not having anything to say. Ever since she came aboard he had been looking at her when he thought she couldn't see him. In his bunk at night he fantasized about her. He knew Miss Jenkins was not as beautiful as Lady Marisha, but there was something about her that was different, exciting. She had short, dark brown hair, deep set eyes and a round face with clear, olive complexion. She didn't wear tight clothes, it was just that her clothes were snug at her chest and hips. He had seen lots of native women naked, but that wasn't the same. He had never really seen a white woman naked. Once when he was thirteen Frieda Jones and he had gotten undressed with each other in the Black-waddle grove. But she was as flat as he was on top and when they had touched each other she began to cry because she was afraid she was going to have a baby because he had touched her there. She had not really been interesting, and at the age of thirteen his interest in Frieda was mostly curiosity.

He was fifteen before he really learned anything about women and sex. The last term at the mission boarding school he had a roommate who was the son of a coffee planter. His roommate had told him all about women and had assured him it was natural for the two of them to talk about the girls and play with each other. His roommate said it helped them get ready for girls. He knew his parents and the teachers would say what he did was wrong, but with his roommate's encouragement he did it anyway. That year Frieda developed almost overnight and he told his roommate about his session in the Black-waddle grove with Frieda Jones, but he never mentioned that at the time she was only twelve. When he talked about it with his roommate he often closed his eyes and fantasized himself again in the Black-waddle grove with Frieda fully mature and doing to him the things his roommate was doing to him.

His roommate had said his father had a magazine with pictures of beautiful, naked women in it. Matt had never seen such a magazine, but he thought Miss Jenkins would probably look like those girls in the magazine. Sitting next to her he wondered if she had ever caught him staring at her, or knew what he was thinking. He knew no one could read another's mind, but maybe she somehow knew. His roommate said women had special instincts about those things.

She leaned her head back against the top of the deck chair and that caused her chest to stick out. After a while she said, "This is nice, isn't it?"

"Yes."

"How long has it been since you left your home?" she asked.

"Eight months. It took us a month to get to Cape Town and then we waited around there for seven months. My parents were beginning to think they should go back."

"Did you have a girlfriend back home?"

"No," he said blushing.

"How old are you, Matthew?" she asked leaning away from the back of the chair and looking at him. The way she was leaning he could just see a little way down the front of her dress.

"I'll be seventeen in a month."

"Seventeen and don't have a girlfriend?" she said sounding surprised.

He shrugged.

"I'm twenty-one. Do you think that's too old?"

"Oh, no, not at all. I wish I were twenty-one."

They were silent again for a while and he kept looking straight ahead so he didn't see her hand at her side working secretly to twist the thread loop for her belt around the head of the bolt that held the arm of the chair to the back. "Oh, dear, I seem to be caught," she said. "Can you help me?"

He got up and walked around her chair. He bent over trying to get the twine loop out from between the washer and the wood. She slid her legs to one side making a little room. "Here, you can sit down while you work on it," she said patting the wooden slats of the chair. He sat, feeling the pressure of the outside of her thigh against his buttocks. It was hard to figure out just how the belt loop had gotten so strongly caught. He could smell the scent of her like the faintest of gardenias. Once when she turned to look and see what he was doing he felt the pressure of her breast pushed against his upper arm. He finally got it undone and she said, "Oh, thank you. Thank you. I don't know what I would have done without you. It would have been a shame to put a tear in this frock. It's one of my favorites."

He started to get up and she took one of his hands in both of hers and held it to her cheek while looking into his eyes gratefully and said, "I hope I can do something for you sometime."

He got up and went back to his chair, his heart pounding. He sat looking straight ahead for fear she would be able to see into his eyes and know what he was thinking. She got up a little while later saying, "Well, I best go check on the little one."

***

Mary VanderMeer sat alone in the corner of the wall couch in main salon. She was leaning back with legs up on the seat. It was after eleven at night and everyone else had gone to bed. She felt free and very adult to be out from under the supervision of her parents. Being in a different cabin from them meant they couldn't check on her and it gave her a feeling of independence.

The overhead lights had been turned off so that she sat under one of the wall sconce lights looking at a magazine. She was startled to hear Third Mate Travers say, "Good evening, Miss VanderMeer. I didn't expect to find you here."

She dropped the magazine, swung her legs down, straightening her skirt at the same time. She brushed a wisp of hair away from her face and wished he had not caught her in such an ungainly position. "Oh ... ah ... I ... ah ... I was just going to bed," she said and then felt embarrassed for having said it. *Why can't I ever say the right thing to him?*

He was wearing a fleece lined leather jack over his white shirt and black tie. He took the jacket off and laid it along with his cap on one of the chairs. "Bit nippy out there tonight. I was going to have a spot of tea before going on watch," he said. "Would you like a cup of tea, Miss VanderMeer?"

"Ah ... yes ... thank you," she said feeling a little dizzy.

"Come with me then, I'll show you where it is. That way if you ever want some in the middle of the night when the stewards are not about you can sneak in and get some for yourself."

She followed him across the lounge to the galley. He took down two mugs that were different from the cups they used in the dining room and poured out the tea. "Frightfully strong," he said. "Would you like some water in yours?"

"Yes please."

"Milk and sugar?"

"Yes please."

He handed her one of the mugs and led the way back to the salon. He held the chair for her to sit down at one of the tables, sat next to her, and she searched mentally for something to say. *Do you like sailing? Oh, no, not that. She couldn't ask that. Where's your home? Mother has already asked him that.* She most emphatically didn't want to sound like her mother. "Good tea," she said.

"You're lying, Miss VanderMeer, it's horrid tea."

She laughed and felt more relaxed. "You're right. It's not the best I've had."

"Do you want more hot water in it?" he asked starting to get up.

"That will just make it weaker, Mr. Travers, not better."

He laughed and his laughter made her feel good. He finished off his tea, looked at his watch and said, "I have a few minutes before I have to go on watch. Would you like to go to the bridge, Miss VanderMeer?"

"Oh, yes. Could I?"

"For a few minutes. Better get a wrap. It's a bit chilly up there," he said picking up the cups and setting them on the sideboard.

"Oh, I'll be all right," she said and followed him up the inside stairs to the bridge level. Parkington greeted her as she entered and she stood not saying anything, trying to understand as Travers explained to her about the compass and the steering. He directed her by the elbow around the pilothouse and over to the chart table. He pointed to a little X and said, "That was our position at twenty ... at eight o'clock this evening."

"Where are we now?" she asked.

"About there," he said moving his finger down a little. "We're almost half way between Durban and the Cape."

He held on to her hand as he helped her over the lip of the hatch when they went out to the wing. The wind whipped around the pilothouse, tugging at her hair and blowing her skirt. She held her skirt down and walked behind him to the starboard rail. "We have a repeater compass here and on the other side so we can check the course without having to go inside. And that thing out there is the taff rail log. It tells us how far we have gone through the water. It is usually streamed from the stern of the ship, but when they mounted the gun back there they moved the log up here."

They stood there on the wing for a few minutes. He moved so as to protect her from the wind and she stood watching the top of the mast tracing connecting lines between the stars with the swinging of the ship. Thirty feet below her the bow wake curled back in glowing, foamy scrolls. "Are you getting cold?" he asked.

"A little, I guess."

Back inside he asked, "Would you like to steer the ship?"

"Oh, no, I might do something wrong."

"Oh, you can't do anything wrong. Come on," he said going over to the wheel. "What's the course, Jones?"

"Two-five-eight, sir."

"I'll relieve you for a moment, Jones."

"Yes, sir," the helmsman said stepping aside.

She stood next to him, listening carefully, trying to understand while he explained to her about the lubber's line and all she had to do was to bring the line to the number. "If the line goes off to the right, you turn the wheel to the left. If it goes to the left, you turn to the right. Now, you try it."

"Oh, I couldn't."

"Of course you can. Even I can do it. I'll be right here behind you."

He stepped back a little holding on to the wheel with one hand and guiding her between himself and the wheel with the other. He stood behind her, his arms reaching around her, looking over her shoulder. She could feel his chest against her back and smell his cologne. "Put your hands on the spokes," he said, his lips close to her ears. "I'll keep steering until you get the feel of it."

She put her hands on the wheel and his arms were parallel with hers. She could feel his arms rubbing against her as he turned the wheel. "It doesn't take much. There, she's starting off to the right so we turn a little to the left. She is getting back on course now."

His arms suddenly fell away and she had the wheel with no help from him. "A little to the right," his voice said gently, "A little more. Now ease off. This spoke here," he reached over her shoulder, "with the cap on it, when it is straight up and down your rudder is amidships. Your rudder is straight. A little to the left now. You see the line is going off to the right. That's it. Now put your rudder amidships."

He was quiet for a while and she kept turning the wheel first one way and then the other. She was beginning to understand it. The line began to drift off to the right and she turned the wheel a little. It kept going to the right and she turned the wheel a little more. It was going to the right faster and faster. Something was wrong. The ship wasn't turning the way it was supposed to and then she heard him say very quietly, "Remember, bring the line to the number. The line to the number, not the number to the line."

How could I forget so soon? He must think me a complete ninny. She turned the wheel the other way and the line started back the way it was supposed to. She got it back and his arms were around her again. "You did very well," he said. "Here, let me get it right on the button before we give it back to the helmsman."

She took her hands off the wheel and he lowered one arm to let her out. "You'll have to come try it again sometime."

"Oh, I'd like to."

"Can you find your way below all right?"

"Oh, Yes."

"Good night then, Miss VanderMeer."

"Good night, Mr. Travers. Thank you," she said and walked out of the pilothouse and down the stairs. Behind her she could hear his voice talking to Mr. Parkington and she walked slowly to continue to hear his voice as long as possible. At her cabin she got undressed, one item at a time, dreaming of the night when they would be alone somewhere on the ship and he would put his arms around her and not just hold her arm, or her hand, to help her through a hatch.

CHAPTER FIVE

Saturday, 17 January 1942

The rising sun found Helen Stanley in a deck chair holding that morning's paper rolled up into a tube. Her rising early had started in nurses' training when she used to get up to study in the quiet of the morning. For her there was something special with the beginning of a day. Angola sunsets could be awesomely colorful, inspiring and beautiful, but there was with them the leftover heat and tiredness of the day. There was also the noise and voices of people waiting for the day to end, whereas mornings were cool, quiet and fresh. But she did not feel the usual tranquility this morning. She was irritated because Reverend VanderMeer was again up before her. Two days in a row he had intruded into her time of the day. He was on the opposite side of the ship and didn't even know she was there, and yet she still had the feeling he was intruding. She had seen him heading the opposite direction when she had come out of her cabin that morning. She had waited quietly by her cabin door until she heard the opposite hatch close behind him and then went over and picked up one of the papers. Her irritation did not extend to any members of the crew who might awake. They had to be up. It was their job. She didn't resent Harold VanderMeer personally, but only because he was a member of the clergy.

Her resentment of the clergy started when she wanted to get married. Her lifelong minister refused to perform the ceremony because her fiancée was a Catholic. His priest refused to perform the ceremony because she was not Catholic. At the time she was madly in love with him. He was the only man who had ever proposed marriage, the only man who had shown any interest of any kind in her. At some time amid the confusion and frustration of religious demands, the offer of marriage was withdrawn. "Let's just forget the whole thing," he had said. She was willing to change her religion and take instruction, but her parents and minister were so against it that her fiancée could not withstand their onslaught. After that whenever the minister condescendingly said such things as, "Well, we know it was not God's will you marry him, don't we?" or "God will send the right man along, my dear." She would nod in agreement but be filled with anger and wish there were some way she could hurt him as much as he had hurt her.

In 1927 she made application to the Baptist Board of Foreign Missions and was accepted as a nurse to Angola. From the moment she arrived she had a running battle with the station director who visited the hospital daily, preaching hell, fire and damnation to the sick. On one occasion she physically threw him out of the room of a patient who was scheduled for surgery that day. In less than a year after she arrived on the field she was ordered home to defend herself before the mission board. But instead of going home she applied for and got a job as nurse with the Portuguese Colonial Government.

As the years passed she came to consider herself as non-religious, not because of any philosophical searching, but because of the insensitivity of those who called themselves servants of God. She shunned clerics and churches more intensely than a teetotaler avoids drunkards and bars. Her resentment now was not aimed at a man named Harold VanderMeer, but at a clergyman who had intruded into her time of day. In her experience that was what clergymen always did, intrude into other people's lives.

She heard the blackout panels being turned back, the door opened and the steward stepped out. "Good morning, Miss Stanley. Would you care for a cup of tea?"

"Tea? What makes you think you could find any tea on this tub?" Her voice was sarcastic, but there was a smile on her face. It was the combination of sarcasm and smile that the passengers and crew were just beginning to understand.

"I'm very good at ferreting out those types of things, ma'am."

"Well, just make sure you bring me the tea and not the ferret."

"I'll be very careful, ma'am."

"In that case, John, yes, I would very much like a cup of tea," she said smiling warmly and pushing a strand of brown hair the wind had blow loose back into place.

"Yes, ma'am."

He went back inside and she unrolled the cylinder of paper. Her private day had come to an end. Others would be coming on deck soon. She rolled the papers the opposite direction to restore their flatness and started reading.

Saturday, 17 January 1942
At approximately 1630 hours today we shall pass within five miles of Cape Agulhas, the southernmost point of Africa.

SINGAPORE - 16 January 1942
War communiqués,
British Far East Headquarters
    During the later stages of the engagement reported yesterday in the eastern part of Negri Sembilan our troops destroyed six enemy

tanks and inflicted heavy casualties. Enemy troops were supported by fighters and bombers that attacked our forward troops.

She suddenly didn't want to read about a war somewhere else. Looking across the deck to the blue water, the war seemed far away; more distant than it had ever seemed before, as though the water had somehow separated them from it, immunized them against the disease of it. The northeast coast of the United States, and Tripoli, and Hamburg, and the Philippines were all very, very far away and she wanted to keep the war in those places far away from her.

***

Rudolph Duer came out, crossed the deck and stood with his buttocks against the top rail, his legs crossed at the ankles and his sweater thrown over his shoulders. He lighted a cigarette cupping his hands to protect the flame of the match from the strong winds. He was waiting for Lady Marisha to finish her coffee so he could take her tray back to the Galley. From the corner of his eye he saw Helen Stanly finish her coffee and he went over to her.

"Good morning, Heavenly Helen," he said. "May I take your tray?"

She turned and looked up at him for an instant and said, "You know, Dr. Duer, I don't think I have ever met anyone quite so full of bullshit as you are. Who do you think you're kidding with this 'Heavenly Helen' bit?"

He smiled his most captivating smile, laughed a little and said. "Miss Stanley, you may be right, but I have discovered in my short lifetime that friendships, like flower gardens, often grow better with a little bullshit."

"That may be because many people can't tell the difference between the bullshit and the rose even when they smell it," she said. "My name is Miss Stanley, not Heavenly Helen."

"As you wish. May I take your tray?"

"I'll take care of it. Thank you," she said setting the tray on the deck next to her chair.

He went back to leaning against the rail where he could watch Lady Marisha and Magical Maggie annoyed by Miss Stanley's rebuff. Most people liked the names he gave them. He had names for almost everyone. There was Marvelous Matt and Lucky Lukie. The names seemed to come spontaneously. Matt got his name when he was playing chess with Duer one evening and Duer had said, "Come on, Marvelous Matt, you better take that move back. You can do better than that."

His use of special names was a way to be familiar. If some names came spontaneously, there were other names that had to be manipulated.

The first name that came to mind for Miss Stanley was "Hellish Helen," but that kind of name would not flatter her. Her spurning of his special name for her angered him. Somehow he would have to get even with her for that. Mable VanderMeer was another one he knew instinctively didn't care for him and would not accept a flattering name.

He leaned against the rail, waiting. Lady Marisha's cup was almost empty but she hadn't poured any more from the little pot on her tray. She just sat there looking across the water while Magical Maggie played with the kid. "Are you finished, Lady Marisha? May I take your tray?"

"Yes. Thank you, Mr. Duer. You may take away my tray."

He picked up the tray and headed for the galley. She had answered him as she would have answered the steward. He was not her servant. She might be a "lady" but he was determined before this trip was over she would accept him as her equal, even as her lover.

***

At eleven o'clock Mary VanderMeer settled into a deck chair near the starboard ladder to the bridge to wait for Third Mate Travers to get off watch. It would be an hour or so before he came down the ladder, but she could wait. This time he would not surprise her. This time she would be ready for him. She had taken hours to do her hair just right and had put on her prettiest sweater. Over her legs she had thrown a steamer rug to hide her less attractive skirt and shoes. She pulled another chair close to her and put her crocheting bag on it to prevent anyone else from sitting there. When he came down the ladder she would pick up the bag and he would, for a little while anyway, sit down next to her.

The time crept by. Rose Duer sat next to Mary's mother who sat next to Mary's father. Mary was on the urge of asking one of them what time it was, but restrained herself. She turned her head and looked intently at the ladder, trying by her thoughts to force his appearance. When she turned back she saw him on the other side of the ship. *How could that be? He always uses this ladder. Why did he go over there? Did he know she was waiting for him? Was he trying to avoid her? He was talking with Miss Jenkins. No! Not Miss Jenkins, to Nicky.* She immediately felt better. *Now he was talking to Miss Jenkins. She was answering him, smiling at him, flirting with him.*

Mary felt empty and certain that at any moment the tightness in her chest and throat would burst through as tears. She stood quickly, grabbing her crocheting bag, and rushed through the hatch and lounge where some of the passengers were sitting around waiting to go into lunch. She went into her cabin and threw herself on her bunk with her face to the wall so if anyone came in they would not see she was crying.

***

"Do you have any free time?" Travers asked quietly so the others on deck would not hear him.

"And what would I do with it if I had it, Mr. Travers?" she asked speaking just as quietly.

"We might be able to find something to do."

"Oh, really?" She raised one eyebrow quizzically and suggestively. "Would you take me into town to the cinema?" She paused for just an instant and then before he could answer added, "Or maybe we could go dancing at some club. I like to dance."

He smiled, amused by her teasing. "I don't think I have enough petrol to get into town from here, what with rationing and all, but maybe we could find something interesting to do right here."

"And what might that be?"

"Well, I don't know for sure. Maybe whatever one does after one's been to the cinema and finished dancing."

"Like playing games. They have some nice games in the salon. Is that what you were thinking of?"

"I was thinking of something just you and I could play."

"They have chess and checkers there. Those are games for just two people, but I don't know how to play chess. I don't know how to move the little men," she said teasing him.

"I was thinking of something much more personal. Something where it was just the two of us in the room."

"Well now," she said pretending to be shocked. "Aren't you the bold one? Cheeky to boot."

"Me?" He exclaimed pretending to be hurt.

She laughed and said, "Me times me own after he's abed."

He shook his head disappointedly. "Tonight I'm on watch until midnight."

"Oh, that's too bad. Too bad. Maybe some other time," she said raising an eyebrow and then stood up. "Come, Nicky. Time to wash for lunch."

***

The soft rays of the setting sun sent long shadows along the deck. The passengers who lined the rail were silent for the most part, looking at the sun-brightened and dark-shadowed cliffs of Cape Agulhas. For each of them there was a subconscious excitement and apprehension of heading totally away from this land toward open ocean and to another land they could not yet see.

Margaret Jenkins stood by the rail looking at the land and thinking that leaving was one of the most fortunate things that had ever happened to her. She was fundamentally one who saw the best in things. It did not occur to her that her pleasant disposition was the main reason for her good fortune. It was the war and her disposition that had kept her on as a lady's maid when she didn't have any of the qualifications for that position. She would never have said it just that way to anyone else, but the war had been good to her. Young ladies who had the education and background to be nannies were employed in more important jobs with the military and the government. They had the glory of helping with the war effort and got better pay, but she was still grateful that their good fortune also meant her good fortune. Colonel and Lady Marisha had been extremely patient and good to her. They had taught her how to talk, proper table manners, even how to stand and how to walk.

They had taught her the things that mattered, things that made the difference between her station in life and theirs. But she had never forgotten who she was, or where she came from. Until a few months ago there had been that dread in the back of her mind that when the war was over she might no longer be able to keep her position. Not that the Colonel and Lady would out-right sack her, but she knew she had gone as far as she could go. Even aboard ship she knew as a lady's maid she ranked just a little higher than the ships stewards. True, she was a passenger, but she and the stewards knew she wasn't a proper passenger on her own. No way could she have afforded this on her own.

Of all the good luck that had come her way, the best was when the colonel had called her in and told her Lady Marisha and Nicholas were going to the United States until after the war was over and had asked if she would consider going with them. She could hardly control her excitement while he kept talking of how he couldn't force her to go, and he would certainly give her good recommendations if she decided she couldn't go, but he would consider it a great personal favor if she would agree to accompany Lady Marisha.

She let him finish his entire speech before she respectfully said she felt it her duty to go despite what her personal feeling might be. He appreciated her self-sacrifice and on the spot gave her a raise. For six months after that it was all she could do to go about her duties quietly without asking when they would be leaving. But now she knew she was on her way to America. When she got up next morning this continent would be left behind and out of sight and the next land she would see would be the final step to the United States. America, the place where anyone could become whatever they wanted to be without any class and social restrictions. She would not just desert the Harwells. She would certainly stay with them until they found someone else, but now that she was going to America, she didn't intend to stay a maid for the rest of her life.

***

A few feet away Lady Marisha Chatham stood not really seeing, nor appreciating the sight, only knowing she was leaving her husband behind. Eight months before she had sailed into Cape Town a hundred miles to the northwest of them with Ransom at her side. Then she had been thrilled at the sight of Table Mountain and the blanket of clouds rolling over the top of it. But there was no thrill in any beautiful sight now, only fear. She felt part of her was attached to that land and she was being stretched out as the ship moved away.

Instinctively she sensed there was something wrong with this trip. She knew beyond any question that no matter what else might happen in that campaign, her husband was not going to be killed in North Africa. For that reason she knew this trip was unnecessary. She couldn't identify it. Maybe it was just the extreme distances involved, but there was something wrong with this trip for Nicky and herself. She had fought and argued against this trip with everything she had, but he had remained adamant and in the end she had no choice but to comply with his wishes. Consequently, there was mixed with her longing, love and loneliness, resentment and anger.

***

Mary waited until her mother had gone and then picked up their teacups and carried them to the sink in the galley. She could have just put them on the sideboard as Travers had the night before, but she wanted to go into the galley. She dreamt of last night and waited with the uncertain hope he might walk in to get himself a cup of tea.

She left the galley and made her way through the blackout partitions to the deck. She was half way to the rail when she saw Margaret sitting in one of the chairs. "Oh, excuse me," she said automatically.

"It's too nice a night to stay inside, isn't it?" Margaret said

"Yes."

"Why don't you sit down?" Margaret said motioning to the chair next to her.

"Okay. I came out for just a moment before going to bed."

They sat for almost half an hour without saying anything. For both of them there was the pleasantness of just sitting without feeling a need to speak. Finally, Margaret got up saying, "Well, I guess I'll go to bed."

"Me, too. I'm getting cold," Mary said and followed Margaret through the door. When they were past the blackout panels Mary said, "Do you want a cup of tea?"

"Can't get tea this time of night."

"Sure you can," Mary said leading the way into the galley. "Mr. Travers showed me where it was." She drew the tea and handed one cup to Margaret. "He took me to the bridge last night," she said having to tell someone.

"Oh, when was this?"

"Before he went on watch."

"Do you fancy him?" Margaret said looking over the top of her cup.

"Oh, he's very nice of course, but I don't fancy him," Mary said looking down into her cup and blushing.

Well, the girl was moonstruck over the cheeky blade. "How old are you?" Margaret asked and then quickly added, "You don't take offense at my asking, do you?"

"Oh, no. Almost nineteen. How old are you?"

"Twenty-one, I'm afraid."

"Afraid?"

"You know, twenty-one and not married."

"Oh ... but you've ..." She stopped, not knowing just how to ask the question and shocked she could even think such things. Good girls didn't do what she was thinking, but the question had started to come out before she knew she was asking it. She knew her question was the kind her mother would say should never be asked and her father would have told her it was wrong to even think those things.

"Had lovers?" Margaret said finishing the question for her.

"I guess that's what I mean."

"Oh, hundreds, love."

She couldn't mean the same thing by lovers that they meant in the books her father didn't want her reading, the thing her mother had tried to explain to her a man only did to a woman after they were married, unless the woman was bad. Margaret couldn't mean that and talk so carelessly about hundreds. And yet there were things she wanted to hear about and hoped Margaret could tell her. She knew it was wrong to want to hear about those things, or even think about them, but she couldn't help herself from asking, "What's it like?"

"What's what like?"

"Oh, you know ... a man ... and." She felt herself blushing and wished she hadn't asked the question.

"Ah, nobody can tell another about that. You have to find it out for yourself."

"How old do you think he is?"

"Haven't the foggiest. Never gave it a thought," Margaret said and she suddenly felt sorry for Mary and protective of her. She was not at all interested in Mr. Travers. She knew exactly what he had implied in his conversation with her and by that conversation she knew his opinion of her, and he had been right. She was a servant girl who had been born in the East End and had the good fortune to become a lady's maid. Nor did she resent Mr. Travers' opinion of her. That's the way things were. But there was an enormous difference between an East-ender who lost her virginity at the age of fifteen and a minister's only virgin daughter. "Well, I guess I best be getting to bed. Thank for showing me where the tea is," she said putting her cup in the sink. "Good night."

"Good night," Mary said watching Margaret leave and then waited for a moment, wishing he would come in for a cup of tea, wishing last night would happen again.

***

Harold VanderMeer closed the devotional he was reading and suddenly realized another day had passed and he had not said anything to the captain about holding a Sunday morning service. He had intended to ask the captain's permission for a service, but somehow the opportunity had never presented itself. He only thought of it late at night, or first thing in the morning, and then more out of a sense of obligation than something he wanted to do.

It was only two months ago he had started leading the family devotions again. All the time he had been sick, it was Mable who'd held the Bible reading and prayer time every morning right after breakfast. At the Andrew Murray Rest home, where missionaries went on vacation, there was always an evening service led by the director. Then one morning after breakfast the director said, "I know you always have devotions with your children in you rooms after breakfast, so why don't you have them here in the salon then so anyone who wants to can join you."

By then they had been at the Andrew Murray for almost four months waiting for passage and had become almost a fixture while other missionaries came and went. The director had asked him because they had been there the longest. Right then the Andrew Murray Home was almost full and he was terrified at the suggestion of standing in front of people and conducting a service. He had looked at Mable for help, for her to say something that would gracefully get him out of the situation, but she had just smiled at him and nodded a little. The first time his hands had shaken with fear as he sat in the chair conducting the Bible lesson. One of the intimidations was that his audience was all missionaries. But in a few days he had regained his confidence and after a week, the director asked someone else to conduct the devotions and so there was soon a weekly rotation.

He turned off the light and thought if the captain were to ask him to hold a service tomorrow he would be glad to oblige. Suddenly he understood he did not love God any less, nor was he an unfaithful servant for not making arrangements for a service. Not everything was his responsibility. All he had to do was be ready if called upon. He fell asleep content with that thought.

CHAPTER SIX

Sunday – 18 January 1942

Rose Duer, looking over her shoulder as though something was chasing her, approached Mable and asked. "It's Sunday. Is there going to be any service today?"

"Well, I don't know. I think if the captain wanted there to be a service, something would have been said about it. But we have family devotions that are kind of like a service in our cabin every day right after breakfast. You may certainly join us if you wish."

"Why don't you do it right here?" Rose said waving her hand indicating the salon.

"We wouldn't want to disturb anyone," Mable answered looking around the salon. The stewards were taking away the last of the dishes and removing the cloths from the tables. Hal had already gone to the cabin and Mary and the boys were just waiting until their mother said, "It's time, children," and they would all go. She knew as soon as the stewards were through, Lady Marisha would get her writing things and sit in the corner writing letters. Duer would sit in the opposite corner pretending to read while he watched her. Margaret would be in the lounge right outside the door playing with Nicholas until they all went out on deck. Mable knew Duer would not like them having family devotions in the salon and she didn't know how Lady Marisha would feel about it, but she didn't want to impose on her. "Why don't you and Robbie join us this morning?"

"Thank you. I'd like that," Rose said, smiling and then added, "but don't tell Rudy. Please. He doesn't like Robbie and me going to church."

"Then we won't tell him," Mable said smiling reassuringly.

***

At a little after ten, Third Mate Travers climbed the starboard ladder to the main deck. He greeted Mary and Mrs. Duer and talked for a few minutes with Reverend and Mrs. VanderMeer. On his way through the lounge he saw Dr. Duer in the galley joking with the stewards. Exiting from the lounge on the other side of the ship he greeted Lady Marisha and then went over and squatted down between Margaret and Nicky, who was coloring. "What are you coloring?" Travers asked.

"It's Windsor Castle," Nicky said without looking up.

"Of course. I should have recognized it right off."

"I wrote my Daddy a letter this morning," Nicky said.

"All by yourself?"

"My Mummy helped a little bit," he said finally looking up. "She's going to post it when we get to land. It's the first letter I ever wrote."

"But now that you've started you'll be writing lots more, won't you?"

"Oh, yes," he said and went back to his coloring.

Travers turned to look in Lady Marisha's direction. She was busy reading her book and not paying any attention to them. He looked at Margaret. She was watching him. "And when does he go to bed?" he asked smiling.

"Now why would a man like you be interested in when a little boy went to bed?"

"Oh, just idle curiosity, I imagine."

"Then you do not care if you get an answer."

He chuckled. "I'm free this evening until midnight. Have you any pressing engagements."

"Not that I recall."

"I'll meet you here after dinner," he whispered standing up as Duer came through the hatchway. She nodded and he spun around and ran up the ladder to the bridge.

***

Rose Duer sat on the starboard side of the ship with Reverend and Mrs. VanderMeer and she felt happier than she had been in years. The steward, as he had done previous mornings, had just set a coffee tray in front of her and such service made her feel special. Everybody else had a coffee tray, too, but it was special to her.

The other thing that made her feel so good was the way Reverend and Mrs. VanderMeer, particularly Mable VanderMeer, treated her. The first day they had invited to her pull her chair over closer to theirs and talked to her. Mable VanderMeer had asked her about her home in Mankato. People hadn't talked to her in years. They had always talked to her husband. And, if they did start talking to her, he always forced his way into the conversation, pushing her into the background. But on this trip, there was too much time for him to always be interrupting her conversations.

Once he had tried to interrupt a conversation and make her look like a fool in front of her new friends. When he was through, Mable VanderMeer firmly said, "No, Dr. Duer. I think you are wrong and your wife is right." And Reverend VanderMeer had jumped in and said, "No question about it." From then on he had spent most of his time on the other side of the ship. But when they were in their cabin at night, he would torment her by telling her how dumb she was and that the Reverend and his fat wife were as dumb as she was.

That morning in the devotions she had felt she was loved and she was not as dumb and worthless as Rudy kept saying she was. She was also grateful they did not have one of the better cabins. Both she and Rudy had discovered early that if they were not careful, what they said in their cabin could be heard on deck. With the other cabins she had to be right outside an open porthole to hear what was being said inside, but the bare, steel wall of their cabin seemed to carry the voices even when the porthole was closed. She had discovered it when she was outside and Rudy had been talking to Robbie in the cabin. What she liked was how when he made fun of her and scolded her, he did it quietly. Somehow his disdain for her did not seem as bad when he had to whisper his abuse.

She felt more secure than happy. The thin walls of their cabin restricted the way he treated Robbie and her. But no matter how secure or pampered she felt, she still wished he were dead. Sometimes she would see him on the other side of the ship leaning against the rail. His legs would be crossed at the ankles showing off his stylish pumps that she had polished. He would be wearing flannel slacks she had pressed and a tasteful check or striped shirt under his sweater. If it was warm, the sweater would be thrown over his shoulders with the arms tied casually in front. As often as not he would have a drink in his hand.

At times like these she wished she could find him in that stance, leaning back with the top of the rail just below his waist, when no one else was around. It would be so easy to just give him a little shove in the chest and watch him topple over the side. She wished she had the courage to do that if the opportunity ever presented itself, but she knew she did not.

She had loved him once, but that was long ago. In high school she had worshipped him from a distance, adored him, loved him. He was the school football hero and star of the senior play. She couldn't believe it was happening when he started calling on her during the summer after graduation. Her wildest dreams and hopes came true in the fall when he asked her to marry him. They had lived with her parents after they were married and all the time he was going to college and for two years after graduation. That was nothing to be ashamed of. There was a depression and times were hard. Lots of young married couples were unable to start their married life in a home of their own. Neither her father, nor any of her brothers had gone to college and they were all proud to have a college man in house.

They were not rich, but somehow the grocery store managed to survive when lots of other family businesses were failing. And although

Rose's paychecks from clerking in her father's store were sometimes late, there was always food on the table.

She was pregnant with Robbie before she realized, or at least accepted the realization, that Rudy had used her. He had married her to finance his way through college. He had never loved her except possibly as one might love a useful tool. It was after Robbie was born he started shouting at her and blaming her and Robbie for preventing him from making something of himself.

He was classified 4F with the draft and he considered that an accomplishment. He got jobs at first because with so many young men drafted into the service, there was a shortage of teachers. She knew he liked teaching because it put him in contact with a great many single women. She had stayed with him even after he had started beating her. The beatings hadn't been too bad at first, just a slap. But it wasn't too long before the slapping had turned into beatings. Once after he had beaten her she had tried to stand up to him and had told him she was going to leave him and get a divorce. He laughed at her and said, "Why you ignorant little simp. You stupid bitch. You're going to leave me? What are you going to do? Where are you going to go if you leave me, back to clerking in your father's store? You're no spring chicken any more Rose, and you never were much to look at anyway. Do you think any other man is going to want you at your age with a brat to raise?" He became angrier as he shouted at her, his voice getting louder and louder. "You can't leave me, Rose. You know why? Because nobody else will have you. Even your parents don't want you," he shouted and started beating her again. He beat her so badly she could hardly move and as he walked out of the room he said, "That's just for thinking about it, Rose. If you ever try to leave me, I'll kill you and then for the rest of his life I'll beat the shit out of Robbie and tell him I'm doing it because of you."

She never mentioned, nor even thought about leaving him again. What she thought of was being rid of him. She went along with whatever he said, saying pretty much what he told her to say. He had always put up a big front and she had spouted the same things to her parents he did because she didn't dare say any differently. He was always going to better jobs with better salaries.

When she was asked about it she confirmed what he said was true. But if her parents didn't know what a failure he was before, now there was no longer any hiding it. Rudy had just lost his job at a small, none-too-good, private school in Cape Town and the grocery business which had put him through college was now expanded and flourishing and financing their passage home.

She wanted to tell Harold and Mable VanderMeer that Rudy did not have a doctorate, that he couldn't hold a job, that she and her family had put him through college, that he abused Robbie and her, but no one would believe her. He would just tell them she'd had a breakdown and ever since then had spells when her imagination runs away with her. But there were times when she thought if there was anyone she could confide in who might believe her, it would be Mable VanderMeer.

***

At noontime, the day was clear and transparent with air so light that at the horizon the sky was hardly separable from the ocean. The sun radiated a languid warmth and the wind was reduced to soft whisperings. The ocean napped, its chest rising and falling in the long and even swells of its deep and even breathing. Behind the ship three shearwaters skimmed the undulations crossing back and forth across the turbid wake. At the bow a school of porpoises left and reentered the water in parabolic patterns. On the bridge, First Mate Renshaw, with sextant to eye, slowly turned the drum following the climb of the sun. He was always mildly excited when the sun stopped climbing and hung for an instant at its zenith before starting its descent.

It was a day where all the elements, the rising and falling sea, caressing breezes and the warm sun amplified the strange restlessness and longing within Mary VanderMeer. She was totally unable to concentrate on the book she held in her hands and at the sound of every set of footsteps would look in their direction in the hope of seeing Third Mate Travers.

The day brought to Lady Marisha memories of lazy holiday mornings with Ransom and tea taken in the garden on pleasant spring afternoons. But there was mingled with those memories the constant concern as to his whereabouts and the emptiness of his absence. The ship's paper had reported the garrison at Halfaya had unconditionally surrendered the previous day. More than five thousand Axis prisoners had been captured and seventy-six British soldiers that had been prisoners of war had been released. But casualties could occur even at times of surrender and she just could not be as encouraged and excited about the news as Parkington seemed to be. Looking up from her reveries and seeing her son, she had a desperate urge to go pick him up and clutch him. *Son of my husband, flesh of his flesh.* But he was sitting contentedly on the deck watching the youngest VanderMeer boy braiding something and she could not impose her fears and concerns on his tranquility, even with a gesture of affection.

On the bridge, Captain Chipman was not insensitive to the day. Having spent a lifetime at sea, he knew it to be the precisely rare day it was and he was reluctant to disturb its perfection, but there were other considerations. He looked through the porthole at the ship's clock.

Twelve-eleven. Time enough before lunch. He stepped into the pilothouse where Mr. Renshaw was just finishing plotting the noon fix. The captain looked at the plot and picked up the stopwatch in passing. Three feet from the helmsman, the officer of the watch Travers was standing with his legs spread against the easy rolling of the ship, his hands clasped behind his back, and the captain knew his thoughts were far away. "Mr. Travers."

Travers turned quickly, startled by the captain's voice. "Aye, Captain?"

"Sound life boat drill, Mr. Travers."

"Aye-aye, Captain," he said walking to the intercom. His voice blared over the speakers in the crew's quarters. "This is a drill. This is a drill. Life boat stations," and as he spoke the last line he reached over and pushed the alarm button and the captain started the stopwatch. On the bridge all except the captain, Travers and the helmsman, rushed to the main deck. Throughout the ship there was the sound of feet running up steel ladders and across steel decks as the crew rushed to their stations. The first to arrive started taking the covers off the boats. The passengers, all of whom were on deck, lined up to receive their spare life jackets and were amazed at how fast the boats could be swung over the side.

On the bridge, Travers stood looking down at the boats. He saw Mr. Parkington raise his hand and reported, "Boat number three over the side and ready, Captain."

"Very well."

Mr. Renshaw waved. "Boat number four over the side and ready, Captain," Travers said. He stood anxiously, waiting for Hawkins signal. He wanted to report his boat ready before the captains, but the signal came from the two boats at simultaneously. "Boats one and two—"

The captain pushed the stop button. "Very well," he said and looked at the watch. Two minutes and forty-seven seconds. It was good. Would even have been considered exceptional by other people's standards, but too slow as far as the captain was concerned. "Secure from life boat drill, Mr. Travers."

The captain moved to the after rail of the bridge and stood looking down at the main deck. He watched the passengers put their life jackets back in the bins while the crew brought the boats back in and settled them in their cradles. Hawkins went around from boat to boat pulling on the cover lashings, making sure the falls in the blocks were not twisted and checking the pelican hooks to make sure they would let go easily. The youngest VanderMeer boy came up to Hawkins and showed him a braid. Hawkins looked at it critically, nodded, then made a loop of it and slipped it over the boy's head, indicting it had to be longer. When Hawkins crossed over to the other side, the Chatham tot fell in beside him, looking up at him, moving when he moved, stopping when he stopped, and standing with his hands on his hips when Hawkins stood that way. Hawkins spun around suddenly, crouched down and said, "Boo!" Nicholas ran laughing gleefully to his mother. He waited there for a moment and then walked as though stalking some prey along the hatch trying to sneak up on Hawkins.

The captain watched the game of boo-and-run and wondered where the colonel was at that moment. He looked at the sky. It was at times like these that catastrophes occurred. It was in the clear, calm predawn hours of September 1, that Germany invaded Poland. It was during a magnificently dawning Sunday that the Japanese attacked Pearl Harbor. It was just before daylight on a day that turned out to be much like this one that Ronald was shot down over the Channel. It was on a beautifully clear tranquil night the Port Rhodes was shot out from under him. *Abominable, bloody war! It taints even what nature would make beautiful.*

He saw Hawkins say "boo" for one last time, turn and go down the ladder to the after well-deck. The crew was gone and the passengers were expecting to hear the dinner chimes announcing lunch at any moment. They were all complacent and logy. That attitude was permissible for the passengers, but not for the crew. Not when he and each member of the crew was in a way responsible for each of those passengers. "Mr. Travers!"

"Aye Captain?" he said stepping half way out of the pilothouse door.

"Sound life boat drill, Mr. Travers."

"Beg pardon, sir?" he asked looking puzzled.

"Sound life boat drill, Mr. Travers," the captain said slowly and distinctly.

"Aye-aye, Captain."

The captain waited until he heard the first clang of the alarm before starting the stopwatch. He could just imagine the outburst of cursing and swearing the second time the crew heard the alarm. He saw them tear off the covers and throw them aside with no concern of where they landed, men were still readying the boats for lowering even while others furiously turned the cranks that swung the boats over the side. The boats were ready almost simultaneously so Mr. Travers could not call them off and said, "All boats over the side and ready, Captain."

The captain pushed the stop button and stood by the rail waiting until every head was turned his direction. "That's better," He said. "More than one whole minute better. Bosun."

Hawkins jumped to the hatch touching his hand to his forehead and said, "Aye, Cap'n."

"After block-and-fall on number three boat appears to be a little tight. Have it checked."

"Aye-aye, Cap'n."

"Secure from drill, Mr. Travers," the captain said and shortly after that the steward walked along the decks striking the dinner chime.

***

The captain saw the steward come into the pilothouse and take away his lunch tray. He didn't remember having eaten lunch, but he must have because the tray was empty. He did remember the engine room had called in the noon fuel and engine reports. They were a little late because of the lifeboat drills. Mr. Renshaw had reported a distance covered of four hundred and fifty-eight miles since the noon fix of the day before which put them a little more than three hundred miles West of Cape Agulhas. The lookout in the crow's nest had reported a floating box and the captain had seen a faint smudge of smoke on the horizon the lookout had not reported. All these things he remembered, but he did not remember eating his lunch.

He looked over at Travers who was standing in the walkway directly in front of the pilothouse, his hands resting on the rail. *He's a thousand miles away*, the captain thought and said, "Mr. Travers."

"Aye, Captain?"

"Lovely day, isn't it?"

"Yes, sir, it certainly is."

"How would you describe this day, Mr. Travers?"

Travers became cautious. "Sky clear. Wind, southeast eighteen to twenty knots. Sea," he looked at the water, "a force four. A little flat, Captain, but I would call it a force four. Barometer, steady."

"What about the visibility, Mr. Travers?"

"Visibility? Why, unlimited, sir."

"Tell me, Mr. Travers, if there were an aeroplane flying at an altitude of three thousand feet twenty-five miles to the North of us, would we be able to see it?"

"Probably not, sir, too small. Unless, of course, it reflected the sun, or something like that to draw our attention to it."

"Do you think that same aeroplane would be able to see us?"

"Quite probably, sir. We are much larger and leaving a smoke trail."

The captain stood looking at him for a moment and then said, "It is a shame, Mr. Travers, that except for your training years, you had so little peace time sailing. It is days like this that can seduce a man and bring him back to the sea year after year. But in war time, it is often days like this that can be the most unfortunate."

"I understand, sir."

"No you don't, Mr. Travers, but in time, God willing, this war will end and then you will understand. Bring her into the wind, Mr. Travers. Prepare to launch kites."

Travers stepped into the pilothouse and gave the orders to bring the ship about and headed into the wind. He went over to the intercom and pushed all the buttons except the ones for the passengers' quarters and said, "Now all hands to kite stations. All hands to kite stations."

On deck below, Matt VanderMeer had been sitting in the same place as the day before hoping Margaret would soon be out. It had reached the point that whenever she caught him looking at her across the room, she smiled and he smiled back instead of quickly looking away. He had expected she would join him, but now he felt the ship turning and suddenly members of the crew were running forward along both sides of the main deck. He got up from where he was sitting to go to the walkway in front of the salon and soon all of the passengers were out there with him. Margaret came and stood not far from him with Nicky in between them. She smiled invitingly at him as she picked Nicky up so he could see over the rail. He moved closer to her and said, "Would you like me to hold Nicky. He's kind of heavy, isn't he?"

"Oh, thank you," she said handing Nicky to him. Her hand rested for a moment on his arm before she separated herself the proper distance from him.

The combination of the ship's speed and heading into the wind created a forty-knot gale that blew their hair back and pressed their clothes against their bodies. Only Helen Stanley and Lady Marisha did not come to stand along the forward rail to watch the launching. The kites were opened and it was all their crews could do to hold them until they were released. Once airborne the kites jerked back and forth, sometimes almost hitting the crew on deck. When clear of the mast and bridge, the kites rose steadily, the wire spinning off the spools until they reached their height and then the spools were stopped and wires straightened, creating a humming sound in the wind.

The kites were left to fly for five minutes and then the ship slowed to reduce the wind speed and for the next half hour the crews took turns cranking the winches that brought the kites down. There was not much fun watching them bring in the kites, but the time for naps was passed and with it, Matt's time alone with Margaret.

***

Third Mate Travers almost ran from the pilothouse to the top of the ladder when he was relieved of the watch. With a hand on each rail and his arms stiff he lifted his feet so as not to touch the steps and slid down the ladder rails on his hands. He walked quickly across the deck, slid down the ladder to the after well-deck and ran aft to his cabin. Half an hour later, after showering and shaving, he crossed the after well-deck and saw her standing by the rail above waiting for him. She turned to go down the ladder backwards and with one hand on each rail, carefully picked her way, one step at a time. At the bottom he put his hand on her arm to guide her around the hatch and she stood smiling as he spun the wheel and swung open the steel hatch. "Careful stepping over," he said taking her hand. "There's a high lip there."

The lights came on in the passageway when the door was tightly closed behind them and she said, "Where is this cinema you're taking me to, Ducky?"

"Right here," he said opening the door to his cabin. "My own private theater."

"I do hope it will be a good show," she said walking through the door he held open for her.

CHAPTER SEVEN

Monday – 19 January 1942

At a little after seven in the morning Third Mate Travers threw the blankets back, swung his legs over the side of the bunk and sat there for a moment, groggily rubbing his eyes. He stood up slowly and walked with his eyes still half closed to the bathroom that he shared with the doctor. Standing at the basin he splashed water on his face, ran damp fingers through his hair, and dried his face. Wrapping the towel around his waist, he went to the crew's galley for a cup of tea.

He returned to his cabin with the tea and as he entered he was aware of her lingering scent. He picked up the paper Sparks had slipped under his door an hour earlier, turned on the light, and settled back comfortably into his bunk. He sat for a moment sipping his tea, remembering the evening before. He turned his head and smiled to himself when he smelled her scent on his pillow and then looked at the paper. He read the Far East Communiqués quickly. Singapore had been raided again, a hundred and thirty dead and more than a hundred injured. Some enemy planes had been shot down along with the loss of some British planes.

The news from Cairo gave more details about the surrender of Halfaya, even giving the names of the commanding generals, De Gorgis and Puttafuco. Travers had never heard of either of them before.

LONDON - 18 January 1942
Home Securities Ministry Communiqué
This morning a single engine aircraft dropped bombs at a point in the Shetland Islands. Some minor damage was caused, but no one was injured.
Early last night a small number of enemy aircraft flew over Southwest England. A few bombs were dropped. No one was hurt and little damage was reported.

Admiralty Communiqué
A twin-engine bomber that unsuccessfully attacked one of our convoys in the North Sea yesterday was shot down by the destroyer HMS Walpole. There were no casualties, or damage to the convoy, or escorts.

Admiralty Communiqué

The Board of the Admiralty regrets to announce His Majesty's Submarine Perseus with (Lt. Com. E.C.F. Nicolay commanding) is overdue and must be considered lost. The next of kin have been notified.

Perseus lost? Nicolay dead? It was hard to believe. He had known Everett Nicolay. They had gone to the same public school. They had not been close friends because Everett was two years ahead of him, but still, he had known him. He knew when he received his commission in the Royal Navy and knew when he was given command of the Perseus. It was one thing to read that ten, or a hundred, or even that five hundred strangers were killed. That kind of information was just so many numbers that didn't evoke much emotion except possibly anger. But now it was someone he knew, a sailor like himself, and he suddenly felt vulnerable. Somehow he had always been able to tell himself he was safe, that he couldn't be killed. Bombs only killed other people, people he didn't know. Torpedoes only sunk other ships, not the one he was on.

That Admiralty Communiqué reminded him death was not remote. He wondered when, where and how it had happened. *Overdue and must be considered lost.* He was certain he would prefer to be shot on the surface than to drown in a submarine. He set the paper aside, finished the tea, and went into the shower. The water sprayed out of the nozzle and he wondered if water would spray like that through a cracked seam in a submarine.

He finished showering, shaved, and got dressed. He left his cabin and after opening the steel hatch to the outside felt even more despondent. It had been perfectly clear when he had walked Margaret to the main deck, but now the sky was a solid gray, releasing its slow steady rain. He went back for his raincoat and went on watch unable not to think of Nicolay and the Perseus.

***

Margaret Jenkins stepped out of the shower and quickly dried and dressed. She was in her bunk, fully clothed, when Miss Stanley came in. It had been raining all morning and the passengers had stayed inside. She put Nicky down for his nap and she was certain after the big lunch everyone else would be ready for a nap, also. Mary VanderMeer and Lady Marisha came in soon afterward and as Lady Marisha came in, Margaret got up. None of the others even turned to look her direction when she left. She looked into the salon and then went out on deck. She knew he would be there waiting for her. He was sitting in a deck chair out of the wind and rain, clutching his jacket around him to keep warm.

The fact that he was out in the cold just waiting for her was touching. He got up when he saw her, as though offering his chair and that also was touching. She smiled at him. "Come," she said and started toward the ladder. She looked around to make sure nobody was about and then turned and started slowly backward down the wet, slippery ladder to the forward well-deck.

Margaret Jenkins knew before they left Durban that Matt VanderMeer was infatuated with her. She knew it wasn't love, even though he might not know it. She liked him. He was polite and shy without being too shy. He was tall with dark blond hair. He had a wide-eye look about him as though everything in life was a surprise. She liked the looks of him. She was certain he was a virgin and because he was still a virgin at seventeen and because she liked him and because he was shy and infatuated with her, she decided he deserved to have something special by which to remember this trip. She herself had lost her virginity when she was fifteen to a man ten years older than she was. It had been a pleasant experience. Charlie had caressed and kissed her until she could hardly stand it and when he finally stole her virginity she was delighted it had happened. The relationship didn't last long. After that she had other lovers, she had no idea how many. A few had been a little better than Charlie, most had not. She had never forgotten Charlie and eventually she came to the conclusion no one ever forgot the first time. She was also certain she would never forget Matthew VanderMeer because it was the first time for him. She had never had a first-timer before. And he would always remember her, too. She was determined to make it so especially wonderful he would always be grateful she had been the first and the standard by which he would judge later affairs. She liked the idea of always being remembered by the likes of him. He would undoubtedly go to university and into a profession. The thought that she could call on him if she ever needed help after she got to America was more comforting than selfish. It would be good to have someone like him who remembered her gratefully.

She also intended to make him as good a lover as Charlie had been. She wouldn't be able to teach him much these first few times. He would be both too eager and nervous, but before the trip was over she would make him into a lover every other woman would be grateful to have been with. She knew most men didn't realize they weren't naturally good lovers. It took a woman to teach them. It pleased her that the women who followed her would be beholden to her without ever knowing it.

Next to the ladder was the door to the baggage compartment. They stood in the drizzling rain while she got the key out of her sweater pocket and he turned back the dogs that held the hatch shut. "Where did you get the key?" he asked.

"I told the steward m'lady's always wanting me to get things from the trunk and it would save him time and trouble if he just let me have a copy of the key. It took a little coaxin', but he finally agreed."

The door squeaked as they swung it open. They stepped quickly inside and the door squeaked again as he swung it shut. In his nervousness he pulled it shut too strongly and it clanged loudly. She smiled at him reassuringly. A soft gray light came through the only porthole and he stood for a moment while his eyes got used to the dimness. On one side there was the passengers' suitcases and steamer trunks. On the other there was open shelves with steward's supplies: sheets, blankets and tablecloths. Standing on end and strapped against the bulkhead opposite the door were two mattresses the size of the passenger's berths. He helped her undo the straps and lower the mattresses to the deck.

She smiled at him without saying anything as she took off her sweater and threw it on the pile of trunks. She opened the top buttons at the front of the dress and then slipped it off her shoulders. He stood there staring at her knowing she was going to drop the dress and he would see and learn everything he had been fantasizing about. She slowly slipped the dress off her shoulders and then she let go of it.

***

They lay holding on to each other until she finally said, "We have to go, love. The little one'll be waking soon." They got up, got dressed and put the mattresses up against the wall and she said, "From now on, love, we can't come here together. You stay on the other side of the ship and when the coast is clear I'll come down. When you see me come down wait a little to give me time to open the door, but make sure no one sees you come here."

***

The day that had been so dark and rainy gave way to a night that was absolutely clear with a full moon. Most of the passengers had gone on deck after dinner to look at the moon and the sea beneath it. It was a spectacular sight. But even the most inspiring sight can quickly be abandoned when it gets too cold. One by one everybody went back into the warmth of the salon. By nine-thirty when they were beginning to think the games should come to an end and it was getting to be time to go to bed, they felt the ship speed up and turn sharply away from its course. Cups and glasses started sliding across the dry, wooden tabletops and as people reached for them they looked at others expecting an explanation. The ship turned again.

We're zigzagging," Matt said looking across to the table where Margaret was playing cribbage with Miss Stanley.

"It's a submarine," Luke said excitedly to his brothers.

"Oh, I don't think so, Lukie," Mable VanderMeer said. "Probably just a drill of some kind."

"Can we go on deck?" Mark asked.

"May we," his father corrected him and then added, "I guess so. For a little while, but stay on the main deck, it's almost time for bed."

Mark and Luke bounded from the room, slowing down only when they got to the blackout panels while Matt waited to see if Margaret was going to go out. When she nodded a little he followed his brothers out.

"I think I'll go out on deck, too," Mary said picking up her coat and following her brothers.

Several times after they came on deck the moon swung from one quarter to the other, brightly silhouetting the gun as it passed directly astern of the ship. On one leg of the turns the shipped rolled heavily from side to side while on the other, it pitched up and down and headed directly into the sea. On that leg they could hear the staccato of the flag whipped by the fifty mile an hour gale created by the combination of wind and ship's speed. Heading into the wind Luke would put his arms out to the side and rising up on the slippery leather soles of his shoes, the force of the wind pushed him back along the steel deck.

Twenty minutes after the zigzagging started the ship slowed, turned back to its westerly course and Mark and Luke went back inside, disappointed the fun was over. On the other side of the ship Matt and Margaret stayed on deck a few minutes longer, kissing and groping passionately until Margaret said, "I have to go in now, luv," and then they too went inside.

***

Mary VanderMeer stood by the rail for a moment after her brothers left and then went and retrieved one of the chairs that had slid under a lifeboat when the ship was rolling. She lined the rest of the chairs up neatly along the bulkhead and pulling her coat around her, she sat in one of them. It was comfortable there protected from the wind and with the warmth of the steam pipes that ran behind her to the galley. She adjusted her chair, leaned back with her head resting on the cushioned top, stared at the full moon, and fell asleep.

CHAPTER EIGHT

Tuesday, January 20, 1942

"You are relieved. I have the watch," Parkington said and hearing those words Richard Travers relaxed. He had not realized he had been so tense. He checked that the course changes for the zigzagging had all been correctly recorded in the log and then wrote the last line, "Watch properly relieved by 2nd Mt. Parkington," and then signed it, "Richard Travers, 3rd Mt."

He stepped out of the pilothouse and stood for a moment at the top of the starboard ladder. He had time now to look at the moon for what it really was rather than a source of light to aid him in the responsibility of self-preservation. He had a sense of gratitude toward the silvery orb. If it hadn't been for the moon he might not have seen the little feather of white water that seemed to trail off from a stick protruded from the water. He also realized if it hadn't been for the moon his ship could not have been as clearly seen in the lenses of the periscope. Even now he was not sure it was a periscope, but he was not the only one to have seen it, just the first. But now he no longer had to be on the lookout for such things. The sea was no longer a frightening cauldron containing unknown and unsuspected dangers. He saw the sea now as a magnificently majestic power rolling endlessly to infinity: a power effortlessly supporting the vessel and through it, him.

Mingled with his awe and appreciation was a sense of security. He was glad for the moment he was not the captain. He had no doubt he would someday captain a ship, but in this moment he appreciated he could, for a while, shed the majority of his responsibility just by the signing of his name to the ship's log.

He started down the ladder still looking out across the water. At the bottom he took one step and kicked the first of the deck chairs Mary VanderMeer had so carefully aligned, sending it crashing into the next one.

"Damn!" He saw Mary sit up because of the noise and said, "Oh ... good evening, Miss VanderMeer. I didn't see you there."

"I think I fell asleep out here."

"I didn't mean to disturb you."

"What time is it?"

"A little after midnight."

"Oh, my," she said getting up quickly.

"Beautiful night, isn't it?"

"Yes, it really is. I think it is the most beautiful night I have ever seen. I was just sitting here looking at the moon and ... and ... I must have just fallen asleep."

"Well, I can think of a lot worse places to fall asleep."

She moved to the rail, embarrassed he had again caught her unprepared. He came and stood next to her, looking down into the water. She could see his blond hair curling out from under his cap and over the collar of his jacket and she had an overwhelming urge to reach out and touch that hair.

He stood for what seemed an awfully long time before he straightened up and turned toward her. Her right hand slid along the leather of his jacket and then touched his hand. She could not remember when, or how their hands had touched and she had taken his. She looked up into his face, feeling weak and a little frightened and she felt herself shaking. He said, "The moon is reflected in your eyes, Miss VanderMeer."

She was suddenly weak and out of control. She was aware that her right hand had left the rail and was holding his. She was rising on her toes and her head was leaning back while her body was leaning toward him expecting, hoping, wanting. His face was closer to hers and her hand left his and her arm went around him. She felt his go around her and for some reason she could not explain she closed her eyes just as his lips touched hers. His lips were on hers for only an instant, but in that moment there was the faint smell of his cologne and the gentle caress of his breath on her cheek. Then he was pulling away and she held on to him tightly with her head on his chest. She was aware of a strange dizziness that had started in her stomach and reached to her head creating a floating sensation. The dizziness seemed to flow through her abdomen to her legs. Her knees had no strength in them and the only way she could keep from falling to the deck was to cling to him. She felt his arms loosening and she clung to him much harder.

"I'm sorry, Miss VanderMeer. I shouldn't have done that. I apologize," he said gently pushing her away.

"I love you," she said, clinging to him.

She thought she felt his hand stroking her hair and heard him say. "I think we'd better go in now."

She clung to him even more tightly, her face pressed against his chest. *Not yet ... not just yet ... I love you ... I love you ... please, not just yet.*

"Come, you must go in now," he said pushing her gently from him. She released him, nodding obediently, submissively.

He held her hand as they walked across the deck and then opened the hatch for. "Good night, Miss VanderMeer," he said trying to release his hand.

She wouldn't let him go. "What's your Christian name?" she asked.
"Richard."

"Richard." She repeated the name almost reverently.

"Good night," he said, again pulling his hand away and quietly closing the hatch.

She stood there in total darkness between the first blackout panel and the outside hatch, her hand still outstretched to him, waiting for the hatch to open and show him silhouetted there in the moonlight. She leaned back against the bulkhead, her head pressed against the hardness of the steel while torrents of silent tears ran down her cheeks.

***

Third Mate Richard Travers walked slowly aft toward his compartment wondering how he could have let it happen. He had trifled with a young girl's affections and that was something a gentleman did not do. He had acted the cad. He had acted disgracefully and he was thoroughly ashamed of himself.

***

Rudolph Duer set the empty glass down and became even angrier; there was no more gin in the bottle. He was not drunk, but he was angry. It was one in the morning with no chance of getting any more.

He had gone on deck when the zigzagging started and had seen Margaret and Matt kissing good night. He had watched as Margaret sent Matt in first and then Rudy had gone around the other way and was waiting for her in the lounge when she went in. There was no one else in the lounge. Everyone else was in the salon talking excitedly about the maneuvers. He confronted her just as she emerged from the blackout panels. "Come now, Magical Maggie," he said smiling. He was blocking her way with his arms extended with one hand on the edge of the blackout panel and the other on the bulkhead. "You can do better than trying to seduce a little boy." She looked at him without saying anything and he added, "What you need is a man like me."

"Dr. Duer," she said, "you are a married man and I make it a policy not to fool around with married men. After all, you have a wife. It wouldn't be fair of me to deprive a single man to give it to a married man who can get all he wants, now would it?"

"You wouldn't have to deprive anyone," he said dropping his arms.

"No, Dr. Duer. The answer is *no*," she said getting by him.

"Why not?"

She went into her cabin without answering and that irritated him. He had gone back and sat in the chair outside the salon getting angrier the more he thought about it. It was not just that she had denied him; it was the way she had done it. She had been condescending to him. *Why the little nobody. He didn't really want her. Did she think he wanted her? She had acted superior. A housemaid had turned him down. Well, he would put an end to that. Reverend VanderMeer would probably be extremely upset to hear what was happening to his son. The Reverend would talk to Lady Marisha about it and that would be the end of that little game.*

He continued to sit there sulking. One by one the passengers went by on their way to bed until he was left alone. He had gone into the salon and looked in the cabinets under the sideboard and found the bottle. He had poured himself a drink and took the bottle with him and went back to the lounge. He went into his cabin and took off his clothes dropping, them at the foot of the bunk. He went into the tiny bathroom and threw some water on his face. He hit his elbow as he reached for the towel and the smallness of the bathroom added to his irritation. He pulled out the top drawer, "Where's my blue, plaid, shirt?" he said making a mess of the neatly folded shirts. "I want to wear it tomorrow."

"I haven't ironed it yet. You just wore it the day before yesterday," Rose said sleepily from the top bunk.

"Well get up and iron it," he said punching her in the thigh.

"I can't iron it now, Rudy. I'll do it in the morning. I promise. I'll get up early and do it in the morning."

"Do it now," he said grabbing her by a foot and pulling her out of bed.

She just managed to twist herself so she landed on both feet. "I can't do it now, Rudy. I don't have the iron, or board, and I don't know where they keep them. The stewards are all asleep," she said moving away from him.

"Don't you ever tell me you can't do something," he said and punched her in the stomach.

She doubled over grabbing her abdomen. "Please, Rudy don't," she wailed. "Please don't hit me again, I'll iron it in the morning. Before you get up. Just don't hit me again." The sound of her crying filled the cabin.

"Shut up," he said grabbing her around the throat and pushing her up against the wall. He started choking her. She stared at him with frightened, wide-open eyes unable to breath. "Don't you make one sound. You want to die? You want to die right now? All I have to do is strangle you. I won't even need both hands. You want to die right now? When you're dead all I do is carry you out and drop you over the side."

Robbie kneeled up in his bunk above the dresser and stared pounding with both fists on his father. "Stop it! Stop it!" he screamed.

With his free arm Duer swung at him, hitting him in the side. The force of the blow threw him against the outside bulkhead. "Shut up, or I'll kill you, too," he growled and Robbie huddled in the corner, his knees under his chin, and his hands over his face.

"You want to die now?" Duer said again turning back to his wife. "You make one sound and so help me God, I'll kill you. It will be easy to get rid of your body here, Rose. No one will even care you're gone."

He slowly let go of her throat and she slumped to the floor. He kicked her, in the stomach, the chest, the back, and each time she just gasped squirming trying to get away from the kicking foot.

He stopped and she cowered in the corner, whimpering quietly. He finished getting undressed and then grabbing her by the legs pulled her away from the wall so she was laying flat on the floor and raped her. When he was through he turned off the light and stepping over her lay down in his bunk.

She rolled over so that she was resting against the dresser and wept silently. If she went to anyone now and told them what had happened would they believe her? It didn't make any difference if they believed her or not. Rudy would always be there and as soon as they were gone he would beat her up again for having gone to them.

***

Rose did not go to breakfast. A little before ten Rose settled gingerly into her chair next to Mable VanderMeer. She hurt all over, her stomach, her sides and her back. Rudy had been careful not to hit, or kick her, where any bruises would show. At breakfast when Mable asked Rudy about her he said, "She's just a little under the weather." Now Mable was concerned as she watched Rose slowly and carefully lower herself to the chair.

"Are you all right?" she asked reaching a plump hand over to take Rose's hand.

"Oh, yes. I'm just a little sore. I fell out of my berth last night."

"Maybe you should go and see Doctor Bowman."

"No. No. Please. I'm all right. I just missed the ladder and fell to the floor."

"You sleep in the upper berth?" Mable asked.

"Yes. I prefer it actually," she said and then tried to make a joke of it, "except when I fall out of it."

***

On the other side of the ship Rudolph Duer stood against the rail. The wind tugged at his wavy, blond hair as if trying to mess it up, but it always fell back perfectly arranged. He was wearing gray slacks and a blue blazer with a crest on the pocket. Under the jacket he had a gray sweater over a blue shirt, open at the collar with a light blue scarf around his neck. Robbie was standing next to him with one arm wrapped around his father's leg. From time to time he would look up at his father who would stroke his son's head.

Duer walked over and sat down in a chair and Robbie sat down at his feet on the leg rest.

Helen Stanley looked up as they sat down and then said, "Come over here, Robbie."

Robbie looked at his father afraid of doing something wrong. "That's all right, son. Go to Miss Stanley when she asks you to."

He got up and walked over to her and she turned him around and lifted up his sleeve. "That's a nasty bruise, Robbie. How did you get it?"

Duer was at his son's side immediately. "Yes, son. Why didn't you show me this before? How did you get it?"

"I fell."

"Where?" Stanley asked.

He pointed to the high lip of the hatchway. "On the other door. On the other side."

"Where was your mother?" Duer asked accusingly.

"With Mrs. VanderMeer. It's all right. It doesn't hurt."

"That's my brave boy," Duer said as the two of them went back to the chair.

***

Richard Travers lay contentedly on his back with one arm around Margaret Jenkins. She lay on her side, crowded against him in the small bunk with her head on his shoulder and one leg thrown across his thighs. The hand of the arm that was around her was gently stroking the smooth skin of her hip. "What was all the running around last night?" she asked.

"Oh, we thought we saw something."

"It wasn't a drill then? We all thought it was a drill."

"No it wasn't a drill."

"What did you see?"

"We don't know. Just a little thing in the water. We all saw it. I thought it was a periscope."

"You mean a U-boat?"

"Maybe. But that's unlikely this far away from land and the shipping routes. Maybe it was just the fin of a shark or a sailfish, but we weren't taking any chances."

They were silent for a few moments each of them thinking about the night before. "I came on deck when the ship sped up. I thought something was wrong."

"Any of the others go out."

"Oh, yes. Dr. Duer. The VanderMeer boys and Mary. She stayed out there to wait for you to come off watch," she said teasingly.

"Oh come off it."

"She's daft over you, you know."

"Yes, I know. Are you jealous?"

"Of course not. But don't take her to bed, Duck."

"You are jealous," he said laughingly.

"I ain't either."

"Then why are you telling me not to take her to bed."

"Because she's a virgin."

"Oh, come, Maggie Dear. You can do better than that. I guess she probably is a virgin and I have no intention of taking her to bed, but why should that matter to you? Everybody's been a virgin at one time. Even you were a virgin once," he said feeling guilty again about the night before and hoping that joking with Margaret would lessen his genuine concern.

"Maybe for a little while between my legs, but never up here," she said tapping her head. "But she's a virgin all over. I'll bet she's never even been kissed. I mean in a romantic way. And her father's going to be proper blazin' when he finds out about it."

"Why would he find out?"

"Don't be a chump, Duck. Of course he's going to find out. She's going to be all upset, pouting and weeping and her mother's going to keep after her until she finds out what's ailin' the girl and she's going to tell the Reverend."

"Every time I turn around I stumble over her."

"Oh, you poor thing. Just can't keep the women away can you," she said playfully and then added frowning seriously, "be careful, Duck. She fancies herself in love with you, you know, though I can't imagine how anyone could fall in love with the likes of you." She lifted her head to kiss him under the chin.

"What a ghastly thing to say," he said slapping her gently.

She giggled and stretched up a little to look at the clock. "Ten o'clock, Duck. You go on watch in a couple of hours. I'd better go now and let you get some sleep," she said crawling over him to get out of the bunk.

He lay with his hands folded behind his head watching her get dressed. "You're good stuff, Maggie Jenkins."

"Good enough 'til we get to land and you can find something else I'll wager," she said teasingly as she leaned over and kissed him. "Good night, Duck."

She left his cabin and walked slowly across the after well-deck. It was a bright moonlit night, the kind of night she thought was made for love. The only trouble was there was no porthole in Travers' cabin to let in the moonlight. She thought it would be nice if she could meet with Matt some place where they could make love in the moonlight. It would be a night he would remember for the rest of his life.

Margaret Jenkins had no compunctions about the fact she thoroughly enjoyed sex, or that she was currently enjoying it with two men. Third Mate Travers had chased after her and she liked that. What's more, he had been there first and in her sense of fairness it wouldn't be right to throw him over just because she had found someone else. He was an adequate lover, but there was something delightfully stimulating about Matt's inexperienced, but eager excitement. She liked them both and as long as they were both happy, she saw no reason why she should give up one, or the other.

***

The captain lay flat on his back in his bunk. His black tie lying perfectly straight down his chest covering the buttons of his shirt, his hands clasped loosely on the center of his tie. A half hour's nap was what he had promised himself and then he would go back to the bridge. He stayed just on the verge of sleep, dozing comfortably, easing in and out of consciousness so the dreams he had when he was dozing were delightfully distorted continuations of his thoughts when he was conscious. He slowly opened an eye and looked at the bulkhead clock. *Twenty-three forty-five. Oh, good. Still ten minutes left to nap.* He closed his eyes and eased back into drowsing.

Through his semi-sleep he heard the click and snaps of static on the squawk box and was already starting up from his bunk when Parkington's electrically distorted voice said, "Captain, bridge. We've sighted a distress flare bearing zero-six-zero relative. Estimated range two to three miles."

In one motion his feet swung to the floor and his right hand reached for his coat. He was going through the door before Parkington's voice faded from the intercom. His first reaction was it was a submarine. They could have been on the surface recharging their batteries. At that range, even in this bright moonlight, it would have been hard to see the black conning tower of a submarine while the high, broad sides of the ship would be easily visible. At that distance they were in no danger and for just that reason the sub might be trying to lure them over with a distress signal. It was not unheard of for a submarine to send up a distress flare and then dive, hoping some unsuspecting ship would come over to pick up survivors. It was a trick that had been used before and would probably be used again before this war was over.

He was conscious of all this as he crossed from his cabin to the pilothouse. "Who saw it?" he asked as he stepped through the doorway.

"We all did, Sir. Both lookouts and all of us here on the bridge."

"Did the lookouts see anything else, before, during, or after the flare?" He knew he was picking at straws, hoping for the impossible. At that range lifeboats, or rafts would have been so low in the water they could not have been seen. If it was a sub it was almost under water by the time the flare lighted up the sky.

The report came back that the lookouts had not seen anything else and the captain went out onto the starboard wing. He stood at the rail with the binoculars wishing for another flare. *If there are survivors out there why don't they send up another flare? If you are out there send up another flare. Prove you're still on the surface. Send up another flare, damn you. Who are you? I'm not going to let you influence me. I'm not coming over there till I see another flare.* But for all his demands for proof and his concerns for the safety of the ship he knew he would go over there. He would never be able to forget his own experience of a little over a year ago when he had been a survivor.

It had been an absolutely clear, moonless night with each star precise in its minute clarity. At a little before midnight, twelve hours out of Plymouth, the captain felt more at ease that they were out of the English Channel and well into the Atlantic. He sat down at his desk and started writing in his personal log. Although his personal log contained much of the same information regarding weather and courses as was in the ship's official log, there was also other information: recollections of conversations with harbor masters, first impressions of passengers, comments about his officers and members of the crew. Quite often there were thoughts he would not have wanted anyone else to read. His last entry in the log for that day was, "With the intensive bombing going on along the coast and the sinkings that are continually occurring in the Channel, it is a relief to be once again in the open seas. It is most regrettable I fear my homeland and my home waters more than any other place in the world."

He capped his pen and clipped it in his inside coat pocket. He closed the log and placed it back in the left-hand top drawer. He sat for just a moment with his hands clasped behind his head leaning back in his chair.

The gentle rolling of the ship was soothing and assuring. He got up and walked over to the sideboard and poured himself a cup of tea from a pewter pot. He had the cup half way to his mouth when he felt the first tremor and then the violent shaking of the ship as the torpedo exploded. The explosion lifted the stern and then let it settle back into the water. He dropped the cup and was in the pilothouse before the rumblings of the explosion quieted and the ship rode with its stern low in the water.

"I've lost all steering," the helmsman said spinning the wheel one direction and then the other. At the same time he felt the ship loosing headway and coming to a stop in the water. From the squawk box was the blare of a panicked voice saying, "Bridge, engine room. The after section of the ship has been blown away. Water's coming in all over."

He ran to the squawk box and pushed the button. "Engine room, this is the captain. Steady, Lad. Steady! Are there any casualties?"

"There were two men taking after bearing temperatures, Captain. They must be dead. That part of the ship is blown away."

He felt a sick emptiness in his stomach while at the same time thinking the ship was dead in the water, a sitting target. The next torpedo would probably go into one of the holds setting off the cargo of munitions and the whole ship would be one great explosion. "Any other casualties?"

"Roberts has a broken arm, or something, Captain. It's really bad down here, Captain. Water's coming up fast."

"I understand. You lads report to your lifeboats. Stand by to abandon ship. Be sure to help Roberts up the ladders."

"Aye, sir."

"Sound the alarm, Mr. Jones. All hands to lifeboat stations. Stand by to abandon ship."

"Aye, aye, Captain," the first mate said and reached over and threw the alarm switch.

The talker started to take off his phones. "Be sure the lookouts have the word before you go off the line, Lad."

"Aye, aye, Captain." the talker said and put the phone back on his head. "Lookouts, bridge. Report to lifeboats. Stand by to abandon ship. Acknowledge." He paused for a moment and then said, "Lookouts. To your boats." He waited until the helmsman was gone and then he said, "Gentlemen, I suggest you take off your jackets and hats before getting into the boats. If they should surface we don't want to make it too easy for them to spot an officer. As soon as your boat is ready with all crew and passengers accounted for, pull away. Don't wait around for each other. Get away as fast and as far as you can before she goes up. To your boats, gentlemen. Good luck, and God save the King."

They saluted and walked quickly from the bridge and he was left alone in the pilothouse. He took off his coat and hung it on the ship's wheel, a spoke where his neck should have been and the spokes on each side filling out the shoulders. He set his cap on the binnacle, the gold-braided beak pointed forward. He walked out onto the bridge and stood at the rail watching the efficient speed with which the boats were being readied. The six passengers, all of them Army officers going to assignments in Africa, stood quietly to one side putting on their life jackets waiting to be told when they should get into the boats. The hope they would get the boats over the side in time was an intense mental urging, but almost just as desperately he didn't want to leave his ship. Not this way.

He had been with the Port Lines for ten years. He had started out with them as first mate aboard the Port Halifax. For the past five years he had been captain of the Port Rhodes. This ship was his life, the culmination of thirty years at sea. It was his business, his profession, his club, his church, and his home. The house ashore was Elizabeth's, really. The house had the accumulation of her lifetime, lace curtains, silver-framed photographs and china figurines on the fireplace mantle. The accumulation of his lifetime was in the little cabin aboard the ship. There were things that had been acquired in his ascendancy from midshipman to captain and they had moved with him from one ship to another: a jade Buddha from Hong Kong, a piece of ivory from the Congo, his favorite books, a brass belaying pin from the sailing ship Trively, his first birth as third mate in 1911, a blue velvet box with his medals earned during his three years in the Royal Navy Reserve during the last war. It was not so much the things themselves, but what they represented, seasons of his life. He had always believed that when he retired they would take their places comfortably among the silver-framed photographs and figurines.

He felt now as though that whole portion of his life was being snuffed out with the sinking of this ship and he wondered if he had a right to continue. Could he start a new life which began with the loss of two men and the abandonment of his ship, an ignominious abandonment in which he was sneaking off of a still floating ship without his coat and hat as though he were ashamed of his calling, his position and his life? It would have been easier in that moment to have gone back into the pilot house and put on his coat and hat and wait for the explosion he knew would come. He did not in any way consider staying with the ship would be heroic, or proper, or an honorable gesture, only easier. It would be easier never again to remember the loss of two men, never again to have to account to himself for his failure, a failure that was not of his making, but for which he was responsible. Precisely because staying with the ship would have been the easier thing to do, he couldn't do it.

Above the noise of the canvas covers being ripped off, of pelican hooks hitting the decks, of blocks and davits squeaking, he heard the Second Mate shouting the radio officer was unaccounted for. He ran back into the pilothouse and opened the door to the radio room. There was Sparks sitting in his chair, earphones on his head, his right hand on the telegraph key sending out the distress signal. The radioman turned and looked at him without breaking the rhythm of the transmission he was sending. The radioman smiled at him and the captain felt suddenly ashamed. His reason for staying behind had been because of a sense of failure, self-pity, and a fear of the future. This boy at least had a worthwhile purpose for staying behind. He stepped in and lifted the earphones off the radioman's ears. "The boats are ready, son. It's time to go."

"Just one more transmission, Captain."

"There isn't any time for it, my boy. If no one has picked up the signal by now they aren't going to pick up one more."

"Yes, sir," he said standing up with his hand still on the telegraph sending out the last three dots.

Two boats were already in the water when they came out on the wing. "Get to a boat," the captain said and stepped aside to let the radioman precede him down the ladder. He hesitated for an instant longer, patted the rail and said, "Well, good-bye, old girl," and followed the radioman to the main deck and into a boat.

The boats pulled away from the ship, the crews bending backwards against the oars, the blades dipping rhythmically in and out of the water. From his boat the captain stood in the center looking back at his ship. On either side of him the bodies of the men leaned forward, then pulled back, leaned forward and pulled back and they, too, were looking back the direction they had come to the black silhouette of the ship, its bow high in the water, its stern low as though it had been loaded incorrectly with all the cargo in the stern. In the stillness of that clear night the only sounds were the bows of the lifeboats slapping into the waves, the creaking of the oars in the oarlocks and the heavy breathing of the men as they strained against the oars.

The distance increased to 100 yards, then to 150, and suddenly the night was bright with the first explosion. The explosion broke the ship in half, the stubby funnel rolling through the air like some easily tossed great oil drum. The deafening roar was followed by a second, and a third explosion at the bow and then at the stern of the ship. There were three distinct explosions, but so close together they had to be considered as one. The forward mast shot straight in the air as though it were an arrow shot from a bow. Thirty-foot steel loading booms twisted through the air like toothpicks. The brightness of the explosions put a yellow glow on the faces and bodies of the men, on the grayness of the lifeboats' hulls, and gleamed on the varnish of the oars. Even at that distance they could feel the blast of hot air rolling over them. Eyes that had been peering wide open were now squinting against the brightness.

Almost as quickly as it happened it ended. The brightness was gone. All that remained was the glow from the flames of a few scattered oil slicks, their flames flickering feebly in the darkness, showing an occasional piece of floating wood, or canvas. They too burned out and there was darkness again, and still the men sat looking at the place where only a few moments before a ship had been. The smell of expended powder burned their noses and throats with every breath and was the only real, physical evidence there had once been a ship there and yet now that it was gone, they were more emotionally aware of it than they ever had been when it was afloat. Initially there was not any sense of relief they had escaped, only a feeling of loss, an emptiness, and an inability to believe the ship was really gone.

And for none of them was the feeling of loss more acute than for the captain. The Port Rhodes had been his first captaincy. He had commanded her for five years, two in peace and three in war. He had seen the colors of blue hull, red masts and funnel, and white cabins covered with the dull gray. He had seen the attractive lines of the ship disfigured with the additions of guns and cork life rafts. For five years he had worried her through storms and narrow channels, maneuvered her through minefields, had made demands on her and let her make demands on him. He had felt the pain when a tug bumped her a little too hard. He had been proud of her when she behaved well and ashamed of her when she was sloppy. On that dark, clear night he had stood for a long time looking at the emptiness of where his ship should have been, unable to believe what he had just seen. His life was over, yet he was still alive.

Standing on the bridge of the Port Jefferson peering into the darkness and hoping to see another flare, the captain saw again the whole scene of the sinking of the Port Rhodes and remembered the tedious, fearful hours he and his men had been through in a lifeboat. He could not ignore the possibility there might be seamen out there that needed to be rescued. He opened the cover to the voice tube and spoke into it. "Mr. Parkington."

"Yes, Captain."

"All hands to emergency stations."

"Aye, aye, Captain."

CHAPTER NINE

Wednesday – 21 January 1942

The captain stood on the wing watching the crew going to their stations. In the bright moonlight he could see the silhouettes of the gun crew at the stern moving the gun, the aimer and the pointer sitting in their steel seats spinning the wheels in front of them to make sure they were working smoothly. Others were opening the cases that held the ammo. Even after making the decision the captain hesitated. He could understand the great depression any survivors would feel at seeing a ship passing them in the night, ignoring their flare, leaving their survival to some other ship that might, or might not come along. But he also knew the decision to search for survivors could jeopardize the safety of his own passengers and crew.

Renshaw and Travers had both arrived when he reentered the pilothouse. "Mr. Renshaw, take the conn," he said. "All engines ahead full; show turns for twenty-five knots. Come to base course three-five-zero, zigzag pattern Alpha. Mr. Travers ..."

"Aye, Captain?"

"Stand by to launch boat number one. In the event we see survivors we will launch underway."

"Underway, sir?" he asked apprehensively.

"It is not uncommon, Mr. Travers, for a U-boat to sink a ship and then hang around the survivors and sink the ship that comes to rescue them. I do not intend to sit still for some U-boat captain who wants to paint another British flag on his conning tower. You have launched underway before, have you not, Mr. Travers?"

"Once, or twice in training, Captain."

"Good. Then you know how it's done."

Travers walked over to the intercom and ran his finger down the face snapping on all the buttons to the speakers in the crew's quarters. "All crew of lifeboat number one report to your boat. All crew of boat number one report to your boat." He turned off the buttons and started to leave.

"Mr. Travers."

"Aye, Captain?"

"Report back here when the boat is over the side and ready for launching."

"Yes, sir," he said and left the bridge.

"Mr. Parkington, take the men from the kite stations and make preparations for taking survivors aboard. We will take them aboard on the after well-deck, starboard side."

"Aye, aye, Captain."

"And make sure Dr. Bowman is up and about and aware of what's happening. Put someone to sobering him up if you have to."

"Yes, sir,"

In cabin A, Harold VanderMeer heard the sounds of activity outside the cabin and when he couldn't figure out what the sounds meant put on his robe and went out to investigate. He stood against the bulkhead outside of the Duers' cabin watching them preparing the boat. He saw everybody was too busy to be interrupted and, since only one boat was being worked on and the passengers had not been called, he assumed it must be some kind of drill for the crew.

In cabin B, Helen Stanley dreamt she was in the little brick house at the hospital. Outside her window a couple of native orderlies were shuffling their feet on the gravel path and arguing about which one should pound on the window and tell her she was needed at the hospital. She came out of her dream slowly realizing she was aboard the ship and the sounds outside were members of the crew walking along the deck and talking. She looked at her watch. *A little after midnight. Probably the watch coming off duty.* She was relieved she could go back to sleep, but the sounds continued and she became curious. In the darkness she got up from her bunk and above her she heard Mary whisper, "What's happening?"

"I don't know. I'll find out and let you know," she said putting on her robe and went out.

On deck she saw that on the other side of the ship the boat was being swung out and crossed over. She found Reverend VanderMeer standing along the bulkhead and said, "What's all this about?"

"I don't know. Just got here myself."

They stood watching. The boat crew was busy putting the oars in place in the center of the boat and one of them tied a rope to the bow of the boat and threw it to a man in the forward well-deck. He walked it forward and attached it to a cleat. "Ready for lowering she is, sir," the bosun said.

"Very well," Travers said and started for the ladder to the bridge.

"Ah ha, Mr. Travers," Miss Stanley said stepping away from the bulkhead. "I see the captain has finally found out the truth about you and is setting you adrift."

He stopped with his right foot on the first step of the ladder. "Oh, Miss Stanley, I didn't see you there. We may be picking up survivors soon. Doctor Bowman may be needing your help."

"Certainly. I'll go get dressed."

"Is there anything I can do?" Reverend VanderMeer asked.

"I don't think so, reverend. Not at the moment," he said and continued up the ladder.

In the sickbay Doctor Bowman sat on the edge of his bunk trying to get himself started with a cigarette and a cup of black tea. When he had heard the blare of the loudspeaker sound emergency stations he had awakened enough to remember his station was in the sickbay. Since that was where he slept and he was already there he had turned over and gone back to sleep. When the speaker blared the second time he rolled over grumbling, "Knock off that bloody noise, will you?" Then Parkington had come in and shaken him until he was forced to sit up before Parkington would leave. Parkington had put the cup of tea in his hand and he was trying to remember what it was Parkington had said about survivors. He got up slowly when he heard the knocking on the dispensary door. He walked unsteadily from the sickbay to the dispensary and opened the top half of the Dutch door. The person standing there looked hazily familiar. "Doctor Bowman, I'm Helen Stanley. I'm a nurse. The captain thought I might be able to help you with the survivors."

He grunted and slid back the bolt and swung back the lower half of the door. "Thash wha' we have," he said waving his hand around the room. "Thash all there is, thash all we have," he said and went back into the sickbay shutting the door behind him.

On the after well-deck Parkington looked around wondering if there was anything more that should have been done. A section of the rail had been removed and one of the loading booms had been swung out with its end over the side in case anyone had to be brought aboard in a sling. Two metal-framed canvas stretchers waited on the deck beside the loading hatch. In the darkness the wind whined through the volleyball net that was still stretched across the cargo hatch. Above it in the light of the moon, the wind-whipped flag beat a rapid staccato. "Just stand by now men," Parkington said. "Rogers lay up to the bridge and tell them we're ready back here."

"Aye, aye, sir."

On the bridge, the captain stood on the wing with the binoculars. The moon, almost at its zenith and to the north of them, put a silver highway on the surface of the water. That highway of light led directly to the ship swinging to either side of the bow as they zigzagged back and forth.

A few feet from the captain, Third Mate Travers also stood with binoculars hoping that by concentrating on searching he would ease the nervousness. He kept hoping there would not be any survivors. It was possible the Port Jefferson could be torpedoed, but not very likely. At this speed using the complicated Alpha zigzag, the possibility of being hit by a torpedo was more luck than skill. What he wanted was for them to search the area and then leave knowing they had done their duty with regard to possible survivors. There was no real danger in looking for survivors. It was finding them that could be disastrous. Even the lowering of the boat was filled with hazard. The ship could roll unexpectedly, smashing the little boat as it was being lowered. What was even more frightening was the knowledge that if a sub were sighted after the boat was launched the captain would have no alternative but to escape, leaving the lifeboat and everyone in it behind. He knew he would not be abandoned forever, but from then on, his boat and the men in it would be the bait in a game of waiting and outwitting between the captain and the sub. The captain would have to wait 'till the sub came to the surface to recharge its batteries before they could use their five-inch gun on it.

"Forward lookout reports three object just off the starboard bow, Captain. Estimated range is one thousand yards. Identified as possible lifeboats," the talker said.

"Very well. Remind lookouts to keep scanning all directions," the captain said staring through his binoculars over the bow until he saw three dark shadows on the edge of the moonlight ribbon. "Tell lookouts we have them in sight," he said and walked over to the repeater compass on the starboard wing, sighted along the top of it and then spoke into the voice tube, "Renshaw, lifeboats bearing zero-one-zero true. Make that your base course. Reduce speed to fifteen knots. Reduce time on each leg of zigzag by one third." Renshaw acknowledged the captain's orders and the captain said, "Mr. Travers."

"Yes, Captain."

"We shall take you to within a hundred yards, or so and reduce speed to five knots. As soon as you feel the ship slacking speed, start lowering away. We shouldn't be doing more than three knots when you hit the water. Find out how long it has been since they've seen the sub. If it's still around they should have seen it when it surfaced to recharge its batteries. If it has been less than forty-eight hours, we will have to retrieve underway. Tie the boats close together in line. Take a torch with you and signal one long flash when ready for us to come by and pick you up followed by one short flash for every twenty-four hours since they've seen the sub."

"Yes, sir."

"Good luck, lad."

"Thank you, sir," Travers said, saluted and left the bridge.

On the main deck the passengers stood along the bulkhead, or sat on the hatch cover, watching, trying to understand, wanting explanations.

They had come out one at a time, each of them asking what was happening of those who had gotten there ahead of them. They understood they might be picking up survivors, but they wished someone would tell them more.

Along the rail, sailors were talking with the crew in the boat that hung over the side. Three men sat along each side of the boat waiting to pick up the oars. Another man stood in the bow holding on to the end of the line that ran from the boat to the forward well-deck. In the stern, the bosun stood with the tiller in his hand waiting to slip it into the rudder the moment the lowering blocks were out of the way. Travers went and stood by the rail. The men in the boat all turned and looked at him and he wondered if they were expecting him to say something. "Have we enough line to tie the boats together, Bosun?"

"Aye, sir. Plenty of line for that, sir."

"The ship will be doing three knots when we launch, Mr. Hawkins," Travers said.

"Aye, aye, sir," Hawkins said flatly and Travers wished he could tell from his voice whether, or not he was concerned about the launching.

The ship turned to the left. The moon crossed over the bow and the men in the boat turned their heads to look over their shoulders trying to see the lifeboats that were waiting for them. Travers looked up to the bridge and saw the captain moving to the after rail. "Mr. Travers," he called down through cupped hands.

"Aye, Captain?" Travers shouted.

"We will slow down for you after the next turn."

"Yes, Sir," Travers said and climbed over the rail into the boat.

The ship turned back to the right and then straightened up, keeping the survivors on the starboard side. "All hands stand by," the bosun said and the rowers picked up the oars and lay them across the lifeboat with the blades all toward the ship. The ship started to slow and the men picked up the oars, bracing them against their bodies with the blades pushing against the ship. The retaining lines that held the lifeboat snug against the ship were let go and the lifeboat swung out a little and then started back with the rolling of the ship and the crew leaned into the oars pushing against the side of the ship to keep the boat from banging into the side of the ship.

"Lower away, Lads," the bosun said to the men on deck. "Easy and steady lower away."

The boat started down swinging back and forth like a pendulum with the rolling of the ship, the arc of the swing getting larger the lower it went. Each time the boat swung toward the ship the men would stop the swing by putting the blade of the oars against it. They strained against the oars to hold the boat away. Each of them cursed the captain for not slowing down more. They were no longer concerned with the safety of the ship, only with themselves. If the small boat were left to swing free, or if the oars used to hold it away were to break, the boat would smash against the side of the ship and they would be thrown into the water to be caught in the suction and wake.

"Keep the painter taut," the bosun called to the man in the bow.

"Taut she is, Bosun," he answered and put another turn of rope around the bit.

From the bridge the captain watched the boat being lowered and leaned over and spoke into the voice tube. "Mr. Renshaw, slow down to three knots."

With the slower speed the ship rolled more gently and the men had more time to brace themselves as the boat swung.

The ship rolled to starboard and a large wave reached up pounding against the bottom of the boat, jarring it, lifting it, tilting it, throwing the men off balance for a moment. The falls went slack for an instant and the blocks rattled and clanked on the hooks. The wave dragged against the bottom so the painter vibrated with the sudden tension, twisting the bow toward the ship and then the ship rolled the other direction lifting the boat off of the wave.

"Lower away," the bosun shouted to those up on deck that were lowering them. "Lively, lads, lively. Lower away! Lower away!"

The ship rolled back to starboard again. The boat touched the water. "Let go falls," the bosun shouted and the boat rocked crazily into the water. The painter twanged with the sudden tension of pulling the boat alongside the ship. The spray flew up on both sides of the bow and then the boat rode steadily alongside the ship. The blocks were released and swung around wildly like uncontrollable wrecking balls as they were being raised. They swung back and forth crashing, filling the night with the thunder of their banging against the metal hull.

As soon as the blocks were out of the way Hawkins slid the tiller into the rudder and said, "Oars to ready, men." The men on each side held their oars straight up in front of them. "Ready forward?" he asked.

"Ready here," the man holding the bowline called back. The Bosun eased the tiller over a little and the boat began to wobble back and forth, pushed away from the ship by the angle of the rudder and then pulled back toward it by the line that was pulling it.

"Let go painter," the bosun shouted and the man at the bow threw off the line, the momentum of the boat carrying it in a turn away from the ship. "Dip oars! Pull ... Pull ... Pull," Hawkins shouted.

The protective mountain of the ship moved away from them, the stern throwing up a glowing wake as the ship picked up speed and quickly pulled away from them. They became a small boat surrounded by a slapping sea and silent moon. The loudest sounds were the creaking of the oars in the oarlocks.

Standing in the stern of the little lifeboat, Third Mate Travers was overcome with a strange and disquieting feeling of apprehension. It was not a normal, physical fear such as the fear of falling, or of being hurt, or even of dying. Nor was it an emotional dread such as the fear of being lost, or failing in some project, but rather a sense of total discord. Above them, the moon glowed in an impersonal, silent aloofness while the waves hissed along the hull, not menacing, but taunting him. He felt separated and disassociated from everything. Even the men in the same boat with him, the bosun standing behind him and a little higher looking over his head with his hand on the tiller, the six men bending rhythmically and in unison at the oars, the bow man bent forward with both hands resting on the gunnels with one leg straight and the other bent at the knee as though ready to spring from the boat, all seemed more like shadows in a painting than human beings he could reach out and touch or speak to. The ship, of which he had thought himself so much a part, had sped away as soon as they had cast off, acting as though it were glad to be rid of them. That dark shadow of a ship circled them now, watching them, never approaching, as though they were some curse that could be observed from a distance, but could not be touched. Even the objects toward which they were headed seemed phantoms that appeared for an instant on the top of a wave only to disappear into a trough, elusive and silent, no sound of shouting, or waving of arms. *Are they really there, or are they some great imaginary hoax? Is the ship there? If I flashed the light would the ship approach, or remain eternally watching us under a stationary moon as we row endlessly on a rising and falling treadmill sea toward phantom survivors?*

Slowly the distance lessened, shadows started taking on the shapes of heads and shoulders. An arm was seen waving for an instant before the boats again disappeared behind the wave. For a moment there was the indistinct sound of voices, muffled and incomprehensible and with those sounds the eerie fear that had gripped him and the others began to ease. "Could you make out what they said, Bosun," Travers asked.

"Nay, sir. Be too far yet fer that, sir."

"Sounded foreign to me, sir," the man at the bow volunteered.

The boat climbed up a wave, hung at the top just long enough for them to hear one of the survivors shout something and then slid into the trough cut off by a wave from the sight and sound of the survivors. "They sound like bloody Germans," one of the rowers said.

"Oh, I don't think so," Travers said quickly. "There are no Germans in these waters." But even as he said it, he didn't believe it. He had never considered the survivors could be the enemy. The captain was always telling them to be prepared for the unexpected, but he was certain even the captain had not considered this. In the brief minute when they slid down the wave and up the next before they saw the survivors his head was full of questions. *Are they Germans? Are they armed? Is it a trap?*

What better way to capture an unarmed merchant vessel with its cargo intact than to pose as shipwreck victims? He had eight men with him, not one of them had a gun. It would be no trouble at all for the survivors to take them hostage and then take over the ship. Or they could be brought on board with small arms hidden in their clothing. It would not be much of a challenge for a few well-trained men to capture a ship with a crew that was unarmed and unsuspecting. He remembered seeing a picture in a newspaper once of a destroyer with sailors lining the rails holding guns aimed at the men in the lifeboat whom they were rescuing. At the time, he had thought the precaution had a certain inhuman callousness. But he wished now the men in his boat were armed and that on board the ship the crew was standing by with rifles.

He turned to look at Hawkins standing on the raised platform behind him. In the moonlight, he could not tell from the expression on his face if he were having the same thoughts, or not. "Stand off a little until we know who they are, Bosun," he said.

"Aye, sir," Hawkins said quietly and then added, "Look lively now, lads."

They crested the wave and there was a moment of silence and then from the other boat there was the sound of several people calling at once. Then the voices quieted a little and Travers called across the ten yards that separated them, "Speak English. English!"

"Vee iz Nederlander, Hollander."

"They're Dutch, sir," one of the oarsmen said.

"Yes," Travers said.

"Pull along side, Bosun, starting with that boat there and not too fast."

The three boats were tied to each other twenty feet apart. There was no one in the last boat. "Cut it loose," Travers said and they pulled alongside the second boat and then to the first one asking the same questions. "Who is the captain? Do any of you speak English?"

In the first boat one man kept answering, "Vee iz Nederlander. Vee iz Hollander." The others that had called out before were now unresponsive, not speaking, just looking at them as they pulled alongside. Most of them appeared to be too weak to respond even to the fact that they were being rescued. It was hard to see clearly in the light of the moon, but Travers felt there should have been some response, a gesture, a smile, but they just lay in the bottom of the boat and it was hard to tell if they were alive, or dead.

There were thirteen in all, six in the second boat and seven in the first. There was no way of getting the answers the captain had asked for. It looked like they had been adrift for a long time, but in the darkness it was hard to tell. Travers finally gave up trying to get any information and said, "Very well, Mr. Hawkins, take them in tow."

A line was attached to the first boat and the rowers pulled at their oars keeping the lines between the boats stretched out as they moved slowly to the west. Travers reached into his pocket for the torch. He knew the captain had given the flashing instructions so the light would be on as little as possible, but those signals could not be used so he flashed the signal he was going to send Morse. He waited until he got a single response flash they were ready to receive and then flashed: Claim to be Dutch. No other info. 13 in all. End. They did not flash they had received the message and he did not send it again.

The ship, rolling from side to side, bore down on them awesomely large and overpowering, the side of the hull like a sheer, dark, mountain cliff rose ever higher as the ship approached. The bow rushed toward them, a curl of foaming water rolling back from the cutwater. The ship slowed when the bow was almost upon them, the curl dying away, the high wall of steel cutting off the wind so it was suddenly still and quiet. The ship continued to slow down until it was dead in the water and they pulled the short distance toward the huge shadow that was waiting for them in the moonlight. "Get Reverend VanderMeer," Travers shouted. "None of these chaps speak English."

"Do not understand. Say again," Parkington shouted back.

"VanderMeer! Get VanderMeer! None of these blokes speak English."

A line from the ship coiled through the air toward them landing loudly on the gunnels of the boat. The crew caught it and passed it forward to the bowman who wrapped it quickly three times around the bit. The line was pulled taught as the ship started up again with the boats riding alongside.

Richard Travers quickly climbed the rope ladder to the well-deck and was glad to see half a dozen of the crew had been issued small arms and were standing along the edge of the hatch opposite where the survivors were going to be brought aboard.

"What have you found out?" Parkington said as soon as Travers had both feet on deck.

"Nothing. Only one of them has said anything. I think he's trying to say they are Dutch, but I don't know for sure. Get VanderMeer. He speaks both German and Dutch."

The first of the survivors' boats was brought alongside and some of the crew climbed down into it while the ship's boat was pulled forward to be taken aboard. It was only six feet from the level of the after well-deck to the boats, but none of the survivors were able to make it up the rope ladder by themselves.

The first man aboard was the one that had been shouting to them in the darkness. As he was being brought aboard he kept saying "Dank U. Dank U," and when he got on deck with a man on each side of him to support him he again said, "Vee iz Nederlander. Vee iz Nederlander."

"Ask him the name of his ship," Parkington said and VanderMeer translated the questions.

"He says he is Third Mate Willen Baay and his ship was the Van Leyden, a fifty thousand barrel tanker. They were torpedoed two weeks ago. They were in route from Curacao to Cape Town with a load of fuel."

Parkington stared at the deck for a while and then said, "Tell him in German we know he is German and the more he cooperates with us the better it will be for him and the rest of the crew."

VanderMeer repeated what Parkington had said and Baay said, "Nein. Nein. Vee iz Hollander."

"But you understood what Reverend VanderMeer said, didn't you, Mr. Baay," Parkington said in English shaking his finger at him.

"It is not unusual for someone to know both German and Flemish," VanderMeer said, "I do."

"Yes, I know," Parkington said. He indicated to the men holding Baay they could let him sit down on the hatch and then said. "I'm going to keep Baay away from the other survivors, Reverend VanderMeer. I want you to talk to them in German as they come aboard. You know, regular stuff, do they have any injuries? How long were they adrift? That sort of thing. Hopefully they will answer our question without our having to ask it."

VanderMeer stood by the rail for a little while talking to the survivors as they came aboard and then went back over to Parkington. "There's no question they are Germans," he said.

All of the survivors needed help climbing on board. Some of them had burns on their hands so they were unable to hold onto the rope ladder. They were all too weak to make it on board by themselves. All of them were suffering from dehydration and exposure. Several of them sat down on the deck and started to cry when they found themselves safely aboard a ship again. One had to be brought on board with a stretcher. He was unconscious, suffering from infections of second and third degree burns. The other serious casualty appeared to be an officer who was in a catatonic condition. The rest of the crew said they had to pry his hands loose from the rail and force him into the lifeboats. He hadn't said a word to anyone since the ship went down.

With VanderMeer talking to them some of the survivors did not realize they were on an English ship and VanderMeer learned the Van

Leyden was the name the Germans had given the ship after they captured it from the Dutch. It had not been a tanker as Baay had said, but was a ten thousand ton freighter that had been turned into a decoy ship. It looked like an ordinary merchant ship, but it was really heavily armed to prey on any ship that came within its range. They had been operating successfully in the North Atlantic until a month ago when they had been ordered to the South Atlantic. Some of the survivors said they hadn't sunk a single ship since they had been ordered to the new assignment. Two of the survivors even said a couple of times when they did see a merchantman they were certain the captain would go after, he had instead changed course and gone away from them. They couldn't understand it.

There had been an explosion aboard the ship. Most of them thought they had hit a stray mine that had set off the ammunition blowing the ship in two and setting the fuel on fire. Others were certain they had been torpedoed. Less than a fifth of the crew survived. Four that were severely burned died in the lifeboats just a few days after the sinking.

VanderMeer gathered this information in bits and pieces as he helped bring them aboard and later in the infirmary. The news that the survivors were German spread from person to person throughout the ship. By-and-large the crew of the Port Jefferson was angry, at first, that they had jeopardized their safety by rescuing the enemy. Doctor Bowman had best expressed the general attitude of the crew when he had said, "We should shoot the bloody Nazis and be done with it." But he was a doctor and when the survivors were brought into his sickbay, he attended to them as best he could. He even ordered that the stretcher case should be placed in the lower bunk in the sickbay, the bunk that had been his.

To the crew, the men they brought aboard were the enemy. Wasn't it treasonous to give comfort and aid to the enemy? It was the bosun who changed the attitude aboard the ship. To him anyone who had survived shipwreck at sea, whether that disaster "be of storm, fire, war, or man, 'tis of God they be saved and Ah nay be goin' against his workin'. They be smiled upon by the gods." He had been at sea for more than fifty years and had seen others pulled from a watery death. "Aye, laddies, what country they be of makes no never mind. They be seamen like you and me. Would ye be wantin' to change place ah them? I'll nay be holdin' them a grudge for where they come from. They've nay had any food to eat, nor bunk to sleep in an' I be giving one of 'em my bunk for sleepin' 'til he be well." It was not long until almost all the crew had offered their bunks. They did not all do it cheerfully, many of them felt forced into it because others did it, but one by one every survivor had a bunk.

Two and a half hours after the flare had been sighted, quiet again prevailed aboard the Port Jefferson. Everything was in its place with the survivors bunked in accommodations befitting their rank. The severely burned man had Dr. Bowman's lower bunk in the sickbay and Lieutenant Baay had the upper bunk. Dr. Bowman moved his gin and cigarettes into Travers' cabin and Travers moved to the settee berth in Parkington's cabin. From the other survivors VanderMeer learned the catatonic officer was the Executive Officer, Lt. Commander Henrik Hahn, and he was put in with Renshaw. The rest of the survivors were berthed in the crews' quarters, those who had given up their bunks doubling up with shipmates on alternate watches so one could sleep while the other was on watch.

Except for the survivors, hardly anyone fell back to sleep quickly. On the bridge, First Mate Renshaw stood next to the chart table. The survivors had been taken care of. The ship was back on its westerly course at twenty knots and yet he was more frightened now than he had ever been before in all his days of sailing. His fear was not of being injured, or even of death, but a fear that went along with his wondering if some event could turn him into a useless human being similar to the man who was now his roommate.

Lying flat on his back on the narrow settee berth in Parkington's cabin, Third Mate Richard Travers stared wide-eyed at the ceiling. He was completely exhausted, too tired to fall asleep. He knew he had done a good job, but he wished it hadn't had to be done. Things were different now. Everyone had been inconvenienced. He no longer had the privacy of his own cabin. That was not what he really minded. That was just a symbol of it. It was the war. The war was the great inconvenience. It disrupted the simplest things in the lives of ordinary people.

In his cabin, the captain sat at his desk looking down at the list of the thirteen names of the survivors Reverend VanderMeer had given him. By the time the Port Jefferson had come along they had given up hope. They had been adrift for fifteen days and had run out of food and were down to their last rations of water. Three other ships had passed them in that time and had either not seen them, or had ignored the distress signal which they had sent up. The flare, which Mr. Parkington and the lookouts had seen, was the last flare the survivors had.

The longer the captain sat there thinking of the night's events, the more he was troubled with a sense of hopelessness: for things the way they were and for the way they were becoming. He was ashamed of those other ships and the captains who had commanded them, yet he didn't condemn them. His sense of shame was mostly that he had almost acted as they had. How close had he come to continuing on his way, ignoring that call for help, telling himself it wasn't really there, and if it was, he couldn't risk the safety of his ship? He couldn't say exactly when his attitude had changed, but he did know not too many years ago there would have been no question in his mind about going to the aid of shipwrecked men adrift. He had always considered himself a decent enough chap, not out to hurt anybody and ready to help the person who needed help. It frightened him to think he had even thought of sailing by without even investigating. It frightened him even more that he could have rationalized it, convincing himself he had done the right thing, that he did not have the right to jeopardize the safety of his ship, his passengers and his crew. He wondered if he and other people like him, well-meaning people, in their desperate effort to preserve themselves, their ships, their homes, their nation, their superior way of life, were not destroying their souls.

***

Not many people read the ship's paper that day. Those who did tended to remember only two items in the many communiqués.

LONDON - 20 January 1942 – British Admiralty communiqué
    The Board of the Admiralty regrets to announce the loss of HMS Trawlers HENRIETTA (Lt. A.V. Pierce, Royal Navy Reserve, Commanding) and IRVANA (Skipper J.I. Borritt, Royal Navy Reserve, Commanding)

The other item was from the US War Department communiqué:

Atlantic Theater
    Enemy submarine activity is continuing off the East Coast of North America from Newfoundland to Cape Hatteras. The sinking of three tankers, NORNESS, COLMBRA and ALLAN JACKSON has been accompanied by attacks on other vessels within the territorial limits of the United States.

***

At ten o'clock in the morning Captain Chipman sat in the forward seat of a table in the main salon. On one side of him was Second Mate Parkington and on the other was Reverend VanderMeer. Across the table from the captain, Lieutenant Willem Baay sat with both hands holding on to the arms of the chair as though to keep himself erect. Beyond the closed doors the two armed crewmen who had brought him forward were waiting to take him wherever the captain told them to.
    The captain sat with his hands folded on the table in front of him. The dark blue and gold stripes of his sleeves contrasted sharply with the

polished mahogany top of the uncovered table. He had been apprised of all that had happened and all that had been learned. Sitting across the table from him now, the captain wondered if he could trust the word of this German naval officer. If the survivors had been from any other kind of German war ship, he would have felt the officers were honorable men, men of their word who could be trusted. But a decoy ship's whole method of operation was one of deception. Could an officer from that kind of a ship be expected to tell the truth? He had come aboard lying to them, claiming to be Dutch instead of owning up to who he really was. He had claimed their ship was a tanker when in fact it had been a converted freighter. He undoubtedly thought he would be treated better if his rescuers thought he was an ally. On any other trip, it would have worked because none of the crew of the Port Jefferson spoke either German, or Flemish, but unfortunately for Baay, Reverend VanderMeer had been along on this trip. Sitting there across from him, Baay looked weak and helpless, but the captain knew the human body was a remarkably efficient, self-restorative machine. A few days of good food, rest and medical attention and these survivors would not be as weak, helpless, and maybe not even as grateful, as they were at the moment. When they became stronger, they might consider it their duty to capture and take control of the ship that had saved them.

There was something else that was bothering the captain and he didn't know exactly what it was. He knew it had something to do with the fact there was a decoy ship in these waters at all. It was true there was some munitions and fuel going into South Africa, but the bulk of war shipping was in the North Atlantic. That's where decoy ships would have been of real value. It also bothered him VanderMeer reported the crew said not one ship had been engaged in these waters and they had turned away from possible prey. It just didn't set right. There was something more here that they hadn't gotten a hold of yet and they wouldn't get it from this man, Baay.

The captain had sailed with an old man one time who had said he could feel in his bones when his ship was getting close to a reef, or a rock, or shallow water. The captain felt now as though he was close to a reef, but he didn't know why.

Captain Chipman leaned back in his chair and started speaking slowly, waiting between phrases and sentences to give VanderMeer time to translate.

"Mr. Baay," he purposely avoided using any rank, "you have to admit we have treated you and your crew well since we brought you aboard. Is that not so?"

"Ja."

"Better even than is required by the Geneva Convention."

"Ja."

"As you well know under the terms of the Geneva Convention I am under no obligation to jeopardize the well being of my crew, my passengers, nor my ship to accommodate prisoners of war."

Baay nodded thoughtfully agreeing with VanderMeer.

"Even now some of my men have given up their bunks to your men. We are not a naval ship, but a merchantman. I do not want to think of you as prisoners of war, but only as survivors." He paused after VanderMeer translated and Baay nodded understandingly. "However, if you insist on being treated as a prisoner of war with the right and duty to do what you can to harass our progress, or even try to take over the ship, than I will have to take the necessary precautions to protect my passengers, crew and ship. In order to do that I would have to confine you and all your men to the chain locker. We would string hammocks for sleeping. There are no toilets, but we would provide buckets for the purpose and basins for washing and bathing. Those who are able would be allowed, under guard of course, to come on deck for exercise and sunshine one hour every other day. There would be adequate food and medical care. This is all in accordance with the articles of the Geneva Convention, but not what I prefer. I prefer your men have comfortable berths in the crews' quarters. You and Lt. Commander Hahn will be given the treatment and respect due your rank. This we have already done, putting my officers at some inconvenience. We are willing to do this, but in return, I must have some guarantees from you and your men." He waited for a moment after VanderMeer had finished translating and stared across the table at the young officer who sat across from him.

"These are my conditions," the captain said. "One: the crew must agree to confine themselves to the crews' quarters and the after well-deck of the ship. Between sundown and sunup they will not come on deck at all."

Baay nodded a little, indicating he understood rather than he was agreeing.

"Two: You and all other officers and men agree to in no way jeopardize the safety of the ship, including not showing any light after dark, nor sending any kind of transmission, nor signal of any kind."

Again Baay nodded.

"Three: In the unlikely event this ship should come under any kind of an attack you will in no way try to hamper us from defending ourselves, nor in any way aid our enemy."

Baay nodded.

"And fourth: you will obey the instructions and orders given you by the officers and crew of this ship."

The captain paused for a moment after VanderMeer finished translating and said, "If you can agree to those terms, Mr. Baay, and speak as the ranking officer of your men, then I promise you, as captain of this ship and as a man of honor, that you and your crew will be treated well. You have already experienced that."

Baay nodded, this time agreeing.

"In the unlikely event we should meet an Allied ship of war of any kind I will not turn you and your men over to them as prisoners of war, nor will I turn you over to our garrison at Tristan da Cunha, nor at Stanley in the Falkland Islands, but to the German Consulate in Buenos Aires."

It seemed to the captain there was, for a moment, a little stiffening and a fearful expression on Baay's face when the Falklands were mentioned before VanderMeer translated the rest of his statement. He leaned forward resting his arms on the table in front of him. "Do you understand everything?" he asked and VanderMeer translated it.

"Ja."

"Any questions?"

"Nein."

"Then do I have your word as an honorable gentleman and an officer of the Reich Navy you and your men will abide by these conditions?"

VanderMeer translated and Baay straightened up even more than before and emphatically said, "Ja!" Still sitting he saluted and then reached across the table to shake the captain's hand.

The captain stood up and the others stood up with him. "Parkington, make sure the pertinent details of this conversation are recorded in the ship's log," he said.

The two sailors came in and escorted Baay back aft to the crews' quarters. VanderMeer went along to repeat to the survivors what the captain had said and to make sure Baay told them he had agreed to it.

"Mr. Parkington," the captain said, "did you notice any reaction from Baay when I mentioned Tristan and the Falklands?"

"Well, they were certainly words he recognized, Sir, and he did appear a little apprehensive for some reason."

***

The mid-afternoon sun sent oblique shadows across the after well-deck where most of the survivors, wearing borrowed clothes, sat talking and smoking donated cigarettes. During the morning, Doctor Bowman and Helen Stanley had attended them again. Now, after two good meals, showers and with clean clothes to wear, they were all, except for the badly burned man in sickbay, on deck feeling happy and secure. On the starboard side, four of them were trying to play shuffleboard. Since all of them had burned hands and couldn't hold the cues, they stood on one foot while using the other to kick the disks to the other end of the court.

On the port side of the main deck Lt. Commander Henrik Hahn sat in a deck chair by the stern of lifeboat number 4. He was staring straight ahead, seemingly seeing and hearing nothing. He was without any visible injuries, the survivor who needed the most attention. In his catatonic state, he was like a big child who had not yet learned to do anything for himself. The night before, Miss Stanley and Lieutenant Baay had put him to bed. At noon they had fed him his lunch, bathed him, dressed him in clean clothes, and led him down the stairs and to the chair where he now sat.

For the most part Hahn was left to sit by himself. Most of the passengers were confused about him and unsure as to how to act. From time to time Lieutenant Baay would come to him, talk to him for a few minutes, squeeze his shoulder encouragingly and then leave. Whenever Miss Stanley passed him she would stop and speak to him while she straightened the front of his jacket and pulled him forward a little to adjust the pillow he had behind his head. Reverend VanderMeer had sat with him for forty-five minutes reading from the Psalms, translating into German as he read. Only Nicky seemed completely at ease with him. He was always going over to Hahn to show him something. "Here, sir. See the picture I drew. That's my Mummy. And that's Margaret; she's my nanny. And that's my Daddy. He's not here right now. He's a soldier. And that's my dog. I don't have a dog yet, but Mummy said I could have one as soon as we get to America."

It never bothered Nicky the man never answered. He sat on the deck close to Hahn, coloring in his book and asking Hahn whether the wall should be colored red, or yellow. He went from one page to the next asking Hahn's opinion on everything he colored. When he was through with the coloring book he stood up and asked, "Do you want to hear a poem, Mr. Hahn?" He started to recite.

"The captain told the colonel,
The colonel the brigadier
The brigadier told the general
That the weather would be clear."
"My Daddy taught me that. He's a colonel."

Nicky spent some time building a house with the snap together blocks and always asked Hahn's advice as to where the windows, doors and chimney should go. When he was through with the blocks he went over and had Margaret make him a pin-wheel and when it was through demanded another one. "Now, Nicky, I think one is quite enough for you to have."

"It's not for me, Margaret. It's for Mr. Hahn. He wants one, too."

"Oh, I don't think he wants one."

"Yes he does."

He sat watching critically as she made the second pinwheel, cutting the paper, folding over the points and finally pinning it to the eraser end of a pencil. Nicky took the two pinwheels and with one in each hand walked backward so as to keep them spinning in the wind. He stood in front of Hahn, offering him first one and then the other. Finally, when Hahn didn't take either of them Nicky, put one of them in his hand, forcing Hahn's fingers around the pencil and placed Hahn's hand so the wind would keep the pin-wheel spinning.

***

After being up much of the previous night almost all the passengers were in bed by 9:00 p.m. Mable VanderMeer woke up from a deep sleep and knew even before she opened her eyes Hal was not in his bunk. Two weeks ago that knowledge would have caused her concern, but he had improved so much during the past week at sea that now she was only curious. Once he had gotten aboard the ship, he had changed almost overnight. Just being at sea had been therapeutic. He had always loved the ocean. She remembered the first time they had crossed the Atlantic more than twenty years before. After a couple of days of particularly rough weather when all the passengers were seasick except him and John Buyse, he had told her excitedly if God had not called him to be a missionary, he would have been a seaman.

She was almost afraid to believe he had improved so much. Just that morning after everyone had gone to bed and the survivors were taken care of, he had taken her on deck and sat talking to her about the night's events. It had been like the old days when he used to return from a safari and come back and report to her all that had happened in the week he had been gone. It had been like that in the early hours of the morning. He reported to her all that had happened that she had not been a part of. He talked of Doctor Bowman and Miss Stanley. While the rest of the passengers and crew were falling asleep, he sat and talked with her and then they sat quietly holding hands for a long time. Now, knowing Harold was not in his bunk, she was not concerned as she had been on the train, just curious.

She felt around in the darkness for her robe and put it on as she headed toward the door. She closed the door gently behind her so as not to wake the boys and noticed in the dim light of the lounge the doors to the dining salon were closed. She walked over to them and heard the faint sounds of the piano being played. She pushed one door open a little and saw him sitting at the piano, his head thrown back, his eyes closed as his hands moved over the keys. He was playing Tchaikovsky, who was his favorite composer and whom he claimed was the most difficult for him to play. She eased into the salon and sat down quietly in one of the chairs. He finally finished and let his hands drop to his lap and then opened his eyes, turned his head and looked at her. "Boy, am I out of practice," he said shaking his head.

She went over behind him and put her arms across his chest. She leaned her head on top of his and said, "Come to bed now. You'll have plenty of time to practice tomorrow."

CHAPTER TEN

Thursday – 22 January 1942

Like a believer who feels more righteous for having made a demanding and sacrificial pilgrimage to some sacred shrine, the crew and passengers of the Port Jefferson felt more secure and confident about themselves for having picked up survivors. It was a good deed that could not be ignored by whatever gods there were who kept track of such things. Not only had they brought people back from the brink of death, but they had also extended compassion and generosity to the enemy. They were doing more than common decency required. Although the crew grumbled about having "the enemy" and the "Nazis" aboard, the fact that "the enemy" was there caused the crew of the Port Jefferson to be pleased with themselves.

The survivors also had a sense of invincibility. They were filled with gratitude, but there was also a feeling that after what they had gone through there was nothing more that could harm them. Even the elements had an indolence about them. Beneath the ship, the swells were long and stretched out, creating a gentle rocking motion. Above, the sky was clear blue as though it was on holiday from associating with clouds.

The day was such that Helen Stanley was at peace with the world and most particularly with Harold VanderMeer. She no longer thought of him as Reverend VanderMeer or attached to him those qualities she usually attributed to members of the clergy. He was, instead, someone with whom she and Doctor Bowman had worked and in that association she had developed an admiration for him. When he walked into the sickbay with the first survivor, she had expected him to say prayers over the patient while she and Bowman did all the work. Much to her amazement, he said the prayer even as he worked, no folding of the hands, no pious platitudes, but instead he had prayed as though were talking to someone. "Well, Lord, as you can see, we have somewhat of a problem here. We'd appreciate it if you would give us whatever knowledge we need, help our efforts to amount to something."

He had gone right to work helping them, handing them dressings and medicine. He was familiar with basic medical procedures and could treat and dress wounds. Sometime while they were treating burns and scrapes and broken bones she discovered he had spent a year at medical school before entering the seminary and she wondered how many other abilities he had that he wouldn't mention until they were needed.

The captain, too, was feeling a rare sense of security. They were halfway across and it was unlikely there would be anything in these waters that would be a danger to them. No self-respecting U-boat captain would come to these distant waters, but would stay along the coast of the continents where most of the shipping was. If by any chance some submarine had strayed so far away from where the hunting was good, well, the surface was smooth and any feather created by a raised periscope would be easily detected. He was in such a good mood that when he did call for lifeboat drill at ten-thirty he was concerned about not wanting it to interrupt the passengers' mid-morning coffee. When the alarm sounded, he did not bother to time it. The drill was, after all, mainly to familiarize the survivors with the procedures and the lifeboats to which they were assigned.

During the afternoon off-watch members of the crew dozed, gazed lazily into the blue sky, or hid in secluded areas of the ship hoping the Bosun would not discover their hiding places and send them back to work. On the after well-deck the survivors napped in the afternoon sun, played checkers, or talked about nothing. In addition to the exultation of having been rescued, there was now the ironic little pleasure of being a passenger aboard a ship while still getting paid to be a member of the crew of their sunken ship. Nor was there any real resentment to the fact there were two armed crewmen outside the quarters at night and even now two armed sailors stood looking down on them from the main deck.

On the port side of the main deck, Lt. Commander Hahn sat in a deck chair close to the smokestack staring out over the water. To the passengers on that side of the ship he was a reminder not only of the catastrophes of war, but also of their ship's noble actions. The steward stepped through the hatch with the first of several tea trays and Mark and Luke were right behind him, each with a handful of cookies. They headed toward the bow hoping to see dolphins jumping.

Nicky sat on the deck next to Margaret drinking his squash and eating his cookies. He finished his juice, put his glass on Margaret's tray and standing up took two more cookies and went over to Hahn. He stood in front of him holding out the cookies and when he didn't take one, he stepped closer and pressed a cookie against the closed lips. Margaret got up and went over. "Maybe he doesn't want a cookie, Nicky," she said.

"Yes, he does. I know he does," Nicky said again pressing the cookie against Hahn's mouth. This time Hahn opened his mouth and Nicky put the cookie in his mouth. "See, I told you he wanted it," Nicky said smiling while watching him eat. He fed him the second cookie and when he went back to the tray, Margaret insisted Mr. Hahn had had enough for one day.

***

Dinner was over and the tables cleared. Matt was playing chess with Duer to pass the time until he could sneak out and go meet Margaret. Duer was sitting in such a way that even when he appeared to be contemplating a move he was also watching Lady Marisha who sat playing solitaire. "Would anyone mind if I were to play the piano a little bit," VanderMeer asked.

"Whether or not we mind would depend, I suppose, on how well you play. But go ahead, you may need the practice and I wouldn't want to interfere with a musical career," Helen Stanley said. When she saw the expression on Harold's face she quickly added, "No, seriously, please do. We'd love to hear you play."

"Wonderful! Let's all get around the piano and sing," Duer said getting up from where he was sitting and heading for the piano. He got there before Reverend VanderMeer did and opened the lid for him saying, "I didn't know you knew how to play the piano, Sir Harold."

"Well, we'll see if I do."

"Do you know Swanee?"

"I think I can remember it," he said and started to play.

"Come on, everybody, gather around and let's sing," Duer said and started leading the others. He knew all the verses and spoke each line, phrase by phrase, so they could all sing it together. As soon as they finished with one song, he would ask for another one. They were songs they all knew and could sing along with: Polly Wolly Doodle, When You Wore a Tulip, I'll Take You Home Again, Kathleen, It's a Long, Long Way to Tipperary, Bye, Bye, Blackbird, Jeannie with the Light Brown Hair and on and on. The only people who didn't join in the singing around the piano were Rose Duer who sat looking through a magazine, Helen Stanley who kept on knitting, and Lady Marisha who sat by herself playing solitaire.

Duer suggested another one and Harold ignored him and said, "Mrs. Duer, is there something you would like to hear?"

She looked up, startled, looked at her husband and shook her head without saying anything.

"Miss Stanley?" Harold asked.

"Yes. Something without words would be nice."

"How about this?" he asked and started to play a Chopin etude glad to get away from the sing-along.

Helen Stanley continued her knitting, but knitting was as automatic to her as breathing. Lady Marisha laid down her cards and leaned back in her chair listening to the music. Those who had clustered around the piano slowly melted away to go back to their seats. As soon as he finished the Chopin, he went to the Tchaikovsky piano concerto Mable had discovered him playing the night before.

Nicholas appeared in the doorway of the salon. He stood there for a moment rubbing his eyes against the brightness of the room and then walked to his mother. She looked up and helped him climb into her lap. He snuggled back with his head against her shoulder and her arms around him. Margaret entered a few minutes later. "I'm sorry, me lady. I was in the bathroom and he went out," Margret said putting out her hands to take him, but Lady Marisha shook her head and Margaret sat down in the chair next to her.

Harold VanderMeer came to the end of the piece, held the final chord and then raised his hands from the keys, letting the sound fade away. He rubbed his hands together to relieve the strain in fingers that hadn't had so much exercise for a long time. Nicholas raised his head from his mother's shoulder and started clapping his small hands. His mother joined him and then some of the others in the room also started clapping. When they stopped, Nicky looked up at his mother and whispered, "Is Reverend VanderMeer going to play anymore?"

"I don't know, dear."

"Would you like me to play some more?" Harold asked.

Nicky nodded his head smiling shyly and his mother said, "Don't just nod your head, Nicky dear. Say, 'Yes, please, Reverend VanderMeer.'"

Nicky did as he was told and VanderMeer moved the piano bench over a little and then patting the seat next to him said, "All right, you come and sit next to me here and I'll play one just for you."

Nicky climbed up onto the piano bench and VanderMeer said, "Do you know *They're Changing Guard at Buckingham Palace*?"

"I know it. I know it," Nicky exclaimed delightedly.

"Fine! I'll play and we'll sing it together."

"They're changing guard at Buckingham Palace
Christopher Robin went down there with Alice
Alice is marrying one of the guards
'A soldier's life is terrible hard,' says Alice."

"Okay, everyone who knows it sing along with Nicky and me on the second verse."

"They're changing guard at Buckingham Palace
Christopher Robin went down there with Alice
We saw a guard in a sentry box
'One of the sergeants looks after their sox,' says Alice."

"They're changing guard at Buckingham Palace
Christopher Robin went down there with Alice
We looked for the King, but he never came,
'Well God take care of him all the same,' says Alice."

"They're changing guard at Buckingham Palace
Christopher Robin went down there with Alice
They've great big parties inside the grounds.
'I wouldn't be king for a hundred pounds,' says Alice."

"They're changing guard at Buckingham Palace
Christopher Robin went down there with Alice
A face looked out, but it wasn't the king's.
'He's much too busy a-signing things,' says Alice."

"They're changing guard at Buckingham Palace
Christopher Robin went down there with Alice
'Do you think the King knows all about me?'
'Sure to, Dear, but it's time for tea,' Says Alice."

They finished singing and Harold closed the lid. "Thank, you, Reverend VanderMeer," Nicky said. "Can we sing again tomorrow?"

"I think so. Maybe we can sing together right after tea and then you won't have to stay up late."

CHAPTER ELEVEN

Friday – 23 January 1942

The rolling of the ship caused strong shadows to swing constantly, but never exactly the same way, back and forth, across and along the deck. In her chair on the port side of the ship, Lady Marisha was thinking of Ransom and the future and she watched the shadows using their movements as omens for good, or bad. If the shadow reached that seam on the next roll it was for good. If it didn't, things would not be good. She knew there was no validity to her shadow watching, but she enjoyed it because more often than not the shadows reached the predetermined point.

On the starboard side of the hatch, Mark and Luke sat waiting for the stewards to arrive with the trays of tea and the large tray of cookies. Teatime was a time to get a handful of cookies and then go off to see what else they could discover. When they thought no one was around Luke had taken Mark to see the bosun's locker and opened the hatch so Mark could look down into chain locker. Of all the passengers aboard the ship, they had seen the most. They had been to the bridge, the engine room, and the crews' quarters. They could hang around the door to the steward's galley and get offered cookies and so lived in a constant state of having a handful of cookies and discovering something new. The only place aboard the ship where they felt uncomfortable was where Hahn was. "He's spooky," Luke had said and whenever he was in his chair on the port side of the ship the two of them avoided walking past him.

Almost everyone, except Nicky, felt uncomfortable around Commander Hahn. Baay brought Hahn on deck right after breakfast and left him there 'til just before dinner when it was starting to get dark. Lunch was served him on a tray with either Baay or Helen Stanley feeding him. Sometimes Lieutenant Baay would sit with him for a short while and try to talk to him, but there was never any response. Reverend VanderMeer sat and read to him for half an hour each day. Except for Nicky he was left pretty much alone.

Nicky was constantly going over to Hahn to show him the flower he had cut out or the picture he had drawn. Margaret no longer followed him nor tried to stop him because as soon as Nicky had finished describing what the picture was all about, he came back and drew another one to show Hahn.

The tea trays were brought out and as on the day before when he had finished his juice Nicky took some cookies over to Hahn. He stood in front of him holding them out and when Hahn didn't take them Nicky stepped forward and pressed one against Hahn's mouth as he had seen Miss Stanley and Mr. Baay do. This time Hahn didn't open his mouth and Nicky said, "Eat it, Mr. Hahn. It's a cookie like you had yesterday." He stood there, reaching up to press the cookie against Hahn's mouth and then slowly lowered his hand and stepped back when he saw tears starting down Hahn's cheeks. Hahn's body jerked with silent sobbing and Nicky took another step back, frightened by the sight of a man crying and wondered what he had done to provoke it.

Hahn stood up quickly reaching his hands out toward Nicky and saying in a quavering, crying voice, "Mein Sohn. Mein Sohn."

Nicky, frightened by the emotional outbreak and with Hahn moving toward him, stepped backward hurriedly and caught his heel on the two-inch lip at the edge of the deck at the top of the ladder. He lost his balance and fell backwards, head first, his head hitting the edge of the third step from the bottom before his body landed on the steel deck, his head bleeding, his body twisted and limp. Hahn stood there staring into space wondering what had happened to his son, who for a moment, had been in front of him and then suddenly vanished.

On the after well-deck the survivors turned their heads at the sound trying to figure out what had fallen next to the ladder. On the main deck those who had seen him fall sat stunned for just an instant, unable to believe what they had just seen. Lady Marisha had not been watching Nicky, but all the others had seen him fall through the rail opening of the ladder. Matt was the first one to jump up, sending his tea tray crashing, and running along the deck shouting, "Dad, Dad! Come quick!"

At his son's urgent call, Harold VanderMeer ran across the cargo hatch with Helen Stanley right behind him. It was then that Lady Marisha, wondering what all the panic was about, began to realize she did not know where her son was. She was going to ask Margaret, but Margaret was running aft with the rest of them. She started after them, but Doctor Duer got in her way, preventing her from following and then Mable VanderMeer and Rose Duer were on either side of her, their arms around her, leading her inside and forcing her to sit down in one of the lounge chairs.

"What's happened? Where's Nicky? Let me go," she cried, but they didn't let her go.

"No, you don't want to go," Mable VanderMeer kept saying. "There's been an accident. Stay here. The others will take care of everything."

The captain came down the inside stairway a few moments later. "There's been a bad accident, Lady Marisha," he said. "I understand your son's condition is serious. Dr. Bowman and the others are doing what they can."

"Is he alive?"

"Yes, he is alive. They are doing all they can," he said and when she didn't look at him he turned and went up to the bridge.

Lady Marisha sat looking straight ahead, her back straight, not touching the back of the chair, her hands folded in her lap, her legs angled to one side and crossed at the ankles. She was aware of the other women around her in the same way one is aware it is a sunshiny, or cloudy day without having looked at the brightness of the sun or the shape of the clouds. She could not identify any of them, but felt their anxiety crowding in on her like low hanging clouds, enveloping her. *Ransom, Ransom, why have you deserted us? Our son needs you. We both need you. Oh, God, save them both. I can't live without them, both of them. Why him? He's so innocent and defenseless. What have I done? God have mercy. Oh, God, Please! Please! Please! No tears. Don't let them see tears. Remember who you are. Oh, God, don't let it happen! Oh, God, give me strength. My son. My only son. I can have no more. Live! Live! You must live, Nicky! Live! Live! Live!*

In the sickbay Nicky lay on the operating table in the middle of the room. From the adjoining sickbay could be heard the semiconscious groans of the burned man suffering in his bunk. All three of them had known Nicky was dead when they brought him in. Harold VanderMeer stood at the foot of the table with his hand clasped behind his back, slowly shaking his head back and forth. There was an ache almost as acute as that which he'd had in his heart when little Esther had died. She was eighteen months old when she succumbed to spinal meningitis. They had tried to comfort Mable and him by telling them God knew best. That in God's infinite wisdom he knew better than man did and it must have been God's will. Even then, it had not sat right with him. What kind of God was it whose will it was Esther should die of meningitis, or a tragic accident like this happen? Now with the ache there was anger, not at God, but at death. He was convinced this was not something of which God would have approved, but what did he say to the Nicky's mother? He knew he would be the one who would have to tell her. He was clergy. He was supposed to have the answers. He was supposed to know how to do these things.

Doctor Bowman stood by the side of the table watching Helen Stanley and understanding her desperation because of his own desperation. Three times in his lifetime he'd had the overwhelming feeling of complete inadequacy. It was not just the inadequacy of a physician, but an inner anguish that if he couldn't do anything, then his own life could not be preserved. Three times he had failed: Harold dying of wounds on the beach at Dunkirk, Julian dying of hunger and pneumonia after their escape from the German prison camp, and now this. Of the three, this time was the most important. This was his last chance to believe in himself, to believe in anything. He groaned and slumped into a nearby chair defeated.

Helen Stanley turned around and leaned back, her hands on either side of her clutching the edge of the table, her nails digging into the wood of it as though by the sheer strength of that grip she would be able to subdue the choking rising in her throat and hold back the tears in her eyes. "No use." the Doctor had said. Then what was the use of anything? Her mind was filled with memories of sights and sounds of him sitting on the edge of his bunk rubbing sleepy eyes, his dark, pageboy hair tousled. *"Half way up the stairs is the stair where I sit"... floppy yellow life jacket ... "They're changing guard at Buckingham palace"... Holding on to the edge of the hatchway to step over the foot high sill ... "He was shipwrecked and lived on an island for weeks"... windblown black hair, smiling eyes, clapping hands. Nicky! Nicky! Nicky!*

There was no consolation in knowing nothing could be done, that it was an accident, a bizarre, impossible accident. All she knew was someone she loved and who had loved her was gone. Never again would he come asking to learn another line, or crawl into her lap for a story, or laugh excitedly when she let him pull out her knitting after she had purposely made a mistake.

She felt something moving behind her and wiping her eyes she turned to see Reverend VanderMeer pulling up the sheet. She looked across at Doctor Bowman sitting slumped in the chair and she wished there were something she could say, but there was nothing that could mitigate defeat. She looked back at Reverend VanderMeer who stood for a moment, looking at her. He took a deep breath and said, "Will you come with me while I tell her?" She nodded wondering how many times the two of them had been the ones required to inflict the pain.

They walked forward quietly ignoring the questioning glances of the people they passed. The women stood expectantly when they entered the passageway. Lady Marisha stood with her hands folded in front of her facing them. "I'm sorry," he said and put out his hands to take hers, hoping somehow through the hands he would be able to express what was impossible to express in words, how genuinely sorry he was, but she did not release her hands to permit him to take them and so he had to cup his hands over hers, holding the knot of her clasped hands inside his.

She stood for an instant looking at them. A muscle tightening and relaxing in her cheek was the only sign of any emotion and then that, too, stopped and she said in a quiet voice, "Thank you both for your help." She turned and walked steadily and erectly with her hands still clasped in front of her toward her cabin door. Mary VanderMeer ran to her parents' cabin sobbing and Margaret sat back down in one of the chairs, her face buried in her hands, her body shaking. Mable VanderMeer tried to catch up with Lady Marisha, but the door slammed shut before she got there.

Lady Marisha stood in the middle of her cabin, refusing to be aware of anything, forcing herself to be void. She saw nothing, heard nothing, felt nothing, thought nothing and yet no matter how she tried not to feel, hear, or think it, she knew her son was gone.

Reverend VanderMeer waited until Lady Marisha had left and then climbed the stairway to the officers' area. He stepped through the pilothouse door and every person on the bridge turned to look at him. They knew before he spoke what he was going to say. "Nicholas Harwell is dead, Captain."

The captain nodded and turned back to look out at the sea ahead of them. He felt a great sense of failure. He had, in all good faith, made the colonel a promise and had not been able to keep it. It should have been an easy promise to keep. Of all the legs of the Port Jefferson's trip, this was the easiest and safest. He knew without being explicitly told the colonel was sending his family away to keep them as far as possible from the war. And yet even here, two thousand miles away from anywhere, the war had been able to reach out its ugly hand and take one of them. And with the sense of failure, there was also the feeling of acute loss. The sudden absence from life of this little boy painfully recalled the ache in all its intensity when he was informed of his own son's death. There was always with him an emptiness that he discovered never got filled. The emptiness was always there, although the ache did lessen a little by the passage of time.

"Have the ensign lowered to half staff, Mr. Renshaw," he said quietly without turning. It was such an inadequate gesture and yet he hoped there was a little something in the symbol of an empire bowing at the passing of a four-year-old boy.

"Request permission to leave the bridge, Captain."

Renshaw? The one he had always considered unfeeling wanted to lower the ensign himself. He turned to look at his first officer. "Permission granted, Mr. Renshaw."

Mr. Renshaw walked slowly down the port ladder to the main deck. He did not look at the VanderMeer boys who looked at him curiously as he walked by. He started down the ladder to the after well-deck and the crew and survivors rose slowly to their feet, apprehensive at the sight of the first officer in this area of the ship. He walked to the foot of the mast, stood at attention for a moment and then reached out and uncoiled the flag halyard from the cleat. The crew and survivors seeing what he was doing came to attention and took off their caps. He lowered the flag slowly and then wrapped the line back around the cleat. He turned on his heels and walked quickly across the deck, the men turning to watch silently as he passed.

Renshaw reentered the pilothouse and the captain turned away from staring out the porthole. "Services will be at 0900 tomorrow, Mr. Renshaw. Notify the bosun to prepare the burial bag. He is to be relieved of all duties and all watches until the bag is sewn."

"Aye, aye, Captain."

The captain left the pilothouse and went to his cabin. He sat down at his desk and wondered for just a moment if he should ask Reverend VanderMeer to read the service. Would she prefer a member of the clergy do it? No, he couldn't ask someone else to read the service. It was his responsibility. He got up from his desk and went over to the bookshelf to look for the Book of Common Prayers.

***

Jack Hawkins pulled the white canvas from the roll carefully inspecting it on both sides. He was almost to the end of the roll before he found a section that was large enough that did not have some water stain, or a dirty spot. Three times before in his fifty years at sea he had been called on to sew a burial bag, but never had it been for a child and never before had he been concerned the piece of canvas be spotless.

He examined the canvas with his own son in mind. He knew his son would be forty-two years old now if he were still living, but he could only see him with his emotions as a boy of only three years of age, held in his mother's arms as she stood on the London quay while the ship slowly pulled away. He was only a seaman then, signed aboard a four-master headed through the Suez to Bombay. As a young seaman, getting underway there was not much to do except glance back from time to time as he heaved on one line and then the next.

His son Andrew, with wind-blown brown hair and one arm around his mother's neck, waved to his father while his wife, Mary, intermittently waved and wiped away tears with her free hand. Sometimes the tugging at his heart seemed more than he could bear when he would see his wife standing on the dock, crying every time he put to sea. But there was nothing he could do about it. He was a seaman. The sea was his calling. He was gone almost two years on that trip. When he got back Mary and Andrew were gone. His widowed mother didn't know where Mary had gone. Mary had left him a letter he knew had been written by someone else because Mary didn't know how to read, or write. In the letter she said she just couldn't bear the loneliness of his being gone all the time. She said she couldn't stand the pain every time he left and the fear he might never come back. His mother had been visiting her sister in Cambridge when Mary left. As soon as his mother got home and found Mary had left, she had tried to find her, but no one knew where she was. Mary's parents probably knew, but they never told him where she was.

For many years after that, whenever he would see a woman with a boy that resembled his wife and son, his heart would jump with expectation and then fall with disappointment when they were not his. As the years passed, he understood that his wife and child would have changed with time. He wondered if he had ever talked to some stranger, looked right into the eyes of some man and not recognized his own flesh and blood. He had a son he had never seen grow up, a son that might even have sons of his own by this time, a son that could even be a grandfather that would make him a great grandfather. He had never seen any of his grandchildren, or his great grandchildren.

As the passengers had come aboard he watched each of the boys and thought, "I had a lad that age once." From a respectable distance, he had watched each of them, wondering if his son had acted that way at that age. He had seen Matt and Margaret sneak into the baggage compartment and wondered when Andrew had fallen in love and if, like his father, Andrew's first love had been his only love. He enjoyed Luke's eager curiosity and wondered if Mark would always be a follower. For some reason he could not understand why he felt sorry for the Duer boy. He only saw the lad up close during lifeboat drills. The lad didn't smile much and that was a shame. But of all of them, the wee laddie was his favorite. He was sewing a burial bag for him now. The same one for whom he had sewn the life jacket, but the life jacket hadn't done the wee laddie any good.

He cut out the section of canvas, being careful not to let it touch the dusty deck as he cut. He folded the piece in half and spread it flat on the rough, plank bier that rested on his work table. He folded the edges over and started sewing, concentrating on his stitches, his gnarled old fingers making each stitch exactly the same length. When he had sewn a foot up both sides he went over and picked up the forty-pound shell that had been sitting on its end just inside the hatch. Lying on its side it wanted to roll back and forth with the rolling of the ship and he put a little wedge of wood under each side of it to keep it steady while he sewed across the width of the bag, sectioning it off into a pocket of its own.

He finished sewing one side of the bag and unconsciously opened and closed the fingers of his right hand to relieve the stiffness as he stood looking down at the small, white bundle resting on the coil of new rope. The tablecloth in which they had wrapped the body was neatly folded and closed. On one side he could see the design woven into the white linen of the flag with the diamond and P in it. *Ah, sweet laddie, 'tis silks and satins yeh should be layin' in and a silver casket for goin' to the mool. And yet, was not the body ah our dear Savior Himself wrapped in linen for the layin' in the tomb. And did not the good Lord who made heaven and earth also make the sea.* He swallowed several times to push back the lump in his throat. *Ah, there's no understandin' it. No understandin' it ah tall, ah tall.*

He bent over and gently picked up the tiny body, carried it to the table and placed it on the canvas. He pulled the top piece of canvas over as though replacing kicked off covers. He sewed up the remaining side and across the top, folding the edges of the canvas over as he went. When he was through his hand ached from pulling the needle and twine through the four layers of canvas and his eyes burned from straining to see that each small, tight stitch was exactly the same. He stood for moment looking down at the burial bag. *'tis done. Fit and proper 'tis done, but 'tis not enough.*

He turned the wheel on the hatch slowly so the dogs would not squeak as they pulled back and released. He stepped through and closed the hatch quietly behind him and walked down the passageway that led to the forward well-deck. He felt embarrassed at having to ask someone, but he had to have it right. Even as he started up the ladder to the main deck he wondered who he could ask. He didn't want to go to the bridge. They might ask him why he wanted to know and tell him it wasn't necessary. He felt relieved when he got to the top of the ladder and saw Reverend VanderMeer standing by himself leaning on the rail. "Beggin' yehr pardon, Reverend," he said touching his closed hand to his forehead, "could yeh be sparin' me a minute, sir?"

VanderMeer turned slowly, pausing to identify the speaker. "Ah, Yes, Mr. Hawkins."

"'Bout the wee laddie, 'tis, Reverend, would yeh be knowin' the spellin' ah the wee laddie's name?"

The wee laddie. Oh, the wee laddie. "I think it's N, I, C, H, O, L, A, S," he said.

"'Tis an ignorant man I am, Reverend, and old with a memory that be none too good. 'Tis much obliged I'd be if yeh'd be writin' it down fer me. It's the whole ah the name I'd be wantin', if you please, sir."

VanderMeer lifted his hand toward his pocket for the pen and then said, "I'll have to get a piece of paper."

"Thank yeh, sir," Hawkins paused and then added, "for the markin' ah the burial bag it is, sir, and I'd not be wantin' ah doin' it wrong."

"I understand, Mr. Hawkins."

"Thank yeh, Reverend. 'Tis much obliged to yeh, I am, sir," Hawkins said.

Reverend VanderMeer paused for a moment. He wanted to say there was no reason for Hawkins to be grateful, but he should be grateful to

Hawkins. He didn't know exactly why he felt that way, or how to say it and so he just nodded a little and went inside to get the paper.

***

Hawkins sat on a coil of rope with a strip of canvas across his knees. His left elbow pinned the piece of canvas while his left hand pulled it taught. With his right hand he pushed the needle back and forth through the cloth following the outline of the letters. *Ah, Sweet Jesus. So tiny he be and so might big the ocean. I know Yeh'll nay be overlookin' him, for surely the likes ah him Yeh'll be wantin' first. Surely Yeh'd nay deal harshly with an old man for offerin' a bit ah help e'en though Yeh'd nay be needin' it. Ashore 'tis stone they use, deeply cut to let Yeh know where the dear one's laid. Surely there be no harm in a bit ah thread.*

He finished the lettering. The name, NICHOLAS B. HARWELL arched across the panel of canvas and below it the date, 23 January 1942. He lay the canvas panel on the table next to the bier and stood up carefully, straightening up slowly, his joints aching from having bent over the canvas for so long. He went out on deck, opening and closing the hatches quietly and stood for a moment looking up at the sky. The waning moon was to the north of them and the stars above told him it was about midnight. *Midnight. Time enough. A cross? Nay, 'twas not the likes ah him put the dear Savior on the cross. A lily. 'Tis pure, but cold. A lamb? Aye, a lamb, pure and gentle.*

CHAPTER TWELVE

Saturday – 24 January 1942

Hawkins bent over the table sketching in the outline of a lamb between the name and the date. He sat down on the coil of rope again and started stitching, each loop of thread another soft turn of the fleece. His legs became stiff and fell asleep. His shoulders ached from bending over and his fingers became so numb he could not feel the needle any more.

He finished the stitching, took a deep, exhausted breath and stood. His numb legs started to buckle under him and he had to hold on to the edge of the table until the blood was circulating again. He lay the panel over the bag and stitched along the edges to hold it in place. He picked up the flag, unfolded it, and spread it out with the red of the cross centered over the body and the red and white ribbons angling off to each corner of the bier. He attached the flag along the sides and top of the bier, leaving the bottom loose so the burial bag could slide out from under the flag. Now that his work was done, he felt very tired, very old, and very, very sad. He wiped the moisture from his bearded cheeks and left the rope locker.

He stepped out to the forward well-deck and looked around him, pleased it was not yet daylight. Behind the ship on the eastern horizon there was just the beginnings of the pre-dawn gray. He crossed the well-deck, climbed the ladder to the main deck, and then took the next ladder to the bridge. He stopped at the top of the ladder, surprised when he saw the captain standing on the starboard wing. "Beggin' yehr pardon, Cap'n, 'tis requestin' permission to come on the bridge ah am, sir," he said to the broad back that was in front of him while raising his hand to his forehead.

"Permission granted, Mr. Hawkins," the captain said without turning.

"The bag be ready. The flag be placed, Cap'n."

The captain nodded, reached into his coat and pulled out three, new, one-pound notes folded in half. He held them out without turning and Hawkins took them feeling the six new edges. *Three pound, an uncommon sum. Three florins was the custom. Three piece of copper. One each for Father, Son and Holy Ghost.* He wondered if substituting paper for metal would in any way displease the Almighty. He put the notes in his trouser pocket without saying anything and went back down the ladder.

***

Third Mate Richard Travers stood at the bottom of the ladder on the starboard side of the after well-deck waiting for the passengers to arrive. Above and behind him, the flag at half-mast whipped in the wind. The crew stood in ranks; their feet apart, the hands clasped behind them on top of the after cargo hatch, all of them leaning forward and then backward in unison to the rolling of the ship. They each wore their dress uniforms, some faded and most were wrinkled. None of them could say they knew the boy. Some had never even seen him, but they all knew the circumstances that were the reason for their being there. They were there to show support to her Ladyship even though they didn't know her. They were there to show their unity in their anger against the survivors. There was not one of them that didn't in one way, or another, blame the Germans for Nicky's death. If they hadn't rescued the damned Nazis it would never have happened. There was none of them, except the bosun, of those who had given up their bunks who wished now they hadn't. They should never have been so kind. The Germans didn't deserve to have it so good. They should have been put in the chain locker and never let up on deck. They were the cause of all the discomfort and trouble aboard the ship. It was the bloody Nazis who were the reason for the trouble all over the world.

Two of the ship's crew stood on the deck below and in front of the others. They stood three feet from the nine by twelve piece of white canvas that lay on the deck blotting out most of the painted lines of the shuffle board court. In the center of the white canvas was the bier with the flag over it. One end of the bier protruded six inches over the side of the ship where a section of the rail was removed, the same section that had been removed when they took the survivors aboard.

The passengers started to arrive and Travers ushered them to their places along either side of the white canvas square leaving a space for Margaret and Lady Marisha and then went forward.

The captain was standing in the middle of his cabin when Travers arrived at his open door. "We're ready, Captain," he said.

The captain nodded and then walked over to his desk and picked up the small, black, leather-bound book with a fine-line, gold cross imprinted on the front cover. He opened the book to check again the markers were in the correct places before walking out of the cabin.

On the starboard wing of the bridge, Mr. Parkington saw the captain walking aft along the main deck. He waited until the captain was at the top of the ladder to the after well-deck and then stepped to the door of the pilothouse and said, "All engines ahead one third. Show turns for five knots."

The ship slowed and the flag that before had been whipping in the wind waved slowly back and forth. The captain took his place at the head of the bier, the toes of his black shoes an inch from the white canvas, the two sailors on either side and behind him.

Mr. Renshaw appeared at the top of the ladder with Lady Marisha holding onto his arm. He went down the ladder ahead of her, walking backward down the ladder, his hands on the rails on either side to catch her if she should lose her balance. He walked beside her to the edge of the canvas, standing outside of her along the rail. Mr. Travers with Margaret came right behind them. Travers took Margaret to stand next to Lady Marisha. Margaret looked at him anxiously, daubing at her eyes with her handkerchief. He stepped back and motioned Miss Stanley to move next to her. Mr. Travers turned and climbed the ladder to the main deck where he stood looking down at them.

The captain opened the book and started to read. "The Lord is my shepherd." His voice quavered a little and he paused for a moment before he continued. "Therefore I can lack nothing. He shall feed me in green pastures and lead me forth beside the waters of comfort." The wind ruffled the pages of the book and he had to spread his hand over the top of them so he could see them to continue reading. "He shall convert my soul and shall bring me forth in the paths of righteousness for His name sake. Yea though I walk through the valley of the shadow of death, I will fear no evil ..."

Margaret spread the hand with the handkerchief in it over her face and started sobbing and Helen Stanley tightened her hold around Margaret, forcing Margaret to lean on her. Margaret buried her face in the tall woman's shoulder trying to control her sobbing.

"... for Thou art with me, Thy rod and Thy staff comfort me. Thou shalt prepare a table before me in the presence of them that trouble me, Thou hast anointed my head with oil and my cup shall be full. Surely Thy loving kindness and mercy shall follow me all the days of my life, and I will dwell in the house of the Lord forever."

Mr. Renshaw stood next to the rail, tense and alert, his head turned watching Lady Marisha. She stood erect, her hands folded in front of her, her eyes dry, looking at the flag spread over the small mound on the deck. He had the uncomfortable feeling she was not aware of what was going on, not aware Margaret was standing next to her sobbing, that the rest of the passengers were gathered there, or that the captain was reading.

"Jesus called them unto Him and said,'Suffer the little children to come unto Me and forbid them not: for of such is the Kingdom of God.' He shall feed His flock like a shepherd, He shall gather the lambs in His arms and carry them in His bosom."

Mary VanderMeer dropped her handkerchief. The wind caught it, blowing it along the deck. It hung for a moment on the two inch steel lip before blowing over the side. Matthew reached into his pocket for another handkerchief, handed it to her, and put his arm around her.

"The disciples came unto Jesus saying,'Who is the greatest in the Kingdom of Heaven?' And Jesus called a little child unto Him and set him in the midst of them and said, 'Verily I say unto you, except ye be converted and become as little children, ye shall not enter into the Kingdom of Heaven. Whosoever therefore shall humble himself as this little child, the same is the greatest in the Kingdom of Heaven. And whoso shall receive one such little child in My name receiveth Me. Take heed that ye despise not one of these little ones, for I say unto you, that in Heaven their angels do always behold the face of my Father which is in Heaven.'"

The captain closed the book, marking the place with his finger, "Let us pray," he said. "Our Father, who art in heaven ..." Reverend VanderMeer was the first one to join the captain in the prayer, and then the rest of the passengers, and then the crew joined in saying, slowly, hesitantly, "Hallowed be Thy name. Thy Kingdom come. Thy will be done on earth as it is in heaven. Give us this day our daily bread. And forgive us our trespasses as we forgive those who trespass against us. And lead us not into temptation, but deliver us from evil. Amen."

The captain took off his hat. The rest of the crew took off their hats and on the bridge Mr. Parkington saw Travers remove his hat that was his signal and he stepped to the pilothouse door. "All engines stop," he said and took off his hat. The relief helmsman rang up the orders to the engine room and then stood at attention behind the engine telegraph. The engine vibrations stopped and there was an unusual quiet throughout the ship. On the after well-deck the only sounds were Mary and Margaret crying and some creaking from the rocking of the ship that had not been noticeable before.

The captain tucked his hat under his left arm, raised the book again and opened it. The wind rustled the pages and the sound of it was like dry leaves in an autumn breeze. "Oh Merciful Father, Whose face the angels of Thy little ones do always behold in heaven, grant us steadfastly to believe that this, Thy child, hath been taken into the safe keeping of Thine eternal love. And Almighty and Merciful Father, Who dost grant to children an abundant entrance into Thy Kingdom, grant us grace to so conform our lives to their innocence and perfect faith, that at length, united with them, we may stand in Thy presence in the fullness of joy, through Jesus Christ our Lord. Amen."

The captain paused for a moment and the two sailors who were behind him stepped forward and stood at the head of the bier. "Jesus said unto His disciples, 'Ye now therefore hath sorrow: but I will see you again and your heart shall rejoice and your joy no man taketh from you.'" The captain turned the pages to the next marker. "Unto almighty God," his voice cracked a little when the two sailors bent over and took hold of the end of the bier, "we commend the soul of Nicholas Bertram Harwell departed."

The sailors straightened up, lifting the head of the bier. "And we commit his body to the deep." The wind billowed the flag as the bag slid out from under it, the bag slid with a harsh rasping sound on the rough, plank bier. It splashed into the smooth, silky water alongside the ship. "In the sure and certain hope of resurrection through our Lord Jesus Christ, at who's coming in glorious majesty the sea shall give up her dead, and the corruptible bodies of those who sleep in Him shall be changed and made like unto His glorious body, according to the mighty working whereby He is able to subdue all things unto Himself."

Lady Marisha saw the flash of white canvas with the name HARWELL along with some other letters. White water splashed up from the blue, wavelets in rings moved away from the side of the ship in ever widening circles, bubbles rising in the center of the rings. She gasped and started to take a step forward. Mr. Renshaw put his right arm around her. She looked at him, bewildered, and then drew back her foot and stood staring at the flag lying ruffled on the flat bier. From far away she heard the words being said, "Therefore are they before the throne of God ..." *Wet, Cold, Dark.* "... and serve him day and night in His temple ..." *Bubbles! Breathing. He'll drown!* "... and he that sitteth on the throne shall dwell among them ..." *Bubbles. Gone. Nicky gone? No! No! Cabin ... Nicky's in the cabin.* "... They shall hunger no more ..." *Why am I here?* "... neither thirst any more ..." *Bubbles! He's breathing.* "... neither shall the sun light on them, nor any heat ..." *Cold. Dark. Drown.* "... And God shall wipe away all tears from their eyes ..." *No tears. No tears. Don't let them see tears.* She raised her eyes and looked across the empty bier at the people standing on the other side of the piece of canvas, not seeing them, looking at nothing, hearing nothing, forcing herself to think black. *Nothing but black. Think black. Black. Black.*

"Let us pray. O, God, Whose most dear Son did take little children into His arms and bless them, Give us grace we beseech Thee to entrust the soul of this child to Thy never failing love and care and bring us all to Thy heavenly kingdom, through Thy Son, Jesus Christ our Lord. And Almighty God, Father of mercies and giver of all comfort, deal graciously, we pray Thee, with all those that mourn, that, casting every care upon Thee, they may know the consolation of Thy love, through Jesus Christ our Lord. Amen."

The captain slowly put his hat back on his head. The two sailors turned around and went back to their places by the cargo hatch. Mr. Travers came down from the main deck and stood by Margaret while Mr. Renshaw walked beside Lady Marisha toward the ladder. Everybody stood waiting until Lady Marisha and Margaret were gone and then the bosun stepped over and raised the flag to the top of the mast. On the bridge Mr. Parkington saw the flag raised. He stepped into the pilothouse and said, "All engines ahead full. Show turns for twenty knots. Come to course two-seven-zero."

The vibration of the engines and the propellers could be felt throughout the ship and the captain turned and walked forward with the passengers following behind him. The crew stepped off the loading hatch and went to their quarters to change from their dress blues into their working clothes. The first gunner went to the magazine and took down the ammunition log. He opened it and directly below the last entry wrote the date: "24/01/42—09:20 hours." He paused for moment trying to think just how to phrase the entry and then wrote, "Expended one round type AB-703-T projectile as weight in burial bag."

***

The warmth of the afternoon sun contrasted comfortably with the coolness of the gentle breeze. The sea rose and fell in long and lazy swells with hardly a white cap to be seen, giving the ship a gentle rocking motion that was soothing rather than tiresome. The passengers did not have to worry about holding the teacup level to keep the fluid from spilling, or holding on to something when walking from place to place. It was as though the elements had agreed to be gentle and comforting after the funeral of the morning.

Lunch had been subdued with everyone conscious of the empty places at the table. Lady Marisha stayed in her cabin; consequently Margaret had her lunch on a tray outside the cabin door. The stewards had unthinkingly set the regular number of places in the dining room and so those at the Harwell table were conscious of the ones that were not at lunch. Those at the other tables had, at one time or another, looked over at that table and been reminded of what had happened.

After the funeral, almost everyone had crowded onto the starboard side of the ship. Matt and Duer had carried most of the chairs over the cargo hatch from the other side as people had arrived and looked around for a place to sit. They had been on the starboard side, or in their cabins, almost continuously since the funeral. They told themselves they did not want to be on the port side because their conversation and activities might disturb Lady Marisha in her cabin. They were still a little uncomfortable being in the place where the accident had taken place.

From time to time Matthew would get up and go in to where Margaret was sitting outside her lady's door. He had sat down next to her and a couple of times he held her hand for a while. Once he held her in his arms when she had an outburst of tears. Each time he had gone to her she insisted he shouldn't be there, that they shouldn't be seen together.

At teatime Margaret was still outside the cabin door. Mark and Luke were on the forward deck sitting on bollards with their arms resting on the rail and their chins on their hands looking down at the water that curled away from the bow. All the rest of the passengers were in deck chairs on the starboard side waiting for tea to be served. A steward stepped through the hatch and walked over to Harold VanderMeer. "Beg pardon, Reverend, but the captain would like to see you on the bridge for a moment if it's convenient."

"Certainly," VanderMeer said and everyone watched him as he followed the steward through the labyrinth of chairs toward the hatchway, wondering what was happening.

On the bridge, the captain was standing at the rail in front of the pilothouse. On the port side of the bridge Commander Hahn was sitting in a gray, padded, steel armchair and VanderMeer guessed the chair had come from one of the officer's quarters. Another chair just like it was next to Hahn. The steward went ahead of VanderMeer through the pilothouse and said, "Reverend VanderMeer to see you, Captain."

"Thank you, John. You may go now," he said motioning VanderMeer to come stand beside him. The steward left and they were alone and isolated from the rest of the people on the bridge. "I would be much obliged," the captain said, "if you would not discuss what I am about to tell you with anyone else, not even with Mrs. VanderMeer. I hope you understand that it is not that I do not trust Mrs. VanderMeer, but there are some things I do not tell Mrs. Chipman just because I know she would tend to be concerned about me if I did."

"I understand, Captain. I shall hold whatever you tell me in strictest confidence."

"Thank you," he paused. "I do not want rumors creeping around the ship and that is why I have not even talked to my officers about what I'm going to say to you. I have never been comfortable with what Baay told us about the sinking of his ship, or why they were down here. We cannot expect Baay to tell us the truth, but it is not reasonable to send a decoy ship to these waters. It isn't efficient and the Germans are a very efficient people. From time to time since the accident yesterday, Hahn has been talking to himself, babbling maybe, but I noticed that twice Baay tried to quiet him down. If it is not against your morals, or scruples, I would like to have you sit with Hahn for a while. He seems to talk most at meal, or tea times. You may have to help him eat, although he seemed much better at lunchtime and was feeding himself most of the time. Does trying to get information like this bother you at all, Reverend VanderMeer?"

"No. Not at all. Particularly if it is important to the safety of the ship. What exactly should I try and find out?"

"I don't know. Just encourage him to talk and maybe you will learn something. I'll have the steward bring tea trays for you and Hahn up here and I've restricted Baay to his cabin so you should have no interference there."

It was almost eight-thirty when Renshaw came off watch and led Hahn to his cabin. VanderMeer had sat with Hahn for more than four hours including tea and dinner. When VanderMeer walked into the pilothouse the captain turned and immediately led him out of the pilothouse to his cabin. He went through the door taking off his coat while at the same time asking VanderMeer to sit down. VanderMeer sat down in one of the same style padded, steel chairs he had been sitting in all afternoon. The captain walked around his desk and sat. "May I get you anything, tea, or coffee, or sherry?"

"No thank you. Nothing."

The captain leaned back in his chair with his hands clasped behind his head, his arms like stubby wings out to the side. "Let me say first of all Reverend VanderMeer that I very much appreciate your letting me impose on you this way. Did we get anything from it, or did I just waste your time?"

"Well, I don't know, Captain. He talked about a great many people. Whether they were shipmates, or people he knew from his childhood, is hard to say. Much of it was disjointed and it was hard to make any sense of it. There were some words I jotted down I thought might interest you." He took the small notebook out of his pocket and turned the pages. "Several times he said the commodore must be informed, or words to that effect. I have it marked here as having been said five times. Three of those times were said successively. The commodore must be informed. The commodore must be informed. The commodore must be informed. Like that, but then much of his talk consisted of repeating himself."

The captain brought his arms down while still leaning back and clasped his hands across his stomach. "Did he give any name to this commodore?"

"No, only the title."

"I see. What else?"

"He mentioned Argentina once and a couple of times he used a word that would be translated as small fleet. I couldn't make out if he was part of that group, or anything else about it. The only other word that sounded out of place was Falkland. I think that's the word I heard," VanderMeer said rubbing his two thin hands together as though contemplating a problem. "I can't be absolutely sure that's what he said, Captain, but that's what it sounded like to me. He said it twice."

The captain leaned forward with his arms resting on his desk, his hands clasped in front of him. When he spoke it was more as though he were expressing his thoughts out loud rather than talking to VanderMeer. "The Falklands. No strategic value really. But it would be quite a blow to moral." He turned his head and looked at VanderMeer. "During the last war there was a sea battle between the Germans and us in the Falkland Islands. We won that one and Germany never did get back control of the Falklands. But I don't imagine it would take much for the Germans to beat us there now. I don't know what the defenses are, but we are being pressed so hard at home I would guess places like the Falklands are down to the bare minimum. Up to now Germany has not gotten hold of one piece of the Empire. They have fought us at home, in Kenya, the Sudan and in all of the other colonies and possessions, but they have not been able to conquer, nor occupy one piece of the Empire. From what little I know, my guess is, Hitler would love to be able to say he had conquered part of the British Empire even if that part is as small and as far away as the Falkland Islands. It might be a matter of some embarrassment to him that his allies, the Japanese, have occupied the Crown Colony of Hong Kong for more than a year now while the Germans don't control any British soil."

"But what would that have to do with Hahn and a decoy ship?" Hal asked.

"I don't know. But a decoy ship looks like something it isn't. And you told me when the survivors were brought aboard some of them said something with regard to not having sunk a single ship since they were down here?"

"Yes. Something like that."

"Maybe their purpose was not to sink ships, but to report on any shipping. They could have monitored radio transmissions and just kept this *little fleet* as you call it, informed of what was going in and out of the Cape. Do you think you could learn anything more from the rest of the crew?"

"I doubt it. When they came aboard they were careless. Just glad to have been rescued. Some of them were so confused they did not even know a British ship was rescuing them. I am sure by now Baay has ordered them not to say anything."

"Yes. I'm sure you're right. Well, we will just have to see what more we can learn from Hahn. I'd appreciate it if you would continue to help me on this. I don't mean for you to spend all your time sitting with him, but when he starts babbling I'd like to be able to call on you."

"Certainly, Captain. Anything I can do to help."

"And what we'll do is keep Baay away from him, so you will be the only one he talks with. He may become increasingly more lucid and I wouldn't want Baay to stop us from of learning something that may be useful to us."

"I understand."

"Thank you."

***

The half-spent moon, often covered by passing clouds, glowed in listless indifference on a lone ship in the middle of the South Atlantic. The sea rose and fell rhythmically and soothingly, but failed in being any comfort. In the crews' quarters Hawkins, exhausted by his all night vigil with canvas and thread, lay flat in his shared bunk, his hands folded on his chest, his gray beard pointed upward, snoring quietly and evenly. At the table a few feet away from him, five of the crew sat playing cards, but the cards that were dealt were viewed with no enthusiasm and the amount of money wagered on each hand was not enough to evoke any excitement. They were playing not from any desire to play, or even to win money, but for something to do, something to keep their hands and minds busy until they could go to their bunks and fall asleep.

For most of them, it was no longer pleasant to just lie in a bunk in the same compartment with a bunch of Nazis. Once there had been a sense that in rescuing the survivors they had defied the war, had won a victory, and were immune from disaster because of their actions. Now there was uncertainty, anxiety and fear. Just a short time before they had been happy to give up their bunks to the survivors. Now there was beginning to be a smoldering anger. The Germans, too, were beginning to sense the strong resentment against them.

On the port side of the main deck, Margaret Jenkins stood by the rail out of the moonlight in the shadows of the lifeboats. The tears were over for the present. Right now, instead of sorrowing, she was worrying. It wasn't natural, even in the worst tragedies, for a person to behave the way her mistress was behaving. She just sat unhearing, unseeing, unfeeling, and uncomprehending in the leather chair that had been moved from the lounge to the cabin. Whenever anyone would come in, she would turn her face to the wall. She had not eaten anything since the teacakes just before Nicky fell. As far as Margaret could tell, she had not slept since then, either. Maybe she had slept a little sitting up in the chair, but she had not gone to bed properly the way someone should. For the funeral Margaret had laid out her clothes and had to help her put each piece on just as though she were a child. After the funeral she had come back to the cabin and sat, her back straight, her arms resting on the arms of the chair and the most frightening thing for Margaret was that she had not shed a single tear. It wasn't natural. It wasn't right. Once when Margaret entered the cabin Lady Marisha looked startled and asked, "Where's Nicky?" as though she were going to reprimand Margaret for leaving him alone on deck and then had turned quickly away, the glazed look coming back into her eyes and Margaret had looked at her for a moment unable to bring herself to say the Nicky was dead and buried.

She wondered whether anyone blamed her for what happened. *It ain't my fault.* She wondered if it was her fault in any way. She knew that it wasn't. Not really, and yet she wished she had not let Nicky take cookies to the man. She should have stopped Nicky and yet how could she have known there was any danger. Nicky's actions were so innocent and typical of Nicky. Even when she saw him starting to step back and knew something had frightened him it never occurred to her he might fall through the opening in the rail. When she saw him take that last step and understood what might happen she was too stunned by the idea of it to call out and warn him. Just one shout might have saved him, but neither she, nor anyone else had uttered that call. She knew rationally it was not her fault, and yet she could not help but wonder if there was something she should have done.

***

Black! Black! Think black! In cabin B Lady Marisha was able to keep her mind blank by concentrating on the black. It had been easy at first; just blank her mind for a while. It was something she had learned as a small child the first time she had buried her face, eyes tightly closed, in her nanny's bosom to blot out the sight of her pet dog bleeding and dying after it was run over by a run-away horse and wagon. Not to see it was not to be aware. As she got older, her ability to become unaware became more sophisticated and she could shut out unpleasantness by blanking her mind to what was happening. Usually she could keep her mind blank until the unpleasantness was past.

During the blitz bombings of London when others huddled with fright, she could sit perfectly serene, completely unaware of the bombs falling, just by blanking her mind until the all-clear sounded. It was during those times she learned to blank her mind even with her eyes open and so function satisfactorily, walk to wherever she had to go, say "yes," and "no," nod her head when she had to without ever being aware she was doing it. But it wasn't working this time. Even in a darkened room, with her eyes tightly closed, she had to concentrate on the black with all her energy, or she would see again the faces of Reverend VanderMeer and Miss Stanley coming toward her in the passageway, or see again the bag sliding over the side and hear the rasp of the canvas sliding on wood. *Bubbles. Bubbles rising and exploding on the surface. Fast at first, lots of them, slowing, slowing, one tiny little bubble left, tiny bubble, floating, exploding. Gone.*

Sometimes no matter how hard she concentrated a little crack would start at one edge of the black, pushing inward, getting larger. *A root? No, a branch, sprouting leaves, growing, other leaves, other branches, not branches, stalks, seaweed, a whole moor of seaweed swaying back and forth, parting, the white bag lying at the foot of the stalks, the seaweed closing, the bag rising, bubbles, the bag on top of the seaweed, white, so white in all the black, the bag lying on top of the seaweed, the bag standing upright, swaying like the weeds with the currents. Swirling blues and orange rolling toward the bag. Nicky falling through the blue-green water, dark hair floating above him, arms outstretched. Mommy! Mommy, help me. I'm coming, Nicky. I'm coming. Mommy's coming. Black! Think black! Black! Black!*

She had started to fall asleep a couple of times. If she could just stay black until the moment of the unconsciousness of sleep. But in the moment of relaxation, the horrors came back. *Bag rolling erratically, end over end down a watery cliff, bubbles rising at each turn, the bag bulging with flailing arms and legs within, icicle pinnacles flexing suddenly to entrap the rolling bag, tentacles reaching out, entangling seaweed, multi-eyed shadows lying in wait. Mommy's coming, Darling. Mommy's coming. Pinpoint of black. Concentrate on black. Larger. Make the black larger. Black swirling larger. All black! BLACK!*

CHAPTER THRITEEN

Sunday – 25 January 1942

By any standards it would have to be described as a perfect day. All the elements: the sun, the sky, the clouds, the sea, the wind were all working together in perfect harmony. From the first rays of light Helen Stanley had recognized the day for what it was and almost immediately began to wish that things aboard the ship were as correct as the day. Now, at nine o'clock in the morning, the passengers were in silent, little clusters. Most of them were on the other side of the ship and she thought it was probably out of some notion of not disturbing Lady Marisha.

But Lady Marisha's self-imposed isolation had to come to an end. It was not healthy physically, or mentally. For almost three days she had sat rigidly in a chair refusing to respond, or eat, or drink. The only time Helen knew of her leaving that chair was when she had gone to the funeral. Margaret was becoming more and more concerned and fearful. Margaret had constantly and patiently waited on someone who would not be waited on. Margaret carried in trays of food and pleaded with her to eat something. "Please, M'Lady, try a bit of the soup." Each time she would carry the tray out feeling despondent and discouraged by her failures. "What am I to do, Miss Stanley?"

"I don't know, Margaret. Try again later, I suppose. Maybe she'll be better then." But there had been too many "try laters" and Lady Marisha had not gotten better. Not only was she injuring herself, but she was also adversely influencing the whole ship.

Helen Stanley got up slowly from where she was sitting, leaving her knitting bag next to the deck chair. She went over to the rail and stood for a moment looking down at the water curling away from the side of the ship and then crossed the deck and entered the hatchway. She hesitated in front of the cabin door wondering if she should wait just a little longer, maybe another day and knew she had to do it now. Margaret turned to look at her questioning. Helen opened the door. It was stuffy and hot in the completely closed room. She turned on the overhead light and locked the door behind her. She went around removing the shades from over the portholes and then went and sat down on a bunk facing Lady Marisha in the chair. She took both of Lady Marisha's hands in hers. Marisha Harwell tried to pull her hands away, but Helen Stanley held on to them.

"Do you know what I miss most about Nicky being gone is the way he used to sing? The one he used to sing most when he was with me was *Half Way Up the Stair*. She started singing it.

"Halfway down the stair is a stair where I sit
There isn't any other stair quite like it
I'm not at the—"
"Stop it," Marisha wailed.
  "... bottom, I'm not at the top
So this is the stair where I always stop."
"Please stop it. Please stop singing," She pleaded. Helen Stanley ignored.
  "Halfway up the stair isn't up and it isn't down.
It isn't in the nursery, it isn't in the town."
Lady Marisha yanked her hands away clenching them into fists. "Get out," she screamed. "Get away from me."
"No, I'm not going to get out and I'm not going to leave you alone."
Lady Marisha stood up glaring at her, her hands hanging at her side.
"Lady Marisha, I am sorry about your son. I am sorry Nicky is dead. We are all sorry—"
"No! No! Go away."
"But you are not the only one that has lost a son. All over the world mothers are losing sons of all ages. The world does not come to an end because a mother loses a son. They have to go on. You have to go on. You have to accept Nicky is dead and you are alive. You have to go on."
No. No! Think black. Think black! But she didn't have a chance to think black. Through her effort to concentrate she heard the words, "Nicky is dead. Cry about it. Cry!" and then she felt the slap that stung the whole side of her face jarring the blackness out of her mind.
The wail that escaped from her was the most inhuman sound Helen Stanley had ever heard. On deck and in the salon the other passengers heard it and looked at each other and Margaret got up and rushed to the cabin to find the door locked. She pounded on the door and then stopped, listening to the wailing coming from inside.
Lady Marisha slumped to the floor, her face contorted with pain, tears streaming down her face, her body swaying, forward with each devastating howl, backward for each grasp of air. Helen Stanley sat down on the floor next to her taking Lady Marisha in her arms, holding her, comforting her and weeping herself. She wept for her own grief and for the grief of the other and because she had been the one to inflict it.
The wailing subsided to muffled sobbing, then to silent weeping, which ended finally in complete exhaustion, with no tears left for weeping and hardly sufficient strength for breathing. They sat clinging to each other until they had strength to stand. Miss Stanley helped Lady Marisha to undress and get into bed. She fell asleep almost immediately and Helen left the cabin. "She'll be all right now," Helen said to an anxious Margaret, "she's sleeping."

***

At ten-thirty Captain Jeffrey Chipman sat leaning back in his swivel desk chair. He had it turned all the way around so when he leaned back it hit the edge of the desk. He sat with his legs stretched out in front of him and crossed at the ankles with his feet resting on a leather footstool which he had picked up in Morocco. His hands were clasped across his stomach and he sat staring out at the porthole on the other side of the cabin. If the door had been open and anyone had seen him in that position, they would have thought he was a man comfortably at peace. He was wondering where and if he had made mistakes and what he should be preparing for in the few days remaining until he was in port and rid of his passengers and survivors. He was feeling a little despondent and thinking if he were at home Elizabeth he would be leaving for Sunday Service at about this time. That's what decent people did on a Sunday morning. He had been surprised and relieved when Reverend VanderMeer had not asked to conduct Sunday morning service when he first came aboard. He was glad now that shortly after the funeral he had asked Reverend VanderMeer to do a service. It would be good for the crew and passengers and maybe even for himself. Right now VanderMeer was sitting on the starboard wing trying to get information from Hahn, who had been an unwitting agent in causing the death of a child.

He couldn't remember the number of times since that tragic hour when he had wished he had never picked up the survivors, that no one had seen the flare. He always drove the thought from his mind, but he knew if he had those thoughts, the crew also had them. There was also the fact that he had promised a father he would protect and deliver that child and his mother to safety. He had failed in keeping that promise.

His thoughts were interrupted by the hardly audible electronic click on his intercom. He lifted his feet off the footstool while at the same time swinging around so he would be facing the gray box when the first words came from it. He had a feeling of dread, expecting another report of a catastrophe of some kind. "Captain, this is Parkington on the bridge. The bosun's here wishing to see you, sir. Says it's a personal matter. I told him you were unavailable, sir, but he is rather insistent."

"Personal matter?" the captain asked feeling a great sense of relief that it wasn't some emergency.

"Yes, sir."

"Very well. Send him in," the captain said. He looked up when Hawkins knocked on his open door and said, "Come in, Mr. Hawkins. Come in." He tried to sound pleasant and reassuring.

Hawkins took two steps into the cabin, stopped respectfully to raise his clenched fist to his forehead and then turned his head to look over his shoulder as though checking to see if anyone else were close enough to hear him.

"Would you like to close the door, Mr. Hawkins?"

"Aye, Cap'n. Thank yeh, sir." He closed the door and then turned back and crossed the distance to the desk. He took a roll of canvas from under his left arm. He stood awkwardly in front of the desk, suddenly at a loss for words. He wondered why he thought he had to bother the captain with this. Maybe he should have talked to one of the officers, or to Reverend VanderMeer.

"What did you wish to see me about, Mr. Hawkins?"

"About the wee laddie we buried it is, Cap'n..." He stopped frightened by his own boldness.

"Yes? Go on, Mr. Hawkins."

"About the markin' of the bag, Cap'n ... there be nothin' said about how should be done and there nay be any against how to be doin' it that I be knowin'."

"I'm quite sure you're right, Mr. Hawkins."

"Such a wee laddie he was, Cap'n. I was thinkin' 'twould nay be fittin' his goin' to the mool with no markin' on the bag. I meant no disrespect, sir.' He lay the roll of canvas tentatively on the desk. "'Tis so I made his name on the bag, Cap'n."

The captain unrolled the panel of canvas slowly and sat looking at the name, the lamb and the date that had been woven into it. He instinctively put out his hand to feel the softness of the lamb's wool. "'Tis a perfect likeness of how the bag was marked, Cap'n and I'm nay wantin' to be forward, Cap'n, but I was thinkin' the laddie's muther might be likin' to know how the bag was marked. That's why I come to yeh, Cap'n. I'd not be wantin' to do what was not fittin' and proper, or givin' her somethin' that would be addin' to her grief. Do yeh think Her Ladyship'd be wantin' it, sir?"

"I think it would be altogether proper for you to give it to her, Mr. Hawkins and I think she would be very pleased to have it," he said carefully rolling up the canvas.

"'Tis much obliged I'd be, Cap'n, if yeh'd be givin' it to her for me. 'Tis a common man I am and I'd not be knowin' the words to say."

The captain nodded slowly. "There isn't any of us know the words to say, Mr. Hawkins. But I'll give it to her and tell her you made it."

"Oh, there be no need of tellin' her that, Cap'n."

"I think she'd like to know."

"Thank yeh, Cap'n. Then 'tis much obliged I am to yeh, sir," he said touching his hand to his forehead and left.

The captain unrolled the panel of canvas after Hawkins had left and sat for a while staring at it. He rolled it up again and set it on the side of his desk and turned around and pushed the button to the intercom. "Bridge, Captain. Is Mr. Renshaw there."

"Renshaw here, Captain."

"Mr. Renshaw, I want you to take a new, never before used chart of the South Atlantic and mark our exact position at the time of the boy's death and our position at the time of the burial. And have someone bring me the flag that was used at the service and have the ship's carpenter report to me."

"Yes, sir, I'll see to it right away."

***

Captain Chipman stood in the center of his ship on the walkway directly in front of the pilothouse. He was feeling better about things than he had that morning. It had been a good service. They had sung two hymns, "A Mighty Fortress Is Our God" and "God of Our Fathers." Reverend VanderMeer had asked Sparks to put the words on mimeographed sheets the night before. Reverend VanderMeer himself had played the piano for the singing and then talked for half an hour on the goodness of God. It was a good message. He and Renshaw had both been able to be there and he was surprised and pleased to see almost half the crew was there. The salon had been so crowded the crew had to stand along the sides and out in the lounge. The only passengers not there were Lady Marisha and her maid. He had been informed Lady Marisha had come out of her "state" just that morning and was resting comfortably. Her maid was sitting by her.

At just a little before 1300 hours the sun was ahead of the ship so the captain felt the warmth of it through his blue, wool uniform. If he turned his head just a little to the right, he could see Lt. Commander Hahn and Reverend VanderMeer sitting in their chairs in the forward starboard corner of the wing. Right after the service was over Reverend VanderMeer had changed out of his suit and returned to his place with Hahn. The steward had just come up to take away their lunch trays and once again the captain was feeling guilty that Reverend VanderMeer had been deprived of having his meal in the salon with his family. But it was at meal times Hahn was most talkative and the captain was certain that eventually Hahn was going to say something that was going to explain something that needed explaining. He didn't know what it was that needed explaining, but there was a secret there with which he was not comfortable. He stood with both hands on the rail in front of him, his body swaying to the rolling of the ship, not looking at Hahn and

VanderMeer, but thinking, *talk, Hahn, talk*! He was surprised, when suddenly, as though in answer to his thoughts, Hahn suddenly jumped up and started toward him, shouting at him. VanderMeer was right behind Hahn, and Travers came out of the pilothouse as though to intercept Hahn.

The captain turned to face Hahn who stopped three feet away still talking loudly. VanderMeer stepped in front of Hahn and said, "I think, Captain, that he's just come to his senses. He is demanding to see his crew. He saw the flag and made it quite clear he was not altogether happy about where he is."

Without looking away, or changing his expression, the captain said, "Reverend VanderMeer, I'm not particularly happy about where he is either. Mr. Travers, have small arms issued to all qualified men off watch and have two of them bring Mr. Baay to the salon. No, belay that. Have them bring him to my cabin. No sense having the passengers see more than is necessary."

"Yes, Captain," Travers said and turned to leave.

The captain followed Travers, forcing Hahn to squeeze up against the pilothouse to let him pass. "Reverend VanderMeer, please ask Hahn to join us in my cabin," The captain said.

The captain sat in his swivel chair behind the desk with VanderMeer in a chair next to him. The stewards had brought in two more chairs from the other cabins and Hahn was in one of them. He had become silent after his initial outburst. "Did you learn anything more before he came to?" the captain asked while they waited for Baay to arrive.

"Nothing I can make out as being of any value."

"Don't mention them because I don't want to tip our hand he's told us anything yet, but you haven't gotten any more names have you?"

"None to which I can attach any importance. I've already told you the commodore's name." He paused for a moment and then added, "May I make a suggestion, Captain?"

"Please do."

"Before we were married my wife was a school teacher. But before she went to normal school for her teacher training, she went to secretarial school. She is very good at shorthand. Over the years she has taken down most of my sermons in shorthand and then transcribed them. I have tried to remember what Hahn said, but I can't always remember it all. I think that's true of everyone. Since you may want a record of what is said here, I assume you would want the most accurate record possible. Afterward, if she could use one of the typewriters in the radio room you would have an exact record of everything that was said."

"Well, yes, I'd like that very much. Do you think she'd be willing to do it?"

"I'll go ask her," Harold said getting up and as he left the room the captain thought that of all the people he had wanted to be aboard his ship the least were the ones he was beginning to depend on the most.

Another chair was brought in and Harold was sitting to the captain's left and Mable to his right when Travers entered the cabin followed by Baay. Baay stopped for moment, stared at Hahn, and then asked in German if Hahn was all right. Hahn nodded and the captain motioned Baay to the empty chair. The crewmen, armed with carbines, stood just outside of the open door. Baay started to say something more and the captain said, "Reverend VanderMeer please tell Lieutenant Baay he is not to say anything more until I say he may."

Baay quieted down and Hahn glared at VanderMeer. "Now tell him, if you will please, Reverend VanderMeer, that he is to tell Commander Hahn everything that has transpired since we picked them up. If at any time he says something that doesn't sound quite right to you, or you don't understand, don't hesitate to interrupt him."

Mable didn't know German, but she wrote down the sounds she thought she heard, thinking later she could read those sounds back to her husband and he would be able to translate them into English. From time to time while Baay was talking, the captain would turn to VanderMeer and ask, "What's he talking about now?" When Baay was finally through the captain asked, "Did he pretty much cover everything?"

"I think so."

"Did he tell how the Harwell lad died?" VanderMeer nodded. "Did he leave out anything you think he should have said?"

"No, I think he's pretty well covered it."

"Very well, tell Mr. Baay he may go now. One of you lads take him back with the others. Smith, you stay here."

Baay left, arguing about why he should remain, and Travers moved the chair Baay had been sitting in away from next to Hahn and sat down. "Ask him," the captain said to VanderMeer, "if he agrees to the same conditions to which Mr. Baay agreed?"

Hahn's answer was longer than the captain expected until VanderMeer translated it. "He wants you to know, Captain, that he genuinely appreciates what you and the crew did in rescuing them. He also thanks you for the kind treatment of his crew, but he says Lieutenant Baay acted incorrectly. He says any agreements between you and Baay are no longer in effect since he is now the commanding officer of the Reich contingent. 'Reich contingent' is his phrase. He says we are at war and it is his duty as an officer of the Reich to hamper you in any way he can and to encourage his men to do the same."

"I see," the captain said nodding, "ask him what Commodore VanGoebler is going to think of an officer of the Reich who told his rescuers about their plans for the Falklands."

Hahn looked startled for just a moment when he heard the question and then the glazed look he'd had before came back to his eyes.

The three of them looked at each other, VanderMeer and the captain both feeling guilty for having put Hahn back into shock. "Well, at least it confirms what we suspected, doesn't it," the captain said. "I hate to do this, but you never know when he's going to snap out of it again and incite his men against us. I can't spare crew to stand guard over them all the time. Mr. Travers, tell the bosun to swing hammocks in the chain locker. All the Germans, including the officers, will be berthed up there."

"Yes, sir." Travers said and left.

"Smith, take Commander Hahn back to the others."

"Yes, Captain."

"I feel I owe Baay an explanation," the captain said raising his eyebrows in a gesture indicating futility.

"Is it really necessary to put them in the chain locker?" Mable VanderMeer asked. "My boy, Luke, was down there with Mr. Hawkins and told us what it is like."

The captain looked at her for a long time. It was not an angry, or irritated look, but just a look of one who was weighing the question. "I think it is, Mrs. VanderMeer. I think it is. This passage has been troubled ever since we left Durban starting with not being able to get a pilot. I thought I was doing the right thing, and yet for all my attempts to do what I thought was right, a little child is dead. I do not think I am putting them up there as a form of revenge, or retaliation, but I do not feel safe any longer with them free to roam wherever they like. And when I say safe I am not thinking of myself, but of the ship, the passengers and the crew. Baay is a gentleman. I could trust him. But this Hahn is of the same fabric as his "paper-hanger" leader. It hasn't ended yet. I am usually an optimistic man, but frankly, Reverend and Mrs. VanderMeer, my optimism is at a very low level. I hope you do not think me ungrateful for all of your help. I'm extremely grateful, but I just don't know how to express it right now."

"There's no need to express anything, Captain," Harold said running a gaunt hand through his graying hair. "You may not be able to understand this, Captain, but I think I know a little bit about the burden of responsibility. If there is anyone who should be grateful, it is us, but I guess we, too, don't know how to express it."

The captain smiled. "Thank you," he said. "Now if you'll excuse me I feel I should get back to the bridge and you will be able to have dinner with your family tonight, Reverend VanderMeer. I really do appreciate all your help."

"I know, Captain."

The captain sat there a few moments longer after Harold and Mable had left. He wished the trip was over and he was safe in a neutral port. He was feeling tired and discouraged. He wished he didn't have to put the Germans in the forecastle, but there was nothing else he could do. There was more to it than just that Hahn might get well again. There was throughout his crew a strong resentment against the survivors. No one had said anything to him directly, but not only could he sense it, he had also overheard comments. "Let me stand guard over the bastards and if one of them moves out of line and I'll blow the bloody bastard to hell. Bloody Nazis. If you ask me we should never have picked them up." For their own safety he had to put the Germans in the forecastle.

***

Margaret Jenkins stood by the rail, hidden by the lifeboats. There was no moon yet, so the sea was inky black and the stars sparkled brilliantly in the cloudless sky. She was tired. More tired than she remembered ever having been before. Ever since Nicky died she had been tense and alert. There were times when she had slept a little, but it had been a restless sleep with certain senses ready and listening in case her mistress should call her. With that alertness there had also been a concern, concern for someone she genuinely cared about. It was more than just sympathy, but a fear Lady Marisha might never again be well, never again be herself. But that fear was pretty much gone now. She didn't know what Miss Stanley had done; she didn't care. What was important was Lady Marisha had woken up and eaten some lunch and then fallen asleep again. She had sat with Lady Marisha most of the afternoon even though Miss Stanley had come in from time to time and insisted there was no reason for Margaret to stay in the cabin. Margaret had finally agreed to go into dinner, but all through dinner she'd had the feeling someone should be in the cabin with Lady Marisha. Mary VanderMeer and Miss Stanley were both in there now. Miss Stanley was already settled down in her bunk with a book and Mary had been getting ready for bed when Margaret came on deck and for the first time since the accident. Margaret had relaxed her concerned vigil.

Her concerns now were of the future, her future. She had been so caught up in everything else that had happened that it was not until just a little while ago she had begun to realize the Harwells no longer had any need of her. She did not for an instant think they would be anything but generous and kind to her, but the fact was they would no longer need her. She knew Lady Marisha could not have any more children. They had never told her that. That was not something that their kind discussed with the servants, but from things she had heard them say to each other, she knew that was the case.

She wondered how long it would be before they let her go. The colonel was responsible for her. He was the one who had gotten her the visa. She didn't know much about those things. She wondered if once they sacked her if she would have to return to England. She had planned to stay with them until she became a citizen of the United States, but now there was no telling what was going to happen.

She pulled her coat tighter around herself and sat in one of the deck chairs. She thought she should go to bed, but she didn't want to go to the cabin just yet. It was peaceful on deck. She didn't think she would feel at peace if she went inside. She was just dozing off when Travers sat down in the chair next to her and said, "What are you doing out here all by yourself?" His cheerfulness irritated her.

"Just getting away from everyone for a little while. Needed to be alone," she said hoping he would take the hint.

"It's been hard for you the past few days, hasn't it?" She didn't answer him and he added, "Well, things will be better from now on."

She thought he was trying to cheer her up, but the more he talked the more irritated she became. He talked about how good it was Lady Marisha had finally come out of her condition. There was a callousness in his voice and she didn't like him talking about her mistress that way, or the way he said "condition." He talked about the Germans being moved to the forward hold and that he now had his cabin back. He didn't come right out and say it, but she knew what he meant about having his cabin back and she thought it was in poor taste he could even think those things at times like this. But she understood that to him she was only a servant who could be treated as he wished. And then she remembered she was a passenger and he a member of the crew. "Mr. Travers, why don't you go do whatever it is you're supposed to do on this ship and leave me alone."

She knew she had shocked him even though she couldn't see his face. She had quite shocked herself. He got up from where he was sitting and went down the ladder toward his cabin. She was a little frightened by what she had done, but she was also pleased with herself.

CHAPTER FOURTEEN

Monday – 26 January 1942

Captain Jeffrey Chipman sat at his desk. His mid-morning coffee tray was on the far edge of the desk. He had taken a few sips of coffee while looking over the morning reports, the number of miles covered since 0800 the previous day, the fuel report and finally a report from the gunner that one round had been expended to weight the burial bag. It crossed his mind the ammunition report was really two days late, but he knew it didn't make any difference. It was just another reminder of a tragic experience and yet there were other reminders of that tragedy right on the side of the desk. There was the chart Renshaw had given to him that morning and on top of it the flag that had draped the bier. On top of the pile was the piece of canvas the bosun had so painstakingly stitched. He had planned to give them to Lady Marisha that afternoon, but Renshaw had reported the carpenter had not yet finished the box. He had been relieved when he learned the box was not ready. He knew he would have to face her eventually, but he wasn't quite ready to do it. Tomorrow would be soon enough. He pushed the reports to one side of his desk and picking up the cup he took two large swallows of the now cool coffee. He set the cup down and leaned back with his hands behind his head, rocking his chair gently to the motion of the ship. What he would have liked to do was put a record on the player, but the ship was rocking too much. The needle of the record player would just jump out of the grooves. Right at that moment he wanted to hear some music and thought of how nice it would be if Reverend VanderMeer would start playing for the passengers again.

He got up and went to the closet. It was while he was taking his jacket from the hanger that he heard the slight click of the intercom. Renshaw's voice shot excitedly into the room, "Captain, we have just spotted an aeroplane bearing two-eight-five true. Fifteen degrees off the starboard bow."

"Impossible!" The word exploded out of him as he rushed from the cabin, but he knew it had to be true. Renshaw was not one to mistake a bird for a plane. They were too far away from any land for it to be a land based plane, therefore it had to have been launched from a ship not far away. But whose, friend or enemy? Even as he wondered, he knew it was somehow tied up with Hahn and the survivors. "Are the survivors still on deck?" he asked as he stepped into the pilothouse.

"Yes, sir."

"Get them into their quarters and don't anyone say anything to them about an aeroplane."

The stand-by helmsman handed him his binoculars as he passed through the pilothouse to the starboard wing of the bridge. "Can anyone identify it?" he asked raising his binoculars to his eyes and looking the direction Renshaw was pointing.

"Too far away yet," Renshaw answered.

"Who spotted it first?" he asked starting to scan just above the horizon until he saw the little speck that was just discernible as an aeroplane.

"Forward lookout, sir."

"Tell him well done." He lowered the glasses and glanced at the forward well-deck where the last of the survivors was going through the hatch. He waited until the last of the survivors was inside and the hatch closed behind them and then went inside, pushed down all the buttons on the intercom and said, "We have just spotted an aeroplane, lads. It is still too far away to know what kind of aircraft it is, or to whom it belongs, but in a few minutes we may be sounding emergency stations. If we do, I want all the passengers to stay in the main salon. You all know your stations, lads. That is all."

He went back out on the wing and now he could see it quite easily with his naked eye. *Why are you still coming toward us? It doesn't make sense. You obviously saw us before we saw you. You don't care that we have seen you, do you?*

"I think it's a float plane, Captain," Parkington said.

A floatplane. Well, at least you aren't a fighter. A fighter would mean there was a carrier close. Maybe a reconnaissance plane from a heavy cruiser, or a battlewagon. They are the only ones that carry floatplanes. Might be from a hospital ship. Not bloody likely. No hospital ships down here. What's its range? Not more than four hundred miles. Two hundred out and two hundred back. So, which way were you going when you saw us, out, or back?

"It's not one of ours," Travers said. "Can't make out the markings yet, Captain, but its silhouette is not ours."

"I understand, Mr. Travers," the captain said.

They all stood along the forward bridge rail with the binoculars glued to their eyes. "Crow's nest reports the plane is German, Captain," the bridge talker shouted excitedly.

"I can see the markings now," Parkington said. "It's definitely German."

The captain turned to the talker. "Tell lookouts to keep a sharp lookout in all directions. This plane had to come from somewhere. Keep a sharp lookout for smoke or ships on the horizon."

"Yes, sir," the talker said and then repeated the captain's instructions into the mouthpiece.

"Mr. Renshaw, sound emergency stations," he said and the officers went to their stations in the pilothouse leaving the captain alone on the wing. He moved to the outside rail where he would be most visible to those of his crew who might be on deck. He heard the sound of Renshaw's voice passing throughout the ship as he called the men to emergency stations, followed by the clanging of the alarm. He opened the covers to all the voice tubes and bent down to the one marked pilothouse. He waited until the clanging stopped and then shouted into the tube. "Travers!" He turned his head putting his ear to the tube to hear the response. "Yes, Captain."

"The ensign is too small. Have the bosun find the largest ensign we've got. I want the largest ensign we've got flying from our mast."

It would be several minutes before the plane would be close to them. On the forward well-deck he could see the crews unrolling and spreading out the kites. From time to time one of the men would look up to the bridge and he hoped it made them feel safe to see their captain was no more protected than they were.

He saw the bosun start up the ladder to the main deck and a short time later he came up the ladder to the bridge. He stopped behind the captain, saluted, and said, "Beggin' the Cap'n's pardon, sir, there be no bigger flags, sir, 'ceptin' the one was used for the burial, sir."

The captain looked at him for a moment. "Ah, well then, Bosun, we'll just have to use that one then, won't we? It's on my desk. Get it and replace that little thing back there," he said jerking his thumb toward the little three by five flag that was flying from the after mast. "We don't want them to have any doubts as to who we are, do we, Bosun?"

"Aye, Cap'n, that be God's very truth."

The captain waited until the bosun had left the bridge and then he leaned over the voice tube and said, "Mr. Renshaw, bring the ship into the wind and launch kites." He did not bother to turn his head toward the voice tube to hear Renshaw's answer, but instead watched the little aeroplane now clearly distinguishable. He felt the change in the motion of the ship as she turned into the wind and on the foredeck the kite crews also felt it and took up their positions. He leaned over the voice tube again and said, "Launch when ready, Mr. Renshaw."

He felt the ship steady up on its new course and the kites start to rise wobbling from side to side from the forward well-deck. He looked aft and saw the large six by ten flag flying from the after mast. He leaned over the voice tube again and said, "Send the steward to ask Reverend VanderMeer if he will join me here on the bridge."

VanderMeer arrived and the two of them stood together watching the kites climbing into the sky. "I wonder, Reverend VanderMeer, if you would be willing to give our radio man a hand and translate any messages he might be able to pick up from our friend out there," he said pointing to the approaching plane which was now little more than a mile away.

"Certainly. Yes."

The captain led the way through the pilothouse and to the radio room. VanderMeer sat down on a stool next to the operator. On the bulkhead in front of him there were three speakers with broadcasts in different languages coming out of each of them. "Sparks here will be scanning all the frequencies we can reach. If you hear anything at all in German just tell him to stop until you have identified it." The captain left and Reverend VanderMeer sat in the middle of the small compartment surrounded by the ever-changing voices and languages interspersed with the crackles, squeals and whines of the radio.

By the time the captain got back to the bridge the plane was only a thousand yards away. The black crosses, outlined in white on the gray fuselage and wings were clearly visible. Five hundred yards away it descended until it was flying at only forty, or fifty feet above the water. It passed so close they could see through the grillwork of the glass canopy and see the silhouette of the pilot inside. The plane passed the ship, circled it once at low level and then banked and climbed, heading north. The captain went to the radio room. "Anything?" he asked walking through the door.

"Nothing, Captain."

He had not really expected anything. The plane was probably under radio silence. What he couldn't understand was why the plane had come so close to them. Certainly the pilot had seen them before they had seen the plane "I see. Well, Sparks, try to raise Tristan De Cunah. Inform them we have seen a single engine German reconnaissance plane. Give them our position and tell them that wherever that plane is from must be within two hundred miles of us. Let me know as soon as you get them."

"Yes, sir."

"Reverend VanderMeer would you come with me." They stepped out of the radio room and the captain said, "Reverend, I need to impose on you and Mrs. VanderMeer again. Would you ask her to join you in my cabin? I'll be there in a moment." The captain held the door for VanderMeer to go through and then stepped over and leaning into the pilothouse said, "You may retrieve the kites Mr. Parkington and then secure from emergency stations. Warn the lookout to keep a sharp eye on the starboard side. When stations are secure have Mr. Baay brought to my cabin. Mr. Renshaw come with me to my cabin please."

The captain dropped heavily into his chair and indicated for Renshaw to also sit. "I'm having Baay brought up. There are some questions I have to ask him," he paused, "oh, ask the steward to bring in two more chairs would you?"

The VanderMeers arrived followed by the steward with more chairs. The captain paused for a moment after the steward left and then started counting off with his fingers. "First," he said, "we know we have survivors aboard from a German decoy ship. That is a certainty." He pushed over the first finger of his left hand. "Secondly we have got some words from Hahn which makes us think there is the possibility of a German attack on the Falklands. We have no idea as to the size or number of ships in that attacking force." He pushed down the second finger. "We have the name of a Commodore VanGoebler. But "commodore" can be an honorary title for someone who has command of two ships, or more. So these two are bits and pieces," he said closing his right fist around the second and third fingers, "about which we can only speculate. But the fourth fact is that this morning we saw and were seen by, a German reconnaissance plane. What I want to know is why that plane came so close to us. It could have spotted us and been over the horizon before we would ever have seen it. I can think of only two reasons why it would have come so close. First, it wanted us to be sure to see it and know what it was. If that's the case, it did it to try and confuse us. The second possibility is it made a mistake; thought we were someone else. Do either of you want to add anything to that?" he asked looking first at Harold and then at Renshaw.

They sat for a moment and both of them shook their heads.

"And you, Mrs. VanderMeer, do you have anything to add. Something you might have picked from your transcribing the last meeting I might have missed?"

"I can't think of anything, Captain."

"Very well then, let me throw something out to you. Do you think it is possible the pilot thought we were the decoy ship? That maybe Hahn and his ship were supposed to rendezvous here some place with the others and the plane was looking for them?"

"But wouldn't they have had coded radio communication of one kind, or another?" Renshaw asked.

"Or they might have been sailing under radio blackout with orders to meet somewhere. Ships sailing alone like a decoy ship would attract a lot less attention than several ships sailing together. And a decoy ship can carry a lot of fire power."

"But certainly, sir, they would have established the exact place and time where they were supposed to meet?"

"Yes, I would have to agree with you, Mr. Renshaw. However, I've been thinking that if VanGoebler did not know Hahn and his people had been sunk they might just send out a search plane rather than risk breaking radio silence. Does that make any sense? Because I'll tell you that plane coming that close to us doesn't make any sense to me unless it's something like that."

"Do you think Baay is going to admit to something, sir?"

"I'm hoping to trick him into letting something slip. If we ask our questions correctly and he doesn't know, or suspect anything about the aeroplane we saw this morning, he may just answer a question without knowing he's doing it."

Baay was shown in and sat down in the chair the captain pointed to. "How is Commander Hahn today?" the captain asked and VanderMeer interpreted.

"His condition has not improved. I must protest the treatment and the accommodations. They are inhumane."

The captain spread his hands in a helpless gesture. "You know how crowded we are on this ship Lieutenant Baay. Commander Hahn is your superior officer and has left me no alternative. I explained all that to you before. If you were in my position would you act any differently?"

Baay didn't answer.

"I have no other place to put you and still know my ship is safe. As you know we are a refrigerator ship and so our holds do not have any ventilation. The chain locker is the only place I can put you. You knew when you gave me your word; I believed you and members of my crew gave up their berths so your men could have a berth to themselves. Now your commanding officer has promised to hamper us as much as possible. I have to believe him just as I believed you. I regret we don't have berths for all of you. Undoubtedly the Van Leyden was a much larger ship with berths to spare." VanderMeer translated sentence by sentence, but it was hard to convey the captain's sarcasm in the last sentence.

"It was not much bigger than your ship, Captain."

"But we are a freighter and yours was a war ship equipped with guns and probably had a crew of a hundred, or more."

Baay just looked at him, but didn't say anything.

"Thirteen bunks for thirteen survivors out of more than a hundred bunks is not much. But we are just a small freighter. Our holds do not have bunks in them. If we had been there in time to rescue all the crew of the Van Leyden where would we have put them?"

Baay shrugged his shoulders.

"What was your ship's compliment, Mr. Baay?"

"A hundred and thirty-four," he said surprising them all with his answer.

"Thirteen survivors out of a hundred and thirty-four," the captain shook his head sadly while VanderMeer translated. "Were you able to send off any S.O.S signals?"

Baay shook his head. "The mine, or maybe it was a torpedo, hit the powder magazine and it all went up at once. I don't think we got off any signals."

The captain shook his head sympathetically. "I hope you understand, Mr. Baay, why I can't move you from the forecastle. But is there anything more you need up there? Food all right? Enough water to wash with? Waste buckets emptied often enough?"

"As you can imagine the stench is pretty bad down there. It would be nice if the buckets could be emptied more often."

"I understand. I'll give orders your men are to be let up three times a day to empty buckets, but only those assigned to emptying buckets."

"Thank you, Captain."

"Now there is another thing I must talk to you about, Mr. Baay. When I talked with you before we agreed I would turn you over to the German Consulate in Buenos Aires. But that was before Commander Hahn had made his threats against the ship and me. Now I have no alternative but to turn you and the rest of the crew over to the British authorities at Stanley in the Falkland Islands."

A frightened look passed over Baay's face when VanderMeer mentioned the Falklands. "Please, Captain, do not put us off at Stanley." His voice changed. "To do that would send you so far out of your way, Captain."

The captain spread his hands in a futile gesture. "Certainly as a naval officer you can see my position," he said. "I cannot jeopardize the wellbeing of my ship. Commander Hahn has chosen to act as a prisoner of war and so I must treat him and the rest of you accordingly."

"I am now in command of the men, Captain. They understand that the Commander is sick and I am the commanding officer. I give you my solemn word that none of my men will do anything to jeopardize this ship. Nor will we let Commander Hahn do anything."

The captain leaned back in his chair and with his thumb hooked under his chin, ran the index finger of his left hand up and down the bridge of his nose a couple of times and then pointing the same index finger at Baay said, "You would help the crew to mutiny?"

"No, Captain. But all the crew knows by now the Commander is a sick man. They will do what I tell them."

"But if Commander Hahn were to get well again he would again take command. You are too honorable a man to lead a mutiny, or even go along with one, Mr. Baay."

Baay shrugged.

The captain leaned forward again. "Tell me, Mr. Baay, what did the Van Leyden look like?"

"Like any freighter."

"A freighter? I thought you said it was a converted tanker," he said acting surprised. "What size was it?"

"I would guess she was about a ten thousand ton vessel before she was converted."

"About the size of this ship then?"

Baay pursed his lips and nodded. "Yes, about the same."

"Did it look at all like this ship?"

"What a strange question, Captain," Baay said looking suspiciously at VanderMeer and then at the captain.

"Well, did it?"

"All freighters this size look the same, Captain."

"Let us not play games, Baay, because your life, and the lives of all your men, and me, and all my men, and passengers might depend on it." He let VanderMeer translate before going on and Baay looked at him suspiciously. "Now, could somebody who didn't know both ships very well, somebody who had maybe just seen a picture of the Van Leyden, mistake this ship for the Van Leyden?"

Baay stared at the captain for almost a full minute and then slowly nodded his head and said, "Yes, Captain, they are similar in outline. The biggest difference is the Van Leyden did not have a gun on its after deck." He smiled a little. "We had them hidden everywhere else, but none showing on the after deck."

"And what flag were you flying when you were hit by the mine, or torpedoed?"

"Your Union Jack, Captain," he said smiling.

"Then it is possible a German submarine could have mistaken you for a British ship and torpedoed you?"

Baay became serious again. "Why do you ask, Captain?"

"Because, Lieutenant Baay, just a little while ago a German, single-engine, reconnaissance, float plane flew by us no more than forty feet off the water and not more than a hundred feet away. Why would that plane have come so close to us unless it thought we were you?"

Baay shook his head unbelievingly. "First I get torpedoed by a Reich sub, then I get sunk a second time by my own people. I am not telling you any more, Captain, except that you and all of us are doomed. Now I would like to go back to my men if I may," he said standing up.

"How many ships are in the group, Mr. Baay?"

"I'm not telling you anything more, Captain."

"If as you say we are all doomed, what difference can it make what you tell me."

"Because you will tell someone else."

"I already have enough to tell someone else. Where were you supposed to rendezvous?"

"I would like to go back to my men now, Captain."

"Your best chance for survival is to tell me anything you can that will help me save my ship and in doing that, save you."

"It is not my duty to survive, Captain. My duty is to fight the enemy in any way I can, and when I can't, to live to fight the enemy another day," he said standing up.

"Very well," the captain said and Renshaw got up to open the door and told the two men outside to take Baay back to the forecastle. Baay walked out and Renshaw closed the door behind him.

"Well, it appears we were right about an attack on the Falklands," the captain said. "And we have gotten us a very, very sticky wicket, but we've not lost the game. I suggest we not say anything to the crew, or passengers yet." He looked at each of them. "If nothing comes of our little encounter with the aeroplane then we will not have upset them unnecessarily."

***

For all practical purposes, the captain had been in the same spot since he left his cabin after the meeting with Baay. His lunch tray had been brought to him and taken away again with nothing eaten from it. He stood with his great coat buttoned tightly around him with the collar turned up against the cold and the continual thirty-knot wind. The chin strap of his peaked cap was pulled down to keep his hat from blowing away and he stood with his feet spread, his hands clasped behind him, his large body swaying to compensate for the rolling of the ship. From time to time he would look down at the repeater compass and then his eyes would return to scanning the horizon. He was looking off the starboard bow when he heard the pilothouse door open and even before Travers was next to him he knew why Travers had come out there. "Forward lookout reports smoke bearing two points off the starboard bow, Captain."

"Thank you, Mr. Travers," he said raising the binoculars to his eyes. He held the binoculars with both hands, his elbows out to the side and slowly rotated his whole body toward the right following the line of the horizon. He looked at the thin plume of smoke and lowered the binoculars. He stood staring the same direction, unable to see the smoke with his naked eye and thought how strange it was that circumstances could play such an important role in people's lives. If the plane had started searching to the north instead of the south when it left the mother ship, it probably would never have seen the Port Jefferson. Their whole passage had been determined by circumstances over which he had no control. If they had been able to get a pilot and had left in the morning they probably would not have sighted the survivors. If they had not picked up survivors, there would not have been a funeral on board. If it had not been for the delays in picking up survivors and the funeral, the plane would probably not have seen them, but it had seen them and now his junior officer was waiting for him to say something. "No need to set emergency station yet, Mr. Travers. It will be some time before we are in range," he said.

"Yes, sir."

"You have the watch, do you not, Mr. Travers?"

"Yes, sir."

"Would you have Mr. Renshaw, Mr. Parkington and Mr. Harvey informed I would like to see them in my cabin immediately?" he said raising the binoculars back up to his eyes. "Let me know when they have arrived."

"Yes, sir," Travers said and went back into the pilothouse.

The captain lowered the binoculars. His problem was fuel. The tanks had not been full when they left Durban. Fuel was scarce in Durban, while in Buenos Aires there was all the fuel anyone wanted. Fuel in South Africa was needed for the war in the north and so they had left with just enough fuel for the trip with a little margin of safety. But the margin of safety had not taken into account picking up survivors, nor having to run from some German ship. The little column of smoke was ahead and to the north of them. What he had to do was get by them to neutral waters. If they had left Durban with full tanks he could have just speeded up and gotten away, or headed south until it was dark. But even if he headed south, all the other ship had to do was head south and it would always be between them and safety. From the fuel reports that morning he knew they had enough to get to Buenos Aires. But even then he had understood they couldn't change speed, or course. To slow down would waste fuel. The ship's most efficient cruising speed was twenty knots. If he slowed down he would not be getting the most distance for the amount of fuel consumed. And if he speeded up just five knots he would double his fuel consumption. It took twice as much fuel to run at twenty-five knots than at twenty.

Mr. Harvey would be able to tell him exactly how many running hours of fuel they had aboard, but whatever the others might suggest, he knew he had to keep headed for the neutral waters ahead. He had enough fuel for some evasive maneuvering, but he had no alternative but to push on.

The steward came to announce his officers were waiting for him in his quarters and he looked again at the smudge of smoke that was just beginning to be visible to the naked eye. *What kind of ship are you? How many of you are there?* He turned and looked at the large flag flying from the after-mast. It was funny how a piece of cloth with geometrically colored stripes woven into it could make him feel weak, and proud, and strong all at the same time. His ship was a molecule of Empire about to come under attack and how he, his ship and his crew conducted themselves would contribute to, or detract from, the honor and glory of the whole. That flag with its lines of blue and white reaching out in all directions from the center was a symbol of the Empire. No matter how far out on a line of color a thread might be, it was connected to the center. Somewhere on one of those stripes there was a microscopic spot that was representative of the Port Jefferson.

He thought about Elizabeth. In his mind's eye he saw her, plump and warm and strongly comfortable while wrapped in sweaters sitting in the chair by the fireplace that had not been lighted to save on heating oil. It was winter there and he knew, although she never told him, that she saved her heating rations so she could keep the house extra warm when he was at home. A lump started in his throat and he swallowed hard. It was five in the evening back home, beginning to get dark. Maybe she was in the kitchen preparing supper. It would be a little warmer in there close to the stove. "God bless you, Elizabeth. God bless you and keep you," he said to the wind and the flag and then turned and went into the pilothouse.

By the time the captain came out of his meeting with the officers the ship was rife with rumors. It was not that they were started maliciously, but it was a desire to know combined with imagination. The forward lookout had seen smoke—the talker had heard the First Mate say—who told it to the after-lookout, who told one of the crew working on a kite winch, who told it to the rest of the after-deck crew, who told it to one of the engine crew, and all of them told each other.

For the passengers, some words spoken in the captain's quarters were heard through the porthole by a steward, who worriedly told the other steward, who was overheard by Mark VanderMeer, who told it to his brother, who told the other passengers. When asked, Reverend and Mrs. VanderMeer, who couldn't tell a lie, said, "I can't talk about it," which made things worse.

The captain hadn't heard any of the rumors; he just knew what ships were like. Consequently, as soon as the meeting was over he went to the intercom in the pilothouse and pushing down all the buttons said, "This is the captain. I have just come from a meeting with Mr. Renshaw, Mr. Parkington and Mr. Harvey and we have been talking about the same thing all of you have been talking about, the plane that flew by this morning and the smoke on the horizon. Most of you have been sailing with me for several voyages now. For some of you, this is your first voyage. But I want you all to know I will not keep you in the dark as to what I am thinking of doing. At the same time I also do not want you to speculate as to what the Old Man is doing. Don't start stories about what that smoke out there is. At the moment, not one person on this ship knows what kind of ship it is. Furthermore, since all we can see is the smoke, and not the ship itself, it means the ship is a minimum of thirty miles away, probably farther. That's all we know for now. As I learn more I will keep you informed. Meanwhile, go about your regular duties and try to avoid starting rumors."

He turned away from the intercom and looked around the pilothouse. The men were at their normal places, but they were all tense. He went out on the wing again and checked to see if the smoke was still ahead and to the north of them. It would have been such a relief if the smoke had started to drop aft a little, but it was still there. If anything, he thought it looked a little more ahead. He looked down at the deck and noticed almost all of the off watch had found something to do on starboard side of the ship where they could watch the horizon. Most of the passengers were also along the rail, or sitting in chairs on that side. *Well, I don't blame you. I'm out here, too, aren't I?*

At the meeting, Mr. Harvey had informed them they had even less fuel than he had thought. According to Renshaw's calculations, if the enemy were forty miles away and were traversing the most direct course at twenty-five knots they would have their first sightings of the ship itself within an hour. By two o'clock they would be able to see enough of the topside to determine what kind of a ship it was and start to calculate accurate course and speed. By three o'clock the whole ship would be in view on the horizon fifteen miles away and if it were a cruiser they would be in range of its guns. But it probably was not a cruiser. If anything was coming after them, it was probably a destroyer. There were some newer German destroyers that could do thirty-seven knots. By four-thirty a fast destroyer could be within four, or five miles of them and that was well within the range of the destroyer's guns. All the Port Jefferson had on the stern was an old World War I relic that had a range of about three miles. By four-thirty the captain knew he would not have time to think and speculate, just to do everything he could to break through. Both Renshaw and Harvey recommended they wait to see what was coming after them before they wasted fuel in a getaway attempt. When it came into sight they would be able to know what kind of speed the other was capable of. The waiting was what was unbearable. At least they were meeting him in daylight, giving him a chance to do something instead of just blowing his ship out from under him in the middle of the night without any warning, nor chance to know who was attacking him as it was with the Port Rhodes.

By two o'clock the speck that had started on the horizon had grown to be clearly visible with the naked eye as some kind of ship. Through the binoculars could be seen everything above the deck. There were two large gun mounts forward, one behind the other, the bottom of the second even with the top of the first. Right behind that was the bridge with the mast sticking out of it followed by two smokestacks. Between the smokestacks were anti-aircraft guns. On the stern was another gun mount.

The captain stood with the binoculars studying the other ship. *What are you thinking, Captain? What are your intentions? What are your orders? Is your navigator as quick and precise as my man Renshaw at calculating courses and speeds? You are not going to get me! By God, you are not going to get me!*

A steward came out and said, "Radio room reports they have just made contact with Tristan de Cunah, Captain."

"Very well," he said. He turned to look at the steward and realized most of the crew was at emergency stations even though it had not been sounded. "Tell Sparks to inform Tristan we have sighted a German aeroplane and ship and ask them if they can give us any information on the number of ships in this area. Get our position from Mr. Renshaw."

"Yes, sir," the steward said and left.

Ten minutes later Sparks came out on the wing and stopped behind the captain. "We are unable to get voice communication with Tristan de Cunah, Captain. Only Morse. We sent the message and have received a reply."

"What did they say?" he asked.

The radioman cleared his throat a little. "There's the regular heading and then this is the message. 'There is no known German shipping, military, nor civilian, in the area. Nor is there the possibility of German aircraft being in the area. We believe your sightings to be in error.'" Sparks paused and then added, "That's all they say, Captain." He stood there with the clipboard in his hand, the wind ruffling the sheet of paper attached to it.

"I see," the captain said. "Do you have a pencil?"

"Yes, sir."

"Very well. Take this message." The captain spoke slowly and distinctly giving the radioman time to write. TO: COMMANDING OFFICER, BRITISH CROWN POST, TRISTAN DE CUNAH. I am as of this moment in sight of, and being pursued by, a German destroyer. Other ships are believed to be in the area, though none have been sighted. I am armed with one model 201, 1918 five-inch gun. At present course and speed I expect to engage the enemy at 1630 hours local time, two and one-half hour from now. God save the King. TSMV Port Jefferson, Capt. Jeffrey Chipman commanding."

He paused for a moment, the radioman waiting for him and then said, "Send that message on all available frequencies, both Morse and voice. If we don't do anything else, we'll let the world know there is something down here."

"Yes, Captain," Sparks said and left.

Why are you chasing me? What could be so important you would come after me? I can see you, therefore, you can see I'm in ballast. There's no cargo on board worth sinking. Do you think by sinking me you can keep your secret? Do only you, the German High Command and I believe you are here. Your secret is out. I've told the whole world, so why don't you just go home and leave me alone? Revenge? Is that what you want? You have to get something for your trouble; is that it? "Well, you are not going to get me," he said aloud. He patted the teak rail and said, "No, Old Girl, they are not going to take another ship out from under me."

A short time later the radioman was back on the bridge with the clipboard in his hand. "Tristan acknowledges the receipt of our message, Captain."

"Just acknowledged it? Is that all?"

"Yes, sir."

"How gentlemanly of them. I don't think they believe us, Sparks."

"It would appear that way, sir."

Renshaw and Parkington came out on the wing. "I believe we're close enough now to get an accurate course and speed," Renshaw said and the captain stepped aside to give them the best place by the rail.

"Take this message," the captain said. "Same headings as last one."

"Yes, sir."

"This is to confirm that the ship in pursuit of us is a German destroyer. The enemy is within fifteen miles of us and closing. The aeroplane sighted earlier was a single engine floatplane of the type carried for reconnaissance aboard heavy cruisers. The aeroplane flew within twenty-five yards of this ship and was definitely identified. Although no heavy shipping had been sighted, some ship capable of carrying such an aeroplane must also be in the area.

"Persons aboard my ship are: ship's complement of thirty-one officers and men, twelve passengers and thirteen German survivors. The German survivors are from the German decoy ship Van Leyden that reportedly hit a mine. The officers rescued are, Lt. Commander Hahn, Executive Officer and Lt. Baay, Gunnery Officer.

"The rescue was made five days ago. From these officers and men, we have good information that the Van Leyden was part of a group of ships intending a secret attack on the Falkland Islands.

"The commander of the attack group is Commodore VanGoebler. The number of ships under his command is unknown. This is a confirmation message that there are German warships in the area. I repeat; there are German warships in the area. I expect to engage the enemy at 1630 hours. Notify Stanley. Notify London. God save the King. As soon as you have sent that off bring a copy of it back to me," the captain said.

The radioman left and the captain waited while Renshaw and Parkington continued to get ranges and bearings to the other ship. *Why didn't I shoot you down when I had the chance? Without you that ship might not have been able to find us.*

Renshaw and Parkington went back inside with their figures and a short time later the radioman appeared with a copy of the message. "The message has been sent, Captain, but we have not received a reply."

"Very well," the captain said. "Keep sending it, both voice and Morse. All frequencies."

"Yes, sir."

He went inside. He looked at the copy of the message that had been given him and then pushed down all the buttons on the intercom. "Lads, this is the captain. I told you earlier I was going to keep you informed as to what was going on so I want to bring you up-to-date. The ship on the horizon is a German destroyer. Fortunately for us, it is one of their older ones. Mr. Parkington believes it to be from the last war. At the present time it is about fifteen miles away. A little while back we sent out a radio message which I would like to read to you at this time."

He read the message slowly. When he finished reading he heard a cheer that reverberated throughout the ship. It was natural and right they cheer when he said "God save the King," but he thought he heard them start cheering when they heard the words, "expect to engage the enemy."

He waited until the shouting quieted down and said, "We are in no danger yet. We are still well out of the range of its guns. We will be in range at 1630 hours and we will set emergency stations at 1600 hours. Our gun is no match for her guns so we will mostly be trying to evade her and get to neutral waters. However, if we should ever be close enough, we will, of course, open fire." He paused. He felt there was something more he should say, but didn't know exactly what it was. He wondered if he should tell them about the fuel, that if they burned too much fuel too soon they would run out and just be a sitting duck. "It won't be easy, Lads, but we'll come through." he released all the buttons and as he did so he thought that maybe when it came time to set emergency stations he might do well to call on Reverend VanderMeer to say a prayer. It was wholly appropriate for a chaplain, or minister to say something to the men at times like this.

He pressed down the button marked ENG.RM. and said, "Engine room, this is the captain. Is Mr. Harvey there?"

"Harvey here, Captain," the box answered.

"Screws, how long can we hold thirty knots if we have to?"

"Water temperature is good and cold here, Captain. I guess we could hold thirty knots for as long as we wanted to, but we would sure be burning up the fuel."

"Thank you, Mr. Harvey," he said and walked over to the navigation table. "Is it still sixteen-thirty, Mr. Renshaw?"

"Pretty much, Captain, if we both maintain course and speed we will be within five miles of her at sixteen twenty-two."

"Thank you, Mr. Renshaw. I shall be on the wing," he said and walked out of the pilothouse. He stood looking at the other ship, wondering if he and Harvey had calculated the fuel correctly. He wished it were winter. It would be starting to get dark by four-thirty if it were winter it would be easy to get away from the German in the dark. But it was summer and in these latitudes it would be light until almost ten at night.

At one minute to four the captain stepped into the pilothouse and said, "John, please ask Reverend VanderMeer to come to the bridge."

The steward left and the captain went over and stood by the intercom. When VanderMeer arrived he said, "Would you say a prayer for us, Reverend?" VanderMeer nodded and the captain pushed down all the buttons and spoke into the gray box. "Lads, this is the captain. I have asked Reverend VanderMeer to say a prayer for us." He stepped back and said, "Just push down this button and speak into here," he said and all those in the pilothouse took off their hats as VanderMeer started to pray.

The captain appreciated the prayer. Reverend VanderMeer did ask for Divine protection, but more than that, he asked for special wisdom, that right decisions be made at the right time, for special alertness, that their reflexes would be quicker than usual. It even seemed he asked for a special sense, an extra sense to anticipate what they should do next. So many prayers the captain had heard in his lifetime had always asked the Almighty to do it all. VanderMeer had only asked the Almighty help them do what they had to do and it seemed to the captain it was a prayer with which the Almighty could agree.

"Thank you, Reverend VanderMeer," the captain said when he was through. "You may stay on the bridge if you like, although if they start firing it may be safer in the salon."

"Thank you, Captain. I'd very much like to stay up here. May I be out on the wings?"

"It would be safer in here probably," the captain said.

"I understand. But I will be able to pray more knowledgeably if I can see some of what is going on. You see, Captain, I do believe prayer works."

The captain smiled a little, "I believe that, too, Reverend. You just be wherever you think you can do the best praying," he said letting Hal go ahead of him out the hatch. VanderMeer went and stood at the back of the wing while the captain stood in the hatchway sideways with one leg out and one leg in, his bulk filling the hatchway. It was a place where he could have unobstructed view of the other ship and still give his command to those in the pilothouse. "Set emergency stations, Mr. Renshaw."

The alarm had hardly started to ring when the talker was giving reports of stations "manned and ready." The last station reported in just as the alarm stopped ringing.

"All engines ahead full," the captain said. "Show turns for thirty knots."

"Aye, aye, sir," the standby helmsman said excitedly. He reached for the telegraph handles, pulled them back once and then pushed them all the way forward the bells ringing as he did it. He reached down and turned a knob to show the number of propeller revolutions necessary for thirty knots. Almost immediately a dial underneath matched up with the number he had set. "Turns for thirty knots rung up and answered for, Captain."

"Very well," the captain said and went out on the wing. Throughout the ship a vibration started building up as the powerful Paxman engines increased speed. The bow rose a little bit and the stern settled down as the propellers dug into the water. At full speed the whole ship was shaking. Water flew back from the on-rushing bow and at the stern a coxcomb of white water rose behind the ship trying to catch up with the ship that was rushing away from it. On the bridge the vibrations worked up through the legs of the captain and the officers as they stood watching the other ship. "Starting to change course now," Renshaw said and went back into the pilothouse to start plotting the bearings and ranges Parkington and Travers shouted to him through the voice tubes. He came out in a little while and said, "Captain, the German has changed course to two-seven-zero. Running parallel with us. Speed still twenty-five knots."

"Thank you, Mr. Renshaw." *So twenty-five is probably your top speed. You've been running full speed to catch us before dark.* He smiled a little when he thought of the startled realization on the destroyer's bridge. He could just hear some officer saying the German equivalent of, "That's impossible. Freighters don't do thirty knots."

He stood there behind Travers who was calling the bearings through the voice tube. The German had been nineteen degrees off the bow, but the bearing began to change: twenty, twenty-one, twenty-two, twenty-three. She was still ahead of them, but they were overtaking her one slow degree at a time, twenty-four, twenty-five, twenty-six. Every degree was crucial, that much closer to escape.

The Captain stood with every muscle taut as though he could, with his own strength, help his ship pass up the other. He set goals for himself and the ship. Thirty degrees. Forty degrees. Every time they reached the mark, he was as proud as a father with a son in a race.

They passed the sixty, the seventy and the eighty degree marks and he felt all the excitement of winning a race. When they reached ninety degrees, broad on the beam they would be neck and neck. From that moment on they would be continually getting further and further away from the enemy. If the German stuck with them he would stay at thirty knots for another half hour and then slow to twenty-five until it got dark, but he expected the German to give up once he realized he had lost. The German had no way of knowing they were low on fuel.

He felt the change in the vibration of the ship first. Then the ship starting to turn to the right. He turned and ran for the pilothouse. He saw the helmsman pulling on the wheel trying to keep the ship on course. He heard the bells clanging on the telegraph and the standby helmsman saying, "Captain, starboard engine answering no turns. Port engine still answering turns for thirty knots."

"Very well, son. Show starboard engine stop. Slow port engine to twenty knots."

He had just reached the intercom when Harvey's voice said, "Captain, we just blew a gasket on the starboard water pump. We're starting repairs now."

"How long will it take?"

"If everything goes exactly right, an hour and a half, but it will probably be closer to two hours."

"Mr. Harvey we don't have two hours. In half an hour, or less we're going to have to start maneuvering to keep from being shelled."

"I'll do what I can."

The captain turned and looked at Renshaw who was bent over the chart table. "What is our actual speed under these conditions, Mr. Renshaw?"

"Through water speed is twelve and a half knots, Captain."

"What is the German doing?"

"Still the same, Captain. Twenty-five knots. They don't seem to have noticed our change in speed," Renshaw said and the captain saw the hard earned degrees of gain quickly slipping away.

"What is your rudder, helmsman?"

"Full left, Captain."

With all the power on the left side there was no way he could effectively make a left turn. What he had to do was put as much distance between the two ships as he could. Right now the important thing was to get away from the German. He would never make it to port if he didn't first get away from the destroyer. "Right twenty degrees rudder. Come to course zero-nine-zero," the captain said and the ship seemed to jump into its right turn.

"Enemy beginning to turn now," Renshaw said.

"Very well," the captain said and walked out to the port wing where Parkington and Travers were already starting to call ranges and bearings to Renshaw. He stood looking back at the other ship. It wasn't quite halfway through its turn and he watched it trying to control it with his mind. *Not so fast. Not so fast. Slow down. Turn around. Head north. We're of no value to you. Blow a boiler. Blow up.* He pictured it having an explosion in the engine room, the ship breaking in half, clouds of smoke and flames rising from its center, but it just kept coming around, steadily making its turn toward them. It almost seemed nonchalant about the way it made the turn as though they knew their prey was crippled. They were in no hurry. There was no way a disabled freighter could get away from them. "Oh, yes, I will," he said aloud to his own thoughts.

He waited until it was obvious the German was no longer turning and then stepped into the pilothouse and Renshaw gave him the answer to his question even before he asked it. "Course parallel with ours, Captain, zero-nine-zero. Speed is twenty-five knots. We will be within range of their guns in thirteen and a half minutes."

The captain went to the intercom and pushed the buttons for the main deck and passenger areas. "This is the captain. All passengers please confine yourselves to the salon and lounge area. It is possible that within a few minutes we will be under attack so please confine yourselves to the salon and lounge." He released those two buttons and pushed down the one to the engine room. "Engine room, this is the captain, how are things going?"

It was a moment before Mr. Harvey answered. "We're working on it, Captain. So far it's gone pretty well. Half my crew is working on getting the pump fixed and the other half is trying to jury-rig a crossover. I think one pump will be able to keep both engines cool if we only run at half speed, but at least you'll have two engines. We should know in fifteen, or twenty minutes."

"Do you need any help?"

"No, only so many people can fit down here and it's better to have people who know what they're doing."

"Well, I just wanted to let you know we will be in their range in ten minutes, or so."

"I understand, Captain."

He stood in the hatchway his legs straddling the lip, his bulk once again filling the opening with the binoculars raised, watching the destroyer gaining on him. He wondered how long the rudder could stand the pressure of always being turned against the tremendous thrust of the engine. It was all the rudder could do to keep the ship on a straight course; the rudder trying to turn the ship to the left while the thrust of the propeller was trying to turn it to the right. He wondered how long it would be before the enemy knew they could only turn one direction.

He saw a puff of gray-brown smoke rise from the end of the barrel of one of the forward guns. At the same time his head turned, he lowered the binoculars and shouted into the pilothouse, "Right full rudder!" He had not finished speaking when a shell hit the water behind them.

With the propeller and the rudder working together the ship turned quickly to the right. There was a puff of smoke at the muzzle of the second gun and the shell landed in the slick of their turn and would have hit them if they had not turned. "Steady on one-eight-zero," he said.

He felt the ship steadying up on its southerly course as he crossed over to the other side of the pilothouse. He waited, standing in the doorway looking back at the other ship. A couple of more shells landed in the water and he again gave the command to turn. "Steady up on two-seven-zero." The thought crossed his mind that was the direction he should be going headed for South America. The two ships were headed for each other four miles apart. He wished he could know if they were aware he could only turn one direction. He waited until he could no longer control the urge and then said, "Port Engine stop. Left full rudder." The ship started to slow down and at the same time coast into its left turn. Two shells landed where they would have been if they had turned right again and he smiled. With the last turn the two ships were headed in opposite directions and the distance between them was increasing. The shelling died down as they moved out of the German's range.

"Estimated range to enemy is six miles," Renshaw said. "They are beginning to turn our direction."

The captain watched the German make his wide easy turn. He knew what the German was doing, coming up directly behind them. That way the destroyer presented the smallest possible target. In this position the Port Jefferson was also their smallest target, but when the Port Jefferson started evasive maneuvering they would be presenting their side to the Germans. He wished he had a gun on the bow as well as on the stern, but the only way they could fire was when the enemy was to one side, or behind them.

The German kept closing in behind them and from time to time he had an urge to give the order to turn, but restrained himself. The distance kept getting shorter, four and a half miles, four, three and a half. He knew the closer the destroyer got the more accurate its firing would be. The Germans were going to come in close and finish them off. He turned to the talker. "Tell the gun crew to hold their fire until we give the command."

He watched the up and down motion on the other ship as it met each wave. *They are coming at twenty-five knots, all engines working, all guns ready. Half my power is gone. For all practical purposes I can only turn one direction. How can I possibly think I can escape? Is it just selfish, defiant pride that is directing me? What about my crew and passengers? If I hauled down my colors and raised a sheet wouldn't the passengers and crew be well-treated? This is a freighter, for God sake, not a warship.*

"Range three miles, Captain."

"Very well." *The outcome is inevitable if I continue this way. The loss of the ship and death and injury to my crew and passengers. Yes there are other considerations. This ship is needed to carry arms to South Africa for the long trek across a whole continent for the campaign in North Africa. My ship and I are vital to that. No. If I surrender they will get the ship. I can't let a fine ship fall into enemy hands to be used against us later. Better it go to the bottom than they get it.*

Shells were beginning to fall around them and behind them. "Range, two and a half miles, Captain."

"Very well. Tell the gun crew that as soon as we start firing we are going to start turning to the right. Be ready to follow the turn." The captain waited just long enough for the talker to repeat the message and then said, "Gun crew, commence continuous firing."

The ship shook with each round fired. He waited until three rounds had been fired and then ordered the ship's turn. As soon as he gave the order to turn he saw more puffs of smoke from each of the destroyer's forward guns and then felt the jolt as one of the shells hit amidships entering the empty midships' cargo hold. The shells from the destroyer were coming one after the other. Most of them fell in the water. One passed over the bridge to fall in the water on the other side and one passed through the smoke funnel going in one side and out the other to land in the water. He was just about to give another course change when he suddenly heard the telegraph bells ringing, the helmsman shouting the starboard engine was back on line and Harvey's voice over the intercom saying, "We did it! Both engines are on line now, Captain. Only one water pump to cool both engines so I can't give you top speed, but try fifteen knots for a while and see what happens."

"Very well. Thank you Mr. Harvey. Well done. Standby for some quick engine orders."

"We're ready down here, Captain."

The captain put the ship into a sharp left turn and didn't even steady up on a course before coming back to the right, back and forth trying to keep the gun crews on the destroyer guessing as to where they would be next. There was a cheer from the crew stationed on deck. "Gun crew says they scored a hit, Captain," the talker said and almost immediately after that Renshaw reported the enemy was dropping back out of range.

For the next hour and a half the Port Jefferson kept making quick right and left turns, scooting one direction for a moment and then another, always with the German staying just out of range of their gun. They took fourteen more hits, on the forward deck, amidships, in the stern just forward of the gun and one through the pilothouse.

At eighteen-thirty-seven, Mr. Harvey's voice came over the intercom. "Captain, Harvey here. Repairs are completed. Both engines are on line. Both pumps working."

"Thank you Mr. Harvey. Keep an eye on those engines. I'm going to break away from this bloke once and for all."

They started zigzagging at thirty knots, the ship rolling one direction and then another in the turns. The shells started dropping behind them instead of alongside of them. Twenty minutes later the shelling stopped and a little after that Parkington announced they were out of the range of the German's guns. A few minutes after that Renshaw announced the destroyer had changed course and was no longer following them and the Port Jefferson dropped down to its regular cruising speed.

The crew cheered when they saw the German turn away and the captain went over to the intercom. He pushed down all of the buttons and said, "Lads, you did yourselves proud. There's no question about that. Every man did his bit. But when I think back on this afternoon I cannot explain to you why we are still afloat. We took some hits, but I am told not one person was injured. By all that's reasonable and understandable we should not have escaped and so I cannot but believe that Almighty Providence in His mercy had a hand in today's affairs. I am sure at one time or another this afternoon, every one of you, as I did a time, or two, called on the Almighty for His help and protection. Before this all started I asked Reverend VanderMeer to say a prayer for our deliverance. During all of this he was up here on the bridge with us praying. I believe The Almighty heard and answered his prayers. Now that we have been delivered I think it only proper and gentlemanly, that we thank the Almighty for granting us that for which we asked. I have asked Reverend VanderMeer to again lead us in prayer."

VanderMeer stepped up to the intercom and hesitated for a moment and then said, "Almighty God we thank You for watching over us, Your children. We thank You for this day. At times like this there isn't much we can say except thank You. The words are inadequate, but You know our hearts, Father God, and You know the gratitude each of us feels.

"We pray, Father, that in the days ahead when we remember this day, when we tell our friends and families about our part in it, that we will not forget to also tell them about Your part in it."

He started the Lord's Prayer and throughout the ship the crew joined in saying it with him. When he was through he stepped back from the intercom and the captain said, "Thank you, Reverend VanderMeer. Mr. Renshaw, you may secure from emergency stations. Set the regular steaming watch. Set the most direct course to the mouth of the Rio de la Plata. And then check that our friends in the forecastle are all right."

"Aye, aye, Captain."

"John, tell Sparks I want to see him. Tell him to bring pad and pencil."

When the radioman arrived the captain said. "This message, Sparks. TO: COMMANDING OFFICER, BRITISH CROWN POST, TRISTAN DE CUNAH. Have engaged the enemy, a German destroyer number 376. We were hit several times, but sustained no casualties and no damage below the waterline. Believed to have scored one hit on the enemy. Were able primarily to out run the enemy and so escape. German warships definitely in the area. Inform Stanley. Inform London. God save the King.

See if you can get any response from Tristan with that, Sparks."

CHAPTER FIFTEEN

Tuesday, January 27, 1942

> LONDON - 26 January 1942
> Air Ministry Communiqué
> Squadrons of R.A.F. bombers last night attacked the dock area at Brest. None of our aircraft is missing.
> This afternoon a patrol of our fighters over Northern France attacked several objectives including railway stations. Two of our fighters are missing from other patrols.
>
> Home Securities Ministry
> Early last night a few enemy aircraft dropped bombs at coastal places in Southwest England. Some houses were damaged, but no casualties were reported. One enemy aircraft was destroyed.
>
> Admiralty Communiqué
> Two large and fully laden enemy tankers have been successfully attacked by submarines of the Mediterranean fleet. It is believed both were destroyed.

***

In the after-breakfast quiet of the deserted salon, Marisha sat trying to write a letter to her husband. The first letter had been fourteen pages of anguish and tears. When she was through, she knew she couldn't mail it. Now was not the time, nor a letter the way, to tell him of his son's death. She had written two more letters and they had been ripped up and dropped in tiny pieces on the table next to her along with the first one. She reached for another sheet of the light blue stationary with the embossed gold coronet and the initials M.B.H at the top and started again.

My Dearest Ransom:
Please do not be upset with me, Darling, when I tell you I have decided to return home. I understand your feelings and that you were only thinking of our comfort and safety when you insisted we go to the United States, but to be safe with Cousin Andrei is not what I want. I cannot endure the prospect of being so distant from you in both miles and time. I understand you may not get leave and be able to come to me

soon, but that time will be much closer if I am at home instead of across the Atlantic. Come home as soon as you are able, My Darling. I am desperate without you.

Your most loving wife
M.

She folded the letter without reading it and put it in one of the blue envelopes. She expected he would be angry with her for not doing as he wished, but when he learned the reason for her decision he would understand. In the meantime, he would not have to suffer alone with the knowledge of his son's death. She was a little afraid he might learn of Nicky's death from someone else, possibly someone offering his or her condolences thinking he already knew of it, but that would be unlikely if she were careful. There was no reason why he should learn of it until she told him and could be with him.

**

At two-thirty in the afternoon Captain Chipman sat at his desk waiting for the steward to return. He was not looking forward to his meeting with Lady Marisha. It was not something he was doing out of a sense of duty. He wanted to do it, but he wasn't looking forward to it. He felt exactly the way the bosun did when he said, "I'd not be knowin' the words to say." *What does one say at a time like this? What was there to say? Nothing really, yet something has to be said. Why? If words don't help why say them?*

The steward appeared at his door and he hoped John would report Lady Marisha was engaged in conversation with someone, or writing letters, or resting in her cabin, or anything else that would give him an excuse to put off a little longer the painful meeting. "Lady Marisha is on the port side of the main deck, Captain." John said.

"Is she alone?"

"Miss Jenkins is with her and Dr. Duer is there."

"Thank you, John." She was not alone, but he knew he was just reaching for excuses. He stood up and took the mahogany box from his desk. It had once contained a sextant and had been renovated and refinished by the ship's carpenter. On the lid was a small brass plaque that had been cut from a gunpowder casing, smoothed and polished and engraved with the words:

In Memory
NICHOLAS B. HARWELL
from the officers and crew of the
T.S.M.V. PORT JEFFERSON

He stopped by the door of the pilothouse. "I'll be on the port side of the main deck for the next few minutes, Mr. Parkington," he said and went down the inside stairs to the lounge.

She was sitting with her back to the hatchway with her ever-attendant maid sitting near her. He wondered if she sat that way so she would not have to look up and greet anyone who came on deck. She was looking out over the water. He hesitated for an instant, reluctant to intrude on her reverie. He went up to her chair and was aware of the perfume that was so much part of her. She turned her head, her heavy black hair swaying with the action. She looked up surprised to see him. "Oh, good afternoon, Captain." she said.

Duer, sitting closer to Lady Marisha than she would have liked, said, "Good afternoon, Captain. Today certainly is a better day than yesterday, isn't it?"

"Would you please excuse us, Mr. Duer?"

"Well, yes, certainly," Duer said acting flustered as he got up quickly going to another chair, not as far away as the captain would have liked, but out of earshot.

The captain pulled the chair in which Duer had been sitting a little closer to Marisha and sitting on the edge of it with the box in his lap said, "I don't want to intrude, Lady Marisha, but I also wanted to tell you how deeply sorry I am about your son's passing."

"Thank you, Captain."

"I always resent it a little at times like these when someone says, 'I know exactly how you feel. I went through the same thing myself.' That is a lie, because no one can know how another feels. They can only slightly remember how they themselves felt under similar circumstances." He paused for a moment looking out over the water. "We lost our son a few months back," he said going on quickly so as not to give her time to interject an 'I'm sorry.'"

"At the time one of the things that added to Elizabeth's grief, Elizabeth is my wife, was that no one would tell us exactly where he was shot down. I suppose it's based on some notion that if they let out too much of that kind of information the enemy might be able to figure out what our flight patterns were. 'Over the Channel,' is all anyone would say. And yet I know that even today, three months after it happened, it bothers Elizabeth that she does not know approximately where in the Channel his body might be." He paused for a moment sliding his arm off the top of the box.

"I have some things here. I don't want to add to your grief and yet I thought you might also have some of the questions my wife has."

"Thank you, Captain, that's very thoughtful of you. May I see them?"

He undid the latches on the box, opened the lid and took out the chart. The wind rattled the edges of the stiff paper as he unfolded it. He spread it out in front of her. Two thirds of the way down and toward the left there were two Maltese crosses, one blue, marking where Nicholas died and one red, marking where he was buried. Under the red cross in Renshaw's precise lettering was the time and date: 15:45 - 23/1/42 and under the blue cross a little to the left of the other: 09:22 - 24/1/42. She looked at the chart for a moment and pointed to three rough circles printed on the chart below where the crosses were. "These islands, Captain? Tris ..."

"Tristan de Cunah. They're three barren, rocky islands. It is Crown territory and we have a small radio post there."

"Still, it's nice to have a name to the area," she said, "to be able to say he's buried close to Tristan de Cunah." She reached for a handkerchief and he busied himself with folding the chart.

He handed her the piece of canvas and she unfolded it slowly while he talked. "The bosun made that. He asked me to give it to you saying he wouldn't know how to do it, or what to say. None of us know what to say." He paused to take a deep breath to steady his voice. She sat with the panel of canvas spread across her lap, her left hand resting on the lamb, the fingers of her right hand tracing the stitching of the name above it, her silent tears falling on the stitched date. "It's a duplicate of what the bosun stitched on the burial bag," he said.

"I know," she said nodding a little. She sat for a moment longer looking at the panel and then took a couple of deep breaths and dried her eyes. "He's the one who sewed Nicky's life jacket, isn't he?"

"Yes."

"Nicky liked him. I remember one time, it was the day we had the two lifeboat drills, it was right over there," she said pointing. "The two of them were playing a little game." She paused for a moment, her chin quivering, biting her lower lip. "He would pretend not to know Nicky was sneaking up behind him and then he would turn around quickly and Nicky would run to me pretending to be scared. Oh, how he laughed that day. Oh, how beautifully he laughed that day."

"I remember," the captain said quietly. He remembered that most perfect of days marred by his lifeboat drills and gunnery practice. For all of his precautions he had not been able to prevent the death of a little child. He wiped his cheek with the back of his hand and slowly closed the box. "You will find the flag in here, the one that covered your son. I'm afraid it is a little tattered along the edges. It was the largest flag we had and I decided to fly it yesterday when we were under attack. It had never been flown before then."

"I understand, Captain."

"Would you like me to have these things put in your cabin?" he asked holding out a hand to take the piece of canvas.

"No. Leave them with me for a while," she said stroking the stitching that was the lamb.

He stood up and set the box on the chair he had been sitting in. "If there is anything I can do, please let me know," he said getting up.

"Thank you, Captain." He was almost to the hatch when she said, "Oh, Captain?"

He walked back to her. "Yes, Lady Marisha?" He picked up the box and sat down so she would not have to be looking up at him.

"How long is the ship going to be in Buenos Aires?"

"Ordinarily it would only be a few days, or so. It doesn't take long to load. But this time we have the repairs to make. My guess is we will be in port for a fortnight, or maybe even three weeks."

"I want to go home, Captain. Do you think it would be difficult to get passage from Buenos Aires to England?"

He hesitated for an instant thinking quickly. If they were fully booked he could always move in with Renshaw and give her and the maid his cabin. "I'll notify our agents. If you don't find earlier passage, I am sure there will be space available if you wish to continue on with us."

Her smile was one of gratitude and relief. "Thank you, Captain. Thank you."

He nodded and getting up headed back to the bridge.

***

She sat looking over the water. *What a large graveyard you have, My Child. Your father is in constant danger and is alive and well in a desert somewhere, while you, who everyone thought perfectly safe, are dead. Alive one moment, dead the next. Buried in the vast blue of the South Atlantic. Your father will come out of the vast yellow of the North African desert and all I have to return to him of his son is a flag, a chart and a piece of canvas.*

She put the piece of canvas and the chart in the box and closed the lid. She picked up the box, stood, and Margaret started to get up to go with her and with a motion of her hand indicated Margaret did not have to come. Duer was immediately alongside her offering to carry the box. "No thank you," she said. He walked behind her to the door of her cabin where she turned and thanked him and closed the door behind her. Inside she set the box on the settee bunk that had been Nicky's. She stood for a moment with her hands resting on the box and thinking it was awfully hard and cold and angular and rigid for a memorial to someone who had been so warm and moving and responsive.

She went over to the dresser and opened the drawer that had Nicky's clothes in it. Right on top there was a sweater he had never liked. He had always complained it was itchy. The evening before he died she had made him wear it. *No, Mommy, No. Please, Mommy, the sweater itches.*

Don't be foolish. Put it on. Now stop your crying.

Please, Mommy.

She clutched the sweater to her and sitting down beside the box, started to cry. *Mommy's sorry, Sweetheart. Mommy's sorry, precious. Sorry. Sorry. Sorry.* She sat there for half an hour grateful that none of the others came into the room.

***

Margaret Jenkins sat in the deck chair after her mistress left feeling that things were just going from bad to worse. She did not for one moment think the loss she felt for Nicky could in any way be like the loss her Lady suffered, but now she had just learned they would not be going on to the United States. She did not want to return to England. There was no future for her there. She was sure once they were back in England she would be dismissed. There were others at the estate and they might offer to keep her on in some capacity, but it would always be as a maid. The death of Nicky was a great loss. Now all her dreams for a new life in the United States were shattered. The shattered dreams, in addition to Nicky's death, was enough to again reduce her to tears. She was weeping almost hysterically and was startled at first and then pleased when she thought it was Matt who she felt take her hand. When she realized it was Duer she turned to him and through clenched teeth hissed, "Let go of my hand and don't ever touch me again you repulsive thing."

When he did not immediately withdraw his hand, but glared at her, squeezing her hand a little tighter and pulling it toward him, she slapped his face hard and screamed, "Let go of me, you bastard."

He let go of her hand and got up slowly. "Don't ever come on deck alone at night, bitch, or you'll be joining the little kid."

On the other side of the ship Harold and Matt VanderMeer heard the scream and rushed across the cargo hatch just in time to see Duer disappearing through the hatchway. "What happened?" they both said together rushing up to her.

"He's a vile man," she said taking some deep breaths to bring herself under control and added, smiling pleased with herself, "He won't try that with me again, I smacked him a good one."

***

There was an atmosphere of reverential gratitude at dinner. The captain's dinner had been postponed, but no one cared. They would be arriving at their destination a day late, but they had escaped and that was all that mattered. By tomorrow evening this time they would be safe in neutral waters. The ship's paper had explained they were low on fuel. As soon as they were safe in neutral waters they would stop and wait for a tug to arrive to tow them the rest of the way, but that, too, did not disturb anyone. The passage was coming to an end. There was nothing more the enemy could throw against them. They were like a team that had fought hard and against all odds had out-scored their opponent. All they had to do was hang on until the final whistle sounded and they would be the winners. Tomorrow evening in the safety of neutral waters they would celebrate the captain's dinner. There had been a casualty that could not be forgotten, but there was now a confident peacefulness.

Lady Marisha and Margaret went to their cabin right after dinner. In the salon, the others prepared to played games. There was a relaxed and careless attitude in their playing; not caring if they won. To an extent, the attack by the German destroyer had separated them a little from the agony of Nicky's death so their last experience was not the heartbreaking loss, but of success. It was a time of companionship and sharing that develops between people who have been through a hardship together.

Matt, Luke and Mary played Chinese checkers, while Mark played chess with Dr. Duer who let Mark take back bad moves. There was a clear redness to the side of Duer's face, but no one commented on it, nor asked him about it. From time to time Robbie would come over and stand by his father, watching the game he did not understand before going back to play quietly by himself in the middle of the room. Rose Duer sat not far from Helen Stanley, both of them reading.

For Lady Marisha there could be no sense of joy, or accomplishment. She could not yet be excited about anything, but neither did she want to dampen the atmosphere of the salon. People were aware when she and Margaret left and they could understand Mrs. Harwell might prefer not to be in the salon.

In their cabin Lady Marisha sat in the chair that had been brought in for her when Nicky died and, pointing to her bunk, said, "Sit down, Margaret. I would like to talk to you."

"Yes, M'Lady," Margaret said sitting down hesitantly on her mistress's lower bunk. It was not proper for a maid to sit on her employer's bed, but that was where Her Ladyship had pointed.

"Margaret, I've decided to return home. I will not be continuing on to America."

"Yes, M'Lady. I heard you mention that to the captain."

"I want you to know how much I appreciate the help you've been to me, Margaret, not just the past few days, but for the years you've been with us. I know how much you loved Nicky and he loved you."

"Yes, Madam. Thank you, M'Lady. I loved him as if he were my own. I mean no disrespect by that, M'Lady."

"I know that, Margaret. And I want you to know, and I know Colonel Harwell would agree, that you need not fear we would ever dismiss you. There will probably not be any children needing your care," she paused to wipe her eyes and then went on, "but I am sure we can find something for you to do."

"Yes, M'Lady. Thank you," she said. She was hesitant, after such generosity, to say that she didn't want go back to England. Nor did she know how she could go on to America by herself.

"On the other hand, although we never talked of it, I know you were excited about the idea of going to America. If you would still like to go, I'll do what I can to help you."

She couldn't believe what she was hearing. "Without you, M'Lady?"

"If that's what you want. You can either come back home with me, or you can go on to America. Your papers are all in order for going to America. I'm sure if I talked to Reverend VanderMeer he would let you travel along with them."

"Oh, Madam," she exclaimed jumping up and throwing her arms around Marisha's neck and then suddenly remembering who she was said, "Oh, I'm sorry, M'Lady."

"That's all right, Margaret. I assume that means you would like to go on to the United States."

"Yes, Madam, with your permission. I'll never forget you, but I think I can make more of myself there than if I return to England."

"I think you can, too. Now bring me my jewelry box if you will."

She got up and went to the dresser and brought the little velvet box to Lady Marisha. "No not that one, Margaret. The wooden one." Marisha said.

"It's not here, M'Lady, it's in the trunk in the baggage room."

"Yes, of course. Will you get it for me, please?"

"Yes, M'Lady," she said and putting the velvet box back in the drawer left the cabin.

Margaret still had a key to the baggage compartment, but after the confrontation with Duer that afternoon she did not want to go out on deck alone. She found the room steward who, after what Lady Marisha had been through, would have done anything for her Ladyship. He brought a heavy, black towel to put over the porthole in the baggage room hatch so no light would escape and accompanied Margaret to the baggage room. Margaret got the box from the trunk and wondered why in the world Her Ladyship would be wanting her jewelry box at that time of night.

The box was not big, only a foot long, eight inches wide and six inches high. Lady Marisha sat with it in her lap while Margaret got her keys. She slipped the little brass key into the lock and opened the case. She looked over the rings and gems in the velvet-lined top tray and lifted it out handing it to Margaret to hold. She looked through the second tray and handed that one to Margaret also. There was not an excess of jewelry in the box. Most of her jewelry was in a vault in a bank in London.

In the bottom of the box she picked out a flawless, antique, two-carat, square-cut diamond ring. She had never worn it after she met Ransom. She had brought it along because it was valuable. If she ever needed cash quickly, before she could get it from the banks in London, or get in touch with Ransom, she could sell it, or borrow against it. She had no sentimental attachment to it. Everything else in the box, though not nearly as valuable, was there because of its sentimental value.

The ring had been given her as a birthday present by the family of a young man they hoped would someday marry Marisha. She had liked the young man, but had never intended to marry him and so even when she received the gift she had felt uncomfortable taking it because of what it implied. At the same time she couldn't reject it because it was only a birthday gift. He had died in a skiing accident when he had fallen and hit his head on an outcropping of rock. Every time she looked at the ring all she could think of was the way he died and in some ways it was similar enough to the way Nicky had died. She knew that every time she saw the ring she would remember that.

"Here," she said holding the ring out to Margaret, "I want you to have this."

"Oh, no, M'Lady. I could never accept that. For the likes of me to have something like that, why people would think I had lifted it for sure."

Lady Marisha smiled a little. "I want you to have it," she said. "It is very valuable and it will help you get started in America. I hope you will never need to sell it because as long as you have it you will never forget us."

"Oh, I could never forget you, Madam."

"If you need money take it to a good bank and they will probably loan you money on it. But don't take it to a hole-in-the-street moneylender."

Margaret took the ring examining it. "My, it is lovely, isn't it?" She said slipping it onto a finger. "I have never had anything like this before," she said giggling. She held her hand up; turning her hand from side to side looking at the light refracted in the stone while Lady Marisha took back the trays and set them back in place in the box. Margaret lowered her hand and slipped the ring off her finger. "I've no safe place to keep it, Madam. I'd be afraid to lose it."

"I guess you may keep it in the box till you leave the ship," she said taking the ring and dropping it in the top tray. "But you must be sure to remind me to give it to you before we leave the ship if I forget. It is yours now, Margaret; I'm just keeping it for you. I will also write a letter of introduction for you to my Cousin Andrei. He lives with his family in Las Vegas. He's heard of you, of course, but I'll ask him to help you get settled."

"Thank you, M'Lady. That's very kind of you, Ma'am," she said and added, "M'Lady?"

"Yes, Margaret?"

"When you talk to the Reverend VanderMeer about my traveling with them could you tell them you gave me the ring so they won't think I lifted it?"

"Yes, Margaret, I'll be sure to tell them. Now put the box in the dresser before you leave," she said holding out the box.

Margaret went back to the salon and joined Matt, Luke and Mary playing Chinese checkers, but she couldn't concentrate on the game. She was too excited to get Matt alone to tell him she would be traveling with them to the United States.

The game ended about eight thirty just as Rose Duer left to put Robbie to bed and as usual did not return to the salon and Matt and Margaret went on deck. They had found a place between the life-jacket boxes where they were sure of privacy. They frequently met there. With some life jackets to lie on and the warmth of the funnel, it was pleasant there. It was the first time they had been able to be alone since Nicky's death and they lay in each other's arms and embraced passionately. But Margaret didn't let the kissing go on too long before she pulled away and started telling him excitedly what had happened with Lady Marisha.

***

Even after Helen Stanly and Mary went to bed, Marisha sat in the cabin holding a book. She was not pretending to read, she would have liked to, but she just couldn't concentrate. If others were glad the journey was coming to a close, she was not. It was not that she wanted the journey to continue, she just did not want it to progress. Each passing moment, hour, day took her further and further away from the place where her Nicky was. She had no illusions about being with him; it was just that she would never again be able to visit the site where he was buried. She did not expect anyone else to understand it. There were times the day before when they were under attack and headed back the way they had come that she delighted in the idea they were headed back toward where her son had been buried.

She got up and put on her coat. "I think I'll go on deck for a while," she said and then seeing the concerned look on Helen Stanley's face added, "I'm all right. I just want to get some fresh air, to be alone for a while," she said and left the room.

She went out on deck and from their place between the lifejacket boxes Margaret and Matt became aware of her standing by the port rail. They waited for Mrs. Harwell to leave while at the same time straightening their disheveled clothes. When, after ten minutes, Lady Marisha didn't seem to be leaving right away Margaret said, "You go in first." She sat on the life jackets for another ten minutes and then followed Matt across to the other side and in through the starboard hatch being careful not to let it make any noise as she swung it open. She was just stepping over the high lip when she bumped into Rose Duer coming out. In the darkness they were both too startled to say anything at first. When they recognized each other Rose said, "I was just going on deck for a little air. It's so stuffy in our cabin."

"It's cold out there. You'll need a wrap," Margaret said and made her way through the blackout panels. Margaret saw Duer sitting by himself in the main salon. He jumped up and caught up with her just as she turned into her cabin. "You'd better run and hide, bitch," he said when she got away from him. He ran a hand through his wavy, blond hair and then continued on past her cabin making his way through the blackout panels to the hatchway to the deck. He had no reason for going out there except he had left the salon and was headed that direction. If anyone had noticed him get up he didn't want them to think he had been following Margaret.

When he stepped out on deck he was both surprised and pleased to see Marisha Harwell standing all by herself at the rail. He walked over and stood next to her. He didn't say anything, but just stood there looking out across the water, occasionally turning his head to look at her for a few moments. She did not speak to him, or so much as even acknowledge he was there. He stood there breathing in the cool wind that carried the scent of the perfume. He was acutely aware of the sound of the wind whistling around the bridge, the creaking of the ship as it rose and fell with the waves, the sound of the water rushing along the hull below him, but more than anything else, he was aware of Lady Marisha's coolness toward him.

As the time passed, he was looking at her more than he was looking out at the water. Fifteen minutes passed and he was staring at her standing next to him calmly, regally and serene. At first, he could only admire the perfect beauty. But after a while he began to be irritated she was ignoring him and then he became angry she was defying him.

He put a hand on top of one of her hands. It was not a sympathetic gesture that might have been acceptable from Reverend VanderMeer, or the captain, but an affront. Without turning her head she said, "Remove your hand, Dr. Duer."

In the past she had accepted his devotion and attention as one would accept those things from any domestic, but this was impertinence and so when she spoke it was not a request, but a command.

How dare you talk to me that way? I'm not just some servant you can order around. You always accepted my attention before so don't suddenly get uppity with me. You need to be put in your place. You need to be brought down from the high opinion of yourself, Lady.

He did not remove his hand from resting on top of hers, but instead closed his hand around the back of hers, defying her. She yanked her hand from the rail and from his grasp and turning to him said, "Don't touch me. Don't you ever touch me!" She spoke softly, but there was in her voice all the vehement disdain and disgust she felt for him.

He grabbed her and pulled her to him. He tried to kiss her, but she started to scream and he put a hand over her mouth to keep her quiet. Her fighting excited him. In addition, there was the added challenge of having to keep her quiet and yet achieve what he wanted to do. One hand was clamped over her nose and mouth. With the other arm he had to keep her pulled close to him to keep her from being able to kick, or knee him in the groin. Her arms thrashed at his back and only made him angrier and more determined.

He forced a leg between hers and then kicked one of her legs out from under her. They fell to the deck with him on top of her. With the hand over her mouth he pinned her head to the deck. She tried to open her mouth wide enough to bite him, but his thumb was clamped under her jaw, all his weight pressing her head against the cold, steel deck, the butt of his hand against her nose suffocating her. She pounded on him with her fists, but he seemed immune to anything she could do.

With all his weight on her, he used his knees to force her legs apart. He raised up with his weight supported by the hand over her mouth and his knees. He kept telling her if she would stop struggling and promise not to yell he would let her go, but she only struggled more. He tried to yank up her skirt, but with one hand clasped over her nose and mouth and all his body weight on top of her to keep her still it was difficult. She rolled back and forth trying to get away from him, but he leaned that much harder on her head. She stopped rolling and struggling for just an instant and her body relaxed just as it so often did with Rose when she finally stopped fighting him. He accepted as submission the fact she was no longer struggling. She stopped struggling entirely and he was suddenly frightened by what he had done. This was not Rose who would never tell anyone for fear of being beaten. If he took his hand away she could still scream. He looked around, but didn't see anyone. There was no sound except the correct sounds of the water against the hull, the creaking of the ship and the whistling of the wind.

"Now don't scream and I'll take my hand away," he said. "It won't do you any good to think of accusing me of anything. My wife will say I was with her the whole time. That we were both in our cabin and I never left it."

She did not respond, or move in any way. In the starlight she seemed to be staring at him with the cold, accusing eyes. He lifted his hand very slowly, prepared at any moment to clamp it down over her mouth, but she didn't move. In the darkness, he could see a dark stain on her upper lip. He rose up still kneeling between her legs and the full impact of what he had done dawned on him. In his effort to keep her quiet he had knocked her unconscious. There was blood on his hand. Her blood. He began to panic. He had to do something. No one would believe Rose and him. They would believe her. *She with her high and mighty ways. Do something. Can't trust Rose. She'll see this as a way to get revenge. Have to do something.*

He watched her as he got up and stood over her. She had not moved and he had the startling fear she might be dead. For just an instant he thought that might be better. She wouldn't be able to accuse him of anything and then thought there would be a body. With a body there would be an investigation. He was certain no one had seen him, but still it would be better if there was no evidence at all.

He stood up and walked aft a little looking to see if anyone was there. He looked up at the bridge, but there was no one on the wing. *Do it quickly. Suicide. It's only logical. Couldn't take the loss of her son. She would just be gone. No one could accuse him of anything.*

He felt the moisture on his hand and unconsciously wiped his hand on his trousers and bent over to pick her up. Her head rolled against his shoulder. He was amazed at how light she was. He carried her over to the rail and hesitated for just a second before dropping her over the side. He listened carefully, but he couldn't be sure he even heard her hit the water. He turned around and leaned back against the rail. He looked around, but there was still no one about. He stood there for a moment leaning back against the rail wondering what he should do next. He was beginning to feel wonderful. There was nothing more to be done. He had done it all. He was too excited to go to bed. He had never had such a wonderful feeling of exciting exhilaration. It always excited him when he beat up Rose before raping her. The first time he had experienced that special euphoria was in high school when he raped Mildred Johnson. But he had never felt as elated as he did right at this moment.

He didn't know if she was dead when he threw her over the side, but if not, she had certainly drowned by now. He felt triumphant and invincible. But there was also the thought that it might be good to get away from that side of the ship. He left the rail and went through the hatch. He made his way through the blackout panels and past her cabin. He wondered if anyone in there was wondering where Lady Marisha was, or were they all asleep? He had a sense of superiority over the women in that cabin. He noted that the lights had been turned off in the main salon and he wondered who had done it. He had a moment of panic when he wondered if they had stepped on deck after turning off the lights. *Impossible. I would have heard the hatch open. They would have sounded an alarm, or tried to stop me if they had seen anything.*

He passed the doors to the VanderMeer's cabin and his own and started through the blackout panels to the deck. He opened the hatch and stepped through and then saw someone was sitting in one of the chairs. It was not until he was almost up to them in the darkness he recognized Rose. He sat down next to her. "What are you doing out here?" he asked accusingly.

"It was hot in the cabin and I just wanted a little air. I'm sorry, Rudy. I just wanted a little air," she said timidly.

You're sorry all right. What a nothing. He thought of how exciting it would be to tell her about it. It would make her that much more afraid of him. He would do it sometime. Someday when no one could do anything about it, he would tell her every frightening detail. "You know I don't want you out of the cabin at night."

"I just wanted a little air," she said beginning to be frightened of what he would do to her. At the same time she noticed the smell of Lady Marisha's perfume. She couldn't believe it. How could she have succumbed to him? She could believe anything of her husband, that he would try to seduce any woman, but how could Lady Marisha have yielded to him. Yet, it must have happened because he was in one of his mellow moods. She knew Lady Marisha had been his fantasy from the moment he had seen her. Soon after they had come aboard he had misquoted a line from Kipling, "Jody O'Grady, or the colonel's lady, are all the same under the skin."

"I think I'll go in," she said. She wanted to get away from him. She was not disappointed in him, he had acted true to form, but she was deeply hurt with Lady Marisha and she had to get away from the smell of that woman's perfume.

"I think you should stay here," he said and there was in his voice the threat with which she was so familiar.

Why not tell her about it now. She wants to get away from me. She's afraid of me. "Well here we are, Rose, just you and me. Do you know how easy it would be for me to strangle you right now and throw you over the side? No one would even care you were gone. It would be so easy for me to do. I know it would be easy to do, because I've already done it once this evening."

In the darkness of just the starlight she stared at him trying to comprehend what he was saying. Facing him the smell of her perfume was faint, but constant. *He couldn't have killed her.* Yet she knew if she had defied him he was completely capable of doing it. And if he could kill Lady Marisha, he could much more easily kill her and Robbie.

"They will find her gone tomorrow, Rosie dear."

He hasn't yet said who. Maybe it is someone else. No, it's her. He killed her.

His voice overrode her thoughts. "If you so much as hint to anyone I was out here with her this evening the same thing will happen to you that happened to her. You know I'll do it, don't you?"

She didn't answer.

"Don't you?" he snarled.

"Yes," she said quietly.

"We were both in our cabin all evening. I think I'll go to bed now. It's been quite a night. I think you should come to bed now, too, Rose."

CHAPTER SIXTEEN

Wednesday – 28 January 1942

LONDON - 27 January 1942
Admiralty Communiqué
  The Board of Admiralty regrets to announce that the battleship H.M.S. BARHAM (Captain G. C. Cooke, R.N. commanding) and flying the flag of Vice-Admiral H.D. Pridham-Wippel K.C.B., C.V.O., second in command of the Mediterranean fleet, has been sunk.
  Vice-Admiral Pridham-Wippel is safe, but Captain Cooke lost his life.

***

  Margaret Jenkins was surprised when she woke up to see Lady Marisha's bed was empty, which meant her mistress was up before her. Margaret had slept so well she hadn't heard her Lady come in. She was just getting used to not having to be alert for Nicky's cry even when she slept. In addition, she had not slept well the previous nights. The fatigue of those nights, plus the tensions of the past few days, had all contributed to a deep and comfortable sleep. But it was unusual that her mistress be up before her.

  When she came out of the bathroom after washing her face and brushing her hair she was fully awake and became concerned because her Lady's bed did not appear to have been slept in. As she got dressed she tried to tell herself Lady Marisha might have straightened the bed herself, but that was not like her mistress. She wanted to wake Mary and ask if she had seen Lady Marisha during the night, but Mary was never totally alert when she first woke up.

  The blackout panels had been pushed back and the hatch latched open when she stepped out of her cabin. She went out on deck and saw Miss Stanley sitting in a chair. They greeted each other and Margaret went to the other side using the walkway in front of the salon. From there, she looked down on the forward decks as she walked across. On the other side she saw Reverend VanderMeer and then walking behind the stack she remembered she had planned to get up early to put the life jackets back in their boxes. Quietly, so as not to attract anyone's attention, she lifted the hinged lids and threw the jackets inside. She completed her circuit, going by Miss Stanley and went back inside to look in the lounge and the salon. She came back out and said, "Have you seen M'Lady this morning?"

"Why no. I haven't," Helen Stanley said looking up and there was genuine surprise and concern in her voice.

There was a tremor of fear in Margaret's voice as she said, "She's not inside either. I haven't seen her anywhere. I'm frightened, Miss Stanley. Her bed ain't been slept in neither."

"Now, now. Maybe she's up on the bridge, or something," Miss Stanley said trying to be encouraging, but she herself had a sudden pang of fright. She had not heard Marisha come in, nor go out, and she always woke up a little whenever anyone went in or out of the cabin. She usually even woke up a little whenever any of them got up in the night to go to the bathroom. She had heard Margaret come in so it was not as though she had slept so hard she hadn't heard anyone.

By breakfast time a search had been conducted of the ship and it was established Lady Marisha was not on board. Everybody, crew and passengers alike, were shocked and stunned when they heard about it. For the crew there was the added sense of failure. No one of such high rank had ever sailed aboard their ship before and they had been proud they had been so privileged. They had been responsible for her and her son and they had failed in their responsibility. The death of the son was at least explainable. This was not. It was assumed she had somehow fallen over the side. There were some who thought, though no one said it out loud, that she had jumped. They could not condone suicide, but at the same time, they could understand how she had been so distraught by the death of her son she just couldn't take any more. Miss Stanley secretly blamed herself for not being more watchful. There was no question of turning around and going to look for her. The chances of finding her were less than those of the sun colliding with the moon.

Those who went into breakfast ate little and said even less. Her death was hard to understand, hard to believe, hard to accept. Mable VanderMeer understood all the reasons why they could not turn back and go and look for Lady Marisha, but she was certain if Lady Marisha had accidentally fallen over the side she was still alive, floating in the water, hanging on, just waiting for them to come back for her.

***

Lady Marisha was gone, but the routines of shipboard life were still there. Rudolph Duer was in his usual chair on the port side of the ship. His solicitous attention was now directed toward Margaret despite the rebuff of the day before which upset Matt. Margaret had told Matt about slapping Duer and what he had said. Because of that, Matt was making it his responsibility to make sure Margaret was not left alone when out of her cabin.

Both Matt and Margaret had contributed to the general information by admitting to Renshaw's questioning they had seen Lady Marisha on deck the night before. They had not mentioned they were together. Neither Matthew, nor Margaret had said anything to each other about the night before, but they were both feeling a little guilty now remembering their contentment while Lady Marisha was in such anguish.

On the starboard side, too, the chairs and their occupants were as usual. Miss Stanley knitted and Harold VanderMeer read while his wife darned a hole in one of her son's socks. Rose Duer put down the month-old magazine she had brought from the lounge and then cautiously looking over her shoulder as she did it, moved her chair until it was almost touching Mable's. She picked up her magazine and raising it in front of her face said in a voice that was just a little louder than a whisper, "Mrs. VanderMeer, if I tell you something will promise not to tell anyone?"

Mable VanderMeer looked at her puzzled. It was such a childish thing to say, but Rose was not a child and there was a desperation about her that Mable could not ignore. She nodded her head while staring at Rose intently.

"Please don't tell, Mrs. VanderMeer. Promise you won't tell him I said anything, or there's no telling what he'll do to me," Rose said again.

"Tell who what?"

"Promise you won't tell I told you?"

There was no question Rose Duer was terribly afraid, but it was obvious she was also desperate to say something. "All right," Mable said nodding a little.

Rose lowered the magazine to look over the top of it and after looking over her shoulders said, "He was with her last night. Her smell, I mean of her perfume, was all over his clothes."

Mable VanderMeer stared at Rose intently while lowing the darning ball and sock to her lap.

"But you must never tell him I told you, or he'll beat me, or maybe he'll beat up Robbie to get at me. There's no telling what he will do if he gets really mad."

"Has he beat you before?"

"Oh, yes."

"Recently?"

"Last week. The morning I didn't come to breakfast when I was so stiff and everything and I told you I fell down the ladder from the upper bunk. I still have the bruises. Some of them still hurt. He never hits where people can see he's hit me."

"Maybe we had better go talk inside," Mable said starting to pack her things back in the mending basket.

Rose started to draw back frightened by what she had done. "I don't think so. If he comes around and finds out I was with you he's going to want to know why and get real suspicious and angry."

"I'll make sure he doesn't do anything to you."

"How? You can't protect me after we leave the ship."

"We'll go to my cabin. If he finds out you were with me you can say you were looking over some of Lukie's clothes that I thought might fit Robbie.'

"What about Robbie? I can't leave Robbie alone."

"Helen, will you keep an eye on Robbie for a moment. Rose and I are going to look over some of Luke's clothes that might fit Robbie. Robbie, you stay here with Miss Stanley for a moment," Mable said getting up.

Robbie looked at his mother. "It's okay, darling," Rose said and followed Mable inside.

Mable closed the glass on the portholes and pulled the curtains. She sat down on her bunk patting the space next to her and said, "Now sit down here and tell me about it right from the beginning."

"I went out on deck last night. It was hot in the cabin and Robbie was asleep so I thought it would be all right for a little while."

"What time was that?"

"I don't know exactly. I don't have a watch, but it was pretty late."

"Okay, go on."

"He came and sat next to me which is something he never does. You know that, Mrs. VanderMeer."

Mable nodded.

"As soon as he sat down I could smell her perfume on him. I couldn't believe she would give in to him. I know what he is, but I couldn't believe it of her. Then he told me he had killed her."

"What?" Mable exclaimed and then put a hand over her mouth hoping no one outside had heard her.

"He didn't say it exactly. He said he would kill me. That it would be easy for him because he had done it once already. I didn't really believe him, but I also did believe him. We went inside after that."

Mable couldn't believe what she was hearing and wanted to ask questions, but kept quiet letting Rose talk.

"This morning I picked up his clothes like I always do. He just throws his clothes down when he takes them off and I have to pick them up. The smell was still on them and I also saw what looked like blood on his trousers and shirt. I didn't think much of it except he would be angry with me if I didn't get them out. I was going to put them in cold water, but he would also get angry if he couldn't use the sink when he got up.

When I heard Lady Marisha was missing I knew what he had told me was true. Oh, I'm scared Mrs. VanderMeer. I took them out of the laundry bag and stuffed them under my mattress."

"Go get me the clothes."

Rose stared at her. "Oh, I couldn't do that. If he saw me with those clothes he'd get suspicious. I'm afraid, Mrs. VanderMeer. I don't think I should have told you," she said standing up and starting for the door.

"Rose," Mable said comfortingly. "When you took the clothes and put them under the mattress it was because you knew you were going to tell me, or someone about it. I'll stand in the passageway and watch out for you. If I see him coming I'll let you know."

Rose got the wadded up bundle of clothes and took them back into Mable's cabin. Even after all that time there was still the faint hint of Lady Marisha's perfume on them. "Where is the blood?" Rose showed her the dark brown spot on the left side of the trousers and on the shirt. "I don't know if that is blood, or not," Mable said looking at the dark brown spots and smears, "but it certainly looks like blood. Dr. Bowman would probably be able to tell for sure. We're going to have to tell Reverend VanderMeer about this."

"Oh dear," was all Rose could say.

Before she ever talked to Mrs. VanderMeer she had concluded she could not win. If Rudy had done what she suspected he had done, then he was capable of anything and Robbie and she would never be safe again. The night he had beaten her up he had threatened to kill her and throw her over the side. But telling people about it wasn't going to save her, either. What could they do to protect her? She had just brought the inevitable on that much sooner. She wished she had never told Mrs. VanderMeer about the clothes. She could have pretended to herself, and mostly to Rudy, she didn't know about it. Now Rudy would find out for sure and she dreaded the next time they would be alone again.

With Mable's help Rose told Reverend VanderMeer. With Reverend VanderMeer's help Rose told the captain. On the surface the captain appeared calm, but inside he was seething. He had never been able to believe Lady Marisha was capable of committing suicide. It was not just that Lady Marisha had been killed, but she had been violated. Why else would he have to kill her? There was no question that there was still the faint smell of her perfume on his clothes. In fairness, he tried to consider the possibility she had yielded to him and then been so ashamed she had committed suicide, but that, too, he knew in his heart was impossible. He considered the possibility Mrs. Duer had made up the story, but then there was still the fact of the blood and the perfume on Duer's clothes.

What he wanted to do was take Duer and hang him from a loading boom. He had no doubts that when the crew heard about it they would have the same feelings. It would have been different if one of the survivors had gotten loose and been seen doing it. Rose Duer had not accused her husband of anything; she had just presented information. But that information and the lingering scent with the spots that certainly looked like blood could not be ignored. He also had the frustrating feeling he wouldn't be able to prove anything. There was no body and if there had been a witness he certainly would have told someone what he had seen by now. He sat for a moment thinking of how he was going to go about conducting the investigation. Renshaw should be the one to do it. Renshaw would be precise and thorough. He had a knack of getting information from harbor officials they were not supposed to divulge.

"I don't want any of you saying anything about this to anyone," the captain said getting up. "There is going to be an investigation and I don't want people, particularly Mr. Duer, formulating answers to possible questions before they are asked. For now we want everyone to think we are investigating a suicide."

He walked over to the squawk box and pushed down the galley button. When they answered he said, "John, have someone find Dr. Bowman and ask him to come to my cabin. And have someone find Mr. Renshaw. Since he had the mid watch he may still be in his cabin."

He sat down again and said, "Mrs. VanderMeer, I'm afraid I have to impose on you again. We will want exact statements of what people say," he turned to Rose. "Mrs. Duer, we will see to it you are safe. At no time will you, or your son be left alone with your husband." He looked at each of them. "Any questions?"

"What's going to happen tonight when Robbie and I are alone with him in the cabin?"

"By then you and Robbie will have been moved into cabin A. But for right now just act as normally as you can. We will tell you when to move. Mrs. VanderMeer, we'll call for you when we are ready."

They left the captain's cabin, each feeling differently. Harold was ready to protect the women if need be, Mable was ready to pounce on Duer and give him the thrashing of his life, and Rose was ready to bolt and run if he approached her. They went to their usual places on the port side of the ship and were each relieved that Duer had not been over there while they were gone.

***

Renshaw started by questioning Dr. Duer. John showed Duer into the salon where Renshaw sat at a table with Mrs. VanderMeer next to him. Both had pads of paper in front of them and each had a cup of tea. "We want Mr. Duer to think this investigation is just a formality," Renshaw had said when the steward had set the beverages in front of them before Duer arrived.

"Would you like a cup of tea, Dr. Duer, or a cup of coffee?" Renshaw asked when Duer was shown in.

"No, thank you. What is this about?" Duer said belligerently.

"Please sit down, Dr. Duer," he said motioning to the chair next to him. "I know we talked earlier about the disappearance of Lady Marisha, but now we have to start a formal inquiry. As you can imagine, when something like this happens the Admiralty will want to know all the facts. For that reason I have asked Mrs. VanderMeer to act as recorder for these sessions. We will be talking to all the passengers and crew and I must ask you not to mention anything that is discussed here with anyone. That includes your wife and all the passengers and crew."

"Well, of course you can count on my discretion, Mr. Renshaw."

"As you may know the captain has the unpleasant duty of explaining the loss of Lady Marisha not only to the Board of Inquiry which will undoubtedly be convened, but to the ship's authorities, the Embassy in Buenos Aires and worst of all, to Colonel Harwell. The boy's death, tragic as it is, is easier to report because we had witnesses and we know what happened, but we don't know what happened to Lady Marisha. We can only guess. The captain has asked me to find out as much as I can about her last few hours on board. I thought I would start by talking to you because you were friendlier with her than most of the other passengers and might be able to give us some insight into her feelings these last couple of days. Of course, we all know the loss of her son was a terrible blow. It was to all of us, but most especially to her. And I also wanted to talk to you first because with your education and keen sense of observation, you might be able to give me some hints as to how to conduct this ... this," he waved his hands and shrugged his shoulders indicating he couldn't think of a better word, investigation."

Mable VanderMeer scribbled furiously, the shorthand symbols scooting onto the page.

"Well, I'll do what I can to help, Mr. Renshaw, you know that."

"Thank you Dr. Duer. I knew I could count on you. And please don't take any affront at any question I might ask you. You understand I have to ask them. When did you last see Lady Marisha?"

"At dinner."

"Did she seem all right to you at that time?"

"Well, Mr. Renshaw, she had been through a lot. We all have. The death of her son and then the attack. That was very frightening for all of us. I guess she was as normal as could be expected under the circumstances."

"Yes, of course," Renshaw said looking down at his paper and then up again. "Then the last time you saw Lady Marisha was at dinner?"

"Yes. She left right after dinner. I assumed to go to her cabin."

"What time did you retire?"

"Well, let's see. Most of us were here playing games until ten, or so, I guess. I can't say when everybody left, but I was the last to leave. I guess it was between ten-thirty and eleven. Margaret Jenkins saw me in here. She passed by on the way to her cabin; at least I thought that was where she was going. She must have been on deck. I went to my cabin right after she passed by."

"So you weren't out on deck at all last night?"

"No! Not at all!" Duer said getting defensive.

"I was just hoping maybe you could have been able to tell us what Lady Marisha's mood was, or if you had seen anyone else out there."

"No. I can't help you there. But, as I said, I'm sure Margaret was out there."

"Is there anything else you can add you think might help me?"

"No, can't think of anything."

"Well, thank you, Dr. Duer. And remember, don't discuss what we talked about with anyone." Duer got up to leave and Renshaw added, "Would you ask Margaret Jenkins to come in."

A distraught Margaret confirmed she had seen Duer in the salon at eleven-thirty. Through her tears and sniffling she added he had gotten up and followed her and she was sure when she went into the cabin he had gone on by and out on deck. She had not seen him on deck, but she was certain as she closed her cabin door she had seen him go behind the first blackout panel.

"You told me earlier you saw Lady Marisha on deck that evening. About what time was that?"

"Don't know exactly. But it was just before I saw Dr. Duer when I went into my cabin."

"Did you talk to Lady Marisha at all?"

"No, sir. She was standing by the rail. I didn't want to intrude."

"Did she see you?"

"No. I don't think so, sir."

"Were you out there before she came out?"

"Yes, sir."

"Where were you when you saw her, in one of the chairs, by the ladder, at the rail?"

"Behind the funnel. It's warmer there. I was sitting on some lifejackets between the two storage boxes. When I saw her, I left. I came in on the starboard side and when I passed in front of the salon, that's when I saw

Dr. Duer. He got up and followed me. When I went into the cabin he went on by."

"I understand you had slapped Mr. Duer earlier, is that correct?"

"Yes," she said, "I smacked him a good one."

"How did that happen?"

"He made an advance, and I slapped him."

"Describe what he did."

"The captain was down talking to Lady Marisha, you know, giving her the box with the things in it. After she left, Dr. Duer came and sat next to me and took my hand. When I told him to let go, he just held it tighter and pulled it toward him. That's when I slapped him."

"What happened then?"

"He let go then and said if I ever came on deck alone at night I'd be with Nicky. Something like that."

"What did you think he meant by that?"

"Why, he'd do me in, one way, or t'other."

"Even after what he said you went out on deck alone? Did anyone see you out there?"

"I wasn't alone."

"Oh? Who was with you?"

She looked down at her hands and quietly said, "Master Matthew was there." She looked up at Mable and said, "We were just talking. Honestly. We were sitting by the funnel talking. When Her Ladyship came out Master Matthew left and then I left."

"And what were you talking about?"

"Right after dinner Lady Marisha had told me I could go on to America without her. She told the captain she wanted to go home. She gave me a big diamond, monstrous large it was. She said I could use it to get started in America. She was going to write a letter to her cousin Andrei who lives in America and she was going to ask Reverend VanderMeer if I could travel with them and tell him about giving me the diamond and all so he wouldn't think I lifted it. That's what I was talking to Master Matthew about. But now she can't write a letter for me, or talk to Reverend VanderMeer about my traveling with them. You do believe me, don't you Mrs. VanderMeer?"

"Let's stay on track here, shall we, Margaret," Renshaw said. "You were talking to Matthew VanderMeer about going to the United States. How long had you been out there talking to him when Lady Marisha came out?"

I don't know. I don't have a watch. I left the salon with M'Lady. That's when she talked to me about going to America. She asked me to go to the baggage compartment and get her jewelry box. That's where the diamond was. You can ask John, he went with me to the baggage compartment. After I came back in here and I went out on deck at about ten to meet Master Matthew. It was a little after ten."

"If you don't have a watch how do you know when you left here?"

She pointed over her shoulder at the clock over the salon door.

"Yes, of course. So, you went out on deck a little after ten. Did Matthew VanderMeer meet you right away?"

"Real soon. I hadn't gotten the life jackets out of the bins before he got there. We use the life jackets to sit on."

"After Lady Marisha came on deck what did you do?"

"We stayed real quiet. Then when she didn't leave I told Master Matthew to go first so his parents wouldn't be worried about where he was," she said looking over at Mable who kept taking notes without looking up. "Then afterward I went inside."

"You went to the opposite side of the ship, is that right?"

"Yes, sir."

"Was anyone on deck on that side?"

"No, but Mrs. Duer was going out there when I was coming in."

"You sure she was going out there and not coming in."

"Oh, yes, sir. She said she wanted some fresh air and I told her she should get a wrap because it was cold out there."

"Then what happened?"

"I came in. When I passed the salon Mr. Duer got up and followed me, but I got into my cabin before he could catch up with me."

"And he went by you and out onto the deck, is that correct?"

"I was looking through the crack in the door and I saw him start behind the first blackout panel. Then I closed the door. I didn't actually see him go on deck."

"I see. Anything else you think we should know?"

"No, sir."

"Well, if you think of anything be sure and come back and talk to me. I guess that's it. You may go now, Margaret and ask Master Matthew to come in."

Renshaw talked with all of the passengers. He knew before they came in some of them wouldn't add anything, but he had to question them all. Matthew corroborated Margaret's story and Mrs. Duer gave a statement that was much the same as she had said earlier. Renshaw was through with his investigation by noon and immediately after lunch Mable VanderMeer was seated at a typewriter in the radio room transcribing all of the statements.

***

The captain sat at his desk feeling both angry and discouraged. He had no doubt Rudolph Duer had done it. Exactly what he had done, or how Duer had done it, he didn't know, but he knew Duer had been involved in Lady Marisha's disappearance, but he couldn't prove it. What discouraged him the most was he had a killer on board his ship who would probably get away with it unless he did something, but he didn't know exactly what he should do. The statements Renshaw had taken were all in front of him. He had read them all.

The captain pulled the pad of paper toward him and tore off the top sheet with the scribblings he had made earlier and said, "What we have then, Renshaw, is this; number one," he wrote the number on the pad. "Lady Marisha is missing. She is nowhere on the ship. Number two, people saw her on deck and one of those two saw Duer headed that way. Margaret ran into Rose when she was coming in and Rose was going out so we have a witness Rose was on deck. Three, Rose has brought us clothes that have the scent of Lady Marisha's perfume on them and Bones says the spots are blood, but he can't say whose, or even what kind of blood for sure. Four, if what Rose says is true, then Duer is certainly capable of violence if he doesn't get his way with women. Fifth, he is lying about being on deck last night."

"Yes, sir, I guess that's about it."

The captain leaned back in his chair. "Do you think he did it, Renshaw?"

"Did what, sir?"

"For God's sake, Renshaw! Why do you always have to be so bloody precise? Do you think Duer was in any way involved in Lady Marisha's disappearance? Did he push her, rather than she fell, or jumped, over the side?"

"I don't think she would have jumped over the side, sir."

"You didn't answer my question."

"I think he is capable of it, but we have no proof. There are no witnesses and no body."

"Then we shall have to try and get a confession out of him shan't we? He's a very arrogant man, Renshaw. He thinks he is invincible. It's those two things that will be his Waterloo. Have you ever had to interrogate anyone before, Renshaw, I mean interrogate them until they breakdown?"

"No, sir, I haven't."

"Well, this is going to be our chance. Have John ask Mrs. VanderMeer if she can join us again and then have him bring Duer here. While Duer is with us have John move Mrs. Duer and the boy into cabin A."

"Yes, sir," Renshaw said and went to the intercom and called the kitchen instructing them to send the steward to the captain's quarters.

Rudolph Duer entered the captain's quarters smiling confidently until he saw Mable VanderMeer sitting next to the captain with her pad and pencil ready. "Please sit down, Mr. Duer," the captain said waving toward the empty chair. "Mr. Renshaw here has been filling me in on what he has found out and there are a few things we would like you to clear up for us, if you can."

"Anything I can do to help."

"You say you were not on deck at all last night, is that correct?" the captain said looking down at the paper in front of him.

"I was in the salon all evening and went directly to my cabin."

"So you did not see Lady Marisha last night?"

"Only at dinner."

"And you never went on deck, or saw Lady Marisha on deck."

"Absolutely not."

"Mr. Duer," Renshaw said sarcastically, "Have you ever been diagnosed by a doctor and found to have memory problems?"

"What are you talking about?" he asked frowning at Renshaw.

"You claim you didn't go on deck last night, which is interesting, because there are two people who say you went on deck after ten-thirty last night,"

"Well, they are lying," Duer exploded. "Who are they?"

"Margaret Jenkins for one."

"She's lying."

"Why would she lie about something like that?"

"Revenge, Captain. 'Hell hath no fury like a woman scorned.' She was after me from the moment I came on board. I also think she resented I was such good friends with Lady Marisha."

"Are you saying the reason she slapped you was because you weren't responding to her being 'after you,' as you put it?"

"What other lies has that little bitch been telling about me?"

The captain stared at him for several seconds and then said, "No, Mr. Duer. You are the one that is lying. You have been lying ever since you came on board. You claimed to have an advanced degree. Physics I believe it was you told Mr. Travers. Whereas in actuality you barely graduated university. You were hardly able to get your teacher's license."

"Who told you that? My wife?"

The captain ignored his question. "Now I ask you again, Mr. Duer. Were you on deck last night."

"Absolutely not!"

"Your wife says you came out on deck and sat with her for a little while before she went to bed."

"She's lying," he shouted rising a little from the chair. "Are you going to take her word against mine?"

"Sit down, Mr. Duer, we're not finished with you yet."

"I don't have to answer any more of these questions," Duer said standing up.

The captain leaned back in his chair and rubbed the bridge of his nose with two fingers and said, "Yes you do, Mr. Duer. For one thing, Mr. Renshaw locked the door behind you when you came in so you can't get out 'til we let you out. The second reason you have to answer our questions is because at sea the captain is the absolute authority. The third reason is because there is an armed guard out there with orders to shoot you if you try to break out of here or attack any of us. Now you can either answer my questions, or I can put you in chains in the forecastle."

"You can't do that to me."

"I not only can, but I have a good mind to do it," the captain said reaching over and pulling open a drawer to his desk. Even as he did it, he detected the delicately faint aroma of her perfume. He laid Duer's shirt and then the trousers on top of the desk in front of Duer. "Do these clothes belong to you?" he asked.

Duer just stared at them and the captain lifted the shirt and said, "Does this shirt belong to you, Mr. Duer?"

"Why, yes. How did you get a hold of it?"

"Did you wear this shirt last night?"

"So what? I'm sure there is any number of people saw me wearing those clothes at dinner."

"Doctor Bowman says these spots," he turned the trousers and shirt so the spots were showing, "are blood. Can you tell me how they got on your clothes?"

"I don't know. Whoever gave you the clothes probably put the blood on there to frame me. My wife hates me. She would love to see me accused of something like this."

"She probably has her reasons."

"What do you mean by that?" Duer asked indignantly.

"Do you ever beat your wife, or your son, Mr. Duer?"

"Did she tell you that? She's lying. I have never lifted a hand against either of them."

"I see. I just thought maybe you'd had a fight with your wife, or cut yourself, or had a nose bleed, or something. Maybe wiped your hand on your nose and then on your trousers. The spot here on shirt could have come from blood dropping from your nose. But you don't have any cuts and if you didn't have a bloody nose, or anything what would explain this blood?"

"I don't know where that blood came from."

"Dr. Bowman says these spots are definitely human blood. He can't tell what the type is, but when we get to Buenos Aries the labs there will undoubtedly be able to tell the type and if it matches Lady Marisha, things will look particularly bad for you since another thing is the smell of Lady Marisha's perfume on your clothes. How do you account for that?"

"There is no perfume on my clothes. Anyone who says there is, is imagining it."

"Why don't you just tell us what happened. You went out there—"

"I was never on deck, I tell you."

"We have two witnesses who say you were."

"They're both lying."

"You went out there and saw her standing all by herself. You felt sorry for her. You put your arms around her to comfort her, maybe she was startled, and in trying to push you away she fell over the rail. Was it something like that, Mr. Duer?"

"I was never on deck, Captain," Duer said. "Even if I was, what of it? You can't prove anything."

"It wasn't like that at all, Captain," Renshaw said. "I wager what happened is he went out there and tried to force himself on her. She wouldn't have any of it, of course, not with the likes of him, and started beating him up. He was so embarrassed by her getting the best of him he just picked her up and threw her over the side. That's what happened, wasn't it, Duer?"

"She didn't come close to getting the best of me."

"So you were out there last night? It does no good to lie. We have two witnesses saw you standing next to her," Renshaw lied.

"That's impossible. I checked. There was no one else out there." He stopped talking looking at each of them intently and beads of sweat began to show just below his perfectly arranged hair.

"So you were out there, and you just said she didn't come close to getting the best of you, but you did struggle with her," Renshaw said pressing in.

"No, of course not."

"But you just said you checked to see if anyone else was there and she didn't come close to getting the best of you. Just what did you mean by that if you weren't talking about some kind of struggle?"

"Well, there wasn't any kind of struggle. Even if there was, what can you do about it? Nothing! You have no witnesses and no body."

"Maybe not, Mr. Duer, but we do have your confession," the captain said quietly. He said it so calmly and quietly that for a moment all of the others, including Duer, thought back quickly over what he had said trying to find his confession.

"I never confessed to anything. And even if I had thrown her over the side I would never have confessed to it. So you don't have any confession from me."

"Yes we do. You confessed to your wife."

"You can't use what I said to her against me."

"Then you admit you did tell your wife you killed Lady Marisha?"

"That was just to scare her. I mean, no. I meant I could kill her. You know, just an expression. You know, like you say, 'He made me so angry I could kill him.' Like that. Just an expression. It didn't mean anything."

"Yes, I understand," the captain said. "You used this meaningless phrase when you were on deck with your wife, is that right?"

"Yes."

"But you told us you were never on deck last night."

Duer looked from one to the other and said, "Okay, so I was on deck last night, but that doesn't mean I did anything to Lady Harwell. When I went out there, there was nobody there. Lady Harwell must have jumped before I got there."

There was silence in the cabin for almost a minute and the captain said, "Mr. Duer, I'm charging you with the murder of Lady Marisha and you are now under arrest."

"You can't do that," Duer said jumping up. "I'm an American citizen. You can't just arrest me for no reason."

"As captain I have the right, nay the duty, to arrest anyone I feel has committed a crime aboard my ship at sea. All the statements taken from all the passengers, your clothing, and all other evidence will be turned over to the British Embassy in Buenos Aries. If they concur with my findings, then you will be sent to England to stand trial for the murder, or manslaughter of a British subject on British territory. The United States Embassy will, of course, be informed. You may go, Mr. Duer. You will find a man outside the door who will escort you to your cabin. As I said before, he is armed and has orders to shoot you if you give him any trouble. You will be confined to your cabin for the rest of the trip. Your meals will be brought to you there."

"You can't do that."

"It is either that, or I will have the chains put on you right here and have you taken to the forecastle. There will be no toilet there and no shower. And I don't know how the Germans are going to treat you when we tell them why you're there. This is really for your protection because there is no telling what the crew will do to you when they find out what you did."

"You can't do this. You have no proof I did anything."

"You may go now," the captain said and Renshaw got up to unlock the door.

***

During the morning, the deep water blue had changed to gray and then there had been streaks of brown in it. By late afternoon they were well within neutral waters and the engines were shut down. With no smoke from the funnel, nor any vibrations from the turning of the propellers, there was a unique silence aboard the ship. In every direction the great, mud-brown triangle of the estuary of the Rio de la Plata lay flat and smooth like a boundless and dune-less desert. Although the closest land was nowhere to be seen, the still air had about it the smell of sun-warmed earth.

On the forward well-deck the Germans, informed they were now in neutral waters, were free to stay on deck as long as they wished. The passengers who were out on deck were all on the port side. After talking to the captain and being moved to cabin A, Rose had stayed close to Reverend and Mrs. VanderMeer, fearful that somehow Rudy would find her alone. When Duer was brought down to his cabin, he had cursed at them and shouted threats at Rose. "I'm going to get you, Rose. If it's the last thing I do, I'm going to get you! When I'm through with you you're going to wish you had never been born."

They had all moved to the port side then and Rose had asked tearfully, "What's going happen to me when we leave the ship? I never should have said anything."

"You did the right thing, Rose," Reverend VanderMeer said. "From what Mrs. VanderMeer tells me, I don't think you will ever see your husband again unless you want to."

"Yes," Mable added, "and from now on you'll travel with us till we get to the States and you and Robbie are back with your family."

"And if it is inconvenient for you to travel with them at any time, you and Robbie can travel with me," Helen Stanley said. "I won't let that husband of yours get anywhere near you."

"Why would it be inconvenient?" Mable asked a little hurt.

"Bookings. What if there is only space for six people? Are you going to wait around until there is space on some ship for eight? In fact, it would be better if they came with me. There is always more likely to be passage for three than for eight."

"You're right, of course," Mable said. "Maybe we'll be lucky and all be able to get passage together on the same ship."

"Huh, that's not very likely," Miss Stanley growled.

"One way, or another we'll work it out," Reverend VanderMeer said and Rose Duer felt happier and safer than she had in years. She guessed it was probably her imagination, but it sounded a little as though Helen

Stanley and Mable VanderMeer were fighting over her company. Even if it was her imagination, it felt good.

CHAPTER SEVENTEEN

Thursday -- January 29, 1942

It was a little after five in the morning when the tug arrived. It took them more than an hour to attach the towing cable. Finally, after sitting motionless in the brown expanse of the river's mouth for fifteen hours, there was the gentle breeze from the towed ship moving smoothly through the brown water. Fifty yards behind the tug the bow of the Port Jefferson cut sluggishly through water like some great plow turning back liquid brown sand. The sand only fell back into the ditch as soon as the plow was past.

At the stern of the ship the gun crew swabbed and cleaned the gun, putting an extra thickness of grease on the unpainted parts and inside the barrel. The gun covers were taken out of storage and were ready to be put on now that they were in neutral waters. A new flag waved gently from the after-mast and on all the decks sailors were shining brass that had not seen a polishing rag since the last time they were in these neutral waters. A week before they left this port all polishing would stop so when they headed out all the brass would be tarnished and dull and unable to reflect any glint of light.

On the main deck the passengers sat around listless and bored after breakfast trying to read, or looking for someone with whom to play a game. The tug only made five knots towing them and they had been told it would probably be another two days before they reached their destination. Even then they would not be allowed to leave the ship right away. Lady Marisha's disappearance would have to be dealt with before any of them could leave.

On the forward well-deck the survivors sprawled, talking, or playing cards. Some sat in what shade they could find, but many of them had their shirts off lying in the sun. The members of the crew resented they had to work while the Nazis just lay around doing nothing.

From the foredeck, the bosun kept looking at the main deck hoping to see Reverend VanderMeer alone, but he seemed to always be with other people on the port side. After waiting for almost an hour to catch Reverend VanderMeer he saw Mrs. VanderMeer standing alone at the starboard rail. He quickly climbed down the ladder to the well-deck, crossed and hesitated for a moment at the bottom of the ladder to the main deck. He wished it were Reverend VanderMeer instead of his wife. It was easier for him to talk to men than to women, but she was the only one who was alone. He climbed the ladder to the main deck, "Beggin' yehr pardon, Mum," he said touching his hand to his forehead.

She turned. "Oh, good morning, Mr. Hawkins."

"Good mornin', mum," he said reaching into his shirt pocket and taking out the three one pound notes the captain had given him. He held them out tentatively. "Meanin' no offense, mum, but 'tis much obliged I'd be if yeh'd be buyin' each of the laddies a little somethin' with this."

"Why, Mr. Hawkins, I can't accept that."

"Please, mum, 'twas paid me fer the sewin' of the burial bag."

"For sewing the burial bag?" she asked looking puzzled.

"Aye, mum, 'tis the custom, mum, so 'twill nay be a pauper's funeral. Three florins is the custom, mum, and 'twas beyond me understandin' when the captain give me three pound. A goodly sum it were, yet I ney could be spendin' it on meself. I thought to put it in the poor box and yet how could I be knowin' 'twould bring any happiness there. Then it come to me, 'twas meant to be a pound a piece fer each of the laddies.'

"That's very kind of you, Mr. Hawkins."

"Ah, nay, mum. 'Tis much obliged Ah'd be if yeh'd be gettin' a little somethin' for the lads. Ah'd nay be rightly knowin' what each would be wantin'."

"All right Mr. Hawkins, I'll tell them it was you who gave it to them."

"Oh, there be no need of that, mum."

"I think it would be good for them to know where it came from."

"As yeh think best, mum, but there be no need of tellin' them before they've left the ship."

"We're very grateful to you, Mr. Hawkins, not just for this, but for all your kindnesses, especially all the things you did for Luke."

"Aye, 'twas me own good pleasure havin' the laddie about. Fine laddie. Fine laddie." He paused and then said, "God bless," and headed back down the ladder.

***

Mary VanderMeer sat all alone in a chair on the starboard side of the ship. Most of the passengers were taking their afternoon nap. She sat there waiting to catch a moment alone with Richard Travers. She sat back by the lifeboats where she could watch the wings of the bridge and she had caught a glimpse of him twice. She was certain if there had not been a death and a funeral there would have been time for more meetings, holding hands and tender moments. But death had intervened. Then just as people were getting over the shock of it there had been the German destroyer trying to sink them and another death. It was hard to believe both Nicky and Lady Harwell had died. If these things hadn't happened there would have been time for her mysteriously wonderful dream, too overwhelming beautiful to be considered anything other than a dream, to be fulfilled. She only had a couple of days left, a few precious hours that were speeding by much too quickly.

Mary saw Margaret Jenkins crossing over the cargo hatch and hoped she would not come and sit next to her. Margaret took a chair under the wing of the bridge and was hardly seated before Duer was at his porthole saying something to her. Margaret got up and went over and closed the outside blackout cover to his porthole. "That should make it start to get hot in there. Not as hot as he deserves though," she said heading back toward her chair and Mary saw tears in her eyes. Mary watched feeling more and more concern for Margaret who sat with her face buried in her handkerchief, weeping silently. Mary got up finally and went over and sat down next to her. "If you don't want me here I'll leave," Mary said.

"No. That's all right," Margaret said through sniffles. "It's just things look so bad I can't help myself. I know I should be brave, but I don't know what to do. You're so kind, Mary. You're a good friend, Mary. You're whole family has been nice to me."

Mary tentatively reached over and took Margaret's hand. "I wish I could do something for you. It must be terrible when people you love die."

Margaret nodded weakly. "Nicky and M'Lady were like family. I know they weren't blood. I would never think such a thing, but they were all the family I had."

Mary didn't know what to say and so she just sat there thinking how terrible it would be to suddenly be all-alone. She tried to place herself in Margaret's place with her mother and father and all her brothers gone. She couldn't imagine it, but she felt genuinely sorry for Margaret.

"And it's not only that," Margaret said through genuine tears, "But I've lost everything. I have no place to go. I can't go back to the colonel. It wouldn't be proper for a single girl to be a maid for a single man. I have no family. Oh, I don't know what to do," she sobbed. "Lady Marisha said I could go on to America. She said she was going to give me a letter to her cousin and talk to your father about me traveling with you, but now she's gone and can't do those things for me."

"Maybe you could still travel with us. We could be your family. I heard my parents talking about it just the other night. Something you said when Mr. Renshaw was making the investigation about Lady Marisha saying you should go to America. I heard them talking about it. I think they are going to talk to you about it."

"Do you think so? Do you really think your parents are agreed to it?"

"Oh, I think so," Mary said and then added, "It will be fun being together a little longer."

"That would be so wonderful. And I'd be no bother. I could help in all kinds of ways. I'm not afraid of work. You're a good friend," Margaret said leaning over and hugging Mary. "I feel much better now," She said getting up and heading toward the salon.

Inside Margaret found Matt in the salon where he had been waiting for her. She smiled, nodding as she entered and he asked, "What did she say? Will she do it?"

"Oh, yes."

"That's great," he said beaming at the thought their being together a while longer. He had suggested he talk to his parents, but Margaret suggested it would be better if she could get Mary to do it. "That way they'll have no reason to suspect anything," she had said. He didn't know what it would be like traveling to the States from Argentina, but while they waited for passage in Buenos Aries they would have to stay in a hotel and Margaret was bound to have her own room. They could be together all the time and not have to sneak off to the baggage compartment, or somewhere else to be together.

CHAPTER EIGHTEEN

Friday -- January 30, 1942

Outside of cabin A, the three steamer trunks took up most of the area of the passageway. Margaret moved clothes from the dressers in the cabin to the trunks and from one trunk to another. In the months of living in rented apartments, houses and hotels some of Nicky's clothes had ended up in her trunk and some of hers in Nicky's. It was not something intentional; just sometimes when she was in a hurry there was more room for a particular item in one rather than the other. Now she had to pack for all three, which was what she had always done, but this time things had to be sorted out because two of the trunks were going back to the colonel. Things had to be put in the trunks just right. She didn't want the colonel to go through the trunks and find things all mixed up.

The last thing she did after sorting all the clothes was to take the ring Lady Marisha had given her. Up to the last minute she felt the ring was safer in her Lady's jewelry box than anywhere among her own things. She also took the Pooh Bear Nicky had slept with for so long. She thought about it a long time. She was sure Lady Marisha and Colonel Harwell would both have given her their permission if there were any way to ask them and she just had to have something that had been Nicky's.

***

Luke VanderMeer climbed down the ladder to the forward well-deck and looked around at the survivors. They smiled at him and he smiled back and wondered why it was the passengers were not supposed to go there anymore now that the Germans were there. One of the crew looked up from where he was taking the cover off the forward hatch and said, "You'd best not be here, lad. Best you go back to the main deck."

"I'm looking for Jack."

"He's in the rope locker," the man said jerking his head toward the bow and then went back to knocking out the chocks that held the cover on the hatch.

Luke crossed the deck quickly, not wanting anyone else to tell him he didn't belong there, and entered the forward hatch. The steel door to the rope locker was hooked open and from where he stood, he could see Jack sitting on a coil of rope smoking his pipe. He approached slowly and Jack turned, took the pipe from his mouth and said, "Come in, laddie. Come in. Well, laddie, tomorrow, or the day aftah, you'll be goin' ashore. Not too long now 'tis on solid ground yeh'll be. Seein' a new country en all."

"I don't want to go."

"Is that so now? Took a likin' to the sailin' life did yeh?"

"I guess so."

"Aye, that's the way of it. Yeh jess be takin' a likin' to a place and it be time fer leavin'. But mark my word, laddie, there'll be many a new place yeh'll be likin' jess as well."

"You won't be there."

"Ah, so that's it is it now? Have yeh the pipe Ah gave yeh, laddie?' he said reaching over and tugging on the lanyard around Luke's neck.

Luke nodded and looked down at his left breast pocket as he unbuttoned the flap and pulled out the pipe.

"Are yeh rememberin' what Ah taught yeh?"

Luke nodded.

"Aye, then pipe the cap'n aboard for me, laddie."

Luke raised the pipe to his mouth, blowing in it, raising and lowering the last two fingers of his hand to create the different notes. The sounds echoed sharply in the small confines of the rope locker.

"Aye. Well done," Jack said nodding seriously. "Now be pipin' me mess call and turn-to." Luke did as he was told and when he was through Jack said, "Aye, laddie, 'tis a mighty great distance a body can hear the pipe if he be listenin' for it. From now on, when yeh blow the pipe Ah'll hear it. No matter how far away yeh be, Ah'll be hearin' it."

"Really?"

"Aye, laddie, 'tis the listenin' for it makes the difference. Ah'll be listenin' and Ah'll be hearin'. An' mayhap yeh'll be a walkin' along a road one day, or a lyin' in yehr bunk and yeh'll hear the pipe ablowin' in yehr head and yeh'll be knowin' 'tis ole Jack ah sayin', 'Top of the mornin' to yeh, laddie.'"

"Will I really hear you?"

"Aye, laddie, yeh can mark my word. 'Tis the way it'll be," he said knocking the ashes from his cold pipe and standing up. He reached up above one of the beams and took down a small fold of brown paper. "'Tis mighty busy Ah'll be 'tween now and when yeh leave so I best be givin' yeh this now." He unfolded the paper and took out a one-foot square of canvas. Forming a circular boarder around the outside with black thread were stitched the words T.S.M.V. Port Jefferson—Jan. 1942. Inside the circle he had stitched the names with little stars by each name.

* JACK HAWKINS *
* LUKE VANDERMEER *
SHIPMATES

Luke took it and stood staring at it. "Go along now, laddie. Yeh'd not be wantin' yehr muther to be a worryin' about yeh," he said.

Luke threw his arms around the old man and looked up into the bearded face. "Good-bye, Jack. I'll never forget you."

The old man awkwardly put his arms around the boy. "'Twould make an old man's heart warm to think he was remembered by the likes of yeh. And Ah'll be rememberin' yeh, laddie. Like yeh was me own son, Ah'll be rememberin' yeh." He suddenly smiled and spoke more lightly. "'Tis a pact then, rememberin' each other we'll be. Run along now. God bless yeh, Laddie."

Luke turned and walked away slowly looking at the little patch of canvas as he walked and the old man watched him cross the deck and reached up and brushed a tear from his cheek.

CHAPTER NINETEEN

Saturday -- January 31, 1942

For almost thirty hours the passengers and crew of the Port Jefferson had grown increasingly more bored with the monotony of the flat, brown water. The first sight of land had been a gray-brown line that had remained disappointingly flat and distant. Eventually the flat land had become more distinct and an occasional building could be seen along the banks. The buildings became more frequent until they crowded together and grew higher, blotting out the land behind them.

Just inside the harbor the towing cables were dropped and two harbor tugs came along side pushing the Port Jefferson into its assigned berth. All about them was a frenzy of activity. Warehouses pressed against the sky towering over the mast of the freighters tied up in front of them. In one area the yellow dust rising from a multitude of black spouts pouring grain into the holds of ships created a buff cloud over that area of the harbor. In another area railroad cranes rolled back and forth swinging gigantic steel arms with nets of crates hanging from them. Behind the cranes were brightly painted warehouses with large signs rising above their peaked roofs: HORMEL DU ARGENTINE, SWIFT & CO., ARMOUR AND COMPANY LTD. To most of the passengers it was a surprise to see the familiar names of American companies in among the others. Ships of nations that were at war with each other in Europe were tied up at the same wharf getting meat from the same company.

The dock was crowded as the harbor tugs eased them toward it. Old men in tattered coats leaned against the steel walls of warehouses. Some of them stood with their arms folded across their chests staring idly at the ship while others passed a cigarette back and forth. Men wearing narrow-brimmed, straw hats, light sports jackets and garish, wide ties pushed their way through the crowd to get a closer look at the ship. Some of them pointed at the holes in the hull and made comments to each other. Young boys pushed and shoved each other roughly, laughing, stopping occasionally to wave at someone on the ship and then went back to their shoving and laughing. To one side two customs men in white jackets with patches on the shoulders and carrying briefcases stood talking to each other. Occasionally they would turn and say something to the small contingent from the German consulate who were standing right behind them. Two men in proper dark suits from the British consulate stood on the fringes at the opposite side of the crowd from the Germans. It was appropriate both groups keep their distance. The Germans were there to meet their survivors that had been picked up by a British ship. The British were there to congratulate the captain.

The ship was tied up and a narrow gangway was put across at the forward well-deck. The customs officials came aboard. Since they had no luggage, nor anything to declare, the survivors were let ashore immediately. From the bridge, the captain watched them leave and it seemed a heavy weight and a cloud left the ship with them. As each one stepped off the end of the gang-plank they were hugged by the men from the consulate and thronged by reporters while trying to get to the waiting cars. As soon as the survivors were gone, the men from the British consulate came aboard and left almost immediately with the captain.

***

Mary VanderMeer stood on the main deck waiting for Richard Travers. She had been waiting for him all morning, but he had been busy with entering port. When the customs men had come aboard and she was told to go to her cabin, she was afraid Travers would disappear while she was gone. But fortunately her suitcases were the first ones the man had looked at and he hadn't looked through them at all. He had just asked her if they were hers and then told her she could close them and had placed a seal on them. She had hurried out as soon as they were finished with her suitcases to take up her vigil again. They would be leaving soon and she had to see him before they left. Once in the middle of the morning she had turned away for just an instant to look at something in the harbor and when she looked back he was running up the ladder on the other side. Tears almost came to her eye because she had been looking away and standing on the wrong side of the ship. *He was in such a hurry. He would come by again. He had to. He would come to her when he wasn't so busy. He wouldn't let her leave without saying good-bye.* She loved him. She knew she loved him and he must know it too. *Soon he will come to me. We're in port now and he can't be as busy as he was at sea. He will come to me.* But with each passing moment the desperation became more intense. Time was getting short. The survivors had already gone. Soon they would be leaving too. He had to come to her.

She turned a little and saw him on the after well-deck talking to the bosun. Certainly as soon as he was finished talking to the bosun he would come to her. *But what if he doesn't?* She started down the ladder to the after well-deck and he looked her direction and smiled a little before turning back to the bosun. She stood awkwardly to one side of the ladder, rubbing her hands together nervously, trying to stay out of the way of the crew putting out more lines and others taking the cover off the cargo hatch. *Do they know why I'm here? I don't care. I don't care if everyone knows I love him.*

He finished talking finally and headed toward her. Her heart started pounding. *What am I going to say? Came to give you my address. Give him Grandpa's address. One-forty-six, or was it Two-forty-six North Seventh Street? Oh, God, please help me remember.*

He came up to her and touched his hand to the peak of his cap. "You really shouldn't be here, Miss VanderMeer, you might get hurt," he said and then looked over the side and added, "Well your trip is finally over. It wasn't very pleasant, was it? We had a bit of a time there, didn't we?"

She didn't answer right away, but stood looking up at him with tears on the verge of spilling over.

"Don't cry, Miss VanderMeer. Please don't cry."

"I don't want this trip to end."

"I know."

"I love you."

"You don't know me, Miss VanderMeer," he said and she reached over and took both his hands. "We hardly know each other—"

"But I know I love you," she interrupted.

"You're fond of me, Miss VanderMeer and I'm fond of you, but you don't love me."

"Yes I do. Yes I do," she said the tears spilling over.

He stood there feeling the desperation of not wanting to hurt her more, but also wanting to end her embarrassing display. "I have been privileged to know you, Miss VanderMeer, but the cruel truth is we will probably never see each other again after today."

"We could write to each other."

"Yes, we could do that," he said wishing to end the conversation.

"I don't know where we'll be living in the States. But you could give me your address and I'll write you and let you know where we are. Please?"

He reached into his pocket and from his wallet took out his card case and gave her one of his cards with the line's seal, the name of the ship and the address of the shipping line. "If you write to this address it will always reach me," he said.

"I'll write you every day," she said, "Will you write me?"

"Yes," he lied thinking she would quickly get tired of writing him when he never answered and he had no intention of answering her letters. "You'd better go back to the main deck now," he said taking her elbow and guiding toward the ladder.

She walked up the ladder ahead of him and at the top she turned to face him wishing he would take her in his arms once more before they left the ship, but he kept walking and she walked alongside him until they came to the ladder to the bridge. He stopped on the bottom step. "I'll see you again before you leave," he said smiling gently and thinking he was going to do everything he could to avoid her.

"I love you."

"I know. I love you, too. I'll come say good-bye before you leave," he said and went up the ladder.

***

Captain Chipman stood on the bridge watching his passengers going ashore. He felt a little guilty for having spoiled the festivities at the embassy. He had been taken there as an honored guest. Sir David Kelly, the British ambassador, had welcomed him. There was an official letter of gratitude from the German Ambassador for the rescue of the German survivors. He was congratulated for having been able to escape the German destroyer. Most of all he was praised for alerting Tristan and through it Stanley of the presence of the enemy. Copies of the radio transmissions between Tristan de Cunah and the Port Jefferson were read and the audience cheered. It was the Port Jefferson that had exposed the attack. The forces at Stanley had later confirmed several German ships, including three destroyers and a battle ship, had been in the area. With the element of surprise gone the attack had presumably been abandoned. But after the congratulations, the honors and the toasts were over what should have been a congenial celebration became a meeting of angry indignation when he told them of Lady Marisha and Mr. Duer. Everyone who heard of it expressed incense and outrage. United States Ambassador Armour concurred it was a British affair. It had taken place aboard a British ship to a British subject and Mr. Duer was under the same law as if he had committed the crime in London. Mr. Duer would be taken back to England to stand trial and Ambassador Armour assured Sir David there would be no problem issuing a separate passport for Rose Duer and her son.

The captain returned to the ship accompanied by two guards from the British Embassy who took Duer into custody. He informed Reverend VanderMeer that Mrs. Duer should stop by the American Embassy to get a new passport for her and Robbie and Mr. Duer would be confined at the British Embassy until passage to England could be arranged for him.

The captain had done what was needed to get his passengers safely on their way, but he had not said good-bye to any of them. After returning and talking with Reverend VanderMeer, he had stayed on the bridge precisely so he wouldn't have to say good-byes. There had been a time when he would have been at the head of the gangway saying good-bye to his passengers. Sometimes they had even exchanged addresses and promises to write. Neither the promises, nor the addresses had been kept. Now those people were just names without faces, or faces without names, but in most cases they were neither, now just names and faces both completely forgotten. It was unfortunate because he would have liked to remember them all. He felt not exactly guilty about not remembering passengers, but rather as though there were something lacking in him. In a paternal sort of way, much as a schoolmaster might think about a graduating class, he wondered what was going to happen to these people who were moving out from under his protection. He had, in effect, turned them over to Reverend VanderMeer who was at that very minute supervising their getting into the taxis that would take them to the Phoenix Hotel. He was no longer responsible for them and he wished Reverend VanderMeer well. He saw the VanderMeer girl staring up at the ship and several times wipe her eyes with her handkerchief. Even after she got in the taxi she leaned forward, her head turned to look back at the ship. He frowned a little wondering what was upsetting her.

He saw Travers coming up the ladder and turned. "Repairs will start at 0800 tomorrow, Captain. Mr. Harvey suggests with all the welding that will be going on it might be better not to take the fuel aboard until the repairs are finished. Bosun reports all lines are doubled up. Ship is secure."

"Very well, Mr. Travers. Shore leave may begin for the starboard watch," the captain said and walked into his cabin suddenly feeling forlorn and tired.

Epilogue of Characters

Doctor Bowman left the ship when it docked in Southampton and resigned from the Port lines. Three months later he was found dead in an alley behind a waterfront bar. He appeared to have been beaten and robbed.

Captain Jeffrey Chipman sailed the same route, Southampton to South Africa to Buenos Aires, for another sixteen months. On November 2, 1942, General Bernard Montgomery commanding the British Eighth Army defeated the Germans at El Alamein. On November 8, 1942, the Anglo-American forces invaded North Africa and six months later, May 12, 1943, all German resistance in North Africa came to an end. From then on until the end of the war in Europe on May 8, 1945, the Port Jefferson sailed directly between Buenos Aires and Southampton. Captain Chipman retired in 1952 to his home just outside Southampton. His wife Elizabeth died in June of 1962 and he died one month later on July 17, 1962 at the age of seventy-five.

Rose Duer returned to her hometown where she got a divorce. She worked in her father's store, which after the war became part of a supermarket chain. With the money from the supermarket chain, her parents opened an implement dealership and a men's clothing store. She inherited all the businesses when her parents died in the seventies. She died in 1989 and Robbie Duer is now President and CEO of the corporation.

Rudolph Duer was tried and convicted of man-slaughter. He was sentenced to life in prison. He served twenty years of his sentence and was then deported to the United State where he settled in California. He tried working for a while as car salesman, but he was not able to hold a job. He was found dead in a parking lot in Downey, California in 1965 at the age of 53. He was buried by the county.

Colonel Ransom A. Harwell continued in North Africa until the end of the resistance there. After that he was assigned to London for almost two years until the invasion of Normandy in which he took part. At the end of the war he retired from the army with the rank of Major General having been awarded the Victoria Cross three times. He entered politics and was for a short time a Member of Parliament. He never remarried. Major-General Ransom A. Harwell, M.P., V.C., O.B., Died on March 7,

1976 at the age of seventy-one. His title and lands succeeded to his nephew.

Ship's Bosun Jack Hawkins died in his sleep two years later aboard the Port Jefferson and was buried at sea.

Margaret Jenkins sailed to the United States with the VanderMeer family. She settled in Las Vegas where she married an accountant in one of the casinos. In 1956, she used a flawless, two-carat, antique, diamond ring as collateral for a loan to open a boutique. The shop prospered and three years later she opened two more stores. She died in 1992 at the age of seventy-one. She exchanged Christmas cards with Dr. and Mrs. Matthew VanderMeer until her death.

Second Mate Parkington retired in 1980 and died in his home at Land's End in 1986.

First Mate Renshaw captained several ships for various lines until he retired in 1969. He died in 1978 at the age of seventy-four.

Helen Stanley took care of her aged father for eight years until he died. After which she tried in several ways of getting back to Angola, but was always refused because of her age. She died of pneumonia two years after the death of her father at the age of sixty-five.

While in London in December of 1942, Third Mate Richard Travers was critically injured by falling debris during an air raid. He lived for two weeks after the raid and died of internal injuries. Among his personal effects was a letter with no return address on it from a Mary VanderMeer.

Harold and Mable Vandermeer returned to the Congo in January of 1946. They were there during the turbulent times of independence in 1960 and during the Simba uprisings that followed. After peace and order was restored they returned to their station in Zaire. On September 21, 1970 Mable suffered a stroke and died. Harold VanderMeer stayed on in Zaire until his death on his eighty-second birthday on January 1, 1982.

On August 3, 1957, while a graduate student at the University of Washington, Luke Vandermeer went sailing alone in a small in boat out of Bellingham. After an unexpected storm the wreckage of his boat was found washed up on one of the several islands. He was never seen, or heard of again.

Mark Vandermeer was for twelve years a corrections officer with the State of California. After that he was a school bus driver in Oregon until he retired at the age of sixty-five. He now lives in a retirement home.

After completing college, Mary Vandermeer went to India as a missionary. In 1970 at the age of forty-six she married an Indian Custom's Officer. She is now lives with her husband, his children and grand children in Darjeeling.

Matthew Vandermeer earned a Doctorate in Educational Administration from Stanford and another Doctorate in Continuing Education from the University of Chicago. He held several deanships and retired as President of a private college in Pennsylvania. He died in 1993 at the age of sixty-eight.

About the Author

At age 13, Paul J. Stam, the author was hunting big game in Africa with his father, not as a sport, but to provide food for the station. He has single handedly sailed a 38 foot ketch from Tahiti to Hawaii.

Paul was born of missionary parents in the northeast corner of the Belgian Congo just a few miles from both the Uganda and Sudan borders, which was about as far into Africa as you could go.

Just before the end of World War II, when he was 15, he came with his parents to the United States.

After graduating from high school he enlisted in the U.S. Navy, serving aboard a destroyer during the Korean War. His tour of duty completed, Paul attend the University of Minnesota and later joined the staff. While on the staff the University of Minnesota sent Paul to the Hawaiian Islands to attend a conference. Paul immediately fell in love with the Islands. When he returned to Minnesota he turned in his resignation and headed back to the Islands.

Within two months of arriving in Hawaii, Paul was crewing on a sailboat. After a year of sailing the Pacific on other people's boats, Paul decided it was time to get a boat of his own. Together with his wife Terry and their ten-year-old son Steven, they built their dream boat, which they launched in 1978.

Among other things, Paul has been a construction worker, university teacher and administrator, and a sailboat skipper. Paul is now retired and lives in Hawaii where he spends a lot of time on the potter's wheel making bowls and mugs and at the computer writing.

OTHER TITLES BY
PAUL J. STAM
FROM
ALL THINGS THAT MATTER PRESS

A River That Is Congo: Of Rulers And Ruled

Pierre d'Entremont was the pampered youngest son of a successful
French banking family. With an older brother to carry on the family
tradition, Pierre is enrolled in the E'cole Militaire with the thought of a
political career to follow his military service. But when the chief
cashier embezzles all the bank's money and escapes to the Americas,
Pierre suddenly has to earn a living. He has heard that a fortune can be
made in King Leopold's Congo Free State. Although he has heard
stories, mostly told by the British and Americans, of atrocities
perpetrated on the natives by King Leopold's agents, stories the King
denies, Pierre concludes that, given his military training, his best
option is to enter King Leopold's Congo military service. Pierre arrives
in the Congo in 1902. Within the first month, he becomes sick and
nearly dies; makes an enemy of Harou, Leopold's most powerful man
in the Congo; and, on the way to his posting, must always keep his
gun within reach. Of Rulers and Ruled is an historical novel of one
man's heroic struggle against the greed, cruelty, and terror of a corrupt
government in colonial Africa. Pierre d'Entremont went to Africa to
seek his fortune, and stayed to fight an evil regime.

A River That is Congo: Of Chiefs and Giants

Kusala should have been chief. He was the firstborn and many in the
tribe knew it. He and Kitomolo were born on the same day but of
different mothers. Because Chief Ronzozo knew that it will be hard to
establish exactly which of his sons was born first, he decided that the
one who became a man first in the traditional way of killing a leopard,
would be chief after him. On the day of the hunt they both throw at
the same time, but Kitomolo, knowing he is not as good as his brother,
damages his spear and then has his friends say that they saw Kusala
tampering with Kitomolo's weapon during the night. Kitomolo is
named chief to be because of his cunning and guile, not his ability and
skill. Harry VanVeldt and some others missionaries are the first white
in that part of the Congo. Kusala goes to them expecting that he will be
able to use them to help him get his birthright, but instead they use
him to learn the language and get established.

www.ingramcontent.com/pod-product-compliance
Lightning Source LLC
Chambersburg PA
CBHW051640260626
47170CB00004B/1266